Also by Ken Scholes

Last Flight of the Goddess
Long Walks, Last Flights and Other Strange Journeys
Diving Mimes, Weeping Czars and Other Unusual Suspects
Metatropolis: The Wings We Dare Aspire (with Jay Lake)

The Psalms of Isaak:
Lamentation
Canticle
Antiphon
Requiem
Hymn

BLUE YONDERS, GRATEFUL PIES

& OTHER *Fanciful* FEASTS

BLUE YONDERS, GRATEFUL PIES

& OTHER *Fanciful* FEASTS

KEN SCHOLES

FAIRWOOD PRESS
Bonney Lake, WA

BLUE YONDERS, GRATEFUL PIES

A Fairwood Press Book
August 2015
Copyright © 2015 Kenneth G. Scholes
"An Introduction" Copyright © 2015 Mary Robinette Kowal

Fairwood Press
21528 104th Street Court East
Bonney Lake, WA 98391
www.fairwoodpress.com

Cover illustration & design by
Paul Swenson

Book design by
Patrick Swenson

ISBN: 978-1-933846-51-4
First Fairwood Press Edition: August 2015
Printed in the United States of America

For Jay Lake:
I miss you every day, my friend.

CONTENTS

AN INTRODUCTION
by Mary Robinette Kowal

*I*ntroductions serve an interesting purpose in life. Once upon a time, it was shockingly impolite to speak to someone without being introduced to them first. It served as a way to vet people, so that people of questionable character could not impose on you. Introductions also served to bring worthwhile individuals to your attention.

In many ways, a book introduction does the same thing. I am here to introduce Ken Scholes to those of you who don't know him. My job, as it were, is to say to you, "Yes. This gentleman is a lovely. You may safely spend an afternoon in his company."

Allow me, then, a moment of your time to give you some framework and context for the stories you are about to read. Ken is one of my first writing friends. When I had just begun to explore the world of creating fiction, he took me under his wing and made sure that I knew people at conventions.

That generosity of spirit reflects in his fiction. His characters are not all shining beacons of perfection but there is, in his stories, an essential element of optimism. Even in the darkest worlds, even the bleakest characters, have something redeeming about them. I think that's directly related to the way Ken moves through the world.

He is also totally goofy. I have spent more than one meal with him in which I laughed to the point of not being able to breathe. That sense of play shows up from the very start in his titles, like "A World Done in By Great Granny's Grateful Pie." I mean . . . how much fun is that? It carries through in the stories themselves. Not that all of them are comedies—far from it—but that sense of whimsy sneaks in to tickle you even during a viral outbreak.

Ken is also a reformed preacher. I say reformed because, while he still has the power to officiate a wedding, he's not a member of the clergy anymore. But . . . but years spent preaching have given him an innate understanding of the power of words. His text sings on the page and has an easy rhythm that not a lot of folks ever get. I say this as someone who is an audiobook narrator . . . Ken's prose is stunning and a delight to read.

All of which is to say that, this is a man you can trust with your time. He will not waste it with stories that are without substance. He will not preach to you without also entertaining you. He will make you laugh and he will make you weep. He will make you think and he will paint pictures in your mind that will remain long after you close the anthology.

It is my very great pleasure to introduce you to Ken Scholes.

BLUE YONDERS, GRATEFUL PIES

& OTHER *Fanciful* FEASTS

ALL OUR TANGLED DREAMS IN DISARRAY

*A*fternoon sun bathed Jessica Riley's face and left arm as she took the slow hairpin curves of California's coastal highway. She kept both hands on the wheel though she desperately wanted to keep one hand on her stomach, on the baby she shouldn't be having and likely wouldn't be having if things went as they had before.

She sighed at the rising panic she felt, and forced her breathing to slow. It started at her shoulders, then moved down her back and chest, finally settling into her stomach.

The unexpected pregnancy at thirty-eight, given her history, was reason for panic enough. But this particular journey—flying to a strange city, driving a strange car along a strange and treacherous highway—was filled with opportunities for anxiety. And the reason for her journey even more so, because it bordered on the crazy.

Jessica had come here from halfway across the country, looking for the Oracle of V'Canto in a desperate bid to know her future.

No, she thought. Her baby's future. Though Jessica was reasonably certain that the baby—the fetus, she reminded herself—had no future.

She felt the anxiety stirring in her stomach like a snake and put her attention back onto the road and to breathing.

Highway 1 north of San Francisco was like nothing she'd ever driven. She'd averaged thirty miles per hour for the better part of three hours, leaving San Francisco around seven on a cool March morning. She'd eaten breakfast at Mel's Drive In, next to the hotel she'd stayed at. Then, she'd gotten on the road.

It was a perfect day. Nothing like Chicago, where it was still dropping into the teens with a windchill that took the cold bone deep. Here, blue sky canopied a landscape that took her breath away, beneath a sun that heralded an early spring for the west. She drove with her window down, inhaling the salt and eucalyptus scented air of Marin County. She took the corners and climbed the hills, and the forest and pastures gave way to coastal towns and steep cliffs. She was glad she was driving north, nestled against the cliff-side in her Kia rental. Even with the south-bound lane between her and the drop-off, she was white-knuckled, eyes fixed on the road, aware that terrifying beauty of the ocean far below might tempt her eyes—and her car— off the narrow highway.

Jessica saw a pullout for a vista ahead and turned into it. She parked and sat for a minute, her hands both resting on her stomach. It was too early for her to show but she still felt it growing there. The flutter of tiny butterfly wings in the deep places of her that manufactured life. She closed her eyes and sat with her baby. With him, she realized, though she knew it was ridiculous to assign gender.

My son.

Another car pulled in and parked on the other side of the small lot. It was a red convertible; a man with long white hair and tan skin climbed out. He wore loose shorts and a windbreaker, and she noticed him checking her out over the top of his shades. He flashed a smile and then turned to the view.

She followed his gaze and took in the sheer rocks and below, the Pacific stretching out to a blurry, blue horizon. Under different circumstances, she'd have documented it with her phone, maybe even posted it for her friends and family. But the instructions had been clear when she decided to seek the Oracle. No one knew anything beyond the automated payroll software conference she was attending. The car was on her boss's card along with the hotel in San Francisco, but everything else was cash. Her phone was off, and its battery removed. Bizarre rules, but she was the one looking to meet a medium.

The man was smoking a cigarette now, and the smell of it flooded her with nostalgia. She took a deeper breath and sighed.

"Ex-smoker?" he said from across the way, smiling at her again.

She nodded. "I am. Just a week now."

He chuckled. "Good for you." He took another deep drag and despite the distance, she saw the paper go orange and shrivel into ash, heard the slow crackle of it as it burned. She watched him take in the smoke and push it out in one final blue haze that tickled her nostrils. Then, she sighed as he field-stripped the cigarette, stomping the cherry with a sandaled foot. "Don't want to be an unnecessary temptation."

She returned the smile. "You're not."

He walked toward the battery of trash and recycling bins between them, near the restrooms. "I'm glad," he said. "And I'm glad you quit smoking. Not good for babies."

Her mouth opened but she had no words. She met his eyes for a moment, then watched him check his cigarette butt before dropping it into the trash. Finally, she found her voice. "How can you tell?"

He shrugged. "You just quit smoking. You're touching your stomach. You look worried."

Jessica blushed but along with the blush, she felt something else rising within her. Something like fear, she thought. She moved for the car and he was walking toward her now. "I have to go," she said.

He stopped and held his hands up. "I'm sorry. I just wanted to shake your hand and congratulate you." He backed up.

Jessica took a breath. "No," she said. "I'm sorry. I'm . . . not my-self." She took a step forward and extended her hand. He lowered his hands and took her hand in his. "Thank you."

"No," he said. "Thank you. What you're doing is . . . well, it is amazing." He still held her hand now, and he squeezed it gently. Then, he winked. "It will all work out."

She noticed the ring as he released her hand. It was silver with small black stone set into it. Very tasteful.

He was walking away now, moving back to his car. "Drive safe," he said over his shoulder. "She'll be waiting for you in Fort Bragg."

The panic was back now as he climbed in and fired the engine to life. She stood with it, feeling it make the slow crawl from her head through her heart and into her stomach as the man pulled back out onto the highway, smiling at her one last time before he was gone.

She'd seen the ring before. Just last week.

It took her back to why exactly she was here, and when she settled back into the Kia and nosed it onto the road, she found she couldn't keep the memories at bay.

So Jessica Riley drove in the cold sweat of fear and pondered the twisting road that carried her.

*

It should have never happened. She kept telling herself this, hoping the repetition would somehow help.

It didn't.

She'd decided at the last minute to attend her twentieth reunion, thinking it would be good to see how everyone had turned out. She hadn't expected Steve Tanner at all, figuring that all of that water had gone under a hundred bridges in the years since they graduated. They'd had spark as far back as their sophomore year at Hoffman Estates High, and twenty-two years later, fresh from her divorce, that spark—in a night of drinking and reminiscing—had turned into a forest fire that a long night in his hotel room couldn't put out. So they'd burned in the heat of it until close to check-out time the next day.

And then, he'd told her over breakfast that he was married. Not happily, but there it was. She'd turned her head at the last second to dodge his kiss goodbye there in the IHOP parking lot and she went home one part angry and two parts sad, though more angry and sad with herself despite knowing that his lack of honesty deserved a generous helping of her unhappiness. Still, she'd always struggled with making herself responsible for other people's bad behavior.

Just a few weeks later, she missed her period but chalked it up to stress. When she missed a second, and felt that butterfly in her belly trying to take flight, she found herself suddenly both frightened and elated as she drove down to Rite-Aid to buy a test.

Because it shouldn't have been able to happen.

She'd opted for a tubal ligation after her eighth miscarriage and Steve had been her first outing since the marriage with Tom had crumbled. And the last five years of that marriage had been sexless so she'd never really test driven the procedure, but had assumed, like most would, that it had worked.

One EPT in the Rite Aid public restroom . . . followed by four others just to be sure . . . had confirmed her deepest hope and her worst fear. After, she sat on the hood of her car, smoking one last guilty Newport while all of the feelings worked her over. She had her phone out, ready to dial but uncertain who to call. Her doctor, her ex-husband, her mother, and even Steve came to mind, though she wasn't sure what she would say to any of them at this point.

So she sat and smoked and cried.

A woman saw her crying and approached. "Hey there," she said.

She was young—maybe in her mid-twenties—her arms covered in tattoos and her ears heavy with piercings and a diamond stud in her left nostril. "Are you okay?"

She felt heat rising to her cheeks. "I'm . . . I'm fine."

There was something in the woman's face, in her eyes, that spoke calm and compassion to Jessica's inner storm. "You don't look fine."

Jessica shrugged and crushed out her cigarette. She looked at the pack at the top of her open purse. Another wouldn't matter, she knew, not if nature followed the path it had taken with her eight times before. Eight times that she knew of, she reminded herself. What was the statistic? Something like a third of all pregnancies terminated naturally before a woman even knew she was pregnant? So her actual scorecard was likely much higher. Still, one more cigarette couldn't hurt and she reached into her purse.

"Better to quit now," the woman said. "And maybe it's time to try something different. You remember what Einstein said about insanity?"

Jessica found the woman's sense of calm and compassion fighting with her fear and despair, feeding the hope. "What do you mean?"

"You've been here before, Jessica," the woman said. "Think about it. Try something new." Then, she gave her a small piece of paper.

Their hands touched as Jessica took the paper and she noticed a single ring on the woman's hand. It was silver and set with a small black stone. Jessica looked up. "How do you know my name?"

"It's . . . complicated." The woman looked around. "If you decide you want to try something different—really want to—call this number." Their eyes met. "But call it first," she said. "Don't call anyone else before you do or you'll be doing the same thing again, hoping for different results . . . more insanity. We can't help you at that point." Then, she stepped forward and lifted the pack of cigarettes out of Jessica's purse. "And I shouldn't do this—it absolutely violates FOC protocol—but I don't think you'll be wanting these this time around."

Then the woman hugged her and despite Jessica's body stiffening with fear, she squeezed her tightly. "It is so good to meet you," she whispered in her ear. "And congratulations."

The woman smiled at her one last time and then moved off across the parking lot, tucking the pack of Newports into her shoulder-slung backpack as she did.

Jessica went home, confused but carrying some of the woman's calm with her now. She sat in the tub and soaked for an hour, her phone nearby with the paper laying beside it. She'd finally decided that she wouldn't be calling Steve at all. Tom was still a maybe because she'd gone through this with him so many times before. Her mom nearly won out. But the odd encounter with the girl kept her thinking of Einstein and the insanity of eight previous attempts at bringing life into the world. Finally, she picked up the phone and dialed the number on the scrap of paper.

She thought the girl would answer, but it was a man. "Jessica Riley," the voice said. "I'm glad you called."

She leaned forward in the tub, closing her eyes. "Who is this?"

"I'm not important," he said. "You, on the other hand, are more important than you realize." There was a pause. "Have you told anyone else?"

She shook her head even though no one was there to see it. "No."

"Good. If you choose this path, you will need to keep it that way." Another pause. "So do you?"

"Do I what?"

"Do you choose something different?"

Now it was Jessica's turn to pause. She wanted to ask him how he knew her, how the woman knew her, and why—a thousand why's, even—they were so interested in something they had no business knowing anything else about. But in the end, she was too tired. And maybe, if she admitted it to herself, too tired of a trail so worn into her soul that she could remember every turn, every twist, along the way.

"Yes," she said. "I choose it."

She heard something snap into place into the man's voice—she couldn't tell if it was enthusiasm or not, but it was something close to it. "Excellent," he said.

And then he told her about the Oracle of V'Canto and started laying out the instructions for her journey carefully, step by step.

Jessica let the towel fall and stretched out on the bed, the spongy mattress pulling her road-weary body into itself. Her hair was wet against her shoulders and neck, her body chilled by the air after twenty minutes of hot, hard water to wash the highway from her mind.

Even now, in bed with her hands folded onto her stomach, she felt the room swaying as her queen-sized bed took the hairpins and switchbacks of the coastal highway.

It was exactly the wrong route for someone afraid of heights and water.

She laid there, eyes closed, and willed the bed to stop. Still, it took the corners, slow as a rocking ship. She wasn't normally prone to motion sickness, but even at fifteen miles per hour, those corners happened with such frequency that she was remembering childhood days at the Cook County Fair. And even now, it held on. When her stomach growled, she found herself wondering how food would play with her body's memory of that drive.

Jessica lay in the quiet and focused on the butterfly wings. *Are you there?*

Yes, she imagined him saying. *And I'm staying this time.*

"Good," she whispered. *I have so much to show you.*

She thought about the drive, the dramatic drop to a blue ocean beneath a blue sky, the fields and rocks and forests. And then, she thought about the Cook County Fair and those rigged, impossible games that inevitably sent you home with a goldfish in a bag after more than ten dollars of dimes and nickels were tossed. And then she thought of Paris, and the smell of coffee on a cool spring morning near the Seine. And of the time she and Tom went to Thailand and saw the temples and jungles, ate lobster barbecued on the beach.

This time, she said it aloud. "So much to show you."

I want to see everything, Mother.

Jessica forced herself to sit up, then stood. She was hungrier than she had realized, and she felt a headache coming on from it. She dressed and dried her hair quickly, and then went to the small desk and started looking at the local restaurants. She would start there, she figured, and begin asking discreetly. Of course, the phone book made it easier. The page was even marked and the restaurant had taken out a small ad in the corner: V'Canto. She scribbled the address onto the small pad of paper provided by the hotel.

It can't be this easy.

Jessica slipped on her shoes, grabbed her sweater and her wallet, and let herself out into the late afternoon.

A wind from the west moved over her as she made her way south on Main Street. She resisted the urge to pull the sweater on, savoring the sun on her arms. Instead, she walked faster.

She passed the Northwest Brewing Company and saw the people crowded at tables and at the bar through its windows, and felt an odd detachment from the people laughing and drinking inside. It was Saturday night and in early March, it was warm and felt like spring, at least when the wind was down.

Jessica walked briskly to Laurel Street and turned left, watching the signs and stopping when she saw the right building, though the way it dominated this small downtown street gave it away before she saw the sign.

V'Canto took up an entire building—three storefronts—with apartments above tucked behind mini-blinded windows on the second floor. An Italian flag hung in the main restaurant window alongside a phone number and a sign that proclaimed lunch to go. There were also menus and flyers featuring their musical line-up.

Jessica pulled the door open and entered the quiet bar. Beyond the bar, she saw a dining room with a scattering of customers, but overall the place was quiet. An older man with olive skin and graying hair sat at the bar. A tall, wiry man with white hair stood behind, polishing a glass.

Both men looked up as she walked in. "Welcome to V'Canto," the old man said. "You chose wisely."

She blinked, suddenly on edge again. "You know?"

He smiled. "I know you chose wisely if you chose V'Canto for dinner tonight." And the warmth of it put her instantly at ease.

"I'm here to meet someone," she said.

The man's smile widened. "Of course you are. A beautiful woman like you, I'm not surprised at all."

Jessica blushed, noting his accent. "You are V'Canto, aren't you?"

He bowed. "I am."

She leaned forward. "I'm here to see the Oracle."

She watched the slightest change overtake his face. As if a door quietly closed and another opened. His eyes took on an appraising gleam. "Of course you are," he said again, practicing a different smile now. "This explains why you're glowing."

It was surprising her less and less and this time, she looked to his hand. Sure enough, he wore the ring.

But when he saw her noticing it, his brow furrowed. He twisted it off his finger and dropped it into his shirt pocket, then touched her elbow. "She won't be here for another hour," he said. "Come. Sit with me and eat."

He nodded to a corner table and she let him guide her there. As they sat, the man behind the bar came around and brought V'Canto's glass of red wine and an ice water for her, along with a menu. "May I recommend some of my favorites to you?"

She nodded and then listened as he described two very different meals. Jessica settled on the rock cod Arabiatto and a glass of iced tea.

As he sipped his wine and she her tea, they made small talk. He asked her questions about where she came from and she asked him questions about life in Fort Bragg and what he'd done before, though the questions she wanted to ask pressed at the inside of her skull like children at a window on a rainy day. Still, she held them back and stayed with lighter topics.

He was an impressive man—he'd spent several years as a chef in France and eventually had settled into the Bay Area only to relocate to the secluded hidden coast and start his own place up. "It is a good place to raise a family," he said.

And it was as if that were the transition in their conversation, timed perfectly for when her food arrived. The bartender—Robert, she learned—brought them bread and V'Canto broke it, handing her half of the small loaf. "Eat," he said.

The more she talked with the man, the more she trusted him, though Jessica wasn't sure exactly why. He felt right. She lifted her fork, poked at the cod there on its bed of pasta and peppers. Then, she put it down. "Can you tell me what's going on?" She nodded to his pocket. "What's with the ring? And why did you take it off?"

His eyes glinted again and she saw something intelligent and calculating there. "I could tell you some of it," he said, "but it is not my place. And I choose not to go beyond my place, though it's not because I don't want you to know. You'll know soon enough." He paused. "Choice is very important. You were asked to choose this, correct?"

"Yes," she said.

He nodded soberly. "Yes. And you've come this far." Their eyes met and she saw something else there that she was uncertain of. Compassion, certainly, but maybe also curiosity. They softened and he smiled. "Why not let it unfold as it is? Try the cod."

She pushed the fork into the cod, beyond it into the noodles below, then raised it to her mouth. The blend of flavors made her mouth water, and she felt the butterfly flapping as she felt the spices warm her face. "It's good," she said.

He smiled. "Choice, as I said, is important. And you will be making a lot of them in a short amount of time. I chose to take my ring off to tell you something. In this moment, I am yours. Not anyone else's. And I choose that so that I can say this to you." He leaned forward. "I wanted to tell you that you can always find more things to choose than what choices are offered."

Then, he slipped the ring from his pocket, put it back onto his finger, and for a moment, his smile became sad and knowing. "Do you understand, Jessica?"

"No," she said. "I really don't understand anything yet."

V'Canto nodded. "You will soon."

Then, as hard as it was for her to shift those gears, they were talking about Fort Bragg and Chicago and anything except the one thing she wanted most to talk about.

When she finished, he stood and took her plate personally. "I hope it goes well for you, Jessica," he told her.

She wasn't exactly sure how to respond. "Thank you."

He bowed to her from the waist, then vanished behind a curtain. Meanwhile, as the spiciness of the cod settled into her stomach, her butterfly was making himself known. And she was suddenly aware that her hands had gone there of their own volition.

The music started up next door in the main part of the restaurant. She heard a single guitar, its strings bent into a warbling blues riff suddenly joined by a harmonica. From her seat, she couldn't see the stage but the music, like the spicy seafood, was setting him off and she suspected these were happy tremors, though she knew it was impossible to feel anything at all this early in.

I want to feel it because I want it to be true, she thought.

It is true, Mother, he whispered to her in her imagination.

She head the door open and close and looked up. There, framed in the doorway, was an old woman. Her pantsuit was a vibrant yellow polyester beneath an orange raincoat that hung open. Her sunglasses were oversized and the frames looked like stems that ended in sunflower rims, something a child might wear or maybe some time-refugee from the seventies. Her hat was made of straw and a plastic rose was tucked into a purple band. She clutched a newspaper in a gloved hand and looked around the bar.

The woman saw Jessica and sized her up quickly, then approached. "There you are," she said. "Aren't you?"

She didn't wait for her to answer; she pulled out the chair V'Canto had vacated and sat down. This time, Jessica looked to the hands first. But the white gloves hid any ring she might've worn.

The woman chuckled. "You're looking for the ring."

"Everyone else seems to be wearing it," Jessica said, feeling the heat rise to her cheeks.

"I choose not to take sides," the woman said. "Now." She tugged at her gloves, revealing liver spotted hands. Close up, the woman was older than she first appeared, and Jessica saw now that it was the amount of make-up she wore. She stretched those hands out across the table.

Jessica flinched by instinct, feeling herself pulling back. Then, she forced her hands forward over the wood surface between them. The woman's were dry and cool and bony, but strong. "Are you the oracle?"

"Yes," she said. "Now close your eyes."

She closed her eyes and felt the woman's hands squeezing hers, felt the flutter in her stomach. "You can tell me if I will keep this baby?"

"Yes," she said, "I can tell you. But quiet now. Breathe."

She breathed and waited. Finally, she opened her eyes and the woman was staring at her, smiling.

"Do you feel better?" she asked.

Jessica nodded. "Yes. What did you see?"

The woman laughed. "Oh, I didn't see anything. You just looked anxious. I wanted to help you relax." She released her hands. "Are you ready to go?"

Jessica blinked. "Go where?"

The Oracle of V'Canto stood. "Off to see your future. That's what you came for?"

She nodded though there was hesitation in her voice as she answered. "Yes." She paused and touched her stomach again. "My baby's future."

"Yes of course," the old woman said. "Let's go."

Sunset cast the sky in shades of pink and red. The high clouds on the horizon became the color of bruises as the light faded, and Jessica drove north out of Fort Bragg.

Beside her, the old woman sat quietly in the passenger seat, and Jessica found herself once more uncertain of this different choice of hers. Learning that she had yet more driving to do, now with this so-called oracle seated beside her, had done little to help the anxiety she worked so hard to keep in check. And the idea of taking more twists and turns on this highway in the dark, after a long day of white-knuckles on the wheel, did little to help.

Still, the woman had insisted that it needed to be this way. At least the drive north had far fewer of the treacherous cliffs she'd faced on her way to Fort Bragg. And after about an hour, the road slanted to the northeast, cutting away from the coast and deeper into the forests.

So Jessica drove on, hope and fear both whispering to her in the silence of the car. It felt like much more time had passed, but just a week ago the girl had suggested Jessica choose something differ-ent. Choice seemed very important to whoever these people were and she'd surprised herself at how easily she'd made these choices—com-ing to California, driving up into the middle of nowhere to find this unusual oracle, and then driving farther into the middle of nowhere to have her future told. Still, she asked herself, was it worth it?

Yes, she thought. *If she tells me I will keep this baby.*

The old woman startled her when she finally spoke. "There's a road ahead to the right. Take it."

Jessica slowed and saw it as she rounded the curve and took the right. It was unmarked, and narrow, the wheel ruts worn deep though it looked largely forgotten. She stopped just as the car left the high-way and glanced at the woman. "Here?"

In the dim light of the dashboard lights, the oracle's face was calm but sober. "Yes. Here."

Jessica eased the car farther down the road, stopping finally at a rusted metal gate. A sign on the gate warned off trespassers.

"We walk from here," the old woman said. "It's not far at all now."

They climbed from the car and Jessica stood for a moment, hear-ing nothing but the ticking of the engine as it cooled. She blinked into the dark as her eyes adjusted to it. When the old woman started walking, her stride long and her gait confident, Jessica followed.

The gate was easily circumnavigated on foot; she stayed behind the oracle as she led them deeper into a forest that changed as they walked.

The trees were getting bigger. The trunks were now massive, stretching upward forever, with small pockets of stars sparkling in the gaps of the ceiling their branches formed. They walked for ten minutes until the woman stopped and raised a finger to point left of the road. "Straight on just a bit," she said. "There's a stone in a clearing. Lay your hand upon it and ponder a bit."

Jessica squinted, thinking she could just make out a brighter patch not far from the road. "Ponder a bit?" She heard how dubious she sounded but was past caring.

The oracle nodded. "I'll wait here."

She left the road, her feet tentative on the soft loam as she moved into the trees. She felt the fluttering start up again and slowed, resting her hands on her stomach, as she approached a lighter patch of dark.

The small clearing was flat and grassy with a mound at the center that, as she drew closer, proved to be a half-buried stone that stood as high as her waist. Jessica stretched out her hand, and then paused and looked around.

The trees rose up above her like sentinels. The stars cast dirty light that washed the clearing in charcoal. The silence was complete. As she lowered her hand onto the stone, she wondered what to expect.

The black surface was smooth and familiar. She wondered if the stones from the rings she'd seen had been chipped from this source or one like it. Either way, something deep and instinctive in her whispered that this stone was rare. Perhaps something so rare that it did not belong here at all.

But nothing else. No flash of future water breaking or a breakneck race to the hospital, already breathing into her labor. No supernatural sense of calm assurance.

She looked up, her hand solid upon the rock, and realized that suddenly here, beneath these trees, beneath these stars, she didn't matter anymore. The trees were towering here before she was born and would tower beyond her death. The stars had shone before—some of them gone already before their light reached her eyes—and would shine on after.

She whispered the words, her hand upon the stone. "I don't matter anymore."

You matter to me, Mother.

Jessica felt the sob take her shoulders and she stifled a cry, the tears suddenly coursing her cheeks.

Then, she took her hand off the stone, turned around, and walked back into the forest. The old woman stood waiting for her on the road.

"What did you see?" the oracle asked her.

Jessica wiped her eyes. "I saw how small I am."

"Yes. That is what I thought you might see."

She looked at the old woman. "I don't understand what that has to do with my baby."

She thought she saw the whisper of a smile on the oracle's face though her eyes held sadness in them. "I know. But you'll understand very soon. If you choose it."

If I choose it. "What do you mean?"

"If I told you that your baby would survive—would even do great and amazing things—but that in order for it to happen you would have to give up your life as you know it, would you make that sacrifice?" Jessica opened her mouth to answer but the woman went on. "Would you abandon your friends, your family, everything, to start over in a place set apart and safe, until your boy reached his majority?"

She didn't give it a second thought. "Of course I would."

"Say that you would choose it."

"Yes," Jessica said. "Yes, I choose it."

"Then your son will be fine," the oracle said.

My son. Her hands went to her stomach again. "You can see that?"

The woman chuckled. "Of a sort. But it's not magic, my dear, at least not my part in it. They'll explain."

She opened her mouth to ask who exactly would explain it but then she closed it as the sound of soft footfalls reached her ears. Five cloaked figures approached from farther down the road. Two of them, she noted, held what looked like assault rifles. One walked ahead of the others.

The leader stepped forward, and when he spoke, she recognized his voice from their telephone conversation last week. "Hello Jessica. I'm so glad you made the journey." He smiled. "How are you feeling?"

She wasn't sure how to answer. She'd driven to the middle of nowhere with a fortune teller and now stood with a group of armed men dressed as wizards. "I feel . . . small."

The man smiled. "And yet history will remember you being among the greatest of our species. But the others said the same thing."

"The others?"

He nodded. "Yes. You've come this far. If you can come just a bit farther, you'll meet them. And get answers to your questions. They're waiting. And the rest are coming."

She took another deep breath. She *had* come this far. Jessica eyed the rifles again. The men who held them were watching the forest around them, not her, and she suspected they were along for their protection. Everything offered so far had been based solely upon her consent. "But it's my choice? I can leave any time?"

He smiled again. "Of course."

Jessica swallowed her fear. "Okay."

Then, as they turned and moved back down the road, she followed them as the forest deepened and darkened around her and carried her deeper into itself.

Jessica sat in the chair and looked at the photographs and open files on the large round mahogany table, disbelief and anger dueling for her attention as she sat across from the man.

He'd identified himself simply as Brother Edmund and in the light of his spacious office, she saw a trim man in his late fifties, his hair short and white, his eyes a penetrating blue. The only jewelry he wore was his ring—this one with a stone slightly larger and a band slightly thicker than the others she'd seen.

They'd walked to the compound and the size of the place had astonished her. It lay within a large walled enclosure, a scattering of enough houses and buildings to make up a smallish town. She'd read a few signs by the light of flickering street lamps—a store, a library, a medical facility. They'd guided her to the center of the compound, a large manor, and then she and Brother Edmund had slipped into his office.

It was a comfortable room with a fireplace crackling in the corner and a few scattered bookcases filled mostly with antique volumes. The desk was large and meticulously tidy, but he'd guided her to a table where a file box awaited.

After she'd sat, he started pulling files from the box and laying them before her.

"Do you recognize this man?" he had asked her.

She'd blinked at the first picture, recognizing him instantly. "That's Dr. Kasmirsky," she said. He'd been her doctor since high school.

"Yes," he'd said. Then, he'd laid another file open and her ex-husband, Tom, had smiled up at her. "And this one?"

"Yes." She'd felt the fear growing in her again and as more files and more pictures appeared, that fear started twisting into anger. People in her life—friends, co-workers, acquaintances.

When they were all laid open in front of her, Brother Edmund sat back. "I know this will be difficult for you, Jessica, but none of these people have been honest with you about their role in your life."

Their role in my life. She forced her eyes up from the photographs and the pages of handwritten and typed notes. "And what was that exactly? Their role in my life?"

His words were gentle and she saw sadness in his eyes. "To prevent you from carrying your child to term."

"I don't understand."

Brother Edmund stood. "I know it's difficult to accept." He walked to the window. Near it sat two armchairs on either side of a small table, and on the table was a chess set. He picked up two of the pieces and looked at them in his hands. "Your baby is actually very important, Jessica," he said. "So important that there are organizations and agencies that exist solely to prevent your child—and the others like him—from ever drawing breath." He walked back to the table where she sat and placed the pieces at the center of it. One piece was white, the other black. His finger lingered over the black piece. "And until now, they've been successful. But my group intends to change that." His eyes met hers again. "We *long* to change it, Jessica, and the entire world longs for it, too, though they do not know it."

She'd hoped coming here would bring answers, but each answer added a hundred questions and she wasn't sure where to start. She saw Tom's face again there in his file and felt the first twist of betrayal in her heart. "Why would they do this?" The question became more specific. "Why Tom of all people? It was his baby, too."

Brother Edmund sat. "It was and it wasn't. But the shortest answer is that once they knew you were a Bearer, they planted appropriate people in your life to maintain control over the situation. Agent Ratchke was assigned to you as a control measure. And I'm sure he discouraged you from future attempts even after the first miscarriage?"

She nodded. They'd fought about it, even. And after the third, he'd encouraged the tubal ligation though she'd resisted it for years after. "He wasn't very excited about children in the first place," she said.

"No," Brother Edmund said. "Particularly this child."

Something he said earlier struck her. "Once they knew I was a Bearer?"

He smiled. "Yes. Your son is very special."

Her eyebrows furrowed. "How do you know it's a boy?"

Brother Edmund shrugged. "How do *you* know? Because you do, if you're honest. You've known each time."

Yes. "It just feels right," she said.

"If you stay, you'll see for yourself. We have a fully staffed medical clinic. You're due for a checkup, though I can assure you that without interference, this baby will be born strong and healthy, ready for his work in the world."

"What work is that?"

Brother Edmund reached out, knocked over the white piece. "Making things right," he said. He leaned forward, his eyes suddenly glinting with something old and buried in them. "We've had lots of time to make them right ourselves, but we are short-sighted primates governed by behaviors once favored by our evolution. The same behaviors are now ushering in our eventual extinction. We increase in our ingenuity, creating bigger and bigger problems to solve. We move through life, all our tangled dreams in disarray, at war with one another and with our very future. It's time for a different path."

Jessica felt the flutter again, this time tentative. "What path is that?"

"The one you help pave with your son," Brother Edmund said. "The Advent of the Thirteen." He closed his eyes now. "Blessed are the Thirteen to come, and blessed are their Bearers," he said and she suspected by his tone that he was quoting something sacred to him.

His words connected to earlier words, out on the road in the dark, when he'd told her there were others. "Thirteen?" She looked at the files on the table. "There are twelve others like me?" She waved at the folders. "Just like this?"

"Not *just* like, but certainly similar. It took us a while to find you all." He nodded to the white piece. "They found you sooner and did their best to keep you hidden. But they always move first on the board and they don't play by as many rules."

The words she'd heard repeatedly over the last week came to mind. *Do you choose it?* She looked at the folders again, then at the white piece he'd tipped over on the table. "They didn't offer me any choices."

"No," he said. "We have a clear Freedom of Choice Protocol that we operate within."

"Which means I can still leave?"

"Yes," he said. "Absolutely. Though it would break my heart, and thousands of others, if you chose that after coming so far and learning all of this." His face became sober, his eyes hard. "And if you choose that, once you've left the protection of this place, they will likely find you. And now that they know not even a tubal ligation can prevent what's coming, I'm not sure exactly what they *would* do. They wouldn't kill you, I know that much. That would start things over again and they'd have to do the work—just like us—of figuring out who the next Bearer might be."

Jessica glanced at Tom's smiling face again there in the folder. *No,* she thought. *Agent Radke.* "If they have these kinds of resources, I don't see how you can possibly protect me with a few rifles and a wall."

"It's the place that protects you," he said. "Though we'll certainly help. But our . . . opponents . . . do not like the old places." He paused and studied her. "If you choose to stay here, your son will have everything he needs. You will too. And when he reaches his majority, with the others, you'll watch him change the world and save our species from itself."

Another question pried at her and it slipped out before she could stop it. "But what if our species doesn't choose to be saved?"

"The Thirteen will choose for us when they come into their own. Our time for choosing will have run out." Brother Edmund stood. "But enough of this. You can talk more with me later. Would you like to meet one of the others?"

She nodded and stood, too. "I would."

He inclined his head. "Then follow me."

He ushered her into a sitting room where a young woman sat waiting. She was maybe eighteen, her long blond hair tied back into a ponytail. Her pink flannel pajamas and slippers made her look even younger. The girl smiled up at her as they walked in. "Jessica, this is Lisa. She's been here for about a week now." He waited until they'd shaken hands and then went back to the door. "I'll leave you for a bit. I'm just outside if you need me."

Lisa patted the couch beside her and Jessica sat. The girl's face glowed. "I'm Ansa's Bearer," she said. "We just found out yesterday."

"Ansa?"

Lisa touched her stomach and now, Jessica saw the slight bulge there. "My daughter. Seventh of Thirteen."

"You've already named her?"

Lisa laughed. "Oh no. They already have names. We just have to learn which ones are which."

"How many are here already?"

"Nine not counting you. But the others are on their way. Edna will bring them out to the stone."

"Edna?"

Lisa leaned over. "Sorry. The oracle." She wrinkled her nose. "Though she's not really an oracle. She's a retired actress—and a member of the Thirteen's L.A. temple—that they brought in to help. She'll bring the last two later this week and then this Advent will be sealed." She paused. "As long as they all choose it, too." Her smile grew. "It's been over eight thousand years since their last Advent." She reached over and patted Jessica's leg. "But you'll learn all about that in orientation."

She imagined a comfortable sun room with comfortable chairs and ten women sitting in a circle, sipping tea with Brother Edmund, wearing name tags that read "Hello My Name is _____, Bearer of _____" with the names scribbled in with Sharpie pens of multiple colors. The thought of it made her smile and the girl smiled back. "So where are you from, Lisa?"

"Minnesota," she said. "I'm the youngest. Brother Edmund says they were lucky they found me. Ansa's last Bearer was killed; she was actually from Scotland." The look on Jessica's face must have clued the girl in on just how lost she felt. "It's a lot to take in," Lisa said. "But after a few weeks of class, it'll all make sense to you." She leaned forward. "But really, at the end of it all, making sense isn't really all that necessary. At the end of it all, we don't matter." The girl touched her stomach. "*They* do."

They talked for a bit longer, Jessica asking questions and Lisa answering, until it was clear that the answers continued to multiply more and more questions.

"Another one for orientation," Jessica finally said after yet another answer that only made sense in a vague and ominous context she could not quite grasp.

Lisa nodded. "But I'm so glad you're here. I can't wait to find out which one you bear. One of the boys, I'm told."

Yes. And despite how crazy, how twisted, it all sounded, something deep in her—down at the very source of that fluttering—assured her that what she heard here in this place was true. A small town had been built for her son and the twelve others who made up this Thirteen, and though she did not understand what they were, they'd been around for a long time and had visited before. The exact details awaited her in orientation, but somehow, they'd been repressed these last eight millennia and the world was now ripe for their return.

"Things need to be made right," Lisa said. "Badly."

When Brother Edmund finally returned, Jessica stood and the girl did as well. This time, she and Lisa hugged and the girl repeated herself. "I'm so glad you're here."

Then, she left.

Brother Edmund smiled. "I hope you had a good visit. A chance to get some questions answered."

"I did."

"You can meet the others in the morning if you'd let me show you to a room."

My choice again. She looked at the man. "And I can say no?"

Brother Edmund took a deep breath. She could see something in his eyes that looked like fear for just a split second. Then it was gone. "Yes. Of course." She could tell he wanted to say more but was resisting the urge. Finally, he found words that didn't compromise him. "But I hope desperately that you choose to stay. If you leave, I'm certain you will lose your son."

As much as she didn't want to accept all of this, she suspected he was correct. Still, something about it felt out of sync. Something about Lisa's youthful enthusiasm frightened her as much as the idea of losing her son did.

And the web of conspiracy and deceit her life had been tangled in, around this deepest and simplest dream of motherhood she'd had for as long as she could remember, enraged her.

"I need to think about it."

His eyes were hopeful. "We'd be happy to host you while you think. You can meet the others. Maybe attend class with them tomorrow?"

Now I test my freedom to choose. "I'd be more comfortable thinking in my motel room."

She watched Brother Edmund bank the hope in his eyes and nod curtly. "As you wish. I'll have my men escort you back to your car."

Jessica Riley extended her hand, and after the slightest hesitation, he shook it. "Thank you for keeping your promise, Brother Edmund."

They moved along the overgrown road in silence, the two cloaked men with their assault rifles held loosely as they moved ahead of her. Red-tinted flashlights helped her navigate in the dark, and when they reached the place where the oracle—Edna—had sent her off the road to find the stone, Jessica felt a stronger flutter than she'd felt before.

She stopped and the others stopped, too.

She tried to take a step forward and the fluttering increased. It settled when she turned toward the direction of the distant clearing. She turned back to the men. "I need to visit the stone again."

They nodded and she slipped off the road, slowly understanding just what—who, actually—compelled her forward.

She reached the clearing and its stone, and stood at the edge of it. She'd made this trip to see the future, and after a fashion she'd seen two—one where she stayed in this place with her son and one where she left this place, and left that dream behind. Either way, she was a piece in an ancient game that went back and forth between sides she still didn't fully comprehend, though one side desperately yearned for her to bear this son and the other would do nearly anything to prevent it.

Staying made all the sense in the world. She suspected that was why the others had chosen it. And the two remaining, she thought, would choose it, too.

But something about it felt wrong to her.

What happened when humanity's time to choose ran out and the Thirteen were choosing on their behalf? *It's a murky future at best,* she thought.

Not so murky at all, her son whispered. *I can show you, Mother.*

She felt him move again and let her feet carry her the rest of the way. She stood before the stone and laid one hand upon it while placing the other on her stomach.

Show me.

The stone was electric now, sending a shudder through her that rocked Jessica on her feet even as she gasped. She saw him then, tiny and brand new in her waiting arms. His dark skin was slick with her blood and his brown eyes were wide but he did not cry.

I am called Tamyr, those eyes told her and then suddenly he was older—maybe six—running across a soccer field chased by other boys and girls in matching team uniforms as he kicked the ball.

Next, he was older—maybe thirteen—and fighting with some kind of heavy stick. There were four men, fully grown and armed with blades, who had him surrounded and she watched him disarm them all, one by one.

The images flashed before her eyes and she felt herself swelling with pride at all that her son—Tamyr—was capable of.

They have their own future to prepare me for. Now she saw all thirteen of them, standing together, all wearing dark uniforms, and watched them lift up into the air together to scatter and fly their separate directions.

She saw them sent out into the world and from that sending, she saw rivers of blood that filled an ocean. She saw cities burning and highways abandoned along with the cars that once roamed them freely. She saw the flags of a hundred nations burned while their leaders—elected or not—were forced to watch before their execution. She saw the same happen with the scriptures of a hundred faiths, their clerics also forced to watch, faces streaked with ash as they wept before being tossed upon the fires themselves.

She saw the Thirteen subdue humanity beneath their booted feet. And after that, she saw peace on Earth, imposed by their will. And an Earth that, because of their Advent, slowly healed itself from the parasite her species had become.

"Blessed be the Thirteen," she heard Brother Edmund's voice whisper. "And blessed be the Bearers."

She took her hand off the stone, her stomach aching from what she'd seen. She closed her eyes against the vertigo that seized her. "You can be more than this, Tamyr."

How can be I more than what I am made for, Mother?

She opened her eyes. Overhead, the stars seemed brighter than they'd been earlier, their light softening the darkness around her. *You could choose it,* she willed. *We could choose it.* Though she didn't know how. And she didn't know where.

What had V'Canto said? *I can always find more things to choose than the choices presented to me.* Perhaps that kindly old man with the familiar smile was the true oracle.

She looked around herself at the ancient redwoods. This old place, Edmund had said, offered her protection by the strange rules of their game. Surely there were other old places where she could hide. She had her boss's credit card still. A phone call home with a made-up emergency would get her access to its PIN and the cash she'd need for the first leg of her journey.

She'd figure out the rest as she went. And try to raise her son outside their cruel and brutal rules. It was not a choice she had expected—or a life she'd ever imagined. But it would be hers. And her son's.

What had Brother Edmund said about humanity's failings?

All our tangled dreams in disarray.

This particular dream, Jessica Riley thought as she walked back to the road and to the car that awaited her, was one that she would spend herself utterly to untangle.

It was, she realized, an easy choice to make.

THE STARSHIP MECHANIC
(with Jay Lake)

*T*he floor of Borderlands Books had been polished to mirror brightness. A nice trick with old knotty pine, but Penauch would have been a weapons-grade obsessive-compulsive if he'd been human. I'd thought about setting him to detailing my car, but he's just as likely to polish it down to aluminum and steel after deciding the paint was an impurity.

When he discovered that the human race recorded our ideas in *books*, he'd been impossible to keep away from the store. Penauch didn't actually read them, not as such, and he was most reluctant to touch the volumes. He seemed to view books as vehicles, launch capsules to propel ideas from the dreaming mind of the human race into our collective forebrain.

Despite the fact that Penauch was singular, unitary, a solitary alien in the human world, he apparently didn't conceive of us as anything but a collective entity. The xenoanthropologists at Berkeley were carving Ph.D.s out of that particular clay as fast as their grad students could transcribe Penauch's conversations with me.

He'd arrived the same as David Bowie in that old movie. No, not *Brother From Another Planet*; *The Man Who Fell To Earth*. Tumbled out of the autumn sky over the Cole Valley neighborhood of San Francisco like a maple seed, spinning with his arms stretched wide and his mouth open in a teakettle shriek audible from the Ghost Fleet in Suisun Bay all the way down to the grubby streets of San Jose.

> *"The subject's fallsacs when fully deployed serve as a tympanum, producing a rhythmic vibration at a frequency perceived by the human ear as a high-pitched shriek. Xeno-*

physiological modeling has thus far failed to generate test-
able hypotheses concerning the volume of the sound produced.
Some observers have speculated that the subject deployed
technological assistance during atmospheric entry, though no
evidence of this was found at the landing site, and subject has
never indicated this was the case."

—Jude A. Feldman quoting Jen West Scholes
A Reader's Guide to Earth's Only Living Spaceman
Borderlands Books, 2014

It was easier, keeping Penauch in the bookstore. The owners didn't mind. They'd had hairless cats around the place for years—a breed called sphinxes. The odd animals served as a neighborhood tourist attraction and business draw. A seven-foot alien with a face like a plate of spaghetti and a cluster of writhing arms wasn't all that different. Not in a science fiction bookstore, at least.

Thing is, when Penauch was out in the world, he had a tendency to *fix* things.

This fixing often turned out to be not so good.

No technology was involved. Penauch's body was demonstrably able to modify the chitinous excrescences of his appendages at will. If he needed a cutting edge, he ate a bit of whatever steel was handy and swiftly metabolized it. If he needed electrical conductors, he sought out copper plumbing. If he needed logic probes, he consumed sand or diamonds or glass.

It was all the same to Penauch.

As best any of us could figure out, Penauch was a sort of *tool*. A Swiss army knife that some spacefaring race had dropped or thrown away, abandoned until he came to rest on Earth's alien shore.

And Penauch only spoke to me.

The question of Penauch's mental competence has bear-
ing in both law and ethics. Pratt and Shaw (2013) have
effectively argued that the alien fails the Turing test, both at
a gross observational level and within the context of finer

measurements of conversational intent and cooperation.
Cashier (2014) claims an indirectly derived Stanford-Bi-
net score in the 99th percentile, but seemingly contradicts
herself by asserting that Penauch's sentience is at best an
open question. Is he (or it) a machine, a person, or something
else entirely?

—S.G. Browne
"A Literature Review of the Question of Alien
Mentation"
Journal of Exogenic Studies, Volume II,
Number 4, August, 2015

The first time he fixed something was right after he'd landed.
Penauch impacted with that piercing shriek at 2:53 p.m Pacific Time
on Saturday, July 16, 2011, at the intersection of Cole and Paranassus
in the Cole Valley neighborhood of San Francisco. Every window
within six blocks shattered. Almost a hundred pedestrians and shop-
pers in the immediate area were treated for lacerations from broken
glass, over two dozen more for damage to hearing and sinuses.

I got to him first, stumbling out of Cole Hardware with a headache like a cartoon anvil had been dropped on me. Inside, we figured
a bomb had gone off. The rising noise and the vibrating windows. All
the vases in the homewares section had exploded. Luckily I'd been
with the fasteners. The nails *sang*, but they didn't leap off the shelves
and try to make hamburger of me.

Outside, there was this guy lying in a crater in the middle of the
intersection, like Wile E. Coyote after he'd run out of Acme patented
jet fuel. I hurried over, touched his shoulder, and realized what a god-
damned mess he was. Then half a dozen eyes opened, and something
like a giant rigatoni farted before saying, "Penauch."

Weird thing was, I could *hear* the spelling.

Though I didn't know it in that moment, my old life was over, my
new one begun.

Penauch then looked at my shattered wristwatch, grabbed a
handful of BMW windshield glass, sucked it down, and moments
later fixed my timepiece.

For some value of "fixed."

It still tells time, somewhere with a base seventeen counting system and twenty-eight point one five seven hour day. It shows me the phases of Phobos and Deimos, evidence that he'd been on (or near) Mars. Took a while to figure that one out. And the thing warbles whenever someone gets near me carrying more than about eight ounces of petroleum products. Including grocery bags, for example, and most plastics.

I could probably get millions for it on eBay. Penauch's first artifact, and one of less than a dozen in private hands.

The government owns him now, inasmuch as anyone owns Penauch. They can't keep him anywhere. He "fixes" his way out of any place he gets locked into. He comes back to San Francisco, finds me, and we go to the bookstore. Where Penauch polishes the floors and chases the hairless cats and draws pilgrims from all over the world to pray in Valencia Street. The city gave up on traffic control a long time ago. It's a pedestrian mall now when he's around.

The problem has always been, none of us have any idea what Penauch *is*. What he *does*. What he's *for*. I'm the only one he talks to, and most of what he says is Alice in Wonderland dialog, except when it isn't. Two new semiconductor companies have been started through analysis of his babble, and an entire novel chemical feedstock process for converting biomass into plastics.

Then one day, down on the mirrored floor of Borderlands Books, Penauch looked at me and said quite clearly, "They're coming back."

I was afraid we were about to get our answers.

It was raining men in the Castro, literally, and every single one of them was named Todd. Every single one of them wore Hawaiian shirts and khaki shorts and Birkenstocks. Every single one of them landed on their backs, flopped like trout for a full minute and leaped to their feet shouting one word: "Penauch!"

—*San Francisco Chronicle*
November 11th, 2015
Gail Carriger reporting

"I must leave," Penauch said, his voice heavy as he stroked a hairless cat on the freshly polished floor of the bookstore.

On a small TV in the back office of the store, an excited reporter in Milk Plaza spoke rapidly about the strange visitors who'd fallen from the sky. Hundreds of men named Todd, now scattered out into the city with one word on their tongues. As it played in the background, I watched Penauch and could feel the sadness coming off of him in waves. "Where will you go?"

Penauch stood. "I don't know. Anywhere but here. Will you help me?"

The bell on the door jingled and a man entered the store. "Penauch," he said.

I looked up at the visitor. His Hawaiian shirt was an orange that hurt my eyes, decorated in something that looked like cascading pineapples. He smiled and scowled at the same time.

Penauch moved quickly and suddenly the room smelled of ozone and cabbage.

The man, named Todd I assumed, was gone.

I looked at my alien, took in the slow wriggle of his pale and determined face. "What did you do?"

Penauch's clustered silver eyes leaked mercury tears. "I . . . unfixed him."

We ran out the back. We climbed into my car over on Guerrero. We drove north and away.

Xenolinguists have expended considerable effort on the so-called "Todd Phenomenon." Everyone on 11/11/15 knew the visitors from outer space were named Todd, yet no one could say how or why. This is the best documented case of what can be argued as telepathy in the modern scientific record, yet it is equally worthless by virtue of being impossible to either replicate or falsify.

—Christopher Barzak
blog entry
January 14th, 2016

We stayed ahead of them for most of a week, turning east and then north. We made it as far as Edmonton before the man-rain caught up to us.

While Penauch slept, I grabbed snacks of news from the radio. These so-called Todds spread out in their search, my friend's name the only word upon their lips. They made no effort to resist the authorities. Three were shot by members of the Washington State Patrol. Two were killed by Navy SEALS in the small town of St. Maries, Idaho. They stole cars. They drove fast. They followed after us.

And then they found us in Edmonton.

We were at an A&W drive-through window when the first Todd caught up to the car. He t-boned us into the side of the restaurant with his Mercedes, pushing Penauch against me. The Todd was careful not to get within reach.

"Penauch," he shouted from outside the window. My friend whimpered. Our car groaned and ground as his hands moved over the dashboard, trying to fix it.

Two other cars hemmed us in, behind and before. Todds in Hawaiian shirts and khaki shorts stepped out, unfazed by the cold. One climbed onto the hood of my Corvair. "Your services are still required."

Penauch whimpered again. I noticed that the Todd's breath did not show in the sub-zero air.

The air shimmered as a bending light enfolded us.

> *"Af-afterwards, it, uh, it didn't m-matter so much. I m-mean, uh, you know? He smiled at me. Well, n-not an, uh, a smile. Not with that face. Like, a virtual smile? Th-then he was g-gone. Blown out like a candle. You know? Flame on, flame off."*
>
> —RCMP transcript of eyewitness testimony
> Edmonton, AB; 11/16/15

I awoke in a dark place choking for air, my chest weighted with fluid. Penauch's hand settled upon my shoulder. The heaviness leapt from me.

"Where am I?"

I heard a sound not unlike something heavy rolling in mud. It was a thick, wet noise and words formed alongside it in my mind. *You are in*—crackle hiss warble—*medical containment pod of the Starship*—but the name of the vessel was incomprehensible to me. *Exposure to our malfunctioning*—hiss crackle warble—*mechanic has infected you with trace elements of*—here another word I could not understand—*viruses.*

"I don't get it," I said.

Penauch's voice was low. "You're not meant to. But once I've fixed you, you will be returned to the store."

I looked at him. "What about you?"

He shook his head, the rigatoni of his face slapping itself gently. "My services are required here. I am now operating within my design parameters."

I opened my mouth to ask another question but then the light returned and I was falling. Beside me, Penauch fell, too, and he held my hand tightly. "Do not let go," he said as we impacted.

This time we made no crater as we landed. We stood and I brushed myself off. "I have no idea what any of this means."

"It won't matter," Penauch told me. "But say goodbye to the cats for me."

"I will," I promised.

"I liked your planet. Now that the—" again, the incomprehensible ship's name slid entirely over my brain "—is operational once more, I suppose we'll find others." He sighed. "I hope I malfunction again soon." He stretched out a hand and fixed me a final time.

I blinked at him and somehow, mid-blink, I stood in the center of Valencia Street.

I walked into Borderlands Books, still wondering exactly how I was wandering the streets of San Francisco in an orange Hawaiian shirt and a pair of khaki shorts three sizes too large.

A pretty girl smiled at me from behind the counter. "Hi Bill," she said. "Where've you been?"

I shrugged.

A hairless cat ran in front of me, feet scampering over floors that were badly in need of a polish.

"Goodbye," I told it, but didn't know why.

A CHANCE OF CATS AND DOGS

A bald guy in a dark suit put down his briefcase and slid into the booth across from me. I'd smelled him coming—four hundred dollar cologne and an omelet with black coffee for breakfast—and smiled as he sat down. He was fiftyish, gaunt as a mortician and human. I'd expected the human part; the patrons had a lot of them working for them.

"Are you Angus Wolfe?"

"I am," I said as I extended my hand.

"Mark Connor." His eyes glanced at the thick hair on the back of it, the wiry curls that poked from my buttoned shirt sleeve. Still, he shook it. "Thank you for agreeing to see me."

I nodded and let my hand drift back to the tea mug. I'd been using Abraham's Table—a small Chinatown restaurant off Market—as an informal office for years. And Henry Ing, the owner, kept a booth free in the back room. I shuffled the papers around and closed the lid to my laptop. "How can I help you, Mr. Connor?"

He pulled a thick envelope from his jacket pocket and slid it across the table. "My employer would like to retain your services."

"I provide a lot of different services. Which in particular is your employer interested in?"

Connor cleared his throat. "He has a lost pet he'd like you to find."

"I'm good at finding things." It was a large part of my business. My father was an Old World rending hound and my mother was a waitress from Spokane. I got her good looks and charm. I got his hair along with a sense of smell like no other. "What kind of pet are we talking about?"

"A cat." Connor lifted his briefcase onto the table and opened it.

He pulled a file from it and then withdrew a picture. "Her name is Monica Evenheart."

I studied it. She was a young woman but old enough to be an Old Worlder. Probably a kitten when she crossed over under the Covenant to escape my father's kind. Dark hair. Dark skin. Darker eyes. The silver moon collar was subtle beneath her cream-colored blouse. Somewhere, off camera, someone wore the ring that went with it to command both the cat and her change cycle. "Was she taken or did she run away?"

"Ran away," he said. "Stole both the ring and the collar."

So it was a breach of contract. When the rending hounds over-threw the Old World, those who could escaped here. The cost of passage—including the means to blend seamlessly into their new home—was steep. Whole families plunged themselves into inden-tured servitude to flee the fangs and claws of invasion and genocide. Because of my father, I dodged all of that. My mother raised me qui-etly away from all the politics and pandemonium. I looked at the picture again then back to Connor. "Any idea where or why?"

He pursed his lips. "We have reason to believe she's in Seattle . . . or will be. As to why . . ." He paused, pulled out another stack of pic-tures. "We're not exactly sure, but she's hunting off-leash."

So she was a mouser. Hunting off-leash in this world was a defi-nite no-no. Leashed hunting was only permitted under the guise of a covenanted patron—usually one of the few Old World humans who'd managed to cross over decades before the war. Only an Old Worlder could wield Old Worlder magic

I laid her picture aside and took the others. Crime scene tape and bloody rags dangling over city streets. They looked like they were men once before Connor's cat trussed them up and played with her prey. I squinted at the streetscape. "These aren't Seattle."

He shook his head. "No. Los Angeles and Portland. She's heading north."

I scowled. "And you have no idea why? Are her prey random or are they connected in some way?"

"We're really not sure." I'm used to being lied to in my line of work so I know what it sounds like. And sometimes, if it's thick enough, I'll even turn down a job. I considered this time as I thumbed through the pictures again. But work had been slow and the lack of work had me living out of a shitty car with what little I owned tucked in storage. The envelope was thick with promise.

"And when I find her, I just ask her to fly back with me?"

"We'll have a tranq pistol waiting for you in Seattle. They're hard to fly with." He pulled a cell phone from the suitcase and passed it over. "When you have her sedated, my number is in the phone. There will be a team ready to bring her back."

"Okay," I said. "I'll do it."

Connor smiled and tapped the envelope. "I think you'll find this to be an adequate retainer toward expenses. You'll be paid two thirds more when our pet is returned."

Pet. I didn't like that part either. But the patrons and their Covenant made their contracts as they could. Most of my work came from them or from other Old Worlders in that system. Despite my parents' best intentions, I skirted the edge of a world they did not want for me.

Connor reached into the briefcase one last time and handed me a wadded bit of pink cloth. "This is her."

I took it. It was a bra, and I felt my face flush. I could already smell it but to be sure, I brought it close to my nose and inhaled deeply of Monica Evenheart. I handed it back.

He waved it away. "Keep it. In case you need reminding."

"I won't need reminding," I said as I laid it on the table.

Connor dropped it back into the briefcase and closed it. Then he stood and offered his hand again. "Be careful, Mr. Wolfe."

I stood and shook it. "I will."

I waited until he left before I picked up the envelope and rifled through the green. It was a lot for this kind of work, even with the bit about her being on the hunt. I pulled out a hundred for Henry Ing and shoved the envelope into my jeans pocket.

Then I opened my laptop and went back online to book my flight to Seattle.

It was mostly cloudy in Seattle, the afternoon light suffused by a veil of gray as I wound through rush hour traffic from the airport to Ballard.

I'd spent the flight going through the Evenheart file, familiarizing myself as best I could. She was near thirty and, as I suspected, just a kitten when she crossed over with her family and took the moon collar of her patron. As custom, the patrons divided up the families and found ways for them to earn their passage and keep. My father's kin had created this mess when they'd taken the Opal Throne. The Queen of the North was the first to flee and those who could, followed. Which led to the Covenant.

I'd skirted all of that, product of a rending hound's unexpected conscience and a waitress's love of strays. My father had worn a moon collar in those days and I reckon that is how I managed to arrive on the scene more human than not. Or maybe it was his deep desire to not pass that part of himself on to his only child. After he'd seen what his kin could do, what he himself could do, he preferred a human son.

But Monica, conceived in the forests of the Old World and in the old ways, wasn't human at all. Not like the New Worlders. And she was bound by the cycle of the moon, forced to leave her truest form and walk upright and hairless and clawless for weeks on end. For her, the moon collar meant control. And until she'd stolen the ring that commanded it and fled, that control had been in the hands of my nameless employer. She was a cat, a mouser, which meant until recently she hunted for him. Now I suspected she hunted for herself and I was certain that there was nothing random about it. And nothing in her file suggested Seattle as a place she had any connection to. Yet there were two addresses they suspected she might be casing.

I drove with the windows down savoring the heavy smell of rain mixed in with every other conceivable scent. Exhaust. Perfume. Cigarettes. The new canvass of the backpack on the seat beside me and the fresh gun oil of the tranq pistol inside it.

Ballard was as gray as the rest of the city, squatting by its locks in the smell of salt and seagull droppings. I drove past bookshops and brew pubs and eventually turned down a side street into the lines of houses.

I smelled her before I reached the address and instinctively pulled the rental over, playing with my phone while glancing carefully around for some sign of her. She was northeast by the wind and so was my destination. I kept up with the phone for a minute, then signaled and slipped back onto the road. As I came around the corner, I saw a black Mustang. But it stood out not just because it was red and fast-looking but because its top was down in the rain and the woman who sat in it didn't seem to mind.

I kept driving, hoping Monica Evenheart would pay no attention to me at all. She didn't. She was too busy watching the house.

I circled the block and parked out of sight, slipping the tranq pistol into the waistband of my jeans and covering it with my jacket. The rain became a drizzle as I started up the sidewalk and turned the corner. The car idled across from one of the older houses on the block, its yard perfect and its windows dark and uninviting.

She made no attempt to hide, watching those windows with feline serenity. Monica Evenheart was pretty and she smelled good. But she was also deadly.

I counted the steps to her car wondering if it could possibly be this easy. Just a quick trip to Seattle, a shot in the back, and a few months of bills paid with a bit to spare. Maybe even enough to get back into the cheap motel I called home when I could afford it.

But I knew when her eyes darted to the rearview mirror that it wasn't going to be so easy after all. She watched me, her gaze level and steady, and I tried hard not to notice as I adjusted the hood on my jacket. I must have failed. She looked to the house, then back to the mirror. Then, she pressed the gas hard, hyrdo-planing the car back into the street and soaking me as she did.

I kept walking and pretended nothing happened.

I listened to her engine winding up as she took the corner and when I was satisfied that she was gone, I cut across the street at a jog and took the stairs leading up to the house two at a time. I still had time before her hunting hours started—she was nocturnal—and with this first address empty, it stood to reason she was on her way to the second. I'd take a quick look around and see what it gave me.

I let myself in quickly with a credit card and a paperclip. Olfactory prowess alone isn't a sufficient skillset in my line of work. And once I was certain no one was home, I moved through the place fast and built my mental database as I went. This was extra work but I knew Connor was lying about the randomness of the attacks, holding something back. It made sense. I was hired to help to bring home a lost pet. By their view, the details were none of my business.

Still, I preferred to decide what was and wasn't my business in the pursuit of a feral Covenanter.

The database came together as I rifled through drawers, peeked around shelves, sorted the mail. There wasn't much. His name was Charles Dennehy and he was a divorced attorney, a father of two children who lived elsewhere and left little evidence of their presence in his house. That he lived frugally for someone worth as much as he was. Little of that really mattered, but I quickly found what did. Tucked behind the leather-bound classics on the shelves of his den was a bound copy of the Covenant and its complex tapestry of laws. That told me everything I needed to know. The smell of Old World paper, easily distinguished from the paper of this world, was still strong in my nose when I let myself out and headed back to my car.

The sun had dropped, painting the western sky purple and rose, the rain clouds bruising its edges. The rain was more a drizzle as I left Ballard for Pioneer Square, my GPS whispering directions to me. I was moving against traffic now, slowed by pedestrians and puddles as I drove south. I parked a block away at the darker end of the street. I used my phone to check what lived at this second address but I already had my suspicion. It took less than a minute to confirm it. McDonnell, Dennehy and Jackson, attorneys at law, had a suite on the fourth floor.

I pulled a dark hoody and a ballcap from my backpack and put them on, leaving my raincoat on the passenger seat. Then, slipping the tranq pistol into my waistband again, I locked the car and moved down the street.

Hunting time couldn't be far away with the light nearly gone. Seattle's streets were quieter than I remembered them—I'd lived here a decade earlier in a downtown loft when times were better. But it was busy enough with a mix of homeless, hapless and just off work with loosened ties. I kept my eyes down and my nose open, pulling in the smell of weed and Pho and wet newspaper as I went. Monica's scent was easy to pick up on that wind and I saw her, standing by the door of the building.

She was tall and slender, wearing a short leather jacket buttoned against the October evening and a black skirt. Her dark hair was pulled back into a pony tail and she carried herself with the same calm I'd seen earlier.

I paused and looked at my phone, watching from the corner of my eye as she took a look around before pulling open the door. I started moving again after she slipped inside. I paused at the edge of the doorway and counted to five before leaning around to look inside. Beyond the glass door, the lobby was dimly lit and the security desk looked empty.

I smelled the guard coming before I saw him—off-brand cigarettes and Brut aftershave—and I ducked back out of the light. I heard his keys jingle in the door as he locked up and the timing of it convinced me that she was expected.

I walked past the door, glancing inside quickly as I went. The guard was slowly returning to his counter and I picked up my pace, cutting down the next alley I saw and making my way to the back of the building. It was easy enough to get onto the fire escape by way of a nearby dumpster. I crawled into a dark office on the fourth floor, my ears and nose taking in what they could. I heard muted voices and the air was full of the smell of her; I followed both sound and scent.

The law offices were empty and the lights were out with one exception. Behind that closed door, I heard voices.

"I don't know where," the man said.

Monica's voice was low, almost throaty. "If you don't know, then you know who does."

I took a few steps toward the door and paused. I heard Dennehy laugh. "I'm certainly not going to tell you. I know all about Criteaux and Bosley and that's not enough incentive for me to talk. There's nothing you can do to me that's worse than the cost of betraying the Covenant. So maybe you should just go home and get back under your patron's protection."

The noise she made could've been a laugh but it was throaty, slurred, telling me she'd made the shift. It was hunting time. "Trust me," she said. "They both talked. Criteaux gave me Bosley, Bosley gave me you. You'll talk, too."

I heard Dennehy gasp and I took another step toward them.

Then a new smell stopped me in my tracks, and somewhere outside the suite, I heard the distant chime of an arriving elevator. This was a dark smell, an earthy smell, and it made my skin crawl. Something that didn't belong had just showed up. I'd not smelled this before, but I knew it wasn't from around here.

It takes a lot to rattle me; I was rattled. Sweaty, hands shaking, as the fight or flight of a rending hound bastard kicked into high gear. I drew the pistol as the smell grew closer and I turned toward the law firm's small lobby. My eyes were adjusted to the dark now and I saw what looked like fog pouring beneath the door, building and gathering until it coalesced into roughly the shape of a large man. But this was no man. Its red eyes burned with cruel intelligence and its dark robes shifted around it like black mist. Its face was flat and mouthless, lit dimly by the eyes. I was familiar with the cataloged Older

Worlders that had been permitted to cross over and this was not one of them. That told me it had been sent over recently. To find her.

She must've smelled it by now because I heard a yowl from the other side of the door.

I'm not sure why I did what I did next, but I have to own it. I stepped in between whatever Old Worlder this was and the door it wanted to get behind. Between it and Monica Evenheart.

It growled at me but its voice was in my head. *Stand aside and let us do our work.*

I shook my head and was aware of the door opening. Monica's smell was overpowering now in her feline form and it must've stirred something of my father's blood in me. Despite the fear I felt, I wanted to give chase to her at some genetic, deep-down level. But instead, as her yowl rose into a snarl and as the Old Worlder roared and rushed me, I raised the tranq pistol and fired three darts into the center of its mass.

It collided with me, tossing me easily aside and into the wall. As I fell, I saw her leaping, claws outstretched and tail puffed up with menace. They were a blur now, rolling and writhing on the floor as I found my breath and my feet again. It pinned her quickly with its dark, taloned hands, and I put two more darts into its back at close range.

I glanced into the open office and saw Dennehy kneeling, hand-cuffed to a massive wooden desk. His eyes met mine and they were wide. The fear in his voice wasn't from the cat. "Help me," he whispered.

I looked back to the fight quickly, not liking the way his eyes made me feel. The beast was slowing with Monica still trapped beneath it and I launched a sneakered foot at its side. Most Old Worlders have little to no resistance to the bugs and medicines on this side and I was glad to see it was true in this case as whatever hunted the hunter drifted off to thick and muddy sleep.

Monica looked up at me beneath him, only she looked nothing like the picture now. Now, she had the face and tail and claws of a cat but the body of a woman. She pushed at the sleeping form that held her down. She echoed Dennehy's words and I shouldn't have listened to her.

"Help me," she said. There was enough purr in her voice that I didn't think. I just acted out of that same place that made me drunk with the idea of chasing her up the nearest tree. I rolled the snoring beast off of her and as I did, her fist shot up to land soundly on my nose. White light and pain exploded and from there, it was nothing for her to wrench the pistol out of my hand.

I was still surprised when she put a dart into my stomach.

"Sorry," she said. I lunged forward but she stepped away easily and I tripped over the massive body on the floor.

This time, when I fell, I just stayed down. And the dark hall went darker still.

I woke up stiff, my head splitting, and my nose flooded with the smell of her and the freeway. When I tried to move, I found I couldn't. My hands were cuffed behind my back and I lay face down in the backseat of a fast-moving car. I groaned.

"You're awake, then?"

I groaned again and tried to find my words.

She continued. "I should've left you."

I twisted again, trying to roll over or sit up. "Why didn't you?"

"You saved me from . . . well, whatever that was. It didn't seem right leaving you for it to find once it woke up." Or the police, I thought, if she'd gone through with her hunt.

I didn't want to ask but I had to. "What about Dennehy?"

She chuckled. "He's in the trunk. He's alive."

I tried to do the math. Somehow, she'd hauled two men from the top floor down to the street and into her . . . I sniffed the car. I could smell Dennehy in it now, too. This wasn't the convertible I'd seen her in earlier. I blinked away more disorientation and shifted again. This was a bigger car. Dennehy's Lincoln, I expected. But why had she kept him alive?

"Where are we going?"

"Twin Falls, Idaho," she said. "We're halfway there, actually."

"And why are you taking us to Twin Falls?" I'd never been there and wasn't even sure where to place it on a map.

"I'm trading Dennehy. You . . . I'm not sure what I'm doing with you yet."

"Maybe," I said, "we should talk about that over coffee."

I heard the car slow and the sound of the freeway diminish as she pulled off and parked. Then I felt her hands pulling me over and sitting me up. "Connor hired you, right? I found his number in your phone."

I didn't see any point in keeping quiet at this point. "Yes."

"And that other . . . thing?" She positioned me in the backseat in the best uncomfortable position she could, and with her leaning over me, her scent even nearer, I had that same sudden urge to chase after her. I held it down. But from the way she looked at me, I thought maybe she felt something too. Maybe at some deep down level of her own, she wanted me to chase her. I shook the notion away.

"I'm not sure. But I don't think it planned to tranq you."

Her face was no longer serene, and I saw worry in her eyes. "No, I think you're right about that."

"I think you've pissed some people off."

"Several," she agreed. "You saved my life."

I looked around. We were at an empty rest stop somewhere in the high desert. "I was going to tranq you and send you home."

She chuckled. "It didn't quite work out that way. Speaking of which, how's the head?"

I heard muffled noises and thumps from the trunk now. Dennehy had woke up, too, it seemed. "It hurts. How about that coffee?"

She ignored me. "What was that back there?"

"Something Old World," I said. "I have no idea. I've never run across one of those before." Of course, there were thousands of Old World denizens I'd never seen; not all of them had been permitted to cross over and not all of them had wanted to. Many had been happy to see the Queen of the North go and the rending hounds take up her crown. "Operating outside of the Covenant, I suspect."

She hissed. "The Covenant is a net they raise and lower based on whoever's serving." I could hear the bitterness in her voice and see the anger in her eyes.

"Okay," I said. I'd heard this before. "So the Covenant's unfair and the patrons are crooked and self-serving."

"Yes," she said.

"So you've gone hunting off-leash because of it?"

"I hold my own leash now, thank you." She paused. "And the hunting I did on my own isn't any more wrong than the hunting I did for them." She shrugged. "Killing is killing. All that's left is the why."

She had a point there. And she left a question hanging that was easy for me to pick up. "Then what is your why, Monica Evenheart?"

She regarded me without speaking for a full minute. "Article fourteen," she said.

I pre-dated the Covenant but still needed to be familiar with it. Fourteen covered the multi-generational aspects of indentured servitude. Usually two or three generations, but I'd heard as many as five. Passage over was expensive and blending in was difficult. The patrons could easily afford it and their initial investment led to even more profit once their indentureds were put to work. "So you didn't want to give up your young to the Covenant?"

"I have no young," she said. "I refuse to bear a litter into this system. I decided a long time ago that I'd slip my leash before it came to that."

That made sense to me. I'd heard of it happening before. No child wants to be held to the decisions of their parents. No one wants to live out a contract they had no voice in crafting. Sadly, the parents had no voice, either, when it came right to it. The terms were dictated in the midst of cataclysm and genocide, completely in the patrons' favor.

But what didn't make sense here was why the hunt. She could've gone under the radar. Surely they'd have still hired me or someone like me to find her. But she'd have stayed hidden longer without the blood trail. Not to mention maybe avoiding whatever it was that now hunted her.

She must have sensed where my thoughts were leaning. "But there's more than that," she said. "My mother brought us all here as kittens—she signed the Covenant on our behalf. We had no say. I'd rather return to the Old World and face the rending hounds than stay under the Covenant. I certainly won't give a litter to it. And I won't give my family to it, either."

I closed my eyes. "How many?"

"Four sisters; two brothers." She watched my face. "I have a sister in Twin Falls."

"And you're trading Dennehy for her?"

She nodded. "He has information that they'd rather not lose."

"After that?"

"I don't know," Monica said. "We'll track down the others. Sort it out as we go."

I shook my head. "I'm not so sure it will go well for you."

Her eyes were hard. "It doesn't have to go well for me." Then, they softened but only by a little. "So what about you? What should I do with you, Mr. Wolfe?"

I saw the sagebrush and could smell rain coming. I should've asked her to let me go; I suspect she just might have. But I didn't. Living outside the Covenant and system of patrons had let me go untouched by the unfairness of it all. I did my jobs for them or their people—and until now, I'd not let the system rattle me. But there was something about Monica Evenheart that struck an undiscovered chord in me. It was in her picture and in her scent, it was in the way she stirred my father's blood and made me wish that I had a cycle like hers that let me stretch into my truest self and bay at the moon while loping across an open field. Running after her as fast as my legs could carry me. Overhead, a night sky mostly cloudy with a chance of cats and dogs in it. I shrugged and poured my mother's charm into my smile. "You might as well keep me nearby at this point," I said. "Otherwise, I'd just have to chase you down again."

She smiled again and I liked it. "You see how well that worked out the last time, right?"

I shrugged again and said nothing as she leaned over and uncuffed me. "Climb up front if you want."

I did. And within a minute, we were back on the road and heading southeast across the Columbia Plateau.

It was dark when we pulled up at the wrecking yard just outside Twin Falls. A worn sign declared in flaking white paint that the large, fenced enclosure of stacked cars belonged to Earl Haskins, Jr. It was far removed from the offices and high rises of L.A., San Francisco and Seattle and I found it hard to believe this backwoods place could have anything to do with the Covenant.

Monica idled the Lincoln outside the gate, headlights beckoning whoever waited for us inside. It rolled open slowly and she pulled forward. Two trailers—one double and one single wide—waited just inside. The pickup parked nearby fit in fine but the dark SUVs with their tinted windows were definitely out of place.

I leaned forward, trying to count the suits that waited. I cracked the window and sniffed. They were all New World humans. Hired thugs. "It looks like they're expecting us."

The calm was in her face and voice again. "Yes."

I studied her as the car crunched to a stop. "I don't see how this can turn out well."

She said nothing but I saw her rubbing the ring she wore. It was dark now. She could shift and that might turn the odds in her favor. Depending on how they were equipped. And who exactly they were.

I waited until she opened her door and then I opened mine as well.

"You." She spat the word and I saw why. One of the suits had separated from the others. It was Connor.

"Good evening, Miss Evenheart," he said as he approached.

"Ms.," she corrected him.

He ignored the correction and turned to me. "I see you've met Mr. Wolfe. Though I'm not sure what's convinced him to bite the hand that feeds him." I could see the anger in his eyes, but his face didn't show it. "However, I don't see Mr. Dennehy."

"My deal was with Haskins," she said.

"Unfortunately," Connor said, "Mr. Haskins can't be with us this evening. But I'm sure we can solve this without him."

"And my sister?"

Connor smiled. "She's inside. But there is no outcome to this that involves her leaving with you. Or you leaving, for that matter."

As he said it, the suits started moving. Only this time, the pistols they drew weren't firing tranqs. These were Glocks, heavy and dark in the yellow glow of a streetlamp that illuminated the yard. And Connor knew what he was up against. His thugs would be packing Old World silver in their clips.

Monica yowled and sprinted, her body changing as she did, her clothes shredding with the shift. I'd never been up close to a change before. It was uncanny to watch her body elongate and then drop to all fours. This time, she was all cat and she was on Connor before his men had their pistols raised, her teeth at his throat as her tail twitched back and forth.

Uncertain, they held their fire, and in that moment, a new smell flooded the yard. I'd only smelled it once and that had been enough. Now, whatever Old World beast had been sicced on her, was here and it moved silently with building speed. The smell of it made my knees shake, and at least two of the suits dropped their guns. The others spun in the direction of the sound and opened fire instinctively. They couldn't miss at that range, but their bullets did nothing.

The cloaked beast rushed them, talons lashing out.

I took advantage of that split second to dodge into the shadows, my eyes on the great cat. Connor struggled beneath her, his eyes wide. His voice was nearly a scream. "What is *that*?"

I couldn't tell him. But in the span of seconds, it had rushed across the yard and lifted two of the suits up, tossing them away and into the dark as their Glocks spun away and hit the ground.

The others scattered and the beast spun on Monica Evenheart. Its voice was in my head; it must've been in hers too. *Your defiance of the Covenant ends here.*

She growled deep in her throat, digging her claws into Connor as she gathered herself into a pounce. Connor shrieked as she launched off him toward the hulking Old Worlder. She hit it hard and it caught her, throwing her easily into a wall of cars. She was on her feet and darting in again, her left paw raking its leg. It howled in my mind but more from anger than pain, I imagined. This time, it lashed out with a foot that landed in her side and sent her sliding into the gravel.

I saw an abandoned Glock and took a chance, rolling for it as the beast charged her again. I picked it up and sighted in, putting three rounds into its back. They did nothing to stop or slow it. Of course, Old World silver didn't work on all of that shadowy place's denizens. And without knowing what this particular creature was, there was no way to know exactly what might stop it.

But there was no doubt about what might stop Monica Evenheart. Already, she was slowing, panting, and trying to get away. I put another two rounds into its back, but it paid me no mind.

She launched herself at it again and it threw her with even more force, this time up over the hood of the car to roll off the other side.

She was closer to me now and I saw her green eyes wide with panic as her nostrils flared. I moved closer to her, putting my hand on her haunch as I watched the beast approach. The bullets were worthless. And there was only one thing in the Old World that I knew had even odds against any other creature born beneath its dark star. A crazy notion entered my head, fueled by desperation or maybe hope. I traced my hand along her body until I reached the collar at her neck. There were no guarantees that it would work on me, but no other option—beyond watching it kill her—presented itself. "This might hurt," I whispered. Then, I pulled it loose, and as her body started changing, I groped for the ring. Her yowl became a scream that cut into the night as her body abruptly twisted itself back to human. As the paw became a finger, the ring slid easily off into my own hand.

It was upon us when I slipped the moon collar around my own neck and shoved the ring onto my finger. What next? Was there something else to say or do? It was a longshot—even more than a longshot. I'd been born without my father's cycle.

I felt the creature make contact and throw me easily, and I felt the air whistling over me. As I landed, I saw it turning again on the huddled, naked form that twitched and jerked in the gravel. The fear inside became a sudden focus of rage. And that rage forced something to life deep inside my DNA.

I roared it out of me and felt every muscle, every bone, every part of me catch fire. But the hottest heat—white and blinding—was the heat from the moon collar and the ring that leashed me to it. And in that heat was a euphoria the likes of which I'd never known. A sense of something coming together in me that had been kept at bay, walled off and unknowable. When I found my feet—no my *paws*, I was on all fours and felt the vertigo of the change. I wobbled then steadied myself as I crouched and snarled.

The beast's red eyes went wide and fell back at the sight of me. I leaped after it, my claws tearing at its shrouded cloak as my fangs sought its throat. It had stopped fighting, which surprised me, and the softness of its flesh within my jaw and the reek of fear that came off of it in waves told me everything I needed to know. It lay still beneath me in a posture of submission. It knew exactly what I was and responded to me.

My mind formed words and shoved them into it with a force that made its blood-colored eyes blink. *What are you called?*

I sensed the fear in the voice it pushed into my mind. *I am Shemol. Of the Yerl.* It paused, then remembered who it spoke to. *Lord Hound,* it added.

I had never heard of Yerl or Shemol. But it didn't matter. *Who sent you after the cat?*

Around us, people were stirring. I punctured its skin and smelled the iron and cloves of its blood on the air. *You know who sent me, Lord.*

I *did* know. His response to me proved it and I growled. *Is Umber still upon the Opal throne then?*

No. His son reigns now.

I increased my grip on its throat. I'm not sure exactly where my words came from; some place tucked inside me with the rest of my hidden nature. *Tell your king that Dengar's bastard sends regards. This one and her littermates are of my pack. Do you understand?*

Yes, Lord, it said.

Now flee. Shemol of the Yerl collapsed in upon itself once I released its neck from my jaws. It dissipated in so much smoke billowing out across the wrecking yard.

Movement from the corner of my eye sent me skittering as a shot went off, gravel erupting where the bullet struck. I wasn't going to find out what Old World silver could do to me. I pounced, and this time, I gave myself over to something I'd never experienced before. I hunted with abandon, chasing down each of the suits and rending them as only a rending hound could. I learned fast and took to my work with enthusiasm, drunk on the blood I spilled.

I didn't stop until I heard my name called. Monica Evenheart stood now, the moonlight white on her naked skin, one of the dropped pistols dangling in her hand. "Angus Wolfe," she said again.

I thought she would be frightened, but I saw no sign of fear and smelled no sign either. Instead, her eyes were wide with awe and her cheeks flushed from watching me. I padded over to her. *Monica Evenheart,* I replied.

She reached down a tentative hand and I bent my head as she scratched behind my ears.

Then, I bent my will toward my lesser form and felt the fire take me again as I shifted. When I was finished twisting and writhing on the ground, I pulled off the ring and collar and pushed them into her hands.

She looked at me laying there and then looked to the trailer.

"I'm fine," I told her, taking the pistol from her. "Go get your sister."

She was on all fours, tail whipping to and fro, when she reached the porch.

The sun rose over the brown Idaho hills casting bloody light over Earl Haskin's Wrecking Yard. I sat on the hood of an SUV wearing a pair Earl's ratty sweats and a wife-beater. I watched the sunrise, wondering just how long we had before the patrons sent their next round of goons. And wondering when the Old World and the hounds who ruled it would throw its next hunter at us. The Covenant benefited more than just the patrons. It kept my father's kin—my kin too—in power. And they liked their power. Enough, it seemed, to keep an eye on things over on this side and intervene to keep things as they were. I'd spent my lifetime on the edges of that hidden world, playing fetch for cash, and for the first time I saw something more that I could do with my heritage. Especially now that I knew the moon collar could bring that heritage fully forward. Of course, the experience of it left me exhausted, head-pounding and feverish. Still, I looked at the bodies we'd stacked against the trailer, tattered leftovers of the patron's men. Now, in my present form, I felt a pang of regret. But not too much. They hadn't come to Earl's to play nice and make friends. And they'd killed Haskin before we'd gotten there. They'd have likely killed her sister, too, along with Monica. She'd brought down the attention of the Opal Throne and that couldn't stand. Not in the Patron's world. So they were cleaning up. No doubt, I'd have been buried in a shallow grave along with the rest of them.

I watched Monica finally come out of the trailer, her sister following with a suitcase and a Remington twelve gauge. She'd changed into jeans and a sweatshirt.

"What now?" I asked.

Monica looked at her sister. "Rachel says we have a brother near Minneapolis. I found some names in Earl's files. We'll keep looking until we find them all. And after that, maybe we'll find the Queen of the North. What about you?"

I shrugged. "I think I'll come along seeing how I don't have much else to do. And I'm stranded in the middle of Idaho." It wasn't as if I had much to go back to—or that the patron I'd betrayed would let me take up my old life. But more than that, there was something about this cat that made me want to keep her close. I'd told the beast she was of my pack. I'm not sure she was part of anyone's pack or that she could be. But I was sure of my need to pursue her even if she could never be caught.

Monica Evenheart smiled and I saw fields and forests that we could run through in her eyes. "Let's talk about it over coffee."

We cut Dennehy loose and told him to disappear. The fear on his face told me he would do just that.

Then we lit the fires that would cover our tracks behind us and drove out of the yard, nose pointed east and into the rising sun.

I rolled down my window as she picked up speed on the highway; Monica and her sister laughed when I howled at the future I smelled upon the morning wind.

ANNUAL DUES

*S*o exactly why is it you've brought me here?"

I was beyond irritability, well on the way to impatient anger. Damn Gilga-Yar and his game-playing—to send me, Frewar Zej, halfway across a world in the care of his minion as if I were a first year mage. And to this wasteland dung-pile, of all places.

I had been here before, back when the trade routes between Aeryé and the K'Tarii nomads hadn't been choked by the dust of war. El Ramir had been a scab of a town then, and from what I had seen before entering its only public house two hours before, it hadn't changed much. The only good memory I could find from my brief stay a quarter-century ago was of a D'an-Nubii dancing girl I had—

The demon in my pocket chortled, interrupting my re-lived pleasure. "Wait. You'll see."

I looked down, my one good eye locking onto the demon's. "It'd better be good," I said. "Or you'll be very sorry."

It laughed, snorted, farted and laughed again. "I don't fear you. My master—"

"Damn you and your master both. I have things to do. I don't have time for his games—to drop everything and travel three thousand miles to this flea-infested chamber-pot just to satisfy his itch for fealty." I kept my voice low, but the ice was in it.

The demon poked his minute finger into my side, his bug-eyes narrowing. "You want to play, you've got to pay."

I had more angry words, but I swallowed them. The little bastard had me there, just like our mutual master, Gilga-Yar. After all, he hadn't sought me out thirty years ago. He hadn't asked for the contract. He hadn't said "name your price" or "whatever it takes." I had done that. And each year, as winter settled in the Northern Reaches

where I made my home, my patron—or, in this case, his messenger—
came calling for a "small token of my commitment."

I took a swig from the tankard before me and let the cool, fermented danaberry juice tease the back of my throat.

I could have sought another patron over the years—one perhaps
more benign. But contract negotiations had never been my cup of
qua'en and my focus was on the Art, not all of the politics around it.
And going solo—well, why make your own flawed paints, brushes
and canvas when there was such a ready, unblemished supply for the
buying? I looked at the hook that pretended to be my right hand. The
price thus far had been reasonable. A hand. An eye. Some toes. A soul
here, a virgin there. Of course, I had preferred those years when he'd
bid me kill a rival or find some artifact he craved. Still, the messenger-
sprite was correct: I did want to play. And I would pay my annual dues
to do so.

It began to caper in my pocket, jumping up and down in a gleeful
dance. "Here she comes! Here she comes!" I looked around the room.
It was crowded with an odd assortment of outlanders. A noisy band of
K'Tarii freeholders, swaddled in silk robes and turbans, occupied a fair
portion of the room, their heavy blades of Akiiren steel hanging from
broad red sashes. Keeping a fair distance, a cluster of out-of-uniform
Suranian warrior-priests, noticeable by their purple-dyed top-knots,
talked quietly into their ale mugs, eyes darting around the room.
Mixed in like clumps of cinnamon in wine were the natives—dark-
skinned, dark-haired men and women, all dressed in a rainbow array
of loose-cut pants and shirts. Most of the women sat on or near the
nomads, casting playful eyes toward the Suranians but knowing better than to approach. The heavy black curtain jingled as it was drawn
back, and a woman walked through.

I don't know how she came to be in this place—it was obvious she
didn't belong, and yet she was dressed as any other El Ramiran. She
was blond, and though her skin was dusky, her eyes were a sharp blue.
She looked young—maybe half my age—and she carried herself with
an easy confidence. Her crooked nose marked her part D'an-Nubii,
but she had smatterings of the Northlands about her cheekbones and
mouth. For a moment, I held my breath. There was a wild beauty
about her that I felt guilty noticing, after all—

"That's her," it gurgled, twitching. "You see her don't you?"

"Yes," I said. "I see her. What now?"

"Master wants her soul. Give it to him."

I'd done this before. "Same terms?" I asked.

"Same terms. No magic. Use the blade. Say the words. Get another year of juice. Get juicier juice."

I nodded. Someone staggered near me and I paused. It wouldn't do to be overheard talking to my pocket, even if they couldn't understand the obscure nether-tongue I used. "Who is she?"

It shrugged. "Nobody." It paused, could have remained silent, but didn't. "A fledgling in the Art." Here my eyebrow raised.

"Does she have a patron?"

It shrugged again. "A minor devil in the Seventh Outer Ring. But . . ."

"Yes?" She walked over to the bar with regal grace and her smile said she knew she was turning heads. She murmured something to the barkeep and he nodded, reaching for a glass. Gods, what a woman.

"She has approached master for a contract. It's been under consideration these past three years."

The words stung me alert. "But I thought he had his allotment?"

"He does," it giggled. "Little does she know . . ." The double dealing bitch-whelp. Memories of my own waiting period came flooding back—years of slavish devotion to prove my intention to sign and stay signed. And now, this young woman, after three years of hard work, hoping against hope to be offered a contract, was to be snuffed out so her soul could decorate Gilga-Yar's mantle. And no doubt, her current patron wouldn't lift a tentacle to save her—her disloyalty by this time no secret. But who was I to develop a conscience? A little late in the year for such nonsense.

"Why her?" I asked suddenly, but didn't know why. "Why not some king or another arch-mage?"

The demon was silent for a moment. "You do not wish to pay? You do not wish to play?" The questions were ominous probes, black fingers in my brain.

I sighed. "She's so young."

There was no response.

"Okay, damn you. Of course I'll do it." I stood and straightened my robes. I knew what *I* saw there by the counter—what would *she* see coming towards her? The great Frewar Zej, Arch-mage of the Twenty-third Order or a fifty-five-year-old man with an empty eye socket and thinning gray hair, who walked with a limp and sported an iron hook instead of a hand? And why did I care?

I shuffled to the counter, my one hand burying itself in travel-stained cloth to rest upon the bone knife-hilt. My fingers absently traced the runes as I pushed up beside her, my mind racing over the litany. She hadn't turned yet, the center of her slim shoulders a waiting target.

I could have done it right then—could've finished it. But I paused. Her hair smelled of apples and my eye followed its waving, broken line over her small ears, down her slim neck. In my pocket the demon poked and pushed impatiently.

Her head came up, as if hearing, and her eyes settled on me.

"Have you come far?" she asked. Her voice was music, and yes, it was D'an-Nubii—her accent proved it out.

I must have started, because she smiled.

"I can see you are a foreigner," she said. "Have you come far?"

"Yes," I said. Damn. This wasn't getting easier at all. I released the handle of the knife and rapped on the counter. "Qua'en, barkeep. And chilled, if you have it."

"Where from?"

"Erlan's Fjord," I lied. She smiled. My drink arrived and I tossed a copper regliré to the barkeep's waiting hands.

"A veteran?" A plausible explanation for my missing pieces, but she knew and I *knew* that she knew. She had turned just enough and my eye had unwittingly discovered that the left side of her chest was noticeably flat compared to the ample curve of her right breast. The demon hadn't lied—she had already begun paying her dues.

"I think you understand the reason for my condition," I stated, quickly flashing her the recognition sign that conveyed my rank and order. She nodded, her fingers quickly making her own sign. She seemed both frightened and excited at the truth, and tried badly to hide it. At this point, enough people had noticed us together. I would need a quieter place for my work now.

"My name is—"

I cut in, angrily. "I don't want to know your name."

Her lower lip jutted out. "I only . . . I mean—"

"I'm sorry," I said. I had to recover somehow. To turn this to my advantage. "It's been a long journey. Please. Tell me your name."

She shook her head and smiled. "No. It's not important. What I'd really like is to talk with you." Her voice lowered to a whisper. "I'm

new to the Art and have never met an arch-mage before. I have so
many questions."

"Then perhaps we should go someplace more amenable to our
conversation." The demon in my pocket broke wind noisily and stifled
a giggle.

"What was that?" she asked, eyebrows arching with surprise.

"Nothing," I said and gave my pocket a thump.

First-moon hung low in the sky, an evil urine-colored orb that
dominated the horizon. We were silent now, watching and hearing
the night around us. In the distance, desert wolves howled as we sat
in the gathering dusk. Four times I had slipped my hand to the knife,
and four times I had stopped myself. I knew that I would have to go
through with it soon, that every moment I stalled made it harder and
easier at the same time. Harder, because already I dreaded the deed.
Easier, because with each word she seemed to trust me more. For
hours we had sat at the edge of the oasis, gazing out over the mauve
wasteland while I answered her myriad questions about my life with
the Art. She seemed so innocent there, framed in the moon-light,
drinking in my every word. She was a perfect woman to my ego—all
rapt attention and wide-eyed wonder.

"So," I asked, breaking the silence, "Tell me of yourself." The mes-
senger-sprite had gone to sleep two hours ago, mumbling curses and
threats under its breath.

She shrugged and her fingers began to play in her hair. "There
isn't much to tell. I was born here in El Ramir. I've lived here all my
life. My mother was a D'an-Nubii dancer and my father was—"

The world reeled around me as a picture came into focus. "Damn
and blast!" I lunged to my feet. "Damn and blast!" I repeated the words
again and again, startling the demon awake with my pacing. The girl
watched me. Did she know? She couldn't know. But she would if
I didn't rein in my anger quickly. My hand dipped into the pocket,
clutched the demon's scaly throat and hauled it out of its hiding place.
I threw it to the ground.

"I won't do it!"

The girl stood up at the sight of the thing and drew near me. "Do
what?" she asked.

"Gilga-Yar knows, doesn't he?"

The demon recovered its wits. "You want to play? You've got to pay!" Then, it fell to the ground and began rolling back and forth, holding itself as it shook with laughter.

"Then I don't want to play." The demon sat up, surprised.

"You—?"

I pulled the knife from my robes and hurled it at the tiny sprite. It dodged away, but I grabbed its heart between my thumb and forefinger and began to squeeze, feeling the Art give it shape and texture beneath my touch. The demon gasped and began to shriek, struggling to inflate itself to full size. It was all fang and eye and claw now, as it twisted in the dirt. With a ceremonious twist of the wrist I burst its heart like a grape and watched it collapse into itself, a puff of sulfuric smoke. Then, I turned to the girl.

She stooped over the knife, picked it up, stared at it.

"What is this about?" she asked.

"I think you know."

She swallowed, nodded. She dropped her hands to her sides. "I've known all along." It was an awkward moment, and dueling visions battled over my imagination. Gilga-Yar would probably hunt me now—perhaps I would become someone else's annual dues. Gods knew I had killed his renegades before.

She stepped into my arms and I embraced my daughter.

"Father, what have you done?" What had I done? I was solo now. A free agent. And a father. I felt her shoulders shake beneath my hand and arms.

"There, there. It will be fine." Her shoulders shook even more and she said something incoherent against my shoulder.

"Besides," I said, trying to make light of it all both for her and for myself, "Gilga-Yar now has room for another contract—if you're willing to pay."

She looked up, smiling, teeth showing, and there were no tears— had never been tears.

"I am willing to pay, Father," she said, and I felt the knife slide into my back, rasp against my spine, pierce my heart. She laughed aloud now and I felt her quiver in my arms as she settled me to the ground. "I want to play."

JAY LAKE AND THE LAST TEMPLE
OF THE MONKEY KING

*T*he tin can vibrated against the brick basement wall and Jay Lake reached for his pruning shears by habit before stopping himself. He'd cut the string two hundred thirty seven times and he'd recycled two hundred thirty seven tin cans before he'd finally given up. The Administration could call. They could use their cowboy ninjas to install their shiny new cans in the dead of night.

"But I don't have to answer," he told the cat that slept on his keyboard.

The can vibrated again and Jay sighed before grabbing it and raising it to his ear.

The sound of heavy breathing far away, wrapped in tin.

"Mr. President," he said in a careful, measured voice, "this is ridiculous."

He heard stifled giggles behind a hand held over the can and then a voice. "I told you, Waylon. The kid picks up every time." Then more heavy breathing.

Jay thought carefully about his words. "Mr. President, once more I feel the need to remind you that sexual harassment is—"

A new voice filled the can. A soft voice full of menace. "Ah," the new voice said, "the inestimable Mr. Lake."

Jay blinked. "Mr. President?"

The voice chuckled. "I'm afraid the President of the United States has been . . . disconnected."

Jay's eyes narrowed. "And how exactly did you manage that?"

Again, the chuckle. "I am a man of many talents." The chuckle became a giggle.

"Well," Jay said, "thank you for your assistance in that matter."

He let the tin can fall and opened his laptop. He did his writing on the Inscrutable Alien Story Device, but unfortunately, its gray-skinned owners had not bothered to build connectivity into it. Yawning, he opened his Instant Messenger.

The tin can vibrated again and he ignored it. It stopped. It started again. Jay stretched out his fingers, entirely unaware of the deeply buried Pavlovian Trigger that had been planted in him during his childhood in Africa. He wrestled his own will and forced his hand to the pruning shears.

A message from UrRchNemesys popped up. ANSWER THE CAN, MR. LAKE.

Jay's fingers flew across the keys. WHOISTHIS?

The letters appeared slowly now. T-H-E-W-O-O-D-S-A-R-E-L-O-V-E-L-Y-D-A-R-K-A-N-D-D-E-E-P.

Jay's will evaporated and suddenly, answering the can was the most important thing he could ever do with his life. His hand flew up and grabbed the cold tin, his fingers moving faster than a fat boy at a rib buffet. When he spoke into the can, his voice sounded far away and tinny. "But I have promises to keep."

The unmistakable giggle filled his head. "Yes, you do, Mr. Lake. Listen carefully."

Jay leaned over the desk. "What do you want?"

"I want," the voice said, "the Last Temple of the Monkey King. Tell me where it is."

"I don't know what you're talking about."

"Do you value the life of every last man, woman and child on this planet?"

Jay nodded. "I do."

"Do you want them to have healthy self esteem and a respect for the boundaries of others?"

Jay thought about this for a moment, then shrugged. "Certainly."

"Then," the voice said, "you'd better figure it out."

It took seventeen hours, fifty three minutes and fourteen seconds to do the research. That meant twelve hundred and thirteen emails, eight hundred six Live Journal posts, and six promised, last minute short stories (three of which later made various and sundry award ballots in a classic homage to style under pressure).

In the end, the location of the Last Temple of the Monkey King cost Jay Lake a MoMo recipe he'd stolen from an Indonesian massage therapist and fourteen full color illustrations of a certain Disney character of Very Little Brain in compromising positions while frolicking with his friends in the forest.

Sighing, he packed his laptop, his Inscrutable Alien Story Device, and two changes of underwear into his battered leather satchel.

Then, scooping up the keys to his GENREMOBILE, Jay Lake whistled his attack cats awake and walked into the waning day.

Fifteen minutes later, when he stopped to fill the tank of his convertible, Jay noticed the pale, thin man who pumped his gas. He was a writer. He noticed character. This one had no hair. From the top of his head to the backs of his hands, the gas attendant was fishbelly white and completely hairless, right down to the eyelashes and nostrils. Jay struck up a conversation. "Do you like goats?"

The man said nothing and Jay continued his observation, noticing the slightest hesitation as he studied the gas nozzle before continuing. Then he noticed the way he stood with his legs just slightly too far apart. Small talk, he realized, was the secret to good character study. He smiled. "Ever been to the moon with a talking dog?"

Still silent, Jay continued noticing and kept right on noticing until he failed utterly to notice the tracking device the bald man placed just under the rear bumper while pretending to trip and stumble.

"Careful there," Jay Lake said.

And he was back on the road again, pushing north for Mount Rainier and the Last Temple of the Monkey King.

The warm night wind tossed back Jay's hair as he flew his little red sports car up I-5. The freeway, devoid of cars and lights during that long stretch between Vader and Centralia, stretched out gray and grim before him. The faintest buzzing tickled his ears and he swatted at it before realizing it came from somewhere above and behind him. He craned his neck and saw nothing, craned it again and saw—

Before he could react, the naked man landed on top of him, a sharpened spoon in his fist. "Taste the steel death of my kansai-buji-do, Lion Lover," the bald man said as his battery powered hanglider sailed on without him to crash into a highway overpass.

"I don't think so," Jay said, struggling to keep both the man's spoon and his nudity at bay. He hit the brakes with both feet and threw the car into a skid that carried him to the shoulder of the road with one hand while slapping at the intruder with his other.

The man fell back over the seat and Jay drove an elbow into his side as he worked the buckle on his seat belt and spilled onto the ground. "What the hell is your problem?" he shouted.

The man laughed and leaped from the car to face him, waving his spoon. "Jay Lake must die," he snarled.

Striking a Clown Fu pose he'd invented last year at Carlos and Juan's Exquisite Science Fiction Con-o-Rama Resort and Nude Tunnel Tours during a drinking contest with David Levine and Hal Duncan, Jay touched the tip of his nose with his thumb. "Wagga wagga wagga," he said in his most menacing tone.

Then, taking advantage of a man who stood with his feet too far apart, he planted his shoe into the offered target, leaped back into his car, and sped into the night.

A drunken clown with a chainsaw pointed Jay towards Mundy Loss road on the outskirts of Bradley, Washington. Twenty miles from the base of Mount Rainier, the town was alive with square-dancing, log-rolling, and tree-topping at the annual Bradley Loggers Circus. The logging chicks with their heavy boots, full breasts, and red suspenders caught his eye, but when he saw the dwarves in their checkered shirts and straw hats, he floored it and headed out of town to find the road he'd missed. The sun rose behind him, pink and melodramatic.

He followed Mundy Loss past houses and into the deep forests of the Cascade foothills. When he saw the orange and black mailbox, he took a hard right onto a winding gravel road.

Finally, when the evergreens threatened to scratch the paint from his car, Jay stopped and turned off the engine. Not far ahead, a rooster crowed, and he heard the twang of a banjo being tuned.

Grabbing up his satchel, he wrestled his way over the door of his car to land in a bed of ferns wedged between two pines. He extricated himself and found his way back to the road, sure-footed in the sandals and tie-dye socks the aliens had sent him for his last birthday. He moved in silence, breathing just the way the Yogi had taught him.

"You must be the wind," the ancient Yogi had told him. It was the last time Jay ever fell for the age-old *pull my finger* routine.

Still, now, those powers served him well as he crept up to the edge of a junk-littered clearing. In the early morning light, he saw a rusting double wide in a sea of car parts, old refrigerators, and stacked tires. Leaning against the trailer's wooden skirting was an orange and black bicycle, and sitting on one of four decks of varying construction was a giant of a man picking on a tiny banjo. The song struck Jay as familiar and he finally placed it—"The Sound of Silence," only played faster, more upbeat, with a bluegrass twang to the notes. Jay watched from the shadow of the evergreens that ringed the yard, and as the large man started singing, chickens and ducks toddled out to peck for their breakfast.

Jay waited until the song was finished and walked into the clearing, willing nonchalance into his approach. "Hey there," he called out.

The large man's head came up. He smiled behind his tangled, red beard. "My oh my," he said. "If'n it ain't the Little Lord Jesus His Ownself come to make his visitation upon me on a Tuesday morning." Before Jay could correct him, the man dropped his banjo and leaped from the deck, falling to his knees. "Lord," he cried out, clutching at Jay's ankles, "be merciful unto thy humble servant."

"Uh," Jay said, suddenly uncomfortable with the large hands near his feet.

But a sudden wind from the forest behind him interrupted the moment of spiritual adoration. "Jay Lake must die," a shrill voice shrieked.

The silver spoon took Jay's left sideburn as he dodged and dropped. The large kneeling man looked up, his face twisted into sudden rage. His voice boomed out as ducks and chickens scattered. "You leave my Little Lord Jesus alone."

The naked man stopped in mid-thrust. "This isn't Jesus," he said. "This is the writer Jay Lake."

Jay rolled into a crouch, his hands coming up in a Flying Clown Claw posture.

For a moment, no one moved or said anything. The big man glanced from Jay to his assailant, his face either red from anger or blushing from the sudden nudity that confronted him. "You're not Jesus?"

"Uh," Jay said again.

The hairless man shifted on his feet, eyes narrowing as he moved his spoon from hand to hand. He started circling Jay. Jay circled as well.

"You that writer fella what as promised me them pictures?"

Jay swallowed and nodded. "And the MoMo recipe."

"And this naked man intends to do you harm with his little spoon?"

Jay nodded again.

The naked man nodded, too. "Jay Lake must die."

The large man squinted. "Why is that?"

But before the spoon-wielding fiend could reply, the big redneck had scooped up a squawking chicken and hurled it with practiced precision. As the spoon fell to the ground, Jay launched himself, his hands flapping wildly. "Wagga wagga wagga," he said.

In full Clown Fu form, Jay danced in, slapping, then danced out. He yanked off his sandal and flung it. The leather missile struck a knee with a satisfying thud. The hairless man went down and Jay dove on him, pinning him to the ground.

"You got any rope?" he asked over his shoulder.

The big man shook his head. "Nope." Then he dug around in his bib overalls. "But I got me some of this." He passed a warm, soft roll of duct tape over.

"You must be Trailer Boy," Jay said, suddenly nervous about where the duct tape had been.

"Yes sir," Trailer Boy said, returning Jay's grin. "Yes sir, I am."

They tied the would-be assassin to a rusted engine block and took their breakfast on an elaborate deck with metal siding, rusted portholes and a green striped awning. Wiping the cream of wheat from his goatee, Jay reached for his satchel. "What can you tell me about the location of the Last Temple of the Monkey King?"

Trailer Boy grinned. "You got my pictures?"

Jay nodded and dug out the sheaf of illustrations. He handed them over, then handed over the MoMo recipe.

Trailer Boy shuffled through the pictures, his face darkening with disappointment. He paused on the picture of the bear and the pig. "Them's not right," he said in a sad voice.

"Hell," Jay said, "I could've told you that. But you said you wanted them." He spooned more of the mush into his mouth and swallowed it.

"I wanted Classic. Not Disney."

Jay blinked. "Classic?"

Trailer Boy nodded. "I'll show you." He dug around in his bib overalls again and pulled out a tattered, stained toy bear, extending it towards Jay.

Jay shook his head at the offering. "I think I'll pass. Thanks, though." Then he leaned forward. "Now," he said, "you named your price and I met it. Tell me the location of the Last Temple of the Monkey King."

Trailer Boy opened his mouth, then closed it again. "Why do you want to know?"

Jay cast about inside of himself for an answer. Finally, he fell back to the only one he knew. "Look here, do you value the life of every last man, woman and child on this planet?"

Trailer Boy nodded. "I reckon I do."

"Do you want them to have healthy self esteem and a respect for the boundaries of others?"

Trailer Boy nodded again, this time more vigorously. "I surely do."

"Then," another voice said, soft and sinister and hanging somewhere in the air above them, "tell us the location of the Temple."

Jay looked up to see a massive, silent zeppelin that filled the sky above them. A knotted silk rope dangled from the zeppelin and a man descended, standing with one foot in the loop at the end of the rope. The man was slender as a willow and his long black hair floated ethereally on the morning wind. He was Asian, and his long, wispy mustache and goatee flowed down like spilled ink. He stepped out of the loop to stand over the duct-taped man who stopped struggling as the newcomer smiled down on him.

"Hello, Scotty," he said. "I am most pleased with your work."

"I've failed, Master."

The newcomer stroked his beard thoughtfully. "No," he said, "you have succeeded most competently."

Yes, Jay realized. It wasn't the most clever bit of misdirection but it had sufficed.

Then the newcomer leaned closer to the duct-taped man and spoke in a still, small voice. "The woods are lovely, dark and deep."

Scotty's eyes went glassy and Jay felt his own doing the same as everything suddenly went out of focus. Both he and the naked man spoke at the same time, their voices in perfect unison. "But I have promises to keep."

"Go home and get some sleep," the newcomer said, cutting the duct tape with a long curved knife. "You have served me well."

Jay and the naked man both stood. All he could think about was his bed at home and his cats and the warm blanket that sang his name. He tried to will himself back to the table, tried to will himself to question and challenge, but found himself powerless, held hostage by Frost's words. As he took the stairs two at a time the slender Asian placed a hand on his shoulder. "Not you, Mr. Lake. Your work is not yet done." He waited until Scotty had fled the clearing, and then snapped his fingers three times and blew a raspberry.

Jay's focus snapped suddenly into place and his eyes narrowed. "Who are you? How do you have this power over me?"

"My name is Frank," the man said. "But you can call me . . . Doctor Wu." When he smiled this time, it was wide and genuine and warm. "And surely you understand the basic mechanism of post-hypnotic suggestion?"

Jay nodded, eyes still narrow. "But why?"

Wu's eyes shone and he pointed up slowly. "They told me to."

"The people in the zeppelin?" Jay asked.

"No. You know who."

"The Lord God His Ownself?" Trailer Boy asked.

"Not His Ownself," Wu replied. "But his gray-skinned servants from afar." He gestured to the card table and the scattering of lawn chairs. "Let us sit together while I explain."

As they sat, the Doctor leaned forward and cocked his head. "You remember what they told you when they gave you the Device?"

Jay nodded. It had been two years, but he remembered it like it was yesterday. The helicopter ride north to the crashsite, the key-lime pies, the bizarre birthday party with the crash survivors and the strange Device they'd given him on which to write his stories and change the world by preparing it to join the ranks of the civilized galaxy out beyond their backwater little blue-green rock. "I remember," Jay said.

"Thousands of years ago, the Monkey King, too, was chosen for this great work, but xenophobia was hardwired into his biology," the doctor said in a quiet, sing-song voice. "He hid the artifacts of power they provided humanity, refusing to use them, refusing to help usher

in a new age of mutual respect and compassion and socialized medicine. He built elaborate temples in which to hide these tools of great
purpose and set his guardians to prevent their use and prevent our
species' prophesized coming of age."

"So let me get this straight," Jay said, "you're not really the antagonist in this story?"

Wu chuckled. "No. I am not."

Jay glanced at Trailer Boy. "What about him?"

Wu shook his head. "No. He's a mere simpleton with a strange
predilection for cartoon pornography."

Trailer Boy blushed and said nothing, but his eyes darted down to
the illustrations before him.

"What kind of story has no antagonist?" Jay asked, finding himself uncomfortable now with the lack of structure.

Doctor Wu stroked his beard thoughtfully again. "A literary story," he finally said.

"I like stories," Trailer Boy said. "I wrote one once." He dug
around in his bib overalls, didn't find what he was looking for, and
went back to his cream of wheat.

Doctor Wu glanced at the large redneck, then fixed his gaze on
Jay. "I have given my life to the restoration of those tools of power. It
is my calling. It is the will of the Lord Most High to bring humanity
to our next place in the Darwinian process."

"Healthy self esteem and boundaries?" Jay asked.

"I want me some of that," Trailer Boy said.

"And socialized medicine," Doctor Wu said quietly. Then he
turned to Trailer Boy. "So again, where is the Last Temple of the
Monkey King."

Trailer Boy grinned. "You're sitting on it."

Jay looked at the aluminum chair with its frayed nylon webbing
and Trailer Boy laughed. "Come with me, fellas," he said, standing up.
"I will show you."

They climbed down from the deck and followed their host as he
went to a loose section of the paint-peeled wooden skirting. Pulling it
back, he disappeared beneath the trailer. Jay and Frank stood outside,
looking nervously at one another.

Trailer Boy's head re-appeared. "Come on," he said.

Jay nodded to the dark opening. "After you."

Frank shrugged.

The loose, cool earth beneath the trailer was scattered with empty Yoohoo bottles and candy wrappers. It smelled damp and Jay wrinkled his nose.

"I like it down here," Trailer Boy said. "It's my Most Special Place."

Jay bit his tongue and said nothing.

They crawled to a wide piece of dirt-strewn plywood and Trailer Boy shoved it aside. Ancient stone steps disappeared into blackness. Jay found a pebble and tossed it in. It clattered away until sound faded.

This time, Frank smiled and gestured to the stairs. "After you," he told Jay.

Shrugging Jay started down the stairs and Frank followed. They both paused when Trailer Boy did not join them.

"I don't like monkeys," he said. "They scare me something fierce." He paused, then offered a smile. "But I'll pray for you." He dug a battered flashlight out of his overalls and handed it over.

"Thanks," Jay said.

Then. clutching his satchel tightly to his side, he descended into earth.

They walked for hours that felt like days, down the stairs and into the deep tunnels, past underground rivers with white-eyed, pale fish and mushrooms that glowed faintly green as the flashlight swept over them. They walked until their feet hurt and the sweat rolled off them despite the cool air. They slipped past traps, ducking cob-web coated blades that fell and iron spikes that thrust upward from the ground and outward from the walls. They took turns dismantling them and complimented one another's work.

"We work well together," Jay observed.

"Yes," Frank said, "but our best work is yet to come."

Finally, as the light from the flashlight guttered and waned, they entered the throne room of the Last Temple of the Monkey King. It was a massive room divided by a broad chasm and at the edge of the chasm stood an equally massive throne and in the throne sat a massive iron monkey, its wings folded back. Jay played the beam of light over the iron monkey with its jeweled eyes and jagged teeth. Then, he shined the light out over the chasm. Something glistened and sparkled on the far side and he squinted at it.

"It is a chest," Frank whispered. "And in it," he said, his voice even lower now, "is the last tool of power."

"You've never told me," Jay said, "where the others have gone."

"They're safe," Frank said.

Jay scratched his head. "How exactly do you propose we get to it?"

Frank walked the length of the chasm's edge, measuring with his eyes. Finally, he went to the throne to study the monkey. "There is a crank here, between its wings."

"Are you thinking what I'm thinking?"

Frank nodded, stroking his beard and mustache. "We wind it up. It asks us a riddle or two—"

Now Jay chimed in. "We defeat it easily with our combined intellect—"

Frank interrupted. "And we bid it fetch us the tool of power."

They both nodded.

Jay paused. "So which of us is going to do it?"

"You must do it, Jay Lake. It is written."

Jay frowned. "Written where?"

Frank waved his question away. "That is not important. What *is* important is that you must crank the monkey."

Sighing, Jay climbed up into the lap of the iron monkey and reached around its neck to the iron handle set into its back. At first, the metal creaked and whined as he put his weight into turning it. Finally it gave and a deep groan emanated from deep inside the beast as gears ground to life and joints shuddered. A dull light grew behind the glassy, jeweled eyes and the wings trembled.

Jay cranked the monkey until he could crank it no more and then hopped down.

Frank drew himself up and spread out his arms cruciform. "O Great Monkey King," he said, "ask us what riddles you will that we may answer them and receive the gift of thy favor."

Laughter bellowed across the room as the iron monkey took flight. A gigantic hand lashed out, tossing Frank easily across the room. The tail whipped around, dropping Jay like a bag of mail and sending the flashlight and satchel spinning across the stone floor. Chortling and shrieking its metal rage, the Flying Iron Monkey soared high above them. Its green and sparking eyes danced in the darkness and behind them, a thick wooden door dropped into place.

Scrambling like over-caffeinated hamsters, Frank and Jay crawled beneath the throne as the monkey dived and struck at the cave floor with its feet.

"Perhaps," Frank said, "we were wrong about the riddles."

Jay rolled his eyes and glanced longingly at the leather satchel that lay out of reach, near the door that had sealed them in.

As the flashlight gave up the last of its battery, Jay Lake pined for clean undershorts and gave himself over to despair and poor personal hygiene.

They huddled beneath the massive throne for two days waiting for the Iron Monkey to wind down. It didn't.

They lay in silence and darkness, hearing nothing but the ticking of gears and the clacking of steel wings that defied science and reason.

"If only," Frank finally said, "we had one of the tools of power."

Jay nodded to the satchel. "It's right over there. Knock yourself out."

Excitement filled Frank's voice. "You brought it? You have the Inscrutable Alien Story Device? Why didn't you say so?"

Jay shrugged. "I don't feel like writing. It's over there. Go get it if you want it."

As if understanding them, the Iron Monkey dove and roared.

Now Frank's words tumbled out, falling over one another in their rush to escape. "You don't understand. I can't use it. But *you* can, Jay Lake. You can write us a way out of here."

"I can?"

"Think about it."

Jay thought about it. "No," he said. "Nothing."

Frank sighed, exasperated. "The tools are subliminal messaging devices designed to prepare humanity—to *compel* humanity—to a place where it is ready to embrace the galactic community and lay aside its primate aggression scripting."

Something sparked in Jay. "I can write things into reality?"

Frank nodded. "Yes. The Device draws raw creative material from the collective subconsciousness around us, re-aligns it around universal values and principles of Zen harmony and psycho-spiritual redemption—"

Jay interrupted as the spark guttered to life within him. "Then it's blended back into story for re-insertion into the collective subconsciousness to bring about societal change."

"Yes," Frank said, laughing. "Yes."

"I could use the Device to craft a story that would bring us help."

"Yes," Frank said again.

"Only . . ." Jay let the words trail off. Then found them again. "Who would read the story?"

Frank pondered this. "They wouldn't need to read it. Not if they were sensitive to the subtle machinations of the collective subconsciousness and story. Not if they were nearby." Frank paused. "Of course, we're stranded in a cavern far beneath the surface of the earth, miles and miles from any sensitive soul."

A sudden memory caused Jay to suck in his breath quickly. *"I like stories,"* Trailer Boy had told them. *"I wrote one once."*

"It just might work," Jay said.

Frank left cover first, singing at the top of his lungs and dancing like a madman and waving his hands in the air. As the monkey roared above them and dived at Frank, Jay scrambled out the other side and raced for the satchel.

Frank went down beneath the flailing tail and flapping wings, but rolled away and sprung lightly to his feet. Panting, they clawed their way back beneath the throne. Jay opened the bag and drew out the Inscrutable Alien Story Device.

Fitting his hands into the grips, he pumped the machine and let his fingers fly across the keys. The Device hummed to life and started spitting paper.

"Is it working?" Frank asked.

But Jay said nothing. Instead, he bent his will into the soup of subconcsiousness and aimed his words like sharp arrows into the soul of his species.

Frank gathered up pages. "It's too dark to read," he said.

"You don't need to read it," Jay said. "I just need to write it."

He wrote for hours until his arms were sore and his fingers ached. He wrote until his brain felt soft and empty and the words failed him. Finally, he put the Device aside.

"There," he finally said.

"Now what?" Frank asked.

"Now we wait," Jay said, exhaustion riding hard behind his eyes.

*

At first, the noise was faint and far away. As it grew, Jay could not place it. A clicking sound accompanied by the noise wind makes in a tunnel. Beneath the door, faint light leaked into the room, becoming more intense as the noise drew closer. The Iron Monkey landed in front of the door and sniffed at it, its tail twitching.

Jay Lake smiled. "Now," he said.

"Now?" Frank asked.

Jay nodded.

"Oh Lord Jesus help me," a muffled voice shouted beyond the door, followed immediately by the sound of something heavy striking the solid wood. Too late, the Iron Monkey flapped its wings to raise itself to safety.

The door came down upon it and a spectacle unlike any Jay had ever seen flashed up and over in a streak of brilliantly illuminated orange and black. It was a large man on a bicycle. Strapped into the bike's small basket was a car battery, a series of wires connecting it to a solitary Pinto headlight duct-taped to Trailer Boy's Space Ranger helmet. Light from it glinted off the tin cod-piece taped to the crotch of his coveralls and he screamed high pitched and like a girl as he sailed out over the chasm still working the pedals and brakes of his bicycle.

He landed tangled up in aluminum and wire and groaned. Trailer Boy wrestled himself free and knocked on the cod-piece. "It worked," he said but Jay was afraid to ask him what he meant.

Instead, Jay called out across the chasm. "Shine that light around."

The beam of light sliced and bobbed until it found the lever Jay knew had to be there. When Trailer Boy pulled it, a bridge unfolded itself and rolled its way across the great divide.

Together, Frank and Jay crossed over to stand before the golden chest. Trailer Boy stood with them and, with trembling hands, Doctor Frank Wu reached out to lift the lid.

They gasped at the beauty of it as Frank lifted the last tool of power from its resting place.

"Behold," he said in a quiet, reverent voice, "The Inscrutable Alien Watercolor Set."

*

They drank Yoohoo in the shade of the double-wide and toasted the eventual maturity of humankind. Trailer Boy cooked MoMos while Jay supervised and Frank embraced his art, filling page upon page with watercolor doodles. Over lunch, they talked about the work ahead of them, and Trailer Boy listened thoughtfully.

"With your stories," Frank said.

"And your art," Jay said.

"We could make a difference," they both said in unison.

One book, Jay thought, birthed from two of the tools of power. One book to draw out the others, those who would take up the tools Frank had tucked away in the vaults of his Bay Area Headquarters and move a species into wholeness.

Trailer Boy chuckled. "I know what you could call it."

"Call what?" Jay asked.

"The book," he said, laughing again. "*Howdy from Wu Lake.* Like one of them new-fangled postcard thingies."

"I like it," Frank said.

"Might need tweaking," Jay said.

Trailer Boy shrugged. Then his face lit up. "I found my story," he said. He dug around in his coveralls again to pull out a sweaty wad of manuscript covered in crayon scribbles and faded New Courier Font. "Would you read it maybe sometime?"

Jay glanced down at it. The first line held no promise and caused him to wonder what the miracles of modern medicine might do for this strange, giant, backwoods bike-riding hermit and his bear fixation. He read it again. *He was a bear and his name was Edward and he lay twitching in the corner of a room that smelled like death.* "Uh," he said, suddenly nervous, "I'll give it a look."

Trailer Boy nodded with a smile and crushed him into a hug. "Thank you, Mr. Jay Lake. Thank you."

Jay extricated himself. "No," he said. "Thank you."

He did the same to Frank, and when he let him go, the doctor smiled and pushed a sheaf of papers into the large, clumsy hands. "I made these for you."

Trailer Boy's face lit up as he shuffled through the hastily crafted series of watercolor doodles. "Classic!"

Jay frowned. "Isn't pornography problematic within your value system?"

Frank shrugged. "They're just cartoons, Jay."

Then the doctor slipped his foot into the knotted silk rope and tugged three times. Jay watched him ascend into the belly of the enormous zeppelin.

"Cool ride," he said.

"I'll bet," Trailer Boy added, "it doesn't have handbrakes."

Laughing, Jay scooped up his leather satchel and walked to his waiting car. With any luck, the Bradley Loggers Circus was in full swing and there was room at the inn. Perhaps the logging dwarves would be busy topping their trees and the logging girls with their boots and suspenders would want to watch him brush his manly hair and maybe swing him around the dance floor in a do-si-do of rural splendor. A shower, some fresh undershorts, and women who weren't afraid of a little sawdust. The perfect close to one more misadventure.

As he climbed into his red convertible and fired it up, sunset washed the sky purple and red.

As Jay Lake drove into it, he smiled and loved the fullness of his life.

TIME DANCING IN THE KEY OF E MINOR

*I*t's quiet," my wife said.

I sat up in bed. "Too quiet."

We both stared at the conch on her nightstand.

Emily looked at me, her gray eyes narrow. "Do you feel it?"

I took a breath, tasted the air. It was humid and I was sweating through my nightshirt. It was cool when we'd fallen asleep two hours ago. "Yes. It's too warm in here. Muggy even."

"Chronotrogs," she said.

We both drew our swords together, pulling them from scabbards tucked safely into the subaether and threaded to our wrists by long strands of moon-elf hair. Emily beat me to the door.

She pushed it open and slipped into the hallway. Her bare feet whispered over the oak floor but each step was steady and deliberate. I knew she was afraid. After ten years with a person, you know how to read them. But she turned her fear into focus, her sword extended and steady before her, its hungry hum a tickle in my ear.

Unlike her, I was forcing myself to breathe slowly. My sword hand shook a bit. My heart pounded. And if it were the first time they'd found us or surprised us it would've made more sense. But I'd lost track of the times this had happened now.

We went straight to the nursery and she moved through that open doorway first, as well. I followed.

The conch lay in Abigail's crib. So did her grandmother's necklace. "Shit."

I didn't wait for her to tell me. I pulled the thread on my left hand and opened our pack. Rummaging through the contents, I drew out first one battered boot and then the other.

Emily scooped up the necklace. "The clasp isn't broken."

"Curiouser," I said. I was already on the floor, tugging a boot that didn't fit me onto my left foot. We'd cut the toe out of it a long time ago to give me more room, but the boot was still too small. Of course, Emily's was too large. We'd built hers up with a wool inner lining, but she still walked funny in it.

Micklefrand's Boots of Time Displacement were intended to be used as a pair, not individually. But working together improved the odds when it came to chasing chronotrogs.

She shoved the boot onto her foot and dropped the necklace in her pocket. "Are you ready, Sam?"

I pulled my goggles from the pack and adjusted the dial on them as they fluttered to life. "Ready."

I looked down. A trail of growing crumbs traced a faint line across the floor, ending at the farthest wall. I tried not to notice that the crumbs were jumping and hopping in the carpet. Despite my mother's assurances, I struggled with intentionally infesting my little girl with tracer-fleas.

Swords ready, we danced the boots to life.

Then, we folded space and time to go find our missing daughter.

It was never hard to find a chronotrog's tunnel. But those few who did find them seldom left. And even fewer actually saw the trogs who dug them.

Emily and I had both the good and ill fortune to have experienced both. Moreover, we'd conceived our daughter in one of these time tunnels the very night we found the boots and made our escape from King Grumber, plundering his treasure vaults as we fled.

"What do you think he wants this time?" Her voice had an edge on it that only an exhausted parent's voice can have.

I shrugged. "Maybe another marriage proposal."

Exhaustion merged with exasperation. "She's two years old."

I shrugged again. "I don't think his son's even born yet."

She glanced over her shoulder. "Maybe it's taxes again."

"We paid them last year," I said.

She sighed.

Each time Grumber had come for Abigail in the past, he'd done so with some wild notion in mind. A proposal for an arranged marriage. A demand that she, as a citizen conceived within his kingdom, pay overdue taxes. At one point, he'd even invoked custody rights.

We'd learned long ago that Grumber and his people didn't mean her any harm. Still, no good parent could let their little girl toddle off with time-tunneling troglodytes.

The trail was fading and I pointed to the point where it ended. "There."

We danced in our nightclothes, the heels on each boot hammering its part as we tapped in unison. An Old Earth Tune named Greensleeves.

Grumber looked up from the book he was reading. Abigail sat in his lap, her blue eyes wide as she laughed and clapped at our grand entry. "Mommy-daddy," she said, the words running together in her excitement.

The guards in the room were on their feet, but their weapons weren't drawn. Slowly, Grumber closed the book and removed his bifocals. Then he lifted Abigail up and stood her on her feet. Laughing, she ran across the room and threw herself at her mother's knees.

I stepped forward, my sword raised, my eyes fixed on the king's.

The stare-down didn't last long.

"What," he finally asked, "seems to be the problem?"

"I have a chronotrog that keeps dragging my daughter through space-time to satisfy his inexplicable whims," I said. I wasn't afraid now. I was angry.

Grumber chuckled. "My whims are quite explicable, thank you. But you have a much bigger problem than that."

I glanced to the left and right, expecting his thugs to fall upon me. They didn't move. "What do you mean?"

He nodded to the girl. "That's what I mean." The chuckle became a laugh. "It seems I was right to tax her as my citizen."

Emily and I looked at Abigail. Smiling, she pointed to our boots and started moving her feet in a mimic of our dance. They slapped against the floor of the vast, dim-lit cave until, with the faintest of popping noises, she vanished.

"Shit," Emily said again.

"Shit," I agreed.

Grumber was still laughing behind us when we slipped into her wake. Her own giggles harmonized with the troglodyte king's laughter as she fled.

It was going to be a long night. And it certainly wasn't going to be quiet.

FISH AND BIRD, CURRENT AND FALLS
(with Liz Coleman)

*S*he comes to me in the middle of the night, in my dreams, and sometimes she whispers French in my ear. She knows I can't understand, but she does it anyway, and some mornings, still baptized in the cold sweat of visitation, I jot down the words I remember. None of them make sense despite those online translators.

Once an angel, now a ghost, she arrives on cat's feet into my soul like that poet said and even though I know exactly how the night will go, I always hope for something different, something better. Something where my voice works, my tears flow, my heart aches and I beg the forgiveness I don't feel I need when I'm awake.

But it is not so. She arrives. She speaks French sometimes, and other times, I awake to her straddling my chest with no weight at all and no words at all. She digs her talons into my chest and cold leaks out from them to freeze my heart with heaviness.

Then, she drags me up.

Up, up, up. Through the ceiling. Through the layer of Seattle cloud, into the night where there is only stars and whispers. She holds me there, close to her own dead chest, her wings trembling.

Then she smiles.

"The falls," she says and I work my mouth open to ask her why.

The falls. And I know what follows. Every night, I know what follows.

She places her cold blue mouth to my ear.

"The falls are beautiful this time of year," she whispers.

And then she drops me and I scream the whole way down.

*

The book lies right where she left it the morning before she fell. Hair cascaded over her shoulders as she brushed it and read from that Basic French reader open flat upon her dresser. Lips moved silently as she taught herself, every morning.

"Are we going to the falls today?" I asked.

She looked at me in the mirror. Curly hair bunched up in a mist beneath her comb.

"Oui," she said. The only thing I understood.

I will see her again tonight. She will hold me down and we will fly. She will grind my love to mist against the rocks of memory. It is the only way to make the pain dry up. I love her ghost for the work she does, and yet the love keeps flowing, and pain keeps coming.

"Elle vous aime," she would say with mischief in her eyes.

Does she hate me? Does the fish curse the current that pulls it over the cliff?

I flip through the book, thinking if I could understand her words in my dreams, she'll fly away to peace. She was the bird, and I was the fish, and our love was the column of air pushing us apart.

She always did like to scare me, and that's why I think she stepped beyond the split-rail fence onto the mist-soaked rocks above Nooksack Falls.

"Get back here," I said.

"Je suis désolé, je ne vous comprends pas," she said back.

Dried coffee glues warped pages together. Doodles spatter the margins. Angels flying over mountains (or were they leaping up to heaven?) Sea horses and dolphins. Curly-haired babies that I wouldn't let her have.

"Do you want to be free of me?" I ask. Wind flies in my face as I flip the pages. The paper smells like sweet peas. And then I stop. I've landed on a dialogue between a waiter and tourist. My eyes land on one word.

"Oui."

I go to bed with the book in my arms, just in case. I reach for the lighter beside her sweet pea candle, and fall asleep with my thumb on the cold metal head.

Her thighs pull against the hair on my chest. Blue lips move above my eyes. Rank air falls from her mouth. In go her claws, and my heart freezes. She keeps my arms pinned, and I cannot reach my flame. But I know my chance will come.

Up we go through the clouds. The falls are beautiful this time of year. They flow upwards to heaven.

Now my hands are free. I set the book afire. She screams and lets me fall. But I do not fall for long and there is beauty in that, too. The smell of burnt feathers turns to fresh mist, and I fly on wings of ash and hair. Infinitives and conjugations flutter away on the wind.

I mark the Puget Sound beneath me, the Cascades far to my right, and the Olympics to my left. Home is not hard to find with the clouds out of the way, and I drop through the roof into my waiting bed.

My heart burns as I open my eyes. I'm stretched out in bed and naked, the sheets and blanket pooling at my feet. I am alone and I know I will be alone every night after this.

A red-rimmed cinder curls upon my chest, burning away the single word: "Oui."

IF DRAGON'S MASS EVE BE COLD AND CLEAR

Muscles tire. Words fail. Faith fades. Fear falls.
In the Sixteenth Year of the Sixteen Princes the
world came to an end when the dragon's back gave
out. Poetry died first followed by faith. One by one
the world-strands burst and bled until ash snowed
down as huddled masses whimpered in the cold.
The Santaman came reeking of love into this
place and we did not know him.
This is his story.
This is our story, too.
　　　　　　　　—Prelude
　　　　　　　　The Santaman Cycle,
　　　　　　　　Authorized Standard Version
　　　　　　　　Verity Press, 2453 YD

I buried my father on Dragon's Mass Eve. I dug the grave myself, there on the hill overlooking our homestead, beside the grave he dug for my mother some thirty-five years earlier.

As I worked the shovel, I tried not to cry. I failed. And I recited the Cycle, just the way he taught me, as I cut the sod and turned the dirt out into a pile.

Muscles tire. It was as if he stood with me. I could hear his voice grumbling on the wind that rose as the sun dropped and the air cooled. "Pause, Melody Constance," he said. "Feel what the writer intended with the words."

I felt my foot upon the shovel, my shoulders as I bent and lifted dirt. I felt the hollow empty place inside that tried to swallow me whenever my eyes wandered to the wagon and the red-wrapped body laying there.

Words fail. Again, a hesitation, a waiting. Silence to honor the moments no words can carry.

Like this one.

Only, it didn't feel like a moment—it felt like a year, in the cold, working the shovel. Alone. Orphanhood settled onto my back and shoulders with a weight I'd never felt before. I had no memory of my mother; she'd died the morning I was born. So it was a loss I assumed and grew into, never really knowing what I'd missed out on other than those times I stayed with neighboring families when my father needed to travel. But even then, it was only the slightest taste of someone else's life. Working the mine and farm with my father was *my* life. And so was Dragon's Mass Eve—his favorite and only holiday—spent quietly at home in our red paper hats and our fruit salad and rice stew while the faithful gathered at church.

Faith fades. Fear falls.

My mind blurred with my eyes as the tears overpowered me. The questions began to rise even as the fear fell upon me. What will I do now? Where will I go? How will I ever learn to live around this vast hole in my heart?

They were all things we'd talked about in passing when he talked in the midst of his illness about not getting better. And I knew that I would find the desk in his office perfectly organized with carefully written instructions for everything that needed to be done and everyone that had to be contacted. He'd learned to be meticulous during forty years working in the Bureaucracy's supply chain, and he'd instilled it into me. I think I was six when he put the first of many carefully scripted lists into my hands and sent me off to do my chores.

But having a plan and executing said plan were not the same thing.

My eye wandered to the wagon again, and I tried to tell myself it was because I was measuring how much further I had to dig. But I knew better. It was because I was close to finished. And when I was done digging, when I eased my father into that hole, he would be gone. I would only ever see him again in memory and dreams, in the half-dozen photographs tucked into our leatherbound copy of the Cycle.

This would be our last Dragon's Mass Eve together. My last time reciting the words with him. Our conversation earlier that morning would be the last we ever had, and it broke my heart open even further.

I went through the Cycle three times before I finished digging, from *muscles tire* to *upon his back, a world,* quoting from the Authorized Standard Version that my father had studied during the single year he spent in seminary. It was the version he'd memorized as a part of his training, and though he'd set aside his faith years before, he still felt it had enough merit that his daughter should know it. So now I said the words, felt none of them, and gentled my father into his grave.

The night was clear and cold but I paid it no mind. The hymn might've promised that the Santaman's grace would find us here, but the reality was I'd already seen at least a half-dozen clear and cold Dragon's Mass Eves, and the Santaman had yet to come back, reeking of anything, much less love. There had been, according to my father, over two hundred and thirty seven cold, clear Dragon's Mass Eves to be exact, much to the great consternation of the few remaining theologians.

We were on our own.

I was on *my* own.

I shoveled the earth over him and went through the Cycle another three times for good measure. But even as I did, I knew it wouldn't be enough. It was my first lesson in grief—that there never, ever was enough when it came to those we lost.

On my last Dragon's Mass Eve with Father, the rice stew grew cold upon the stove and I did not kneel and pray to the north. Instead, I cried myself to sleep, still covered in the dirt and drying sweat of my father's grave-digging.

> *If Dragon's Mass Eve be cold and clear*
> *The Santaman's grace may find us here.*
> *But if Dragon's Mass Eve be clouded sky*
> *The Santaman's grace may pass us by.*
> —*Hymn #475,*
> *"If Dragon's Mass Eve Be Cold and Clear"*
> *Hymns of the Dragon and his Avenger,*
> *Contemporary Edition*
> *Verity Music, 2623 YD*

"Like this," my father told me, unfolding the red paper and then folding it again in a different place, pressing the new crease into it with his massive thumb.

I watched, then took it from him and folded it again. It was my tenth Dragon's Mass Eve and it had gone like all of the others I could remember. First, he pulled out the jars and cans he'd collected over the year, separating the fruit from the vegetables and the cans of potted meat. The fruit came to me along with a notation on my morning chores list, and I mixed it into a fruit salad. His own list called for preparing the rice stew, and while it simmered, we moved on to the hats.

"I can never get it right," I said.

He chuckled, and it was a low rumble in the brightly lit kitchen. "Getting it right isn't always required."

I watched his hands as they moved over his own sheet of paper, a fold here and a fold there, followed by a dab of paste and a cotton ball. I looked at mine and sighed. "Yours is better."

Lifting the hat, he placed it on my head and then pushed up his glasses. Then, he swept my paper and cottonball away with a giant hand and started over with them. "Mine is a wreck," he said with a toothy grin. He nodded to the hat I wore. "Yours looks pretty good, actually."

We laughed, and after, he put the battered hat onto his head. "Now," he said, "we are ready."

We stood and went outside into the night. We climbed the hill out behind the homestead and faced north, kneeling at my mother's grave. The stone that marked it was plain, dark granite.

Harmony Angelique Sheffleton-Farrelly, it read. Then, after the date of her birth and the date of her death: *Public servant, beloved wife and mother*.

My knees were cold. "I don't understand why we do this," I said. Ten was the year that I mastered the art of the subtle complaint.

"We do this," he said, "because it's important to remember where we come from."

Of course, I'd heard the story of how he and Mother had met and about their first Dragon's Mass Eve together in the supply basement of the Bureaucracy. He'd been one of a small number of trolls in public service to the Bureaucracy, his trollishness coming in handy for safeguarding their supplies. My mother had been his replacement after thirty years in the supply chain, but meeting her had caught some part of him on fire and he'd decided to forego retirement. They spent another decade improving efficiencies, easing the government back to some semblance of functional. Then they'd ridden west with some of the world's last hope lining the bottom of an old coffee can to seed a mine that had long before gone dry. They raised a litter of love, selling off each pup that survived, and made due on their pensions.

Somewhere in the midst of it, they decided to have me, and that choice changed everything.

I put my hand on the stone. "But we don't believe in the Santaman," I said.

"No," he said and winked. "We don't have to."

We said our prayer quickly as the wind rose to threaten our hats. When we finished, I looked up. "Clouded sky," I said.

Father chuckled again. "Yes."

"Last year was clear, though."

"Yes," he said again. "There have been quite a few clear, cold Dragon's Mass Eves."

I kicked the dirt. "The song got it wrong."

I felt his hand settle onto my shoulder. "Getting it right," he said again, "isn't required." We went back into the house and I pulled the door closed. He went to the stove and ladled the rice stew into simple wooden bowls that came out each year just for this tradition. He didn't speak again until we were seated at the table, the fire crackling nearby.

"Besides," he said as he tucked his napkin into his open-collared shirt, "they changed the song a long time ago. While I was in seminary there were a lot of people wanting to update the Cycle and the Hymnal. The song used to say 'will,' which implied a guaranty that the clergy couldn't afford to underwrite once the cold, clear nights started showing up again."

I'd heard this one before and I nodded. "So they changed it to 'may.'"

He grinned, his broad face lighting up. "Yes."

I tried to imitate his deep, gruff voice. "So when we sing it, we sing it as it was written—"

He joined in and we finished in unison. "—just as the writer intended it to be sung."

I paused, my spoon paused above the rim of the bowl. "But it isn't true."

He paused, too. "No, it doesn't appear to be."

"So aren't the new words more . . . accurate?"

He took a bite, swallowed, and thought for a moment. "Only if the underlying premise is accurate. I can sing about flying fish that *might* bring little girls vast wealth for Dragon's Mass Eve, but if there *are* no flying fish . . ." Here, he shrugged.

I smiled and mimicked his shrug. "And so we return to my initial question. Why do we do it?"

My father sighed. "Someday, when you have a child, you'll understand it better, I think."

I shook my head. "I don't think I will." Then, I wrinkled my nose. "And I don't want a child."

"Ah," he said, "but do you want your present?"

I nodded. "But let me get yours first."

That was the year that I'd written him a story about the two of us fighting Black Drawlers in the north while we searched for the Santaman's fabled sword. I'd written it out in my best penmanship, and Miss Marplesbee, the sole teacher at the small one-room school in town, helped me bind it between pieces of cardboard with bright red yarn. I was particularly pleased with the cover—one of my better drawings of Father lopping the head off a Black Drawler with me poised carefully on his back, a dagger clenched in my teeth.

And it was the year that he gave me the picture of Mother, wearing the dress she wore when she met my father, leaning against a desk in the drab cubicle wasteland of the Bureaucracy's fifth floor. He'd built the frame himself.

I was pulling the paper aside when I woke up. I lay in bed for a minute and blinked the dream away. It was a good Dragon's Mass Eve. But it was twenty five years behind me now and the truth I swallowed made my stomach hurt.

I looked up to the picture of my mother that had hung above my bed since the night he'd first given it to me.

I forced myself up and drew a bath. When I walked past my father's open door, I did not let myself look in upon his empty bed, upon the spectacles that lay on his nightstand, folded closed and never to be opened again by his large, clumsy fingers.

*

Muscles tire. It's all we really knew. The dragon's back held up the world. The poetry and faith of the Singing Literocrats held up the dragon by the will of the Sixteen Princes. One Literocrat fell to the sword, another to plague, a third to famine. Halved in this way, the choir faltered in its song and the dragon caved in on its spindly legs. The Sixteen Princes had no time to act, to change the course of this sudden, sweeping end. They drank wine and spoke of lemon trees instead.

We sat in the cold until the Santaman came.

—*The Breaking of the Dragon's Back*
The Santaman Cycle,
Authorized Standard Version
Verity Press, 2453 YD

The first week crept by with varied weather. Storms of sorrow blew in at the slightest provocation—the smell of him on his clothes, his pen laid carefully to the left side of his desk blotter, the notes he'd written and organized for me. And on the heels of the sadness, a calm and foreboding hollowness that I didn't know I could feel. Followed suddenly by inconsolable rage that had no place to go but inward or else it might burn down the world.

I went through the pile of papers, mailing what needed mailed and making the calls on Father's list. I loaded the granite marker he'd kept in the mine all these years onto the wagon and drove it into town. He'd had his name and birthdate carved onto it when he had mother's made. *The rest is up to you*, his note told me. And so I dropped it with Anderson, Bauer and Sons' Stonework, picked it up a week later, and planted it at the head of the fresh grave.

Drummond Angus Farrelly, it said, along with his dates of birth and death. *Public servant, cherished father, beloved husband.*

The government men showed up about a month after, briefcases in hands.

"Miss Farrelly?" the man in the suit asked when I opened the door.

"Ms. Sheffleton-Farrelly," I corrected him. "Melody. Call me Mel."

The man looked uncomfortable and his partner looked away,

clearing his voice. Their pinstriped trousers and jackets looked out of place here on the edge of the world and I wasn't sure how they kept their shoes so shiny. "Is there someplace we can talk?"

I nodded toward my father's office—a shack near the gated entrance of the mine. I dried my hands and laid my dish towel over a wooden chair. "Across the way," I said.

I led us across the hard-packed yard and used the key to open the door. There had been little to do in the office and I'd spent most of my time here arranging and re-arranging the items on his desk.

I sat behind it now, still feeling dwarfed by its size, and waited until my guests sat. They each placed their cases across their knees and opened them. "First," the spokesman said as he lifted out an accordion file of papers, "let me say how sorry we all were to hear about Drum's—your father's—passing. I worked with him on several procurements and had a lot of respect for him."

"Thank you." My father, in addition to his contract for the mine, had also entered into consulting contracts with the Bureaucracy from time to time, leaving me with either the Gustavsons or the Graves—sometimes for months at a time—to ride east and do his part to help put the world right. I'd always hoped to go with him, but for one reason or another, we never made it happen. But I'd write my stories as if I'd gone, weaving tales of our derring-do and heroics on secret missions for the Bureaucracy.

"That said," the government man continued, "there are uncomfortable matters to discuss."

I nodded. I knew of at least one matter—the pension. Father thought he'd found a loophole that would allow it to pass to me—something about a Board Order from the past century regarding widows and orphans. But I'd read the order and didn't think it was likely to work in my case. "The pension, right?"

He nodded. "Yes. I'm afraid you do not meet the age requirements for survivorship to apply."

"Understood," I said.

"And then there is the matter of the mining contract."

My eyes came up to his. "The mining contract?"

His smile was apologetic as he drew a letter out of the file. "Unfortunately, amendment six removed the assignment clause from the Bureaucracy's standard terms and conditions. Which means that with the passing of your father—the contractor in this regard—this contract is null and void. I've a letter of cancellation for you, notarized by the Board clerk."

I felt anger rising in my face. "Amendment six?" I rolled my chair to the file cabinet to my left and pulled open the second drawer. "When was this amendment issued? I don't recall seeing it. Do you have an executed copy?"

He shook his head. "It's just been issued in the last fortnight. But unfortunately, Mr. Farrelly is no longer in a position to . . ." Here he cleared his voice and looked away. "To sign it."

Red tape. My father had created his share of it in the Bureaucracy's basement.

I smiled. "Surely you can re-compete it." The first ten years, father had operated the mine on a no-bid contract. It was the only operating hope mine in the western provinces and that made it eligible for a sole source exemption. But the last two and a half decades, he'd competed for it. No one else had, so of course he was awarded the contract.

Red tape.

The government man shook his head. "We are not going to re-procure in this case, Ms. Sheffleton-Farrelly. As you know, the Drawler threat in the north is taking more and more resources. The Bureaucracy is cutting expenses wherever it can."

I leaned forward. "Are you giving up on hope altogether then?"

"No," he said. "We'll fund mining efforts elsewhere certainly where it makes sense."

"Just not here."

"Not here," he agreed. Then, he leaned forward. "Ms. Sheffleton-Farrelly, do you have any idea when the last time was that this mine produced a single flake of hope?"

I rolled back to the file cabinet, this time opening the top drawer to pull out the production journals. "Late autumn," I said. "Twenty-six-fifty-three, Year of the Dragon."

It was the same year my father had gone to seminary.

"Eighty years," the man said. "And thirty-five of them subsidized by tax dollars with nothing to show for it."

There was little to say after that. They left me with a stack of papers less than an hour later, climbing into their jeep and driving back to the town's single inn.

I went over those papers that afternoon, filing them carefully like he would have, and afterward, I adjusted father's financial projections less his ongoing pension payments and the contract revenue. I checked his notations in the savings ledger one last time before folding it up and tucking it back into the file cabinet. If I were frugal, I had maybe two years left here. And after that?

There was a form in the paperwork from the Bureaucracy—an application for the civil service exam with a box already marked and initialed on it, authorizing me to take the test in any satellite branch where it was offered and extending bonus points based on my relationship to one Drummond Angus Farrelly, a decorated procurement officer.

I filed it separate from the other papers and snuffed out the lamp. I looked over everything, neatly in its place, before locking the office door. After today, I really wasn't sure when I'd be back.

Then I went up to father's grave for the first time since digging it. I sat heavily upon the ground and leaned against his marker. "You were wrong about the pension," I told him. "The mining contract, too."

And in that moment, I was certain I heard his voice. First, he chuckled. Then, he told me what he'd told me so many times before.

"Being right," my father reminded me, "is not always required."

> *Myth became life. No one really believed in the Santaman until he came with his tattered red robe and his dripping red sword. No one really believed in his undying love until he burst into our direst need to carve us a new home from the bones of the world.*
>
> *We looked up at the whistle of his wolf-stallion. "Why do you weep and whimper?" the Santaman asked from the back of his mount.*
>
> *"We whimper for the end of our world," one of us said. "We weep for the fall of the Singing Literocrats and the Breaking of the Dragon's Back."*
>
> *The Santaman grinned and shook his sword. Blood rained down from it, mixing with the ashes. "Weep also for the Sixteen Princes who have failed you."*
>
> *"Why, Lord?" someone asked.*
>
> *The Santaman spun his mount. "For I have avenged you in the Name Above All and they are no more."*

We did not waver in our weeping. There was no lull
in our lament.

—*The Coming of the Santaman*
The Santaman Cycle,
Authorized Standard Version
Verity Press, 2453 YD

In grief, time moves at inconsistent pace and the bereaved adjust and shuffle forward accordingly. I did not return to my father's grave again for nearly two years, though I watched it often from the kitchen window or from the yard.

Each month, I hitched the wagon and went into town to re-supply. And on each trip, I endured the sympathy of the closest thing we had to a community so far removed from the rest of the world.

"What will you do now?" was the most popular question, and I never had a real answer. I took their offered condolences and tucked them away. And I watched the numbers on the savings ledger shrink.

I pulled the pictures from the Cycle and tucked the book away out of sight, moving the photographs into the treasure box I kept beneath my bed. But after that, I left the box where it lay for a long time and let it find its dust.

I wouldn't have known the season but for news of the fighting in the north. More Black Drawlers leaking into the world through the ether, moving further south in their hunger. And when I knew the day approached, I even went into town to collect what jars and cans I could.

The mercantile even had red paper, and I bought a sheet.

But as Dragon's Mass Eve drew near, the knot in my stomach grew tighter and my eyes went more often to the hill. Finally, I surrendered and found the best dress that still fit me and rode into town.

Father had never taken me to the church for Dragon's Mass Eve, but we'd visited one Dragonsday for weekly services. On the ride in, I sat beside him on the bench and we talked about what we were going to see.

"There won't be many, I'll wager," he said. "But there will be some. Parson Brown will pray and Emily Hopewell will play a few hymns on the organ that we will all sing to. Then, the parson will preach about the Santaman and take a collection."

When we arrived, the parson's eyes lit up. "Drum Farrelly," he said, "you're just about the last person I expected to show up this morning."

I remember my father's strained smile as he shook the parson's hand. "Melody was curious," he said.

I'd seen Parson Brown around town, but never in the dark robes of his priesthood. It made the short, round man look almost comical. He'd shaken my hand, looking up at me with a smile. "Welcome," he said.

We took our seat on the back row.

Then, just as father said, we prayed and sang and listened and sang again and as we did, father slipped a small wad of the most recently authorized currency into the plate that passed up and down the pews of scattered faithful.

On the ride home, we'd had our discussion and father dissected the components of the service.

"At the end," I told him, "they prayed for the Santaman's return. Do they do it every Dragonsday?"

He nodded. "Some of them do it *every* day."

"Not just on Dragon's Mass Eve?"

"No."

"But they believe one day it will work?"

"Yes."

"They really *really* believe?"

He nodded again. "They really *really* believe. And I used to, too. Even your mother, in some ways, believed. Only she believed that if there was a Santaman, he expected us to work while we waited and make things as good as we could." He looked thoughtful for a moment.

"But we don't believe now," I said.

He smiled at me. "*I* don't believe now. Do you?"

I smiled back. "No, I really don't. I think . . ." I tried to find something to hitch my thought to. I remembered the growing stack of bound cardboard covers he kept in the drawer beside his bed, each containing my carefully written pages of our fictional misadventures spread out over a half-dozen Dragon's Mass Eves. "I think it's a good story, but I don't think it's true." Then, I said what I knew he was going to say next. "But I suppose being true isn't always required."

He smiled. "Exactly so."

I blinked tears away at the memory as I turned the corner onto Main Street and saw the brightly lit building that waited.

Parson Brown stood at the door and smiled at me. "Mel Farrelly," he said. "You're just about the last person I expected to show up tonight."

I climbed down and hitched my horse. "Happy Dragon's Mass Eve, Parson," I said as I took his hand.

"And to you," he said.

The church was full, with men and women crowded onto the pews in their Dragonsday best. I spotted the Gustavsons and the Graces near the middle of the overflowing sanctuary, and though both families waved me over, I took a spot in the last row in the back corner. My nervous hands picked up the worn hymnal and thumbed through the pages until the parson took to the pulpit and offered the invocation.

After, there was a small choir that sang a medley of hymns. The room joined in and it was nothing like the scattered voices I'd heard in this very room as a child—it was one voice made of many, booming out into the night in a cry for help that I could nearly give myself over to. But I did not want help from some mysterious, red-cloaked and red-bladed avenger. I wanted my father, and the power of that longing flooded my eyes with tears. Still, when we reached "If Dragon's Mass Eve Be Cold and Clear," I sang the original words—the writer's words—and not the softer *maybe* his hymn had been neutered into.

"Now tonight," Parson Brown intoned after the singing, "we have a special treat."

My first thought was that he meant to introduce me, point me out to the crowd, and I found myself suddenly wanting to flee. But it didn't happen. Instead, he nodded to a young man who sat to the side. "Tonight," Parson Brown said, "Brother Simon will bring the homily. His first sermon, I might add."

A wave of murmurs rolled over the congregation, and I pressed my mouth together, studying the young man.

His robes were ill-fitting and his eyebrows and cheekbones bore a hint of the fey. He took the pulpit, thumbing through the leather-bound copy of the Cycle that he carried to it, and he smiled out at us. "Good evening," he said as Parson Brown took a seat behind him. "Tonight's message is taken from the Coming of the Santaman, verses one through three."

As he read the scripture, I mouthed the words with him. "Myth became life," he read. "No one really believed in the Santaman until he came with his tattered red robe and his dripping red sword. No one really believed in his undying love until he burst into our direst need to carve us a new home from the bones of the world."

Brother Simon closed the book and looked upon us all. When his eyes moved over the back pew, they met mine and I felt the measurement in his level gaze. "I submit to you, brothers and sisters, that like those before us, we do not *really* believe in the Santaman."

From there, he launched into his sermon and I found his words fading and blurring, taking a seat behind him like the parson, as he filled the room with his presence. His hands moved like a magician, illustrating this or that point, indicating this or that observation, as he moved across the platform. His voice was hypnotic, rising and falling in passion and pitch, and his eyes continued wandering the crowded room, finding mine on more than one occasion. Those eyes, I knew, were unsafe. They held too many contradicting views—hope and fear, anger and grace, and something more I'd never been comfortable with: Conviction.

When he finished, he sat down abruptly and Parson Brown took over. After singing "The Santman Shall Rise Again" as the plate migrated up and down the rows, he dismissed us to the fellowship hall for cookies and tea.

I was moving toward the door when Brother Simon caught up to me and shook my hand. The hand was rough and calloused; it caught me off guard. "You're not leaving are you?"

I blushed and stammered but didn't know why. "I have . . . things to do."

"Come have a cookie at least." Then, as an afterthought: "I'm Simon by the way." And somehow, the voice compelled me, and I let him guide me by the elbow into the fellowship hall before he vanished into the crowd.

A cup of tea was pushed into one of my hands, a molasses cookie into the other, and I blessed both because it meant I need not shake any more hands.

I stood quietly in the corner and suffered the kindness and curiosity of a town that had seen little of me and little of my father before me.

I'd finished the tea and moved for the door when the parson came by with the young man in tow. "And this," he said, "is Melody Farrelly.

She owns the old hope mine out past the Gustavson's farm."

"We've met," I said and forced a smile. But I shook his offered hand again, noticing once more how rough it was.

"Brother Simon is our new acolyte. He's in his last year at the Middleton Seminary. I expect he'll be taking my place when I retire next year." He turned to the young man. "Melody's father, Drummond, spent a year at Middleton."

His face lit up. "Is he here with you?"

I looked away. "He passed away last Dragon's Mass Eve."

The light dimmed and his smile faded. "I'm sorry."

"I've been meaning to ask," the Parson said. "Do you know what you will do now? Will you sell the mine?"

I shrugged. "It hasn't produced in over eighty years. Not much demand for a hope mine without hope."

And then, the conversation folded in on itself and the two of them moved on. I excused myself and slipped out under a cloudy night to find my horse.

I rode home and tried to eat at least some of the fruit salad I'd made earlier that day. It tasted empty without my father. And I knew better than to recite the Cycle. Instead, I braved his room—something I rarely brought myself to do—and curled up on his large bed. Then, I pulled open the drawer and pulled out the stack of stories I'd written him through the years.

As I read them, I found myself laughing and crying, and when I felt sleep pulling at me, I gathered them up and took them to my own room. I pulled out the cardboard box beneath my bed and laid them carefully in it.

My eyes caught the wadded up piece of paper I'd also tucked into the box, and I forced them away. That ball of paper was the first to go into my treasure box, though I couldn't bring myself to open it up and smooth it out. It made me too angry and too afraid.

But now, a strange fancy struck me, and I lifted it careful as a butterfly from a flower. I sat on my bed and held it, remembering my last conversation with my father. Then, I smoothed it out upon my lap.

It was a requisition slip, filled out and in triplicate. He'd completed most of it, leaving the order date blank along with the boxes used to select gender.

Then, I remembered the words I'd said to him—off and on for years—and the quiet way he smiled when I said them.

"I don't want a child," I told the empty room.

Then, I placed the smoothed-out form in the box and lowered the lid over it like a casket before laying it to rest again in the dusty grave beneath my bed.

> *Dust rose from the West as the Santaman approached. The wolf-stallion growled and tore sod and the last of the Literocrats lay down their lyres by the Murmuring Stream as the dragon's eye faltered above them.*
>
> *"Take up your tools and lift your song," the Santaman cried.*
>
> *"We are halved," the Fourth Literocrat said. "Our song is lost. The world ends. The dragon's back, already broken."*
>
> *The sword licked out, then pointed North. The Murmuring Stream ran pink. "Sing a new home," the Santaman cried again. "Beyond the ether at the Edge of the World."*
>
> *Two voices rose and fell in song. A third burbled in the stream. Scooping the golden-haired head from the water, the Santaman came seeking us to tell us of our new carved home.*
>
> *—The Last of the Literocrats*
> *The Santaman Cycle,*
> *Authorized Standard Version*
> *Verity Press, 2453 YD*

The next year moved faster. I learned that loss is like a hole in the middle of your living room floor. Your rearrange the furniture around it and you visit it once in awhile but less and less often with every month. Eventually, you grow accustomed to walking around the hole, living around it as it just becomes a part of your life.

I started writing again, though I'd long ago outgrown the adventure stories I used to tell. Instead, I wrote about my father and about my memories of him. I tended the garden and stretched the savings as far as I could. And in the weeks before Dragon's Mass Eve, as the news turned somber in the north, I didn't even try to find the canned fruits and vegetables and meat. But I did slip into his office to fill out the civil service exam application. I put it into an envelope and took it into the house. I still wasn't certain if I would mail it.

When Dragon's Mass Eve arrived, I rode into town again and like the year before, I slipped onto the back pew. The church was less crowded this year and when Parson Brown's invocation included a blessing upon the men and women serving in the local militia, I made the connection with why.

The singing was more subdued, and when Brother Simon took the pulpit, there was something quiet about him that felt disconnected from the young man I'd seen prowling the platform a year before. "Tonight's message," he said, "is taken from the Last of the Literocrats, verses one through five."

We made eye contact as he read, and the light I'd seen before was dark now. There was something of sorrow or anger in them now that resonated with me, and I couldn't look away.

"Take up your tools and lift your song," he said. "That is what I want to talk about with you tonight."

What followed were brief but heartfelt comments, but nothing like the lively performance I knew he was capable of. When we shook hands later, in the fellowship hall, I could even feel the difference in his grip. And the hands were less rough here in the second year of his apprenticeship.

"I enjoyed your message," I told him, even more uncomfortable with his eyes in such close proximity. "My mother used to believe that the Santaman wouldn't return until we'd done our very best with our own hands."

He nodded and smiled, but I saw the falseness in it. "Yes," he said. There were clouds behind those eyes now, too.

I leaned close to him and lowered my voice. "Are you okay, Brother Simon?"

He looked at me, and I think he was surprised that I noticed, though it was as obvious as his nose to me. His cheeks grew red and he looked around, panic on his face.

Finally, he pulled me aside, and his words were fast and jumbled together. "We lost Fallowston and Reinburg this morning," he said. "The diocese sent a rider. The crier will be announcing it tomorrow. Parson Brown didn't want to dampen spirits tonight with the news."

I knew the towns though I'd never visited them. "Did you have people there?"

He shook his head. "No. But our militia is engaged at Candle-toss." I imagined the points on the map, saw how close it all was.

Simon looked out the window and I saw the firmness in his jaw-line and the anger in his eyes. Outside, it was a clear night and I understood his anger better.

"Something," he said, "has to happen soon."

I nodded but didn't know what to say. Finally, I found my voice. "Maybe," I said, "it's like you said earlier—maybe we're called upon to take up our tools and lift our song. Especially when we're faced with the end of our world . . . just like the Last of the Literocrats."

"Yes. Maybe."

Then he was moving off into the crowd, shaking hands and pat-ting shoulders. I slipped out beneath a star-scattered sky and rode home in the light of the moons.

When I reached the homestead, I stabled my horse and slipped into the house. I found the envelope first, and then I went to the box beneath my head and pulled out the wadded-up requisition slip. Tak-ing both, I let myself back out into the night and climbed the hill behind the house.

I sat quietly for a while, prayerless and facing north. "I don't know if it's the right thing to do," I told my father, "but I'm going to do it. I know you were right about most things—all the important things, really—and I think you were right about this. But I'm still afraid."

I paused in that moment and knew I would have given every-thing I owned to have this one final conversation with him, to hear his words and see his eyes as he formed them. But in thirty-five years with the old troll, I knew what he would ask next and I blushed.

"No," I said. "I don't know *who* yet." Still, I knew who I'd thought about the few times I'd let myself imagine it. "Regardless of who, I'm going to do it and I wanted you to know. But I'm going to have to leave you to make it happen. Because I'm also going to take the test."

I reached out then to touch the gravestone. The granite felt wrong to my fingertips and I rubbed them into the stone, feeling something powdery flaking off as I did.

My first thought was that it was ash or dust. But my second thought was the one that brought my fingers tentatively to my mouth. I'd never tasted hope before, but my father had described it many times before.

Bitter and sweet at the same time.

I looked above me at the clear night and stood on shaking legs. I went into the house and lit the lantern, grabbed my knife, and lifted the keys to the mine off the hook where my father had last hung them.

I walked down into the mine, and I hadn't gone very far when the dark walls started to glisten white. I paused along the way to scrape here or there, each time coming away with a handful of white flaky residue.

I went all the way to the bottom, and when I reached it, I sat down and laughed until my sides hurt, and then I cried until my eyes had no more tears in them.

Two days later, I phoned in my requisition at the town's single phone, dialing the number my father gave me. And when I finished with central stores, I had the operator transfer me to the contracts division.

> "North of the faraway beyond the ether at the Edge of the World" the head sang and died. The Santaman cast it aside.
>
> "The way is too hard," we told the Santaman. "And we are afraid."
>
> He sheathed his sword and climbed down among us. He cast open his arms, his red robes hung like bleeding meat. "Do not be afraid. I walk with you."
>
> North, he walked his wolf-stallion, and we followed after. In twilight, we walked, and as the ruined cities fell behind us, others joined our ragged band.
>
> Lost also behind us, the last of the literocrats sang sunrise and sunset, sang muscles and sinew, sang bones and teeth.
>
> Death crabs scuttled and scavenged. Snick-snack went the sword.
>
> Black Drawlers shrieked and savaged. Snick-snack went the sword.
>
> Some of us fell. Some of us faltered. All of us hoped.
>
> The faraway wrapped us and the ash snows fell away.
>
> Sunlight bathed us and we swam out into the ether at the Edge of the World.
>
> Swam towards our new carved home.
>
>   —*The Ether at the Edge of the World*
>   *The Santaman Cycle,*
>   *Authorized Standard Version*
>   *Verity Press, 2453 YD*

*

The Bureaucracy was faster this time. Within two weeks, the suits were back. They offered twenty years, but I declined, much to their surprise. "One year is about as far ahead as I can see for now," I said.

They looked nervous when I said that. "Do you have other plans for the mine?"

I shrugged. "I might sell it. And I would certainly want to entertain a bid from the Bureaucracy if it comes to that."

My reassurance helped, and when they left, I went to my father's savings ledger and readjusted the figures to account for the contract income. Tomorrow, I'd ride into town and hire a small crew.

A knock at the office door brought my head up. Brother Simon stood framed in the late morning light. "Miss Farrelly," he said with a nod.

"Ms. Sheffleton-Farrelly," I corrected him. "Call me Mel."

"Mel," he said. "May I come in?"

I nodded. "'Please," I said, pointing to a chair. "Sit. I didn't know parsons still made house calls."

He blushed. "I'm not a parson."

"You will be soon enough."

Simon shook his head. "No, I've stepped down. I don't think I'm made for the priesthood."

I'd seen him just two weeks before, and even in that short time, whatever crisis he'd been working through seemed more settled and calm. I knew it was none of my business, and it was a question that I hated, but I asked it anyway. "Then what will do you now?"

He looked around the room and then our eyes met. "What I used to do. I was apprenticed to a blacksmith before."

I nodded and looked at his hands. "So you're traveling the parish and letting everyone know?"

He shook his head. "No. Just you for now."

My breath caught, and for a moment, I wondered if he somehow knew about some of the thoughts I'd thought about him on cold nights beneath my quilt. But I quickly kicked my imagination back to quiet; it was an awkward quiet.

Simon filled it. "I heard you struck hope."

I laughed. "I didn't strike it; it struck me. My father seeded this place for three seasons and got nothing. Then, decades later . . ." I snapped my fingers in the air. "Hope."

"Hope," he said. "I need some actually."

I studied him. "I have some. How much do you need?"

"A pound," he said. "I . . . I don't have any money."

A pound was a lot. Not for me at the moment, but a pound of hope in a world that had for too long gone without . . . its value was staggering. "What are you going to do with it?"

"I'm borrowing Jansen's shop at night," he said. His face went red again and he looked around the empty room as if to make sure no one could hear him. "I'm re-forging the Santaman's sword."

I sat back, surprised. "You're what?"

He nodded. "I'm re-forging the sword based on its description in the Doctrines and Affirmations. I'm going to take it north."

I raised my eyebrows. "Why would you do that?"

"Because maybe if he sees we've tried . . . really tried . . . maybe then he'll hear."

I shook my head. "Simon," I said, "I don't think the Santaman's listening."

But when our eyes met this time, I knew it didn't matter. His conviction was back, and now it bent him away from words and motions, moved him toward deeds and demonstrations now, but it was still the same drive for miracles and wonders to flow into and out of his life. "Please," he said. "I can't do it without hope."

I sighed and measured him. "Okay. But I want something for it."

"Anything I have that I can give you," he said.

I smiled. "Come back tonight for dinner, Simon, and we'll talk about it. I'll have the hope ready for you."

After he left, I weighed out two pounds from the hope I'd scraped these past two weeks. I filled a small sack with it and locked up. Then, I went inside to get ready.

I put a chicken on to roast and took a long bath. I brushed out my hair, and when none of my dresses fit right, I put on trousers and a cotton button-up shirt. I smiled at myself in the tiny mirror, grateful that I couldn't see my entire body in its reflection. I'd gotten many of my mother's features, but I had my father's broad shoulders and thickness along with his towering height.

When Simon knocked at the door, the house smelled of chicken and fresh baked bread. Clouds had wandered in and blotted out the starlight, but the temperature was still down and he was shivering. I let him in and took his coat. "Did you walk?"

He nodded. "I don't have a horse."

I hefted the bag of hope. "I'll just put this with your coat."

"Thank you."

Nothing I did felt right, and my father's words—right was not required—brought little comfort. I wasn't sure what to say or what to do, and it was obvious to me that I was the only one who comprehended the potential of this night. I set the table while we made small talk, and then I opened the bottle of bumbleberry wine I'd kept for such a night as this. I poured out small glassfuls and dished up our plates.

We ate quickly and I watched him. He talked throughout, and I finished easily ahead of him because of it. I think somewhere in the midst of it he must've noticed how I looked at him and it made him talk all the more, his nervous words bumping into each other in their rush to get out.

Finally, I took his plate to the sink along with my own. We moved to the battered old sofa in the living room and sat before the fire. I refilled our wine glasses.

"So you wanted to talk about price," he said.

I sipped the wine, set it down and nodded. "I do. And it's okay to say no. You can have the hope either way."

His brow furrowed. "Say no to what?"

I held my breath and leaned my face toward him. "This."

Then, I kissed him.

At first, he did nothing. Then, he kissed me back. And after a moment, he broke away. "I'm sorry," he said. "I don't know . . . I can't—"

I withdrew and felt the sting of the panic on his face. "No," I said. "I'm sorry." I stood, feeling small for the first time in my life. "Like I said—it's okay to say no."

He stood, too, his face and ears bright red. "No, that's not what I mean." He swallowed, stepped closer to me and stretched up on tippy-toes to kiss my mouth. "It's just that I've never done this before."

Relief flooded me. "Oh," I said. Now it was my turn to blush. "I haven't either."

"Really?"

I nodded. "Really." Then, I bent down and kissed him back.

Taking his hand, I led him to my fresh-made bed and we spent the night teaching each other how.

I never told him why. I couldn't see how it would help him at all, and I could count a dozen ways that it might hurt him. Instead, I just enjoyed him and helped him to enjoy me.

In the morning, after breakfast, he walked back into town with a smile on his face and a bag of hope slung over his shoulder.

> *And in the north, he'll hear our cry*
> *Ride forth in wrath, his sword raised high*
> *To carve our home in violent grace*
> *And lead us to that promised place*
> *—Hymn #316,*
> *"The Santaman Shall Rise Again"*
> *Hymns of the Dragon and his Avenger,*
> *Contemporary Edition*
> *Verity Music, 2623 YD*

It was only after that night with Simon that I allowed myself to think about my last conversation with Father. I'm not sure why, but I don't need the why's nearly as much as I used to when I was younger.

It was morning when he called me to his room. He'd soiled himself again and after nearly a month in bed, I was just beginning to realize that I might not have even another year with him.

I pretended I wasn't angry and tried to find my patience, but it waned. He knew me well enough to know I was frustrated and I suspected he even knew why—it wasn't the mess in his bed. It was the mess my life would become when he left it and I couldn't bear to face that.

I spent the morning cleaning him up and then cleaning his sheets. When I went into the kitchen and saw the cans and jars laid out, preparing for Dragon's Mass Eve was the last thing I wanted to be doing.

"Come in here, Mel," my father rumbled from his bedroom.

I sighed and felt my pulse rising. "What do you need, Dad?"

His laugh was more of a bark. "I need *you*."

I wanted to snap at him but I didn't. Instead, I closed my eyes, counted to five, and then went to his doorway. "Yes?"

He sat up in bed, his lap covered with open books—not real books but bits of cardboard bound together with yarn. "You should write more of these someday," he said. "They're good."

I shrugged. "Is that what you needed?"

He shook his head. "No. Come here." He patted the bed beside him.

I went to the side of the bed but didn't sit. "I have a meal to cook," I said.

Our eyes met. "Sit," he said. "I'm not hungry."

"It's Dragon's Mass Eve and—"

"Sit down, Mel." He looked old there, but truth be told, I couldn't remember a time when my father didn't. He was in his sixties when I was born.

I sat and felt the bed creak beneath our combined weight. "What?"

He smiled. "I wanted to give you your Dragon's Mass Eve present."

"Let's wait until tonight," I said. "I don't have yours ready yet."

Father shook his head and a fit of coughing took his words for a minute. "I don't want to wait," he said. "As tired as I've been, I'm likely to sleep through Dragon's Mass Eve anyway."

I forced a smile. "Okay. But you get yours tomorrow if you fall asleep."

He shrugged, then leaned over to dig around within the deep drawer in the nightstand. He pulled out a form—in triplicate—and handed it to me. "This," he said, "is for you."

I looked at it. I rubbed my eyes and looked at it again. "What's this?"

He cleared his voice. "It's . . . urm . . . a requisition slip. I've been saving it for you. Your mother and I brought two with us when we rode west."

I read it, my eyes naturally drawn to the places where he'd taken the liberty of filling it out. As I realized what it was, I felt the anger burning hot in me and by instinct, I crumpled the requisition into as tight a ball as my white knuckled fist could make it. "I don't want a child," I said. "I don't *ever* want a child."

I tried to stand, but his gnarled hand caught my arm and I turned on him. I nearly said something, nearly let the feelings that savaged me slip past my careful control. But I kept quiet. Still, he saw everything in my eyes, and his own filled up with tears at the sight of my anger.

"I'm sorry," he said.

"Why?" I asked.

He blinked. "Why am I sorry?"

I shook my head. "No," I said. "Why do you think I should have a child?" Seeing his tears made my own fight harder to get out.

He patted my arm. "I thought when I met your mother that I knew what love was. But meeting *you* opened up a vast continent of love I never imagined could exist. How could I not want that for you?" His voice lowered, and then my father said the last words that he would ever say to me. "Melody Constance Sheffleton-Farrelly, don't you know that you are the best gift anyone ever gave to me, Dragon's Mass Eve or not?"

I stood and bent to kiss his brow. Then, I left so he wouldn't see me crying. I tossed the ball of paper into my room and went outside into the yard to walk off the feelings that ambushed me. When I went back inside, I saw my father had gone to sleep amid the stories I'd written him over a lifetime of Dragon's Mass Eves together. And when I checked on him even later, I found he'd slipped away.

I gathered up the books, closed them, and stacked them neatly in his nightstand drawer. I carefully removed his spectacles and folded them up to lay them beside his bed.

Then I went to find something to wrap him in and wondered if the coming night would be cloudy or clear.

Motes swim. Light diffuses. Home rises.

We see it through a smoky glass. We watch it twitch and meep with each note of the framing song.

The Santaman laughs and beats his sword against his thigh: "Ho, ho, ho."

We few remaining weep and set our feet on emerald grass. We smell the reek of love upon the wind. We wipe our eyes. We wipe our eyes and look again.

Ahead a dragon.

Upon his back a world.

> —*Our New Carved Home*
> *The Santaman Cycle,*
> *Authorized Standard Version*
> *Verity Press, 2453 YD*

*

You arrived in Autumn amid the buzz of change.

But before that, while I waited for you, I started wrapping things up at our homestead on the edge of the world. I went through my father's papers and organized them, separating out his working notes from his personal notes. Most, I kept. But some I left for the mine's new owners.

I felt you kick for the first time while I was taking the civil service exam, and after I finished, the test proctor sought me out in the waiting room after everyone else had gone to let me know he'd not seen a score so high in well over twenty years.

I wasn't surprised at all when the offer came through, and once it did, I started negotiating the sale of the mine. I knew going in that whatever I sold it for would be vastly more than I could make in a lifetime on government salary, working in the cubicle maze of the Bureaucracy. But a clean start seemed somehow right to me, especially as your arrival drew closer and closer.

Still, I'm glad we had these three months together on the homestead where we both were born. Wandering the yard, it's been a strange, new mourning as I accept the reality that I'll likely not come back here again. You may when you're older. You might want to see where your grandmother and grandfather lay buried. You may want to see the house where you were born. And I'm sure folks around here will be curious to meet you, too.

There is a knock at the door on the morning of Dragon's Mass Eve and it startles you. I go to answer and find Parson Brown on the porch. He sees the truck the Bureaucracy has provided me, shoved full of everything we'll take with us when we leave. I've only left out enough to celebrate tonight, and tomorrow, we start our weeks-long drive east and south.

"So," he says, "you really are going?"

I nod. "Tomorrow," I say. "Come in, Parson."

I brew him some tea while he plays with you and I can tell you're as uncomfortable with him as he is with you. When the tea is ready, I hold you while he drinks it, mindful of his shaking hands. I want to ask him about your father, but I don't. Last I heard, he'd ridden north with his sword and not long after, bits of gossip drifted back. I don't know who exactly wields it, but there are rumors of a young man in red with a terrible blade, and he's earning quite a name for himself. I'm pretty sure it's him. But maybe it isn't. Maybe someone further north heard the cry of his heart. I doubt it, but it would be a fine story.

Drawler season didn't really subside this year—they pushed south all the way through summer—but the militias are holding them at Harrowfield and Lumner, and in a few weeks, I'll be working supply chain for the headquarters of a new standing army.

I don't ask about your father. And I don't tell Parson Brown your middle name is Simon, either. I know people are wondering and I'm okay with letting them wonder.

I look into your eyes and I find I could fall into them. They are brown like mine and like your grandfather's. The parson has to ask a second time before I realize he's speaking. "I'm sorry?"

"I was asking if you'd be joining us tonight," he says as he drains the last of his tea. "I've a new acolyte. Brother Timothy. He'll be giving the sermon." Parson Brown leans forward and tickles your chin. "I'm sure everyone is dying to meet little Drummond."

I smile. "Maybe," I tell him. "We'll see."

But I already know we won't be attending. Tonight, I'll make our hats, and after I've nursed you, I'll eat rice stew and fruit salad. Then, we'll walk up the hill and I will hold you close as I recite words that don't need to be right or true to have their meaning for me. For us.

I think I understand my father's last Dragon's Mass Eve gift to me now when I see his face in yours. His attachment to his old, discarded religion makes sense to me now, too, though I had to meet you before I could fully comprehend the truest object of his faith.

Clear or cloudy, the only grace I'll ever need has already found me.

And the only home I'll ever want is you.

THE COWARDLY LION'S SLIPPER WISH

Flying monkeys fall like rain
The Scarecrow's burning on the pyre
Dorothy asks me to explain
Why Tin Man's boiling near the fire.

Toto's making yellow snow
Beside a yellow winding path
While far away, the emerald glow
Of ruins mark the Wizard's wrath.

I am the Coward who killed a witch
And scorned my pride and stood erect
And danced behind the Kansas bitch
Who forced us all to genuflect.

I place the slippers on my feet
She cries when I insist she sing.
They are the fire; and she's the meat
And I—I am this Forest's King.

ON THE FREEDOM OF AGENCY
AND THE FINDING OF LOST HEARTS

*R*atzer, the man who trained me, told me I had to be a thief because I was too ugly to be a whore. I told him that he should learn respect, and later, when I'd learned enough about thievery and knife work from him, I taught him some respect by taking his right eye in an even match. He was dead now, from some other woman's lessons I'll warrant.

I always thought about Ratzer when I was on the job. What would he do? How would he lay it out? Would he go alone or work a team? But in this case, he'd have never taken the job. "Never for the unders. Never owe a demon."

Still, Gilga-Yar had been a fair patron. He'd softened by the time he'd taken on my contract; gone were the fealty maimings and game-playing. He taught me the bits of the Art that applied to my chosen profession, and I, in turn, rendered the services only my chosen profession could. Namely, I stole for him every now and again, each job putting me closer to my contract expiring and a life of free agency.

The messenger demon in my pocket farted and giggled, the noise of it loud in the otherwise silent forest. I swatted at it. "Quiet."

I felt its tiny teeth snapping at my fingers. "Master requires messenger returned in fine tip-top shape."

"Mistress requires silence," I said, swatting at the pocket hard enough to get a yelp. "And mistress wonders what master wants from this hovel?"

The cabin lay in a forested gully below us, smoke leaking from its solitary chimney. It was the only smoke on the horizon after days of crossing the Eldenwood on foot, and it was hard to imagine anything of value in this quaint log structure far removed from civilization.

"Master wants what master wants," the demon said. "Master says this may be your last job. It may. It may. It may."

He'd said that before. I wasn't going to believe it this time either.

When I spoke it was more for my benefit than my obnoxious companion. "What could he possibly want from here?"

The demon in my pocket said nothing. I lay still and watched the cabin below, hidden from view by the woodling cloak I'd spent a years' take purchasing for this trip. Under the best conditions the Eldenwood was dangerous, and we were on the edge of howler season.

After another hour, the door opened and a shirtless old man dressed in buckskin trousers stepped onto the porch to gather an armful of firewood. Evening was coming, and the autumn air was crisp. Even at this distance, I saw what I had come for. It was bright on his neck, and though I had no idea what exactly it was, it reeked and shimmered with power that was palpable from where I watched. And not any power I recognized. This was something older even than the Art.

"He wants the amulet," I said.

The demon snickered. "Want, want, want."

I sighed and stood, brushing the leaves from me. "Very well. Let's go fetch it."

Suddenly, the demon was tooth and claw, tearing at my pocket in its mad scramble to leave. "Master says I go now."

I was alone before I could protest. With the slightest cough, the air around me flooded with the odor of sulfur as the tiny messenger vanished. "Fantastic," I said.

I walked down the side of the gully, aware of the knives at my hips and the hands that craved them. Ratzer would never have taken this job. But if he had, he'd have seen the old man and sent in his young apprentice to take what needed taking while he watched and waited.

Godsdamn Ratzer.

I approached the cabin and knocked on its door.

The old man didn't come to the door on my first knock. Or my second. Or my seventh.

I raised my voice. "I know you're in there. I'm lost and could use some help."

Silence met my voice at first. Then, I heard the clearing of a voice.

"No one lost in the Eldenwood gets this far. Who sent you?"

"No one sent me," I lied. Then, I opted for a bit of truth. "But you're right. I'm not lost. I came for you."

I heard a sigh, then heard the turning of the bolt in its lock. The door opened and the man stood before me now. Up close, he was older than I realized, his hair thin and white as it fell over his shoulders. His chest was narrow beneath muscular shoulders, and hanging in the center of a gray thatch of hair, the crystalline medallion guttered and smoldered with its power. One of the first tricks Gilga-Yar had taught me was how to smell the Art and its distant cousins. This was something rarer, and the possibilities frightened me.

The old man watched, his sharp blue eyes narrow at the sight of me. It seemed he was waiting for something, and since the only thing that truly made me uncomfortable were awkward and stretched out silences, I spoke into it. "I am Shayna Westbrook. Of the Clancy Westbrook Run."

He continued to wait, his eyes widening. I mistook it as familiarity with my name and smiled. "You know me then?"

The old man shook his head slowly and leaned forward, sniffing at me with a raised eyebrow. "But you know me or surely you wouldn't have come so far to find me. Who told you how to find me?" He sighed again, then pushed past me with a deliberate stride. "I require you to tell me. And to follow."

He said it with resignation, and I had no interest in telling him that a second-rate demon had sent me here without knowing what I was to steal and whom I was to steal it from. But I fell in behind him as he moved off the porch and around back toward the shed.

He opened it and withdrew a shovel and a knife. "It doesn't matter. Take these."

I thought about hitting him and taking what Gilga-Yar was after. But this old man had me curious, and my patron's lack of forthrightness with me made me want all the more to know what was going on. So I took the shovel and the knife. "What am I doing with these?"

He regarded me with an intensity that made me uncomfortable. "First," he said, "you'll walk north away from the house until you find the other graves. Then, you'll dig a grave. And after, if you truly love me and wish to serve me, you will climb into the grave and cut your throat."

I handed them back to him. "I don't think so."

He didn't take them. Instead, he staggered back, and for a moment I thought he might drop to the ground. "It's you," he said. His face flushed. "Finally, it's *you*."

Now it was my turn to step back. "Yes," I said. "It's me." I felt something stirring in my stomach and didn't like it at all. "Who are you?"

His eyes glistened with tears of what seemed like gratitude or wonder. "Who am I?" He chuckled. "Surely you know. I am Ansylus of Erok."

In that moment I knew I'd been profoundly buggered by a god. Because even though it was impossible, it wasn't: Ansylus of Erok, Ansylus the Conqueror, Ansylus the Enslaver. It had taken half the League of Wizards to bring him down two thousand years ago. It had brought about the treaty with the demons and restored the Art to them.

So this, I thought, is where they'd hidden him.

My eyes went back to the crystalline amulet around his neck. Because of what he wore and the things people still whispered about it, though it was long thought lost. "The Heart of Eylon," I whispered.

"Aye," Ansylus said. "And you are here to free me of it at long last."

Buggered by a god. Buggered by Eylon himself, the god of love and loyalty. A tiny bit of divine heart lay buried beneath the crystal that focused it outward, bending those who beheld it to adore with abandon and obey to the utmost zig and zag.

Only it didn't seem to work on me. And because of that, and because Ansylus the Enslaver now wept tears of joy before me, I was thinking Ratzer had been right all along about working for the unders.

Now, back in the cabin, with mugs of something he'd distilled from potatoes warming our hands and our stomachs, Ansylus wept tears of remorse and regret.

"It's true what they say about complete power spawning utter evil," he said, "and I've had millennia to ponder my sins. And the sins my sins begat."

We'd been talking now for a few hours while drinking and sitting by his fire. Mostly, I listened, though early on I'd told him about Gilga-Yar. I saw no good reason not to.

And in exchange, he'd told his tale. Millennia of introspection after a decade of world domination. The blood of hundreds of thousands upon his hands, and a war with Heaven that would've brought down the world if the demons had not been bargained with by the League. I felt a strange kinship with him—probably because of the spirits we were drinking—as he spoke. He described centuries of loneliness followed by a vast stretch of contentment, recognizing the imperative of his banishment. At first, he'd used the Heart to send those who found him away, bidding them to be silent. But with distance, eventually those silences turned to whispers of adoration. And those whispers turned into pilgrims on his porch.

And so, the small cemetery north of his cabin. "I have them do half the work. I do the other half and try to convince myself it's saving the world."

"It probably *is* saving the world," I told him. And the way I slurred the words told me that somehow, I'd managed to get myself drunk with this old tyrant instead of robbing him and getting out from under Gilga-Yar's contract once and for all.

He shrugged and nodded toward the pan on the stove. "More?"

I shook my head. "I've had plenty, old man. Too much even."

He smiled a drunken smile. "This is the first real conversation I've had since the demons put me here. My first with a human since I put this on." He touched the crystal, and I heard it hum beneath his fingers. He laughed. "And the first woman I've spoken to who hasn't fallen madly in love with me and been willing to follow my slightest suggestion."

I snorted. "It's early yet."

His laugh became a bellow as he stood and clapped me on the shoulder. "Now *that* would be something," he said. "But I think it's time for you to sleep," he said. "Then tomorrow, you can kill me."

I have no idea why I didn't ask. Maybe some part of me knew. Or maybe I was just really drunk and on the job, which was something, oddly enough, that Ratzer *would* approve of. "Sometimes it's just good for the soul," he'd say in his own slurred voice. "Long as you don't mind the job going to hell."

And in this case, I actually *did* mind the job going to hell. To Gilga-Yar, specifically, and I think that's why I drank with the old man and took my time deciding what to do.

So I didn't ask at all about killing him. Instead, I let him guide me to his narrow bed and let him pull my boots and tuck me in like the father I never had. And I fell asleep listening to him wash our drinking mugs.

"I'll kill you in the morning," I mumbled into the drool I'd made on his pillow.

He was staring at me when I woke up, and I sat up quickly, reaching for knives I wasn't wearing.

"Good morning," he said.

My head ached, and I rubbed it with one hand while using the other to accept the cup of cold water he offered me. "Mine's hurting, too," he said. Then he stood from the chair he'd straddled while waiting for me to awake.

I sipped the water, surprised at how terrible my mouth tasted after last night. Then I winced, calling up the memory of it. I drank from time to time but never on the job. I looked at the old man, at Ansylus. Never *with* the job. "So I'm killing you today?"

Ansylus smiled. "Yes. I dug my grave this morning. With the others. I thought it would be fitting."

I took another drink of the water. "And why am I doing this exactly?"

"Because you can. You're immune to it. Just like I was. So you kill me just like I killed the Prophetess Esthra Shau, and the Heart of Eylon then falls to you. You can give it to your master. It won't serve or command his kind, but surely he knows that already."

"Then what does *he* want with it?" I wondered aloud.

His smile faded. "That's a problem for you to solve before you hand it over, I'll wager."

My own eyes narrowed. "Or a problem I should avoid shouldering in the first place."

His lower lip quivered and he said nothing, though his eyes filled with anguish and tears. Finally, he spoke. "You could avoid it. Yes."

"And you would wait until someone else came along who was immune." Even as I said the words, I thought about the two thousand years that had passed while he waited here for me.

He bowed his head. "Yes. And if I must, I'll bear it longer. My sins are my sins, and Eylon's heart is my sin to bear until someone slays me and takes it from me."

Buggered by gods indeed.

So after breakfast, we walked to the grave that he had dug and he knelt at the foot of it. I closed my eyes and pushed my knife into his heart, from behind, angling the blade down as I slid it into his trembling shoulder blade.

"Fare you well, Ansylus of Erok," I whispered as he tipped, laughing, into his grave.

"So you are human," the little girl said.

I looked up from the grave. "I am."

The forest had changed around me, and then she appeared in the way that people appear in dreams, suddenly and without context, as my mind reeled to figure out her place.

"So are you going to take it? Are you going to put it on?" She squatted, brushing the grave's dirt from the unfamiliar fabric of her dress.

I shook my head. "No. I'm not sure what I'll do with it." I met her eyes. "But I'll not put it on."

She smiled. "Good."

And then she was gone, and the forest became something recognizable to me again. For a moment, I considered just leaving it, burying it beneath the dirt on the body of the man who had last commanded it. But even as I thought it, I thought of others coming after me, finding the cabin, finding the graves. Digging them up, one year or a thousand years from now, to find it waiting.

And to find a world waiting beyond the far edges of the Eldenwood.

I sighed, dropped into the grave, pulled the amulet from him, and tucked it into my pocket. Then, I covered his grave and returned to his cabin.

I stayed the night there, drinking more of his potato spirits until sleep insisted and I acquiesced. In the morning, I used his stocks to resupply, and then set out for home.

They trapped me when I exited the forest. They were silent and masked, but their hands bore the markings of the League and I knew better than to resist them, despite who I worked for. The demons had fed the League wizards Art for centuries now but the wizards still held dominion, and even Gilga-Yar had a policy of not crossing them. "Tell them who you serve, and if they still require it, give it to them." Whatever it was, even in the past that had been his advice.

"You're Gilga-Yar's pet, I'll wager," the larger of the men said.

"Or he's mine," I said. After weeks traversing the Eldenwood, I was hoping they'd take me into custody. Hot food. Hot water. Warm bed.

"And you have the Heart then?"

I blinked. This was a change. "I do."

He nodded to the others. "Bring her."

The transition from running to horseback jarred my bones, but I suffered it, longing for the hospitality of a prisoner of the League. Gilga-Yar had friends among the wizards, favors I'd helped him perform over the years, so there was no doubt in my mind that I would be free eventually, the fruit of my labor still snug in my pocket.

The wizard's camp lay nestled in the hills that marked the southernmost boundary of the wood and the beginning of the Emperor's Way. It spread out, a kaleidoscope of tents and wagons, with the wizard's tent the largest and leaking purple smoke from its top.

The Leaguesmen escorted me to that tent, relieving me of my knives before pushing me gently through silk curtains too flimsy for the autumn cold. Warm air met me and I met my first wizard face to face. His skin had gone pale and his hair a thin silver from a lifetime of using the Art, his eyes rheumy but sparking with intelligence.

When he spoke, his voice was as silver as his hair. "You are Shayna Westbrook. Of the Clancy Westbrook Run. Thiefmaiden of Gilga-Yar."

"Yes."

I thought he would introduce himself, invite me to sit. He did not. He lay back in his cushions and regarded me carefully while sipping at a pipe made of white bone.

I shifted uncomfortably beneath his gaze.

"The League is aware of your recent acquisition. Its delivery cannot be permitted."

I reached into my pocket. "If you know I'm Gilga-Yar's thief, then you also know I have instructions to yield to the League in all of my business dealings for him." I withdrew the amulet. "Who should I give it to?"

His eyes narrowed with rage, but none of it touched his voice. "Put the abominable thing away. It is yours to bear now. You who were so short-sighted to have taken it in the first place."

I put it away. "Has Gilga-Yar been summoned?"

"Gilga-Yar," he said in a measured tone, "has been executed by his own kind as per the ordinances of the treaty with respect to treason."

I felt my legs go weak, and it surprised me.

He continued. "The sentence was carried out as soon as it was determined that you had taken the Heart."

Something cold flooded my stomach. "Then Gilga-Yar is dead?"

The wizard nodded. "And you are returning to the Eldenwood with what you stole."

I felt it whispering now in my pocket. It was a quiet voice, a still voice. A sure voice. *Wear me, and the League will do your bidding. Wear me now, and take me off later. But wear me.*

Could I? Put it on and take it off? I knew better. If that were the case, Ansylus would've laid aside his burden long ago. Once I wore it, no matter the power I wielded and how I did so, that Heart of Eylon would be mine until someone immune to it, someone like me, came and took it.

"I will not," I said aloud. The wizard blinked, thinking I spoke to him. He didn't realize I was talking to that bit of a god in my pocket that had buggered me.

But in the wizard's slow blink, the tent fell away and I stood in the forest once again. The little girl smiled. "I'm glad," she said.

The wrongness of the forest raised the hair on my arms. Wrong not in a bad way but in a way that evoked fear and trembling nonetheless. The lines and light of it were . . . *other than.* "Who are you? Where did the wizard go? Where are we?"

"I am Taemyl. The wizard was never here. You are among the Trees of Pantheon."

Orphaned thieves get little in the way of formal schooling, but I knew of Taemyl. And Pantheon. "You are Eylon's daughter." I looked around. The wood was quiet around us, though I suspected other eyes upon us, other ears to catch our words.

She nodded. "I am."

"And you want your father's heart?"

She nodded again. "I do. It was never meant for your kind."

Your kind. Looking at her, it was easy to forget she wasn't what she seemed. But the more I studied this little girl, the less I trusted her. It was the eyes. They were too old and held no humanity within them. Still, it was her father's heart, and I did not want it for my own. I found myself more and more wishing I'd listened to Ratzer about the unders.

I reached into my pocket and withdrew the necklace and its crystal amulet. I held it toward her and waited for her uplifted, empty hand to slide beneath mine. As it did, our eyes met and I shuddered.

Then I released the Heart of Eylon and felt the forest twist itself back into the Eldenwood I stood in, Ansyslus's open grave still before me.

"Didn't I do this already?" No one answered my rhetorical question. So I lifted the shovel once again to finish burying my dead, cursing the Pantheon and everyone in it as I did so.

"And so," Gilga-Yar said in a low voice, "you gave it to her?"

His minion had reappeared when I reached the edge of the Eldenwood for what, to me, seemed my second return trip. And for only the third time in fifteen years under contract, the Grand Old Demon brought me over to his plane to stand in his sweltering office beneath the flames of Raya's Consuming Veil. He sat behind his desk and avoided eye contact with me.

"Yes," I answered. "I did. I believed you were dead and that the League intended banishment for me."

He chuckled. "The gods cannot be trusted to deal plainly."

Nor could the demons, I thought but did not say. Instead, I waited, my stomach churning from the heat and the heaviness of this dark, twisted place.

"Still, you could have put it on," he said.

Now I met his eyes. "Is that what you intended with it?"

He smiled but didn't answer. Instead, he repeated himself and matched the intensity of my level gaze. "You could have put it on."

"No," I said. "I could not."

"Yes," he said. "I see." He started rummaging through the papers on his desk, and it was something about the way he did it that betrayed him. He found an old document and held it up. "Your contract," he said. "I've decided to release you from it."

"But I returned to you empty-handed."

And the last time Gilga-Yar ever met my eyes, I realized that he'd intended it to be that way from the start. I didn't know what price he'd exacted from the Pantheon, but for reasons of his own, he'd removed something dangerous from the world and curried favor with the old powers. "Yes," he said. Then he smiled, his teeth sharp and glistening. "You have served me well."

With a flick of his wrist, his office and its oppressive heat fell away as I found myself standing in the market of Pan Shao Crossing near the Danubii border. There was a pouch in my belt that I hadn't seen before. I took it, opened it, and poured a handful of the diamonds into my hand.

He had served me well too, and, blessing him, I went first for the money-changer and then for the tavern.

I wanted the potato spirits, but the very idea of it was foreign in this forsaken corner of the world. So instead, I settled for fermented samaberry juice served as cold as the cellars in this place could make it, which wasn't cold at all. I stood at the bar while I drank, and every part of me noticed the young man when he sidled up beside me.

He was beautiful, and my heart raced to look at him. His hair was golden and his eyes were bright and blue like skies after a desert storm. Even his smell caused my breath to catch, and when he smiled at me, I felt my hands shaking as they gripped at the edge of the bar.

"Thank you," he said, "for giving me back my heart."

The little girl was waiting for him by the door, and she waved to me and smiled as he bent to kiss me upon the forehead.

As he walked out into the desert sun, I waved back and wondered what I'd unleashed upon the world by bringing him back into it. And another part wondered whether or not it was entirely bad. Regardless, I hoped my life could be finished now with the likes of gods and demons.

"To free agency," I said to the barmaid who'd caught my eye earlier. She caught it even moreso now that my body was flushed and tingling from the love god's presence. And she'd felt the effects of Eylon's charms as well, I'd wager, from the wideness in her eyes and the way her nostrils flared.

She smiled at me. "To free agency," she said.

LOOKING FOR TRUTH
IN A WILD BLUE YONDER
(with Jay Lake)

*T*en years after my parents died, my therabot, Bob, informed me that I should seek help elsewhere. I blinked at his suggestion.

"I've already tried chemical intervention," I told his plastic grin. "It didn't work." I scowled, but that did nothing to de-brighten his soothing, chipper voice.

"Booze doesn't count, Charlie."

"I tried weed, too."

Bob shook his head. "Nothing therapeutic there, either, I'm afraid." He sighed and imitated the movements of pushing himself back from his imitation wood desk. "You are experiencing what we like to call *complicated* grief."

Complicated grief. As if I hadn't heard that one before.

Dad had died badly. He'd been on one of the trains that got swallowed by the Sound back on the day we lost Seattle. He'd called me from his cell phone with his last breath, as the water poured in, to let me know he wasn't really my father.

We lost the signal before he could tell me who he actually was. Naturally, I called Mom. She answered just before the ceiling of the store she was shopping in collapsed.

Both parents in one day. Fuck yes, complicated grief.

And a side helping of unknown paternity.

Bob continued. "Ten years is a long time, Charlie. I want you to call this number and ask for Pete." His eyes rolled in their sockets as his internal processors accessed his files. My phone chirped when his text came through. He extended a plastic tentacle tipped with a three-fingered white clown's glove. "I hope you find your way."

I scowled again and shook his offered hand. "So you're firing me as a patient?"

"Be well," he said. His eyes went dead and his hand dropped back to the artificial oak surface of his desk.

I met Pete in an alley on the back of Valencia, behind an old bookstore that still dealt in paper. I transferred funds to an off-shore account that then moved it along, scrubbing the transaction as it passed through its various stops along the way before his phone chirped. When it chirped, he extended a smart-lock plastic bag to me. A small, withered blue thing sloshed about in it. At first, I thought it was a severed finger or something far worse. (Or better depending upon one's fetishes.) I held the bag up to the flickering light of the dirty street lamp.

The blue thing looked like an asparagus tip, only it wriggled.

"Find someplace safe and quiet," Pete said. "Preferably indoors with a lock. Eat it with water."

"I'm not putting this in my mouth."

Pete shrugged. He was a scrawny kid, his tattooed face stubbly in the dim light, long red hair cascading over his shoulders. "Doesn't matter to me. But the wild blue yonder are especially good for your situation. Complicated grief, right?" I nodded because his eyes—one brown and one bright yellow—told me that he probably knew it from experience. "Eat this. Spend a weekend sweating and naked on the floor. You'll be a new man."

"Naked and sweating?" I looked at the baggie again, then back to Pete. "And how do you know Bob?" I couldn't imagine a therabot needing a dealer.

Pete smiled. "We're colleagues."

"Colleagues?"

The smile widened even further. "I'm a back alley grief counselor."

Slipping my wild blue yonder into my pocket, I left Pete in his alley and turned myself towards home.

I ate the wild blue yonder and stripped down in my living room. I put on some retro music—Zeppelin, I think—and stretched out on the floor.

It worked fast.

Light and sound from within me, building in magnitude until

the nausea clenched my stomach and I sat up. My living room had become a purple field beneath swollen stars. Something like crickets sang all around and I saw a girl sitting on a stump in the middle of the clearing. In the distance, deep blue trees swayed under a windless summer night sky.

"You must be Charlie," she said.

I was naked still, but for some reason I was unafraid and un-ashamed. "I am," I told her, standing. "Who are you? And where am I at?"

"I'm Verity." She tossed her long brown hair and batted the lids of her big brown eyes. "And you are in the wild blue yonder."

She wore a silver gown that flowed like mercury over the curves of her body. When she stood up too, I saw she was taller than me by at least a foot. "I'm sorry about your mother," she said, "and the man you thought was your father."

I blinked. "How do you know all of this?"

She shrugged. "I'm Verity."

We stood there, looking at each other, as an enormous moon rose to the south. A minute passed. "So how does this work?" I asked.

"Simple. I run. You chase me."

And then she ran.

As Pink Floyd said, I ran like hell. Or maybe I chased like hell. I didn't give a shit about Pete anymore. Or Bob. Or all the lost millions in the Pacific Northwest, Hawaii, Japan, and everywhere the sea had come crawling up onto land with bloody salted fingers and needle teeth.

Verity ran before me. With her she carried the hard burden of truth like a seed in the claws of a nuthatch. Her legs sped over this strange blue landscape as perfect as I'd ever seen on a woman. Michel-angelo would have cried to sculpt her. I would have cried to catch her.

But it wasn't that perfect ass I craved. It wasn't those high, firm breasts that I could imagine bobbing with each leaping step. It wasn't that trailing hair that I could wrap around my body.

She carried me: my past and my future.

How the hell had Pete known to give this to me; how had this wild blue yonder reached so far into time and my soul?

My thoughts fell aside as she ran. Reason gave way to desire.

Logic yielded to need. The chase gave way to the run. The ground vanished. We sprinted across a stark, unyielding field of stars. They flared, dying as every hydrogen cycle eventually does, all of time compressed in a dozen falls of those perfect feet; then we ran through the salt sea, the world-girding amnion which had birthed all of evolution's ambitions. The seas boiled and dried and vanished in wispy, weeping gasses; we ran on roads of light, leaping from quantum packet to quantum packet.

Across time, across space, across the seventy-two acres of my neural net, until sufficient self-awareness finally returned to me for me to understand I would never catch up to the truth by chasing it. Grief is the Grendel-monster in the watery cave of the human heart. I pursued Grendel's mother, and she would have her vengeance on me if I dispatched her son.

So I stopped, caught in a moment of wisdom, and let Verity the cup-bearer of my grief come to me. The universe is circular, after all, endless in the manner of an egg, and if you wait long enough your own light will come back to you.

In ceasing my chase of Verity, she soon ran into my arms.

We collapsed in a tangle of limbs and clothing amid lush mounds of mint and violets. Scent, suddenly the world was scent; and the sweet smell of Verity's sweat which made me want to turn to her and place my lips upon the yoke of her neck and breathe her in.

Think, man, think. You're not here for *this.*

"You caught me," she whispered, and her tongue slipped into my ear.

I wriggled away. "We're not doing that chase, either."

"What do you want, Charlie?" Her breath was a furnace of passion warming me down to bones I'd forgotten I ever had.

"Truth," I said. The answer surprised me.

"No one wants truth, Charlie. They want certainty. They want forgiveness. They want love. Truth is like a dead city, a million watery graves. It doesn't compromise and it gives nothing back."

"Relief." This time I almost sobbed the word. "I want relief."

"From truth?"

Truth. Who was my dad? What had my mom meant by this? Whose lie had determined the pattern of my life? Had Mom cheated on Dad? Had he come along after she was pregnant with me, and accepted another man's get as his own child?

I slowly realized that it didn't matter. The ghosts of the past ten years, what Bob had so patiently (as if a machine could be otherwise) talked me through, past, around, away from, out from beneath: those ghosts were of my own making.

Mom's unquiet spirit might haunt the desolate ruins of Auburn, Washington, sleeping beneath the hard, frozen waters. Dad's fetch might ride the rusted rails beneath the Puget Sea. So what?

"I live today," I told Verity.

"Is that the truth?"

"We can only go forward." I set my hand upon her breast, cupping the firm nipple through the flowing silver of her dress.

"I'm not real," she whispered in my ear again.

Tell that to my gonads, I thought, but that didn't matter now. "Is this what I was supposed to find?" She touched my hand, the curves of her flesh proud but not overflowing my grip, and I ached to draw her clothing away and set my lips to suckling.

"You came into this world damp and frightened. Your parents left this world damp and frightened."

"Even my dad?" I meant my biological father, the progenitor that Dad had almost told me about before being erased under a billion gallons of seawater.

It was just a splash, really, good news from outer space. Even if the clouds hadn't dissipated for three years after.

"Even your dad," she said. "Him."

So dad-the-sperm donor had been in the Northwest, too. Or Hawaii. Or coastal Alaska. Or Japan. Or on a ship at sea.

I hoped all three of their ghosts were happy somewhere, around some spiritual campfire trading stories about the boy I'd been. I wished them well, the love of each other, and even the love of me.

The past belonged to them, swept away along with the legacy of a sixth of the planet.

The future belonged to, well, maybe not me, but at the least, to itself.

Roger Waters wailed from my speakers. I swear it had been Robert Plant when I first tripped out. I lay flat, drained. My thigh was sticky where I'd come at some point. I looked down to find my torso covered with blue lip prints.

Lipstick?

I touched myself and flinched. No. Hickeys. What kind of drug trip left you with *hickeys*, for the love of god?

Aching, I dragged myself to my feet, turned down the stereo, and stepped into my kitchenette for some apple juice. Something was missing. Something was wrong.

I probed my thoughts, like a tongue questing for a missing tooth. Grief.

My parents were still present in my absence. But the paralyzing pain, the near-total abrogation of self and initiative, seemed to be gone finally. After all these years. Was *this* what normal life was like? No wonder Bob had fired me.

As for Pete, the back alley grief counselor, I owed him everything.

Heading for the tiny bedroom, I noticed something out of place in my living room as well. I stopped to look around. A woman's silver dress was draped across the back of my couch, as if stripped in a moment of wild passion. I touched the hickeys again.

What *was* real?

What *was* true?

Something stirred in the next room. A wall of seawater finally come to claim me as well? Or the future, waiting with bruised lips and the longest legs I'd ever seen on a woman?

With a silent thanks to Bob and Pete, I stepped into the wild blue yonder, looking for truth. Or at least whatever might come next.

I was finally done with what had come before.

AWASH IN AUTUMN,
THE QUEEN REFLECTS

*E*very day is the same and yet different.

Emily goes to him on her lunch break, her eyes flitting over him and away quickly, though she knows he knows. And Tony smiles and asks her what she wants but she always wants the special—*his* special—and he always adds magic to it.

"Pumpkin spice latte?"

Her eyes are on him. They are away again. "Please."

Then, small talk. But the best conversation of her day. Concluded by the flourish of his art in the foam and money changing hands.

What magic will it be today? She looks at the foam and her eyebrows furrow. She doesn't recognize the tiny image.

"You'll see," Tony says.

She sits in the park on a bench in the gray October day. She eats her sandwich first. Then her apple slices. Only after does she consider the latte.

Emily ponders it, then sips it.

Antlers.

She smiles and closes her eyes. He's never done antlers before.

It is warmer in the clearing; she stands in it in her gown, the crown heavy upon her head. In this place, she is a queen. And the world is on fire around her, the leaves blazing autumn red and yellow, orange for as far as her eye can see. Her feet itch to run the leaf carpet but she waits for Tony, wondering how he will come to her in this place.

He snorts as he runs into the clearing, scattering leaves with his hooves as he tosses his antlered head. He prances around her, then sets off east and she follows.

She runs after him, feeling the crown grow lighter upon her brow as she picks up speed. When she reaches him, she leaps and mid-leap, she lands upon his back and seizes hold of his neck.

They run the forest now, dodging fallen branches and racing through alternating shafts of sunlight and shadow. He carries her for hours before the trees fall away and they run old pastures gone to grass, leaping the fallen stone walls that occasionally intersect them. The sun is low in the sky behind them, the sky shot through with red, when she bids him stop beside a burbling creek.

There, she stretches out upon her stomach to drink her fill while the stag stands beside her doing the same.

Crickets are singing and she sees the forests that surround them in the distance blazing with glory beneath a crimson sky. Emily sees the meadow taking on the same glory. And the white hide of her friend, Tony. Last, she looks at her own arms washed gold and red in the setting sun, and closes her eyes. *Glory shining everywhere about me and upon me*, Emily realizes.

Awash in Autumn, the queen reflects.

When she opens her eyes again, there is just enough time to walk back to the motel and restock her cleaning cart. She drinks the last of her latte, and when she walks past Tony's espresso stand, she looks away and smiles when he winks at her.

VERITY SAVES THE WORLD

She did not always have the magic hat. She did not always have the struck pose or the graceful sway. And the tattoo on the upper swell of her breast, she said, was utterly and completely removable, fake, untrue. But the jazz hands were real. As was the rest of her.

What is truth? I wondered.

She was not always a goddess. Or if she was, it was unknown to her. My favorite brand of deity—one promoted up through the ranks of mortality. One that grasped our precarious and uninvited position in the Cosmos.

When I saw her eyes there was an inner earthquake. Equilibrium gone amok. They were large and round, twin holes in the space time fabric that drew unsuspecting rabbit-chasers into Wonder. And there was sadness there with truth and hope. But when I looked to her smile, wide and white, it was something I could cling to until the world stopped shaking.

"What should I do," she didn't ask.

"Save the world," I cried, "by simply being yourself."

Her smile became more secretive. "I can do that if I ever find out how."

She found the magic hat in a store in Saratoga Springs. It was of the sort that made snowmen become real, begin to dance, attempt to sing. I knew this because just like she once had been mortal, I'd once been a snowman. It wasn't straw, that hat. It was black as starless night with her hair waterfalling down beneath it, long and silky. A redemptive bowler.

I did not see her save the world though I would've liked to. She surged into the lobby and struck the pose, I'm told. The universe looked on with shackled breath. Feet shuffled, shifted as the head cocked and the hands came up. Jazz hands, bright and shimmering like moonlight over water. The eyes went wider if wider was truly possible and the smile poured out from her. It was a defining truth, and then she shifted into the sway.

Somewhere, somehow a stranger was healed of their infirmity. Somewhere, somehow a child laughed in delight at the alphabet they learned. Somewhere, somehow an untrue and unkind deed was redeemed.

"What is your name," a curious world asked.

"Verity," she said as she danced from side to side.

"What is your quest," it asked her again.

"Verity," she said as the jazz hands wove hope into the despairing.

"What is your favorite color," it asked in finality.

"Again," she said, "Verity."

And as always, Alethea was true.

A WORLD DONE IN BY
GREAT GRANNY'S GRATEFUL PIE

*I*t was the Tuesday before Thanksgiving and everything was going to shit all at once, the way things usually like to. Of course it was a
different kind of *going to shit* compared to, say, last year's Thanksgiving
in Iraq. That one started with flares and shots ricocheting off stone
and ended with me slowly heading home on a medical discharge. This
Thanksgiving started with the goddamn underpinning going missing
and ended with burning Great Granny's Grateful Pie. And somewhere in the middle was the matter of Mama's plus one.

"You know, Kay Ann," Mama insisted in her most saccharine voice,
"my *plus one.*"

I put the pie in the oven. "Your plus one?" I pushed buttons that I
assumed were the timer. It was my new stove. In my new kitchen. In
my new trailer back home in Reynolds, Kentucky.

"Yes, like them fancy folks do at *their* parties. A plus one."

"So you're bringing a date to Thanksgiving dinner?" The oven
beeped at me and I pushed more buttons.

She gave one of her patented sighs of exasperation. "No, no, not
a date."

I offered my own approximation of the same sigh. "Okay, what's
his name?"

"Reverend Franklin T. Seymour. I'm sure you've met him."

Yes. I'd met him. The new youth pastor at her church. This wasn't
the first time he'd come up. "Christ, Mama, you're bringing the boy
preacher to Thanksgiving?"

"Language, Kay Ann," she said in her best somber tone. "And I
thought it would be real Christianly with all his people in Oklahoma
and him all alone out here."

"He's not alone. He's got the Lord, Mama. He'll be fine."

"You know what I mean, Kay Ann." I waited for her to say the rest. He had a steady job that wasn't illegal, had a sense of purpose and decent personal hygiene. These moved most gentleman callers to the top of Mama's list. Not for herself, mind you, but for her oldest daughter. I heard gravel crunching in the trailer park's driveway and looked up to see August Cooper's big Ford pulling up. When she didn't say the rest, I saw my opportunity and took it. "Okay. Franklin Seymour is your plus one. Uncle Auggie's here, Mama. Hopefully to see about my underpinning. I'll see you Thursday."

I was off the phone and on the double-wide's narrow porch before my uncle had grunted his way out of the truck, hiking up his torn Levis to help out his stretched red suspenders. "Sumbitch," he said, pushing back his Cooper Construction ball cap to scratch his head. "Where's the goddam underpinning?"

"In the back of your truck, Uncle Auggie, I hope."

His face registered surprise and he actually checked the bed, bless his heart, before answering. "Nope. I thought Ernie put them up Sunday."

Ernie was my cousin, his youngest and about as shiftless as you could get. "It appears," I said, "that he was waylaid."

Way baked was more likely, I suspected.

"It does appear so," he said. He leaned over and looked under the trailer. "How's the rest of it seem?"

"Sturdy," I said.

Uncle Auggie nodded. "Good."

"So any chance I'll have my skirting up before Thanksgiving?"

He scowled. "I sure can try. Have to find it first."

My phone started vibrating and I checked it, expecting it to be my mother again. It was my sister. I gave my uncle an apologetic glance. "I have to take this."

"I'll take a quick walk about, see what's what, then go see if I can scare up Ernie and your underpinning."

"Thanks, Uncle Auggie." I transitioned smoothly into the call. "Hey, Sis."

"Hey," she said. "Where you been? I've been calling."

"I've been moving," I reminded her.

"Oh yeah. All done?"

"Nope. And Uncle Auggie's lost my underpinning."

She laughed. "Ernie sold it to buy weed, I'm sure."

I laughed with her. "Probably so. Or traded it straight across."

Then her voice changed and I should've known what was coming. "So . . . what time's dinner Thursday?"

"I told Mama two but to come whenever."

"Okay. I've got my plus one sorted out."

I felt the front end of my exasperation sigh coming on. "You're bringing a plus one, too?"

And how she answered it, her tone of voice and even the volume, told me everything I needed to know. I was being plotted against by my own family. "Oh, are Mama and Bobby bringing plus ones, too? I hadn't heard."

"Mama is." Bobby was too but I wasn't supposed to know that yet. He'd call next. She'd just given it away.

"Oh goodness," she said, as if she hadn't known all along.

"Yes," I said. "So who are you bringing?"

"Johnny Alvin. Remember him?"

I did, vaguely. He was a few years ahead of us in high school. He drove a sky-blue 1973 Ford Maverick with a 351 Windsor engine and glass pack muffler and listened to a lot of Rush. "Is he still delivering pizzas for the Pizza Shack?"

I could hear the pride in her voice. "No, ma'am. He's assistant manager now. Though he's studying mortuary science at night and interning down at Drummond's Funeral Parlor."

"Mortuary science?"

My sister sometimes mistook surprise for ignorance and answered accordingly. "You know, dead people stuff. Embalming. Funeral directing."

I wasn't sure what to say. She'd gotten the first two in there. Steady work. Ambition. I decided to help her out. "I'm sure he cleans up well, too. Probably has himself a black suit."

"Oh yes," she said.

"Good. You'll both be very happy together. And I just want you to know I'm fine with you bringing your new boyfriend to Thanksgiving dinner. I'm sure we'll all love him."

She was still sputtering when I told her I'd see them Thursday and hung up.

Uncle Auggie let himself out of the trailer as I slipped the phone back into my pocket. "Everything's working," he said. "Heat, water, electric." He took a light jump on the porch. "Everything's solid, too."

He'd put half the trailers into the Shady Grove Mobile Home Park over the last thirty years. Mine was the newest, though it wasn't brand new. Just new to me and new to the park. He'd helped me find it and then he'd moved it for me at a price we both could live with. "I sure do appreciate it, Uncle Auggie."

He tipped his hat. "Thank you for your service to our great nation."

I tipped my own ballcap back. "And yours." He'd served in Vietnam. He'd not been excited to see a niece joining up, much less going overseas into that clusterfuck, but now that I was home, he talked to me differently, looked at me differently. Respectfully.

"I'll see to that underpinning," he said as he climbed into his truck.

The phone vibrated in my pocket again. But I knew who it was. My brother. Calling about his plus one. Though I don't think Mama or my sister had any idea just how different a direction my brother had taken things.

By the time we were off the phone, I was pretty sure Thursday was going to be both hysterically fun and maybe the worst Thanksgiving of my life all at the same time. I had no idea, truly.

When I got back into the trailer, it was already filling with smoke and a terrible stench that made my eyes water as I ran into the kitchen gagging.

Something had gone badly wrong with great Granny's pie.

Of course, I saw that as the least of my problems and fed the burnt offering to the park's community pig before locking up and heading back into town for another load of boxes.

And again, I had no idea, truly. But that damn pig sure was happy about his pie.

I spent Wednesday unpacking and making pies.

I thought about last year and how I was making pies then, too, down at the mess hall. After cleaning my rifle. I'd been in for two years and had already saved up enough for the trailer. I was working on setting aside enough park fees and taxes to keep my costs down while I used that GI Bill and figured out my own sense of purpose.

Last year, I was shot in the ass on Thanksgiving morning. This year, it looked I'd be ambushed by my family and their good intentions.

And Mama wasn't letting up. Her voice boomed in my Bluetooth while I broke down the empty boxes. "And he's such a polite young man," she said, lauding another of Pastor Frank's many shining attributes.

I ran the cutter down the line of tape and loved the power I felt collapsing the box upon itself. "I'm sure he is, Mama."

"And the board's really happy with his work. I expect he'll be getting a raise soon."

I put the flattened cardboard onto the stack and picked up another box. "I'm sure he will, Mama." I decided to have some fun with it all. "So it sounds like Johnny Alvin turned out fine and dandy. I'm real happy for Jessie Lynn. You think they'll get married?"

Mama sounded like she was choking. She didn't say anything. I couldn't resist; I just kept straight on. "Say," I said, "Pastor Frank could do the service. Wouldn't that be nice?"

Mama found her wits and her words. "I don't think Jessie Lynn's all that smitten with Johnny."

"Oh," I said in my most incredulous tone. "Why I can't imagine why she'd bring him around to Thanksgiving if she wasn't."

I picked up the stack of flattened boxes and moved across the shag carpet to the front door. "Well," Mama said, "I'm sure she's just being kind-hearted."

"I'm sure she is," I said. Now, I navigated the steps down. I'd awakened to an inch of snow and now more was drifting down slowly, dusting the driveway and lawns.

Mama changed the subject quickly. "So how did Great Granny's Grateful Pie turn out?"

I glanced at the pig's pen as she asked. I couldn't see him in there. "It didn't," I said. "Went to the pig."

"You have a pig?"

"Folk at the trailer park share one. Cuts down on the trash bill."

She snorted. "You're coming up in the world."

I ignored the sarcasm. "It's okay. I'm making more pie. But Great Granny's was a loss." Her pie was put together from her own butter crust recipe—this year was Jessie Lynn's turn—from ingredients that still grew wild up in the holler where her shack squatted, abandoned now, in a dilapidated heap. It had been a Thanksgiving tradition all the way back to the days of outhouses and dirt roads. There was no time for a do-over on this one so I was substituting with sweet potato, pecan and pumpkin from recipes I'd learned cooking mess for Uncle Sam.

"It won't be Thanksgiving without Granny's pie."

"It was Thanksgiving for the pig." I dropped the boxes into the recycling dumpster and headed back across the lot. "Besides, something smelled awful in that one."

Walking back, I noticed the gate to the pen was open. "Well," Mama said, "at least the pig enjoyed it."

I wandered toward the pen. The pig was nowhere to be seen. "Shit. I think the pig's run off."

Mama chuckled again. "I better let you go chase it down and get back to the rolls. We'll see you Thursday. Wear something pretty." She thought about it. "And proper," she added.

I rolled my eyes at the phone. "I will. And we can check Pastor Frank's calendar for a June wedding. I think Johnny and Jessie Lynn are going to be real happy together." Now, I smiled. "Oh, and Mama?"

"Yes, Kay Ann?"

"Did you hear about Bobby? Ends up he's got himself a plus one too."

"Oh really?"

"New girl at the college. Dana Evans. From Illinois I think."

I could hear the stammering before it started. "Dana Evans? I thought he was bringing Tommy—" She caught herself and backed up. "I thought he'd mentioned that his friend Tommy Ray needed a place to go this year."

"I don't know about that," I told her. "But maybe two of your kids have finally found true love." I grinned into the phone and hoped she could hear it. "Maybe Pastor Frank can pull off a double June wedding."

Of course, I didn't bother telling Mama what I already suspected about Bobby's plus one. It was better letting her think that maybe her baby boy was bringing a true plus one to Thanksgiving rather than someone to set her oldest daughter up with. It was going to be too fun letting her discover the truth for herself.

"I'll see you Thursday, Mama. Sure do love you."

"Sure do love you too."

I paused at the bottom of my porch and glanced back to the pig pen again. Shivering against the cold in my brown army T-shirt, I started off toward the manager's trailer.

Hank Summers was standing by his shed with a shovel as I approached. "I think the pig's run off," I said.

He shook his head. "Nope. He'd dead. Just buried him."

"That's a shame," I said. "What got him?"

Hank shrugged. "Don't know. Something he ate, I reckon, though that pig sure could eat."

The big man's lower lip started to quiver and I wasn't sure what to say. "I'm sorry about your pig, Mr. Summers."

Now his eyes filled up with water. "Oh, Wilbur was everyone's pig."

I blinked. "You named him Wilbur?"

He nodded.

I wasn't sure what else to say so I apologized again and then went back to my trailer and the last of the boxes. I tried not to think about Wilbur again, but later in the day, bagging up the leftover scraps of sweet potato peels and apple peels, I thought of him again. I glanced again to his pen as I trudged across the gathering snow and wondered if maybe it had been Great Granny's pie that did him in.

If so, that pig might've saved my life. And maybe the lives of my family and their respective plus ones. I wasn't certain of my gratitude regarding this salvation.

I dumped the bag of cuttings into the trash and turned back to my trailer and its open door in time to see something small and filthy come snarling around the corner, ramming full force into the tire of a parked truck. It fell over in the snow and growled before scrambling back to its feet.

It was a pig. And not just any pig, but *the* pig. Wilbur.

"Hey!"

I saw Hank coming around the same corner, huffing and puffing, with a length of looped rope in his hands.

The pig was off and running again, this time smacking into the wood skirting of the trailer next to mine.

"Stop that pig," Hank yelled.

As if seeing me, Wilbur growled again and launched himself in my direction. And something about him didn't look right. It might've been the bloody foam around his snout or the glassy stare of its little pig-eyes. I side-stepped him and listened to the satisfying clunk of the pig's head striking the metal dumpster and falling over again.

"That's the fastest dead pig I ever saw," I said as Hank approached. Now I could see the blood dripping from his hand.

"Meannest, too," Hank said. "Fucker bit me."

Wilbur climbed back onto his feet again with a growl nearly as disturbing as his empty, pink eyes.

"Well," I said, "I'm glad he's back."

"It's a Thanksgiving miracle," he said as he dropped the rope over the pig's neck. It spun on him with a yowl, snapping at his ankles, and Hank danced back, yanking the rope tight. "Heel, Wilbur, heel."

My phone vibrated in my pocket again. I was pretty sure it had to be Bobby. By now, Mama would've been at him about his change of plans.

I took the call from my narrow porch, watching the light flakes add to what would make for a slippery, cold Thanksgiving. "Hey, bro," I said as I watched Hank drag the angry pig back into his pen.

I thought about digging the pie scraps out of the dumpster, giving the pig some kind of welcome back treat. But the way those teeth kept snapping at Hank, I reckoned Wilbur was fed up with fruits and vegetables and more in the mood for meat.

Tomorrow, I thought, I could bring him some turkey.

Thanksgiving, I thought, for the pig.

"So tell me about you and Dana," I said with a smile into the phone. "How long you two been going out?"

Then I slipped back into the warmth of my trailer to figure out my oven and bake some pies while my little brother sputtered and spun on the other end of the line.

The flashing lights in the middle of the night were a great reminder to hang the curtains and blinds sooner rather than later.

I rolled out of bed and went to the window.

There was an ambulance and two county sheriff's sedans, and their red and blue lights that played out over the freshly fallen snow lent some Christmas magic to Thanksgiving Eve. Two deputies stood talking with Hank's wife. Even from a distance, I could tell she was crying and she had a field dressing on her cheek.

Ah shit. Hank had seemed harmless enough, but I was smart enough to know about books and covers.

The paramedics wheeled him out now and I barely recognized

him. His skin tone was wrong—deathly pale—and his eyes were wide and empty. His mouth foamed as he snapped and snarled, twisting and pulling at the restraints. One of the paramedics nursed a bloody hand, the latex glove torn and dangling like red, loose skin.

I cracked the window, not wanting to become one of the nosy neighbors that gathered on their porches or in the snow.

Mrs. Summers' voice carried easily. "No," she said, "I thought he was dead." She sobbed again. "I called 911, started CPR and then he bit me."

"Fucker bit me, too," the paramedic said over his shoulder as he helped load Hank into the ambulance.

My last sight of the trailer park manager, his eyes were rolled back in his head as he strained against the straps and howled his rage, showing his teeth, veins bulging in his neck and forehead.

The ambulance left first and once it did, people started slipping back into their trailers as the deputies finished getting her statement.

"Did your husband take anything, Mrs. Summers? Any kind of substance or medication?"

She shook her head.

"Anything unusual happen today?"

"I don't think so. I was at work."

The pig, I thought. I should tell them about the pig.

I turned away from the window to find my sneakers, and then turned back at the sound of snarling. Wilbur tore out from under my trailer at full speed, plowing up the snow like a dirty yellow torpedo, to crash into one of the deputies and sink his teeth into the man's ankle.

"Ow," the deputy said.

I remember thinking that it certainly still seemed to be Thanksgiving for the pig. And on the heels of that thought, I wondered just what was happening here in the Shady Grove Mobile Home Park and whether or not Great Granny's Grateful Pie was culpable in the matter.

It was not a night for sleeping.

After the deputies tried to put down the pig—multiple shots fired, more sleep-faced residents gathering on porches—they left and I settled back into bed and drowsed. But at some point, I heard shouts and maybe thirty minutes later—slow for Arlington County—the red lights were back.

This time, I slipped on my clothes and headed out to meet my neighbors the old-fashioned way, gathered around a police car in the trailer park.

"No," one of the neighbors said. "Stu said she bit Maggie Rae and then ran off into the woods."

I stayed near, picking up what I could both of the night's events and the gossip it may have played into. Hank was doing meth with the neighbor woman while his wife Susie held down work at Ray's Grocery. The affair had gone obviously wrong and now people were biting each other.

"What about the pig?" I asked.

"Pig ran away," someone said. And after that, it was like I wasn't there. Eventually, the cold got to me, and I slipped back inside. The snow was falling harder now, and we had a good six inches on the ground with no end in sight.

I paused outside my bedroom door, looking first to the waiting bed and then to the kitchen and the mountain of food waiting for me there.

Sighing, I turned to the kitchen. I cranked up some Counting Crows and went to work. Potatoes to peel and boil, a turkey to stuff and cook. And later, my family—and all their plus ones—would descend upon me after a snowstorm and a mostly sleepless night. A prospect that promised to be a bigger pain in the ass than last year's AK-47 round.

I decided to be grateful that Thanksgiving only came once a year, and wondered if next year's might not be better spent on a holiday in Spain.

At some point in the wee hours, I heard more shouting. But it must not have been too important. No more red lights to call the neighbors out for gossip in the snow.

I turned the music up and sang louder.

"Oh dear Lord," Mama said as she came through the door with the roll trays draped in towels. "You gotta get Auggie to build you a proper deck, Kay Ann. Nearly broke my neck."

I took the trays from her. "I'd have swept the stairs if I'd known you were coming early."

Pastor Frank, also bearing trays, came in behind her. I tried not to notice the large black Bible underneath his arm. He was a gangly redhead with a face that made me nervous. "We wanted to get a jump on the snow," he said with his easy Oklahoma drawl.

I took Mama's tray to the counter. "How were the roads?"

"Terrible," she said. "Cars off everywhere. I swear, a little snow and the whole county's a wreck. There were sirens all night. Hardly slept at all." Mama blushed. "But where are my manners?" She smiled. "Franklin, this is my eldest, Kay Ann. Kay Ann, this is Pastor Frank."

He extended a hand. I shook it. "We met up at the church, Mama."

His hands were soft but his grip was firm. "It's nice to meet you again, Miss Cooper."

I wanted to frown but smiled instead. "Just Kay Ann."

Mama was already fussing in the kitchen, checking the potatoes and looking in on the turkey. "What time are Jessie Lynn and Johnny Alvin showing up?"

"I expect it'll be a few hours," I said. Then, I offered up my first genuine smile of the morning. "Young love and all."

Mama blushed again. "Well, I don't know—"

Pastor Frank blushed, too. "Where's your broom. I'll get the snow off the porch."

I fetched him the broom and went back to the kitchen. Mama was making a fresh pot of coffee. She'd make it weak and complain that it tasted funny being ground up right there on the spot instead of coming out of a can all ready to brew.

"He's such a sweet boy," she said after the door closed behind him.

I eyed the leather book placed squarely in the center of the dining room table. "I'm sure he is, Mama."

"He's a fine preacher, too."

Sometimes, repeating myself worked best with her. It conserved energy for those long, mostly-one-sided conversations. "I'm sure he is, Mama."

"As a matter of fact," she said, "he's prepared something special to share with us today. About counting our blessings."

I was counting the hours until dinner was over. "Speaking of blessings, isn't it sweet that this year both Jessie Lynn *and* Bobby have found someone special? That's something to be grateful for."

Mama scowled and looked to the door. I could read her eyes. She wanted to correct me, and leaving an uncorrected bit of mistruth, for that woman, was like leaving an unfinished plate at the Chinese buffet. But she didn't dare let on that all three of them had plotted me a mate this Thanksgiving. I thought about letting her off the hook, telling her I'd figured out their scheme on Tuesday, but the fun I could have with this—and the teaching moment it afforded—kept me quiet.

And Mama did what Mama does and changed the subject and started washing dishes. "So how do you like your neighbors?"

I shrugged. "They seem a bit rowdy."

"Well," she said. "It's snowing and it's Thanksgiving. That'll do it. Had the whole town up in arms last night, worse than a full moon."

We kept making small talk until I heard a knock at the door. It was Pastor Frank.

"You don't have to knock," I said.

His eyes were wide and his face red and he stared at me.

I raised my eyebrows at him. "What is it? And where's my broom?"

He looked over his shoulder. "You have some troubled neighbors, Kay Ann. They need the Lord."

I let him in and closed the door behind him. That's when I noticed his sweater was ripped. "What happened?"

"I broke the broom and went to borrow a snow shovel I saw out in another yard. But when I knocked on the door, your neighbor jumped me." He took a breath. "And he didn't look good either. Like he'd been on a three day drunk."

But now I had my suspicions and I raised my eyebrow at him. "Did he bite you?"

Pastor Frank shook his head. "No. But he sure tried."

Mama was there now. "We should pray for that family right this minute, Pastor Frank." She smiled. "Let's all hold hands."

Another knock at the door made it easy for me to brush their reaching hands away. "Who is it?"

My sister's voice was shrill. "It's me."

I opened the door and stepped aside to let her in. Her face was pale as she pushed the green bean casserole into my hands. "Jesus," she said. "What's up with your neighbors?"

Johnny Alvin followed her in and closed the door. I'd not seen him since high school, and he was taller, broader. His thick mustache and curly hair made him look like the love child of a seventies porn star and a Greek god. He saw everyone and looked profoundly uncomfortable, especially when he looked at me.

"Hey, Johnny," I said.

"Hey, Kay."

"Kay Ann," I said. Then I looked at my sister. "What about the neighbors?"

She shook her head. "Looks like they're fighting."

It was sinking in now like cold concrete in my stomach. "Lock the door, Johnny."

He did and I passed the casserole to Mama before going to the window. It did not look right out there. The snow was falling still and some of the trailer doors stood wide open despite the cold. There were no children out making snowmen or throwing snowballs at each other. In the distance I could see figures running, stumbling and falling, in the snow. And I saw others running after.

"Maybe we should call the police," Johnny offered.

"They were out several times last night," I said. But my phone was out and in my hand as I said it. I went to the back door and checked its lock as I dialed.

The line rang forever before a recording kicked in, and shortly after the recording, I had the dispatcher, but I wasn't sure exactly what to say. Some part of me still wanted to believe that this was a string of unrelated and unfortunate coincidences that piled up like the snow. But that part was losing its foothold with everything pointing to the pig and the pie. "We have some kind of trouble out here at Shady Grove," I told the woman.

The woman sighed and she might've been kin given the exasperated nature of it. "We have some kind of trouble everywhere in the county. Can you be more specific?"

I tried to be but it sounded crazier and crazier as I tried to explain it.

"Can you see if they are fighting now?"

"They ran off toward the woods," I said.

She asked me a few more questions and promised to dispatch a unit as soon as possible. "And," she said in closing, "because emergency services are operating at maximum capacity, the Arlington County Sheriff's Department is recommending that residents minimize demand by remaining indoors, staying off the roads and staying warm."

And avoid feral neighbors and pigs, I wanted to add. But instead, I wished her a happy Thanksgiving and put my phone away and looked back to my family and their plus ones. "They'll send someone when they can," I told them. "It may be a while."

"What should we do?" I'm not sure it's a question I ever heard Mama ask before.

"Sit tight, I reckon." I looked at the clock. "But someone should check on Bobby."

Mama went for her purse and slipped into my bedroom with her phone.

Pastor Frank picked at his ripped sweater. "Well, I'm fixing to sit down and pray." He must've understood my stare because his face went red again. "Quietly," he whispered.

Jessie Lynn always took most after Mama and she moved into the kitchen for her own brand of crisis management. "What do you need done, Sis?"

"Everything," I told her.

Johnny Alvin moved to the couch and sat, lifting the remote. "I'll check the news."

I shook my head. "No cable."

He shrugged, put down the remote, and settled back into the sofa with his hands folded behind his head.

"They're on their way," Mama said as she came out of the bedroom. "But they said it sure is a mess out there. Snow's gotten worse and there's some kind of bug going around. Along with a bunch of holiday hooliganism."

No. It's more than that. A thought struck me and I looked over at my sister. "Hey, you gathered up the berries for Great Granny's pie last summer, right?"

She nodded. "I did. I froze them just like Mama did the year before. Why? How did it turn out?" Jessie Lynn looked at the other pies displayed on the counter.

"It didn't. There was something wrong with it, I think. Do you remember anything unusual about the berries?"

Jessie Lynn shook her head. "Not any more unusual than any other time. You sure it wasn't the oven?"

Mama interjected. "New ovens can be tricky."

"I don't know," I said. But I suspected that I did know. As implausible as it sounded, the pie went to the pig and the pig bit Hank. Hank bit his wife and his wife bit the neighbor. And Lord knew how far that might spread. Because Hank hadn't just bit his wife. He'd bit the paramedic. And the pig had bit the deputy.

Some kind of virus, maybe, I told myself. I looked outside at the massive white flakes and the blanket they made over the cars and ground, then looked to the open doors and unswept trailer porches within view.

Now Mama was in the kitchen. "What can I do, Kay Ann?"

Anything and nothing, I thought, and then Mama's phone rang. I heard my brother's voice on the other end.

"Dear Lord, Bobby," she said, "are you both okay?" She looked up at me. "They're in the ditch."

"Fuck," I said. "Let me talk to him, Mama."

"Your sister wants to talk to you." She passed the phone.

"Hey, Bro," I said.

"Hey, Sis."

"Where are you?"

"Just passed Gallagher Road," he said.

"Okay. Sit tight. I'll come fetch you." Then, as an afterthought: "And hey, lock the doors. Watch out for crazies on the loose."

I gave Mama back her phone and went for my boots. I'd not worn them since I discharged out of Fort Dix, and they were the closest thing I had to snow boots. I dug a heavy sweater out of my closet along with my camo jacket and watch-cap.

"We should let Franklin drive us," Mama called from the dining room as she pulled on her coat.

"There's no *we* in this, Mama," I told her. My voice was firmer than usual and I enjoyed trying it out on her. "*I'm* going to go fetch them."

She blinked at me and said nothing.

"Then what?" my sister asked.

"Then," I said, "we have dinner."

The power flickered and Johnny Alvin stood up and grabbed his coat. "You should let me drive you."

"And why would I do that?"

He walked to the door and pointed. "Because of that."

Johnny Alvin had traded in his Maverick for a black SUV with tinted windows. All four tires were chained. I looked from it to my snow-covered Kia. "Okay then," I said. I zipped up my coat. "Y'all tend the turkey and set the table. And lock the door behind us."

We went out into the cold, my eyes already reverting to training, scanning the buildings around me. Outside, there was a heavy silence broken by the crunch of snow beneath our feet. The stillness was pervasive, and when the quiet was broken by a growl, I followed the sound.

There in the gloom just beneath my trailer, the pig watched and waited and growled. Johnny paused at the driver's door. "Never seen a pig like that before," he said.

"Get in quickly," I told him as I opened the door. As I said it, the pig charged.

"Shit," Johnny yelled as he scrambled into the SUV. He pulled the door closed just as the pig slammed into it with a loud thunk. Then it was up and racing across the snow, this time heading for Summers' open shed. Johnny looked at me. "What's wrong with that pig?"

"Something," I said. I stared after it, trying to figure out if the blood on it was its own or another of its victims. "Not sure what." But I was growing more certain that whatever it was, it meant bad news. *Really* bad news.

Johnny looked at the glove box and started the engine. "You think it's dangerous? Should we try to put it down?"

"Him," I said. "It's a boy. Wilbur. And yes, he's dangerous. And they tried to put him down last night."

Johnny raised his eyebrows. "Someone *actually* named their pig Wilbur?"

I nodded.

He sighed. "At least people are reading."

"Amen," I said by way of agreement.

Johnny backed us up and pointed us toward the highway, moving slowly through the park. I watched as we went, suddenly flooded with memories of last Thanksgiving. The smell of the city. The dry desert heat. The sound of raised voices speaking Arabic. It was an odd contrast to now.

Movement in my peripheral drew my eyes to the nearest trailer. Something on the porch.

I jumped when the woman threw herself at my door with a shriek. Her eyes were dark and sunk-in, her skin yellow and her mouth foaming. Her nightgown was a mess of what looked like dried gravy and blood. She clawed and bit at my window and Johnny punched the gas, the chained tires slipping before they caught and rocketed us forward, sending the woman spinning off into the snow.

"What the fuck," he said, glancing to the rearview mirror. Johnny looked at the glove box again, then looked at me. "You can shoot, right?"

I nodded.

He reached over and worked the latch, dropping the compartment open. Sitting on top of the registration, next to a stack of Drummond Funeral Home brochures, lay a 9mm Colt. "That might come in handy," he said.

I watched the woman climb to her feet and lope off toward another trailer. "I reckon it might," I said. "Since when did funeral directors pack heat?"

Johnny grinned. "It's for when I'm delivering pizzas. Dangerous work, that."

I lifted the pistol out carefully, holding it in my hands like something fragile. I'm not a fan of guns. I grew up with up them, of course. My daddy had taught me to shoot and fish before I'd learned to read. I'd not taken to either much—I liked books much better—and my opinion on keeping and bearing arms shifted a little after being shot in the ass with one. I worked the action and left the safety on. "Let's hope we don't need it," I said.

The highway was deserted. Any ploughing and sanding that might've been underway earlier hadn't been maintained, and the road was a ribbon of white stretched out beneath the trees. Rush was quietly singing about today's Tom Sawyer and mean, mean pride and we drove slowly over the snow in silence for the first mile before Johnny cleared his voice.

"You know," he said, "I'm not really with Jessie Lynn. She actually brought me hoping to fix me and you up."

He knows about the plot. I felt the heat in my cheeks, and I wasn't sure what to say. "I'm sorry about that. My family's got it in their heads that I need to marry up." I looked at him. "I hope you're not—"

Johnny Alvin laughed. "Oh no. Not at all." Now he looked at me and I realized those brown eyes had some kind of mischief in them.

"Oh good," I said.

"You're not my type, Kay Ann. No offense."

I felt a rise of defensiveness and a rush of relief all at once. "Not your type? What's that supposed to mean?" Not that I cared but I knew most men noticed me when I walked into a room.

He measured me. "You really want to know?"

"Yes."

Those eyes measured me again before going back to the road. "Your brother is my type," he finally said.

When the words registered, I didn't mean to laugh out loud, but I couldn't help myself. When I saw the hurt on his face, I reached out and put a hand on his arm. "Oh, Johnny," I said, "I'm not laughing about that. It's my family." I continued at his confused glance. "You're one of three plus-ones in an elaborate Thanksgiving matchmaking scheme."

The light came on for Johnny. "The preacher?"

I nodded. "Yep. Pastor Frank."

He released his held breath. "Jesus."

"Exactly," I said.

"And the third?"

"Bobby's bringing a lesbian."

Now Johnny's smile was genuine. "He's not with her?"

"Nope," I said. "I think he's single." Now it was my turn for the light to come on. "You came for Bobby."

He nodded slowly. "Yeah. Didn't have anywhere else to be. Figured it couldn't hurt to spend time with him and his family. Get to know him better."

"Your secret's safe with me."

He shrugged. "Not so much a secret. Just like telling people my own shit rather than them hearing elsewhere."

"Makes sense to me." Despite being caught up in my family's machinations, and despite his own scheme to use that as an opportunity to get close to my brother, I decided that Johnny Alvin was good people.

It didn't hurt that he came well equipped for the kind of *going to shit* that was happening all around us.

We let Rush sing us the rest of the way, slipping past cars and trucks that hadn't made the curves, until we saw my brother's red Civic tipped into the ditch.

Johnny didn't even try to edge off the highway. The road was empty and he stopped right beside the Civic. Bobby squinted at us out of the driver's window. The girl sitting next to him, Dana I assumed, was blonde and pretty in an angular kind of way. Johnny rolled down his window and Bobby did the same.

"Hey, Johnny," my brother said. He saw me and nodded. "Hey, Kay Ann."

"Hey, Bobby," I said. "Need a ride?"

Bobby grinned. "I could use one."

"Hop in," Johnny said.

He and Dana climbed out of the Civic carefully, pulling bags of chips and soda out of the back seat. They climbed into the back of the SUV. "Hey, this is my friend Dana. She's up at the university."

"Nice to meet you," I said over my shoulder as she buckled up. "Happy Thanksgiving."

"Thanks, Kay Ann." She smiled, and there was something wicked in the smile, though it didn't bother me at all. "I've heard a lot about you. Thanks for coming to rescue us."

"Happy to," I said. I looked at my brother. "So why didn't you chain up?"

He blushed and opened his mouth to answer, but Dana cut him off. "He didn't know how to put them on. I told him I could do it. And drive, too." She paused. "I'm from Illinois. This is normal for Thanksgiving."

Johnny carefully turned us around and pointed us in the right direction.

I looked at the abandoned highway and thought about the woman with her yellow skin, the pig ploughing up the snow as he raced toward us. "We're not having much normal around here for Thanksgiving. Sorry he put you in the ditch."

I saw her studying me in the mirror. There was sweetness in her smile that told me she liked what she saw. "I guess I don't mind being a damsel in distress under the right circumstances."

Johnny used the mirror now to catch my brother's eye. "How you been, Bob?"

Bobby snorted. "I was better before the ditch."

Johnny smiled. "Don't sweat it. This weather clears up, me and you'll come fetch your car."

Dana sat forward now and I could smell the peppermint on her breath. "So how long do you think this will stick? We couldn't get a straight answer out of the radio. They're all fired up about some kind of bug that's going around. Otherwise, the news is quiet."

I looked over, aware of her face close to mine. "What are they saying about the bug?"

"Some kind of rabies, they think. It's got folks acting crazy. Hit last night and spreading fast. All the way to Lexington already."

Now my stomach hurt. "They figure out how to treat it?"

"Not yet," Bobby chimed in. "They thought it was killing folk but it seems they were mistaken."

No, I thought, I don't think they were mistaken. And the ramifications of that unsettled me greatly.

"I'm sure they'll figure it out," Johnny said.

I stared at the pistol in my lap and hoped he was right.

"So," Mama said as we all gathered around a table piled high with food, "shall we let Pastor Franklin bless this food?"

Normally, I'd have said no or made light of it, but some part of me hankered for that comfort even though I'd given up faith some time ago, finding it to be something akin to a gall bladder—useful to a point but not really essential. "I think that might be nice," I said. "Maybe throw something in about all the craziness of the day."

Pastor Frank looked around at each of us and smiled grimly. "Happy to. Let's join hands and bow our heads."

His prayer was simple, heartfelt, and long, but I was grateful for it, and I found myself grateful suddenly for lots of things, including my family and their plus-ones on a day that was getting scarier and scarier the more I considered it.

At his "amen" everyone let go of the hands they held except for me. I clutched Mama and Dana's hand and squeezed them harder than proper. I'm sure it gave Dana a different idea than what I intended but I didn't care. Her hand, cool and strong, felt good in mine. Mama's hand, sweaty and worn, felt good, too.

We sat and the feast commenced.

Jessie Lynn and Pastor Frank seemed to hit it off and I noticed my sister's face was a little flushed as she sipped her sweet tea and asked him questions about Oklahoma and the End Times. Johnny and Bobby were chatting, Johnny's eyes more alive than I'd seen them as they talked about work, life, and video games. Somewhere in there, Johnny even offered to show Bobby how bodies were embalmed, and my brother's grin told me that maybe his plan had backfired a bit.

Dana tried to engage me, and I did my best, but I was preoccupied now. I made myself eat even though my stomach protested. I answered her small talk where I could, but found myself watching the others.

Mama was watching, too, and I saw from the line of her mouth that she was perplexed. She was beginning to see that Johnny Alvin wasn't working out at all well, for me at least, and Pastor Frank was all about my little sister. Mama didn't even know what to do with Dana, and didn't pretend to for a change. I leaned over to Mama and squeezed her hand. "Sorry it didn't work out the way you planned," I whispered. "But look at it this way: It still might've worked."

She gave me her phony look of incredulity. "Why whatever do you mean, Kay Ann?"

I'd wanted to play with her in all of this, maybe teach her a little something about how her eldest girl, Kay Ann Cooper, didn't need no man—or no woman—to find her way in this world. I could pay for my own trailers. But now, in the light of everything else, that lesson didn't seem as important and the day had no room in it for playfulness. Instead, I was just glad to be here having what might be our last Thanksgiving before the world changed. So instead, I looked at Pastor Frank and my sister, at Johnny and my brother, and then back to my mother. "Nothing, Mama," I told her.

We'd just served the pie when we heard a commotion outside. A noise somewhere between a howl and a shriek rose up among the trailers, and Mama's eyes went wide. "What was that?"

I made eye contact with Johnny Alvin. He'd tucked the pistol into his coat pocket, and now he stood and went to the coat rack, pulling his jacket on and checking outside as he went. Bobby was oblivious, but Pastor Frank looked nervous. Mama and my sister looked scared. Dana watched me.

Johnny checked the lock and came back to the table. "I reckon we finish the pie and after that we should all head into town. Your neighbors might be getting rowdy again."

"Bless their hearts," Mama said.

"Amen," Pastor Frank agreed.

We ate the pie, and as we ate it, more voices joined the others outside. Hungry voices. Hollow, aching voices. "What's wrong with those people?" Mama asked.

I wished I could answer her, but I couldn't. Instead, I wondered just how far the world might change and what that might mean for next Thanksgiving and every Thanksgiving after. Hell, Christmas wasn't even a month out and I wasn't sure what the world might look like then. Of course, I wasn't even sure what tomorrow looked like: a world done-in by Great Granny's Grateful Pie.

When my phone rang in my pocket it startled me. Uncle Auggie's voice, muffled by the sound of the road, surprised me. "Hey, Kay Ann," he said. "The family all still there?"

"Yessir," I said. "Just finishing pie."

"You have situational awareness, PFC Cooper?"

"I have some, Sergeant Cooper."

"Good. Sit tight then. We're coming for you. Feds are establishing a bivouac at the high school. Me and the boys have been deputized." He paused. "You too, of course."

I had everyone into their coats and waiting by the door when we heard the loud horns indicative of a convoy. Mama and Jessie Lynn had protested, insisting that the dishes be clean, complaining the whole while about being rushed and leaving messes behind and not understanding the why of it.

I didn't have the heart to tell them and neither did Johnny Alvin, but the hand in his coat pocket told me he knew everything that needed knowing.

When Uncle Auggie and his convoy of trucks and RVs, all chained up and brightly lit, passed into the mobile park, we saw the men and women in their parkas, hunting rifles and shotguns held at the ready from their vantage points in the truck beds. I saw Auggie had modified my underpinning into a type of wind-breaker on several of the trucks.

"Why August Cooper," my Mama declared, "what kind of hillbilly parade have you cooked up?"

He winked. "The kind that might just save your life, Betty June. If you haven't noticed, things are going to shit at the moment. Get your things and climb in."

My uncle held a familiar rifle—an M16A1, aged well from the days he'd shipped it home from Vietnam one piece at a time. I sidled over to him. "You should go, Mama."

"But I don't—"

"I'll tell you on the way, Betty June." She looked at me and then let someone pull her up into the open door of an RV.

There was a howl and a flash a movement followed by the crack of a rifle. Something heavy fell into the snow and everyone jumped.

"So what do you know, Uncle Auggie?"

"It's spread past Lexington now, Louisville, too. Feds are in town looking for Patient Zero. Think they have him, and if they do, they might be able to sort out whatever the fuck is happening."

I frowned. "Hank Summers ain't patient zero."

Auggie scratched his head. The others were all in now but Johnny Alvin who hung back, his eye on Bobby where he sat in the passenger side of Auggie's truck. "Then who is patient zero?"

"Pig named Wilbur," I said. "He's been hiding under my trailer when he isn't raising hell."

Auggie looked at the convoy then back to my trailer. "That pig could come in handy. Maybe I'll send y'all on and see if I can track him down."

"Or tell the feds where he is," Johnny suggested.

I shook my head. "They've got their hands full." I looked at my uncle. "You do, too. I need you to get my people to a safe place. I can fetch us that pig just fine on my own." I looked at Johnny. "Can I borrow your ride?"

"You want help?"

I looked at Bobby sitting there, the fear starting to pale his face. "You're already helping, Johnny."

Johnny Alvin handed over his keys. Then, he reached into his pocket and pulled out the pistol. "Here."

I took both, slipping the keys into my pocket and weighing the pistol in my hand.

"You qualified on one of those, soldier?" my uncle asked.

"No sir," I said. "But I'll make due."

He grinned, thumbed the safety on his rifle, and then handed it over. "I know you can handle one of these."

"Damn straight I can." I passed the pistol back to Johnny and took the M16. It felt at home in my hands. Uncle Auggie dropped an ammo belt over my neck.

"Don't be long," he said. "And I want my rifle back."

I smiled, but I knew it was grim. "I'll bring you the rifle *and* a pig."

He put a finger in the center of his forehead. "Right in the head, Kay Ann," he said. "Only thing that works."

I nodded. "Got it."

He nodded back. Then we hugged. I thought for a moment about pulling everyone back out of their respective vehicles so I could hug them, too. Even Pastor Frank. But I didn't. I'd see them soon enough.

I looked Johnny Alvin square in the eye and shook his hand. "I'll bring your ride back too."

"Don't sweat it," he said. "It's the mortuary's."

There was another shriek, and this time, two gunshots cracked open the air, but I didn't flinch. It was all coming back to me, a more familiar home than my nearby trailer. I saw Mama fussing at the window, a panicked look on her face, as they started up the convoy at Auggie's wave. Then, he climbed back into the driver's seat to start the caravan rolling.

I waved and watched as they made their way around the loop, back to the highway. The sun was high, a white wafer behind the softer gray of cloud. The snow was deep and a low wind rustled the nearby pines. Somewhere, something that used to be a neighbor of mine howled at the quiet of the day, and underneath my porch, a pig squealed, dark and ominous.

"Hey, Wilbur," I said. "Good pig."

And then with my belly full of turkey and my heart full of family, I clicked off the safety and took myself gratefully hunting alone.

A SYMMETRY OF SERPENTS AND DOVES

*C*harity Oxham crouched behind a rusting car and cursed the rain that ran down the back of her neck. She adjusted the strap on the ops goggles she wore and blinked through the data as it scrolled by.

The rain wasn't the only thing she cursed tonight.

She glanced toward Hemming where he hunkered down beside her. Like her, he clutched a Colt Stinger in his hands and muttered beneath his breath as the sounds of the gunshot reverberated through the dilapidated neighborhood.

"This was supposed to be a simple bag and tag," she whispered. "Ellis said so."

Hemming chuckled, tipping his head so that the rain trickled off his ball cap. Beneath the visor, his eyes glowed green behind his own goggles. "Nothing's simple with Ellis."

She and her squad were here to pick up one Terrence Ichabod on a handful of warrants that D.C.'s finest had outsourced to Edgewater as a part of its move towards efficiency best practices. Deputized Eddies helped out with patrols, with relatively minor enforcement issues and with outstanding warrants.

Only this one had gone badly. Ichabod wasn't alone. And worse: He and his friends were decidedly up to no good.

And armed.

Another shot rang out.

Charity poked her head up over the fender of the car. She had her squad marked now in overview mode and could see them positioned around the junk-strewn yard that surrounded Ichabod's shack.

She clicked her tongue, opening her mic. "Carter, Murphy," she whispered. "Do we have confirmation on what they're packing?"

Carter's voice reached her first. "One each Remington .12 gauge pump action."

"Three each 9mm Glocks," Murphy added.

"Fuck," Hemming said.

"I'm calling it," Charity said. She didn't want to. The last thing she wanted was to interrupt Ellis's dinner, but she could already hear the sirens. Another click and she pulled up his wireless.

He picked up on the first ring. "What is it, Oxham?"

"Shots fired," she said. "Local's been dispatched."

She heard background noise—glasses and cutlery clinking. She also heard the anger in his voice, though she could tell that he was trying to hold it back. "We can't lose this contract. Take him down."

"But—"

"I'll call local off. You bring him in, Oxham. I don't care what it takes."

"Are you authorizing lethal engage—" The line clicked and she swallowed the rest of the question. *Of course he was. He just didn't want to be on record as saying so.*

She patched voice in to the rest of her squad. "Okay, boys," she said. "Ellis is calling off the heat; we're it."

Charity clutched the Stinger. It was sleek and dark, surprisingly light in her hands. Colt had made quite a comeback with the first in its nonlethal line of handguns. Edgewater's own track record during the Baker-Dansforth Riots and a half dozen other local police actions had helped nudge industry forward in this regard, and though the pistol's range was for shit, the cluster of needles it delivered could drop a linebacker at full run in twenty seconds.

Twenty seconds, though, was an eternity of exposure when three Glocks and a Remington were involved. Charity holstered the Stinger and reached for the small Walther 9mm strapped to her ankle, working the action. "Change up, boys," she said into her throat mic. "We're authorized lethal."

She listened for acknowledgement. When she had it, she peeked over the fender of the car and slid the safety off. "What do you think?" she asked Hemming.

He poked his head around the rear bumper and pulled back quickly as another blast thundered from the shack, buckshot tearing at the metal. "I think they're not very good at this."

She nodded. "Okay. Carter, let's make 'em cry. We'll cover."

"You'd better," he said.

She was vaguely aware of the green ghost of him moving through the debris of the yard in the left eyepiece of the goggles even as she sighted down on a darkened window through her right. She squeezed off a shot, feeling the pistol push her hand back even as she eased its muzzle down once, twice, three times. She listened to the music of shattering glass and the thudding drum beat of bullets on wood.

Even as she fired, she heard Hemming and Murphy doing the same and tracked Carter's movement in the goggles. When he reached an engine block within seven meters, he went prone, popped top and arced the gas canister through a broken window.

"It's in," he said, drawing his own pistol.

She heard the hiss of the gas and counted slowly, waiting for the chokes and coughs that meant she might bring this around without any casualties. What she heard next, though, convinced her otherwise.

Laughter. It was muted by the masks they wore, but laughter nonetheless.

"Fuck," she said. "Eyes inside, Carter."

"On it." She watched him through the goggle as he fished another canister out of his cargo pocket. He glanced beyond the engine block as he pulled the pin on the Sony cam-mite. Inside the house, a pistol cracked and Carter jerked his head back. "I'm gonna need some help here," he said.

They laid down cover while he waited. Then on a silent count of three, Carter popped up and tossed the cam-mite through the broken window. There was a dull whumping sound and a flash of light. Before both had faded, Charity had spun away from her overhead view and pulled up the cam feed. Grainy images coalesced as thousands of microscopic lenses focused.

The first thing she saw was the chair. Wooden and plain, it sat in the middle of the room, and on it lay a crate she recognized immediately. It was open, it was empty, and she felt her stomach lurch. "Boys," she said, "we have a bigger prob—"

Before Charity could finish, the night lit up around her and the noise of the first grenade choked out all other sound but the high pitched ringing in her ears. A second explosion went off somewhere near Murphy, but even it seemed muffled in comparison. The staccato burst of gunfire that followed barely registered. She forced herself to breathe and scrolled through the datastream. Carter was gone.

Murphy was screaming and thrashing about. Hemming was putting
rounds into the house with methodic intent.

"Fall back," she shouted into her throat mic, raising her own pistol to cover their retreat while she spun up the emergency dispatch
officer.

When it was all said and done, at the end of a long night and
surrounded by a crowd of local enforcement, federal agents, and frantic media, she'd lost two good men and Edgewater's contract for the
D.C. Wilds. When Ellis approached her after they'd finally carried
Ichabod and his men out of the house, she didn't even bother to ask
what he wanted.

She put her guns and her badge into his outstretched hand, told
him to go fuck himself, and waited near the ambulance for the next
round of questions about what exactly had gone wrong.

Sunday mornings were the hardest, George Applebaum thought
as he closed the Bible on his pulpit. He looked up at his congregation
and faked the smile once again, amazed at how much more tired it
made him with each passing service. He raised his hands high in a
benediction that had become his trademark over the years. "Now," he
said around that forced smile, "go out and be God's children where
you *live*."

That was the cue. Soft music started up and he made his escape
from the pulpit, leaving the platform quickly and slipping past the
congregation to take his place at the door. This part was the worst.
This was not a carefully crafted sermon where he could pick his words
and line them up with the person he was slowly becoming. Here at
the door, he had to look them in the eye and say things to them that
he no longer believed.

He shook hands as people slowly left. On a good Sunday, it would
be at least an hour. On a bad one, closer to ninety minutes. It just
depended on who was sick that week or who had lost their job or
exactly which passage of scripture had them perplexed or what televi-
sion program or book ought to be boycotted. And he stood, he smiled,
he nodded, and sometimes he even prayed right there with them.

But he didn't believe a word of it anymore. And he couldn't really
even pinpoint a time when he stopped, just moments of awareness
along the way.

Today, he thought, would be a bad one. There were visitors this week. And visitors always meant more time.

The first was a couple from Los Angeles. They were simple and he moved them along with less hypocrisy than he'd expected. But the second was a group of young men that approached him together, though he could've sworn they'd sat apart. He recognized them from the service earlier—each had followed his references carefully in tattered leather Bibles of their own. He'd marked them instantly as hardcore.

"Brother Applebaum," one of the men said, extending a calloused hand. "Brother Frost at Wahkiakum Bible Temple and Holiness Seminary sends us with his greetings in the name of the Lord."

Billy Frost. He'd not talked to Billy in years. They'd met at Southwestern Bible in their first year and had worked revivals and street corners together while they earned their Masters in Divinity. Those were the eager, early, hungry years. But Frost's convictions had drilled deeper into an extremism that Applebaum couldn't fathom even then . . . let alone now . . . and though the man pastored his own church just a few hours away, he'd not seen him more than a handful of times in twenty years. He blinked time away and found his smile. "It's nice to meet you boys. What's Brother Frost been up to?"

The tallest of the four seemed to be their spokesman. He grinned. "You know Brother Frost. He's just preaching up a storm." His face flushed a little. "He told us you were a quiet one but that we ought to listen real good."

Applebaum nodded. "He was always the rowdy one. I hope you enjoyed yourselves today."

They all nodded. "We did. We'll be back. We're staying in town for a few weeks before we go on our mission trip."

The light in the young man's eyes struck something in Applebaum and he wanted to ask more. But the four were moving off, walking with their heads held high, young men with confident purpose.

I was that way once. Now, they were gone, out the doors and into a Sunday afternoon as the next in line approached.

Normally, he'd have forgotten those young men within a week. But they stayed with him, and for the next three Sundays they shook his hand in the foyer after intently listening to his every word.

Then, on an otherwise quiet Tuesday, a nearby apartment complex exploded in a cloud of C4, rubble and human body parts. Churches were good for rumors, and they flew up and down the prayer chain that day until it came back to his office.

"Did you know we had people there?" Sister Rebecca asked him from the doorway of his office.

His head came up and he felt the news like an ice pick in his stomach. "We did?"

She nodded soberly, her mascara already running from the tears. "Twelve dead, I hear," she said, shaking her head. "Including those four new boys. Fellas on the news are saying they think it was a bomb."

The thudding of his heart was a hammer as life drove another nail into the coffin of George Applebaum's faith.

Charity Oxham ran until she lost herself in the relentless splash of one foot in front of the other as the rain and wind worked her over. DC weather sucked, it always did, but it sucked more today. She'd given up an entire day to reports and interviews before busing to the tiny studio she called home. Usually, she could get one of the patrols to give her a lift home. But no one was making eye contact with her after she'd lost Murphy and Carter in a soft entry op gone fatally bad. They sure as hell weren't offering her a ride. The stink of failure was contagious.

She'd collapsed onto her fold-out. After tossing and turning the night away, she showered, pulled on her sweats and hit the street to run it off.

There just aren't enough miles. Charity was pushing ten at this point and she could feel it in her ankles and calves. Still, it was better than what gnawed at the edges of her conscience. She'd lost people under her command before, certainly, and at some level she knew all losses were equal in their senselessness. But it felt different in the wilds of Southeast D.C., as opposed to a village in Pakistan or Nigeria. When she and her boys had geared up Tuesday evening, they thought they were picking up a felon, but nothing in the briefing had indicated the level of violent response they'd encountered.

And now, two men—men with wives and children—were dead. And she was responsible.

Charity blinked at the tears and forced her mind back to the thud-splash-thud of one foot ahead of the other.

She'd put another mile between her and her guilt when her ear-bud tickled. She ignored it the first two times, letting it roll over to voicemail. But when it tickled a third time, she tapped her glasses on to see who was hell-bent on finding her. The number was blocked.

She slowed, and as she did, she noticed the sedan out of the corner of her eye. The vehicle was out of place here on the edge of Obama Park, larger than the other electric cars, and one of the few in this part of town where bikes and buses were the norm. It moved slower than it needed to, keeping pace with her. When she stopped running, it pulled to the curb and stopped as well.

The earbud tickled again, and with one eye on the sedan, she picked up this time. "Oxham."

It was a man's voice. "Sergeant Oxham, my name is John Forrester, chief of staff for Senator Rodriguez."

Senator Rodriguez. It was strange hearing her former C.O. referred to as a senator. She'd known about the election, of course, and would've gladly cast her vote for the woman. They'd been out of touch for most of a decade, but Charity couldn't imagine any political landscape that she wouldn't trust Captain Sandra Rodriguez to navigate with all the savvy and relentless tenacity that she brought to bear as a soldier. Half the citations on the dusty uniform in her closet came from listening to her.

"The Senator," Forrester continued, "would like to meet with you this morning if you are available."

Charity jogged in place, glancing again to the car before scanning the area quickly. "I don't suppose she's sent a car to collect me?"

The caller chuckled in her ear even as the rear passenger window slid down. A young white man with a round face and eyeglasses raised a hand and nodded slightly. "She has, Sergeant, in case you were amenable. She suggested I mention Tehran if you hesitated. Or I can just drive away . . ."

Tehran. Charity wished she didn't remember it. They'd lost a lot of blood on that one and she herself would've been five point six liters of that blood if Rodriguez hadn't saved her ass. They'd possumed-up among their own dead, swapped out their BDUs for burkhas when things had quieted down enough, and made it back to the DMZ. "You owe me," Rodriguez told the young corporal, "and I call in all my debts . . . eventually." Afterwards, Oxham had collected a citation and a promotion, in addition to living to fight another day.

"I assume," she said, "that the Senator understands I'm not quite dressed for a formal meeting?"

"She does," Forrester said. "The Senator is not one to place much emphasis on formality."

It was Charity's turn to chuckle, and as she did, she disconnected and jogged to the car. She climbed into the back even as Forrester slid across the seat. He handed her a thick blue towel as she pulled the door closed, and was smart enough not to engage her in small talk as they started the long drive across town.

Charity watched the bicyclists and buses around them until the car emerged onto the Beltway and accelerated. In the front seat, the driver leaned back and let the automated road take over. When he did, she felt that sudden loss of control, which brought Murphy and Carter back to mind.

Here, on the first day of an administrative leave pending investigation, a woman she owed her life to was calling in a favor.

Outside, the rain became a hail that pounded the car, bouncing off its hood and onto the highway. The shift was as sudden as unexpected gunfire. Charity Oxham closed her eyes against it, wondering just what moved toward her in the gray of this day.

George Applebaum felt the sweat trickling down his sides beneath his damp white shirt. He rubbed his temples and even considered, for a moment, praying that this latest headache would pass. He swallowed the words before he uttered them. Outside, feeble sunlight tried to penetrate the gray clouds that hung over so many Oregon days.

The day had started with the Portland police and Cascadia Law Enforcement Cooperative detectives waiting in his study, followed soon by the Feds, all asking roughly the same questions: What did he know of Casper Logan, Jack Devlin, Spencer Algood and Linus Cooper? How long had he known them? He'd told them what little he could. Something in their questions had perplexed him. The way the agents looked at him made him suddenly nervous, and the phrasing of their questions gave them an edge that he could've sworn was near accusatory in tone.

Still, he'd done his best to stay focused and forthright. Even though each time he asked what it was all about, they rebuffed his questions abruptly, letting him know that they weren't at liberty to discuss it.

Of course, the news had been speculating from the start, and that had him sweating. Four men, names withheld pending investigation, were suspected of bringing down the apartment building when a bomb-making concern in their own apartment went badly. They'd traced the young men to his church and, most likely, they'd traced easily back to Frost's church as well. If he'd not been completely convinced his phone and email were tapped, he'd have already called Billy to find out what was going on.

It was just past five when he stood, gathering up his Bible and the small stack of papers he'd work on from home. Sister Rebecca had already left, so he was surprised by soft footfalls on the carpet when he locked his door.

Next, he heard a quiet cough. "Reverend Applebaum?"

He turned and saw a man and woman in dark suits. Yet another law enforcement agency come to call. "*Pastor* Applebaum, actually." He tried to find his smile.

"It looks like we're catching you at a bad time, Pastor."

He shook his head. "Not at all. I've been answering questions all day. A few more can't hurt."

The woman smiled and, for a moment, he thought he saw genuine sympathy. Her dishwater blond hair was cut short. She stood a few inches less than her male counterpart. "Thank you. Is there someplace we can sit and talk?"

"Let's step into the sanctuary." Applebaum led them down the hall, through the foyer, and into the large auditorium. He took a pew and twisted around, gesturing to the pew behind him. "Have a seat."

They sat, and the woman slipped a pair of glasses from her pocket, tapping the side. "Do you consent to biorecording, Pastor Applebaum?"

This was new. Of course, he'd heard of it. But the other officers had been old school with their notepads and mics. "Certainly." He swallowed. "Tell me again which agency you're with?"

"Patriot, Inc.," she said in a matter-of-fact voice. A soft blue mist shaded the lenses of her glasses.

Ah, he thought. Private law enforcement, working contract for somebody big. "Of course." George hoped his nerves didn't flow into his voice.

"For the record, state your name."

"George Harper Applebaum."

"Thank you." The woman opened a faux-leather bound notepad and brushed the screen to life with her fingertip. She held it out for him. "Do you recognize this?"

It was a picture of a charred credit card, held with tweezers, against the backdrop of an equally charred wallet lying open on a white patch of cloth.

It was familiar. He could just make out the words "church" and "Applebaum." He reached for his wallet, fumbled it open, and paled at what he didn't find. "Where did you get that?"

She ignored his question. "What about this?" Her finger moved again and another image flashed onto the screen. It was an old-fashioned paper transaction report indicating a purchase at a feed and grain store in Newberg that Applebaum had never heard of, though the signature was a close enough approximation to his own.

"That," she said, pointing to the quantity, "is a lot of fertilizer. We found most of it in an antique U-Haul truck they stored in Gresham." She paused, her brow furrowing with concern. "Its rent was also paid with this card."

Applebaum felt his scalp tingle. "I have no idea how—"

Balancing the notepad in one hand, she reached out to briefly touch his arm with her other. "We know that, George." Her sudden shift to his first name along with the physical contact disconcerted him. "We think a member of your congregation stole the card and passed it to one of the four."

Applebaum felt his jaw go slack with surprise. *A member of your congregation stole the card.* It was unfathomable because it had to be one of five who had access to his office. "Why would they do that?"

The woman looked at her partner, then back to Applebaum. "We have reason to believe they were targeting the Cascadia and Western Governor's Conference on Sustainability. Evidence suggests they were financing the operation with credit cards stolen from four area churches targeted by their local handler."

"Handler?"

She nodded. "We've identified three of the four as members of a domestic terrorist organization known as the Sons of New Jerusalem." She touched the screen of her notepad and a familiar face grinned up at him. "The local cell is led by Pastor William Frost. You went to school with him."

"We . . . we were friends." He heard the hesitation in his own voice. He couldn't believe what he was hearing. His friend had sent these four to his church? Worse: someone from his congregation, working for Frost, had taken his card, passed it along? *To make bombs. To kill people.*

Applebaum's stomach lurched. All day long, he'd answered question after question, being told nothing in return. And now, in the span of fifteen minutes, he knew far more than he ever wanted to. The headache was back. He closed his eyes against it. "Why are you telling me all of this?" he finally asked.

"Because," the woman said, "we'd like your help."

From then on, the more she talked, the more George Applebaum's head hurt. And after they left, he sat for a long time in the silence, amazed and terrified at what he'd just agreed to do.

They rode in silence. Charity watched the people slipping past outside the tinted windows until the driver dropped them off in the heavily secured garage beneath the Senate Office Building. From there, Forrester whisked her up an elevator and through security. The guards ran her glasses through a debugger and handed them back. Then they checked her unipass before ushering her along.

The halls were peppered with aides moving about their business. Charity suddenly felt self-conscious about her sneakers, sweats and ball cap. The only people who stood out more had to be the suits—the men and women of Patriot, Inc., a division of Edgewater handling outsourced Secret Service and counter-espionage. Security contractors like her had a saying: You had to be nuts to work for Edgewater; you had to be *fucking* nuts to work for Patriot.

The Patriot agents stood in corners and near exits, scanning the room with their dark glasses.

Forrester guided her through a door and pulled it closed behind him as they entered an outer office. "Senator Rodriguez is expecting you." He knocked on an inner door, and a voice Charity hadn't heard in at least a decade called for them to come in.

He held the door, and Charity passed through. She'd expected him to follow but he didn't. Forrester nodded curtly and closed the door quietly.

Sandra Rodriguez stood and came around to the front of her desk, her smile wide. "Charity Oxham," she said. "It's good to see you."

She resisted the sudden urge to salute. "It's good to see you, Capt . . . I mean, Senator."

They shook hands, then Rodriguez pointed to a chair. Charity sat as the senator made her way back to her side of the desk and a much bigger chair. She craned her neck toward the door, then pulled open a drawer. "Smoke?"

Rodriguez put a plain white box and a lighter on her desk blotter. She reached back down to draw out an antique smokeless ashtray that whirred to life when she hit a switch at its base.

Charity's mouth watered. "You have cigarettes?"

Rodriguez pushed the box across. "French. I have a friend who brings them in through Canada."

"It's been a long time," Charity said. She leaned forward and drew a cigarette from the box, the sweetness of the tobacco soft in her nose. She put it in her mouth and let Rodriguez light it for her, coughing slightly as the first of the smoke hit her lungs. She sighed. "I've missed these."

Rodriguez nodded. "I gave them up when I got pregnant with Matt." Her face clouded over when she said his name. "Picked them back up again when I jumped into politics."

Charity drew in another lungful of the smoke, holding it briefly before exhaling it in the direction of the ashtray. Possession of two cartons or less was a misdemeanor in most states. Hell, they'd been expensive when they were *legal*.

"So," Rodriquez said, "I heard about the other night. Sounds like you got bad intel."

"*Really* bad intel," Charity agreed.

Rodriguez shrugged. "I'm sure the investigation will reach the same conclusion."

Charity nodded, but she wasn't certain that was so. Edgewater had learned over the years that someone had to take the fall, and someone on the frontline was always preferred. "I certainly hope so."

Rodriguez leaned forward. "Are you happy there, Oxham?"

She'd never really considered the question. It was what she did to earn her housing and utility allowance and her meal card. They'd recruited her straight out of the army. Fifteen years had already slipped by. She'd found the work meaningful, but was she happy? She mustered a smile. "Well, at the moment I'm not."

"How would you like to come to work for *me*?"

Charity remembered the suits in the hallway and she felt her eyes narrow. "For you? Or for Patriot, Inc.?"

"For me, initially," Rodriquez said. "But if it works out, I can arrange a transfer easily enough. Tom owes me a favor."

Tom was Tom Haskins, CEO of Patriot. Charity knew her former CO was well connected these days, and this one made sense—Patriot and its parent company were headquartered in Rodriquez's own Denver Free Zone. "That's quite a string to pull," she said.

Rodriquez nodded. "I really need your help, Charity."

The cloud was back, and Charity suddenly saw the link. "It has something to do with Matt." She felt the words in her gut.

She'd never wanted children herself. When her CO announced she was transferring out of combat because she was pregnant, Charity had been convinced Rodriguez would change her mind and be back on the streets of Tehran in no time. But she hadn't, and when Charity shipped stateside, she'd gone to see her captain and the bundle of life that had changed the woman into someone Charity couldn't quite recognize.

"Yes. It has to do with Matt." Rodriguez sighed. "He's disappeared in Seattle. I need someone I can trust to track him down."

Charity nearly dropped her cigarette. "Disappeared? Have you contacted the police?"

Rodriguez shook her head. "No. Not like that. Wherever he's gone, he's chosen to go there. He told me he was leaving. He sent a long email about it." She waved her hands. "Hell, he sent it to *everyone*. His father. His friends. Even his girlfriend—he breaks up with her in the PS." She reached down, touched the screen built into her desk. "There. I've forwarded it on."

Charity's glasses chirped. She resisted the urge to open the email. "He sent the same note to everyone?"

She nodded. "Yes. And it's him . . . but it doesn't sound like him." She leaned forward. "The note's riddled with references to history and the Bible. And the last activity on the account I maintain for him was a rather sizeable donation to a Lighthouse Bible Temple near Seattle. I think. . . ." Her voice trailed off and her eyes briefly made contact with Charity's. When they did, she could see the fear in them. "I think he's joined a cult."

Of course. That's why she chose me. Charity sighed. "Sandra, I'm not sure I'm the best person to—"

Rodriguez raised her hand. "You absolutely are, Charity. You're a good scout. And you understand that world."

Her father had spent his life studying it. And ultimately, he'd given his life for it. He'd made a comfortable home for himself on the bestseller list with his books. And between his firm, rational approach to parenthood and the impact of spending the last four years of her childhood in a foster home once an angry fundamentalist had gunned her father down after a debate, she'd grown up strong and hard. "Folks will ask you to believe in a lot of things," he'd told her. "But you'll always do best just believing in yourself, Tatertot."

She shook the memory of him away, surprised again that she could smell the strange elixir of his cologne and sweat in her recollection. She took a deep breath.

"Okay," she said. "I'll do it."

Rodriguez's fingers flew. "Good. I'm pushing the contract over now. Once you execute it, you'll have access to uni-trans and to a credit line for expenses. I've booked you on a flight to Seattle for this afternoon and authorized you to access his apartment and his co-lo server." She slid a glasses case across the desk. "I've loaded this pair up with access to any database you could need. And at least a dozen ways to reach me, day or night."

Charity took one final drag on the cigarette and then crushed it out, watching the smoke vanish. "I'll find him." She stood and they shook hands.

"Good," said Rodriguez. "And welcome aboard, Oxham."

George Applebaum glanced from the suitcase to the phone. Outside, a Portland autumn expressed itself in a wide gray palette. He felt the weather pressing him, squeezing him. He'd wondered for the last day and a half exactly what he'd gotten himself into, but he also knew he'd go through with it. He had to see for himself that it was true, and he'd know the moment he looked the man in the eye.

Finally, he picked up the old cell phone they'd given him and punched in the numbers. He heard a familiar voice pick up on the third ring.

"Brother Frost." His old friend sounded hoarse, and it gave his southern drawl a gravelly resonance.

"Billy, George Applebaum here. Am I catching you at a bad time?"

The pause spoke volumes, but Frost recovered quickly. "Brother George. It's good to hear your voice." He coughed. "I've heard the news. I can't tell you how sorry I am. I had no idea those boys were up to such mischief."

"It seems they surely were." Applebaum eyed the suitcase and forced himself to the script they'd suggested when they dropped it off. "I've had a lot of people coming around asking questions. I thought I'd better give you a shout."

"I'm glad you did. I've been meaning to call but I've just been busier than a fat boy at the barbecue. Those fellas have people here who are just beside themselves with the fruit of their wickedness."

Frost's sincerity impressed him. "Well," George said, "I was hoping to talk with you more about that, Billy. There were some things that didn't add up with those boys. You know they were attending here, right?"

More silence on the other end of the phone. "Of course I know, George," he said. "I sent them your way. I thought it'd be good for them to get a . . . *broader* view of the Kingdom. As to talking, I'm not sure how much help I could be."

George counted to three, feeling the knot in his stomach tighten as he followed their script. "Some of these visitors I've been having seem to have another idea, Billy. I was thinking I'd come out your way and we could discuss it."

This pause was the longest. "I think," Frost said slowly, "that would be a fine idea, George." Then, as an afterthought: "Bring your Bible and your rod. We'll grab us some fish and some fellowship while you're here."

"That sounds good. How's day after tomorrow?"

When they hung up, George looked to the suitcase again. They'd asked him to pack a bag after that first meeting, and the next day, the woman—Abigail Hunter—had come by to pick it up. They returned it this morning.

"It's all ready to go," her nameless sidekick had told him, patting its handle.

George was still holding the phone when it rang. "Hello?"

The woman's voice sounded nearby. "You handled that well, George. Really well. How are you feeling?"

He rubbed his temples. "I don't know."

The sincerity in her voice was nearly convincing. "You'll be fine.

And what you're doing is going to save a lot of lives."

You know she's right. He didn't want to believe it, but even back in school, he'd seen a parting of the ways coming as a result of Billy's extremism. The idea that his friend might be sending young men off to bomb government conferences was a stretch but not *too* far a stretch based on some of their late night talks in college. In those days, he'd been angry over abortion, over gay rights, and even over magic in books and movies. "When the end comes," he used to say, "they'll all get theirs."

George forced himself back to the conversation. "I'll do my best."

"That's all we can ask," she said.

After Hunter hung up, George looked out of the window. For a while, he watched the gray grow darker. Then he stood and shuffled off to the parsonage's garage to rummage around for a rod and reel he'd not touched in at least a decade. Day after tomorrow, he would climb into the church's single antique hybrid car and make the two hour drive to Cathlamet.

Charity leaned forward in the chair, watching the man's face. "So how long again has it been since you've seen Matthew Rodriguez, Pastor Hill?"

This one's a snake. His narrow eyes blinked and his plastic smile flashed on. "Like I said before. Two or three Sundays back. Delightful young man." He winked and raised his eyebrows with an air of certainty. "He found the Lord here, you know."

She bit her tongue. "He also seems to have made at least one rather sizeable donation just before disappearing."

The man blushed. *That caught him off guard.* "I wouldn't know about such things. I do the preaching. Other folks do the counting."

Of course. She hadn't expected Hill to be forthright or even helpful. But he was a starting place, along with the ex-girlfriend she'd be visiting later that day and a handful of close friends she'd pulled from Matthew's rather large e-print of posts, emails and transactions. A trail that completely vanished two weeks ago with his donation to the church she now sat in.

Charity stood and smoothed her pants suit. She extended her hand, bracing herself for his clammy grip once again. "Thank you for your time, Pastor. I'll be in touch if I have more questions."

He nodded. "Happy to help. I'm sure he'll turn up."

She let herself out of the church and walked to her rental car across the only bit of asphalt that wasn't in disrepair. It seemed business was good for Pastor Hill and his Lighthouse Bible Temple. Here in the wilds of what had once been a community called Shoreline, his was the only bit of level, pothole-free ground. She'd driven past federal Department of Reclamation work crews on her way from SeaTac International Airport, but they'd not made it this far north of the city proper.

Her glasses chirped and she took the call. "Oxham," she said in a flat voice. She continued to the car and unlocked the door with her thumb.

"Ms. Oxham," a woman said, "welcome to Seattle. There is a diner six blocks north and two blocks west. I'm sending the address." Even as she said it, Charity's phone chirped again. "I already have a booth for us."

Across the street, a young man in a tattered army poncho paused long enough to light a joint before hefting his pack and walking away. She watched him go. "Who is this?"

"Abigail Hunter," the woman said. Then, the phone clicked in Charity's ear.

Has to be Patriot, she thought as she slid behind the wheel and started the car. It came to life quietly, and she eased it out of the parking lot and onto the road, going slowly. She synched the car up to her glasses and let it drive. Five minutes later, she pulled up to the curb in front of a run-down diner.

Abigail Hunter wasn't hard to pick out. She and her companion—a slender blond man—were the only ones in suits. They sat side by side in a booth at the back of the restaurant. The woman's blond hair was short and pulled back from her face. She smiled as Charity approached and extended her hand from where she sat.

"Senator Rodriguez's office was kind enough to let us know you were coming," she said after they'd all shaken hands. Her companion smiled but said nothing.

Charity sat and a waitress hurried over with an extra mug and half a pot of coffee that smelled burnt and strong. At Charity's nod and smile, she filled the mug and moved off. "Patriot, Inc., I assume?"

Hunter nodded slightly. "Yes."

"Capt—" She paused and corrected herself. "*Senator* Rodriguez didn't tell me Patriot was already involved." What she didn't say was that she wasn't sure why the senator would hire her in addition to Patriot.

The woman shook her head. "We're pursuing a series of ongoing investigations. Matthew Rodriguez's disappearance is related, but only a small part of a larger whole."

"Ongoing investigations into . . .?" She waited for Hunter to fill in the blank.

"My partner and I have been temporarily assigned to a private foundation, and we're very interested in what Matthew Rodriguez is up to . . . and who he's been up to it with."

Charity's eyes narrowed. "A foundation? Philanthropy and whatnot?" It wasn't unheard of that agents or officers might be attached to private sector business. Edgewater and its affiliates were corporations with bottom lines in a world in desperate need of organized strength and investigative capacity. But she'd never heard of a charitable foundation hiring guns and eyes.

Hunter nodded. "It's . . . complicated. But yes. There are many groups whose work is at odds with our employer's mission. Some of those groups have taken it upon themselves to go outside the law to bring about the changes they'd like to see. We are gathering intelligence on those threats."

"So the foundation is financing its own investigative work? What about local or federal law enforcement?"

"We work closely with our partners at Edgewater and with any of the local jurisdictions that aren't actually being investigated themselves." Hunter stirred cream and then sugar into her coffee as she talked. When she looked up, her eyes were hard. "I wish it weren't true, but many of them have already been compromised."

Charity lifted her own mug to her mouth and sipped. She didn't like the sound of this. "Compromised?"

"A quiet war is being waged, Sergeant Oxham, by an unhappy group of people whose frustrations are manifesting themselves . . . violently."

Those people had always been around, she knew, and some of those voices had gotten quite loud during the decline the United States had experienced for most of the last sixty years. The economy had collapsed first, followed soon by the loss of international credibility after a series of poorly considered military ventures. Then, there was the gradual unraveling of domestic tranquility as a depressed nation began acting out on itself. The crime rate had skyrocketed, demonstrations had gone violent, and even a few coups had been put down by a bi-partisan government losing its grip.

Andrew Shockney and his new Green Party changed all of that. In the last ten years, they had gained a significant foothold in bringing scattered city-states together. Before Shockney, those city-states had operated in relative autonomy within the shell of state lines that no longer made sense, creating alliances and collectives that functioned economically and geographically. Cascadia was the archetype for these regional entities. Sandra Rodriguez was a part of that; a decorated war hero turned Green politician. Thinking of her brought Charity back to the conversation.

"I'm not sure what this has to do with Matthew Rodriguez, Agent Hunter."

The line of Hunter's mouth went firm. "The church he was attending—Lighthouse Bible Temple—is actively recruiting male college students at the University of Washington for an organization called The Sons of New Jerusalem, a terrorist group committed to the violent overthrow of the U.S. government—and worse, an end to the One World Movement and its resulting treaties."

Oxham put down her coffee. She could get her mind around the former but not the latter. It had taken decades of persistent effort to make the progress they had, and even now, there was much more to do. "Why would anyone want to stop that?"

Now, her male companion broke his silence. "If you're familiar with your father's work, you can probably guess the answer."

But Abigail Hunter didn't make her wait. "These particular cultists have a vested interest in the end of the world as scheduled," she said.

Yes. She remembered her father's anger during one of those botched Middle Eastern wars because so many of his research subjects expressed hope and joy that it might bring about Armageddon. "One woman," he'd once told her, "made a big production over how she'd be riding back on a white horse beside Jesus to *teach those fucking sinners a lesson.*" She sighed.

"And you think Senator Rodriguez's son is a part of this movement?"

"We do," Hunter said. "Yes."

That explained why Sandra didn't know about Patriot's involvement here. She could see the path now clearly. "And you already know where he is, then?"

She nodded. "He is in training right now on the Olympic Peninsula. In a few days, we suspect he'll be moving south to a small town on the Columbia River. I'm sure you understand why we wanted to wait and be more certain before upsetting his mother with news like this."

Charity Oxham leaned forward. "Let's be honest here," she said. "You're waiting because you want to learn as much as possible before someone like me comes in and pulls him out of the mess he's landed in. You have your fingers in a lot of pies; pull any one too soon and you lose the entire bakery."

Hunter nodded. "Yes. And our pies are nearly done. We're really close."

"What do you want?"

The woman smiled. "We know where he is and where he's going. We'll share that freely with you. We just want you to coordinate with us before taking any kind of action."

"For national security purposes," Charity added.

Hunter shook her head. "No. It's far bigger than that at this point."

Charity didn't believe it, despite the woman's sober tone. And this meeting, regardless of the information they'd given her, left her feeling less interested in Sandra's promise of a potential transfer to Patriot, Inc. These two were shady at best and didn't improve her opinion of their employer.

It brought her back to her earlier question: *What kind of charitable foundation hired guns and eyes?*

"Okay," she finally agreed. "I'll coordinate with you." She pushed her coffee away. "But I do intend to find Matthew Rodriguez and pull him out of whatever it is he's gotten himself into."

They both stood. "Excellent," Hunter said. "We'll send you what we can . . . *when* we can."

Charity shook their extended hands, noting their grips were cooler and firmer than her own. She watched them leave, in the only other car in the diner's rough asphalt parking lot. Everyone else here was a local, either pedestrian or cyclist. After they'd gone, she climbed into her own car and dialed up one of the secure voice mails Sandra had provided her.

"I have a solid lead," Charity said. She wanted to say more but didn't. Instead, she hung up and nudged her car to life and pointed it back to the smart roads that would carry her back to her waiting hotel.

The Oregon side of the Columbia had kept up with the times for most of the first half of the century. Smart roads equipped with historical narratives about the area carried tourists with relative ease between Portland and Astoria. At one time, these lands were laid bare by out-of-control logging, but two generations of attention, and the skyrocketing price of shipping wood to Japan, had brought back the forests.

George Applebaum relaxed and watched trees move past. He'd just left Saint Helens, the last real patch of civilization on the road to Astoria. But long before reaching that quaint tourist town, he'd cross into Longview and brave the Washington highway leading to Cathlamet.

At least the car can drive until then. He didn't leave the city much, especially not with the church's single electric car leased for his benefit. And how long had it been since he'd taken an actual vacation?

"Have fun," Sister Rebecca had said when he left the office that morning.

"I'll try," he said around a smile as fake as the ones he offered from the pulpit.

What he drove to knotted his stomach. Not for the first time, George wondered exactly what the agents had done with his things. *Brushed it with pixie dust no doubt.* He was certain they had turned every personal item he had into a camera or a microphone or a transmitter beacon pointing them toward his friend.

No, he realized. Not friend. If Billy Frost was willing to use and implicate George's church in his plans, he was no friend at all.

"Pedestrian ahead," the car whispered, following highway protocols, and George looked up to see the hitchhiker. At first he thought it was a young man wearing camo pants, a green T-shirt and a ball cap, carrying a large backpack. But as he drew closer, he realized it was a woman, tall and skinny, with blond hair poking out in a ponytail.

George looked away. Even under different circumstances, he wasn't the sort to pick up hitchhikers. Especially young women. To this day, he still followed the seminary's strict recommendation that he only meet alone with women with his office door ajar and Sister Rebecca within earshot. He looked back to the girl.

Her thumb was out and she held a sign in the other hand.

Cathlamet, it read.

Back in the old days, he'd have called it the Spirit moving him. He didn't know what to call it now. Intuition, maybe. Whatever it was, it prodded him and he took the wheel of the car. "Manual," he said, pressing his thumbs into the sensors to unlock it.

He nosed the car over to the side of the highway just past where she stood and popped the trunk. He felt the car settle with the weight of her pack, and when she opened up the door and crawled in, he extended a hand. "George Applebaum." He smiled.

"Molly Clark," the woman answered. "If you can get me as far as the bridge, that would be great."

"Actually," George said, "I can get you downtown. I'm headed to Cathlamet, too."

Now she smiled. "That would be great, George." She dug a battered book out of her cargo pocket. It had a plain black cover and at first he thought it was a Bible. She held it, her thumb just blocking the title. "I really appreciate it."

He eased the car back onto the highway and let it take over. They were twenty minutes from Longview's Lewis and Clark Bridge, maybe thirty minutes from having to drive manually. He settled back into the seat and glanced again at the book. She had it open now, her finger moving over the thin paper as she read.

A Symmetry Framed. The letters were gold embossed, and below the title, the author's one-word name seemed oddly out of place. Bashar.

He nodded. "That book looks important," he said.

She looked up at him. "It might be one of the most important books ever written."

George grunted. He'd used that line himself before back in the day. To hear it now felt oddly disconcerting. *Because no one book should be that important.* "What's it about?"

He expected her eyes to light up, but they didn't. They were cool and gray even as her mouth twitched into a slight smile. "It's about a new way," she said. "It's about a man named Tygre and the path he walked to heal the world."

George pulled up a search engine in the left lens of his glasses. The old keyboard and mouse technique was so much better than all this ocular mumbo jumbo, but since he had to wear the glasses to synch with the car and highway, he might as well satisfy his curiosity. He ran the name Tygre through along with the title of the book and its author, Bashar.

The search returned very little. The book was a collection of stories and sayings from and about a man named Tygre who'd allegedly found the hidden city of Cascadiapolis some forty years earlier. Bashar's name came back with even less. Most of the references pointed toward Blake's poem. The book itself was published abroad and distributed by the J. Appleseed Foundation out of Seattle.

The girl must have read his mind. "You'll not find much about it online," she said. "But I can give you a copy if you're interested." She nodded her head back to the trunk. "I have a few extras in my pack."

George found himself remembering Texas suddenly, his nose flooding with the smell of sweat and dust as he and Billy Frost warmed up their voices on Dallas's downtown lunch crowd. They had a plastic grocery sack filled with Gideon New Testaments, the faith strong upon them that they'd give them all out in a day's preaching. All that had changed in thirty years was that the plastic sack had become a building full of books. Back in those days, he'd believed every word of it. Now, he believed little. He chuckled at the memory of that former certainty. "I don't think so," he said. "But thanks."

She shrugged, smiled, and went back to reading. There was a quiet confidence in the way she held herself that made him almost reconsider. But in the end, he disconnected from the net and settled back into his own seat to relax before he'd need to take over the driving.

Outside, the clouds broke open, and unexpected sunlight made the wet highway glisten. But it didn't lull George into any kind of hopeful calm.

George Applebaum knew that a storm waited for him ahead.

The sun had won out for a handful of days now, and Charity sat behind the wheel of the antique pickup enjoying the warmth on her forearm where it rested out the window. Her eyes went from the highway to the map layover in her glasses. Out here, most connections failed because of lack of coverage or, in some instances, from the outright blocking of the wireless signal by the Luddites who now dominated the rural extents of the Pacific Northwest.

On the map, she watched the red cursor moving toward her. *That would be the bus from Shekinah Camp.* On it, according to the information she'd received from Hunter, Matthew Rodriguez rode toward the next leg in his training.

Careful to avoid a tail, or observers on the obvious route, Charity had taken the long way, driving her rented electric as far as Aberdeen before stopping to book a room in a cheap motel that made her army shelter-half and fart-bag seem high-end. She took an hour to pick up three second-hand dresses and a battered Bible at the local thrift store before dining in a cafe that boasted local seafood. Then, she'd slept fitfully on the lumpy motel mattress after once more reviewing the information Hunter had sent across. She ended on Hunter's note reiterating that she check in before making any kind of contact with Rodriguez or the people he travelled with. Of course, she had no doubt whatsoever that Patriot, Inc. had its eyes and ears on her as she made her way south.

And I can do this without making contact.

According to the map she watched, the bus was now less than five miles behind her, and she fired the truck up again. She'd driven fossil-fueled vehicles in the military, but that was fifteen years ago. She'd forgotten how they smelled and sounded.

Highway 101 had been privatized, but that hadn't included any high tech. It was asphalt and mostly smooth, though she suspected the tolls collected at strategic points barely scratched the surface of the highway's need.

As she pulled onto the highway, her phone chirped again. She knew the number and had dodged answering for well over a day now. Finally, she sighed and picked up. "Oxham."

Sandra Rodriguez's voice was cold with anger. "Oxham," she said slowly, "how many fucking times do I have to call you? You tell me you have a lead and then . . . nothing."

No, Charity realized, not just anger. Worry. "I'm sorry, Senator Rodriguez," she said. Then, as an afterthought: "Sandra."

"Well?"

She looked to her rearview mirror. So far, no sign of the bus. "It's a good lead. I really can't say more than that."

"What do you mean you can't say more?" The cold was bleeding out and becoming something closer to panic. "It's those fucks at Patriot, isn't it? They've—"

"Sandra," she said again with as much firmness as she could muster. "Listen to me. I can't say more. But I have a good lead. A really good lead."

Charity heard the senator sigh even as she saw movement on the highway behind her. White and cresting the rise behind her, she saw the bus. She increased speed and saw the sign indicating the highway's sole operating rest area was just a mile ahead. "When will you be able to tell me more?"

"I don't know. But I may need a quick flight for two out of Portland in two or three days. Private if it can be arranged."

"Before I do anything, I will—"

But she cut her friend and former CO off as she saw the bus gaining speed. "I'm sorry, Senator. I have to go."

Disconnecting, she punched the accelerator and felt the truck shake as it sped up. She kept an eye on the mirror, and then signaled to exit into a dilapidated and overgrown rest area scattered with a handful of cars. Behind her, the bus followed, and she smiled. A bus full of young men in the late morning; of course they'd be stopping here.

She parked and climbed out of the cab, reaching for a purse she rarely felt the need to carry. The Bible poked out of the top, and she smoothed the somewhat plain dress she wore. She'd been careful to pick one that was not cut too high or too low in the wrong places. "Start recording," she whispered, and the glasses did the rest. All she needed to do was look around. . . .

She stretched and walked toward the sign marked Ladies. The bus had stopped, and three young men in dark slacks, white short-sleeved shirts, and ties climbed down first. They looked around the rest area and one of them grinned at her.

"Ten minutes," one of them shouted into the bus, and pandemonium ensued as a herd of young men scrambled to get off. The bus emptied quickly as a line formed up.

She panned each face, silently counting. There were twenty of them, not counting their chaperones and driver. They were all clean cut and close shaven, skin burnt brown by days spent in the sun. And they were all as fit as fresh recruits straight from boot, only lacking the swagger most privates managed. She nearly didn't recognize Matthew; he'd changed a great deal even from the recent photos she'd seen. But it was him; she could see his mother's eyes and jawline. With that image tucked carefully away, she moved to the restroom.

One of the chaperones—the one who grinned—intercepted her. So much for no contact, she thought.

"Morning, ma'am," he said. "You responsible for that?"

She looked where he pointed, not sure exactly what it was. She tried to pull off demure. "I'm sorry?"

His grin widened. "That well-worn book, ma'am. Did you read it that way?"

She returned the smile. "Yes, sir, I did."

He blushed at the courtesy. *This one is easy.* "Good," he said. "Enough people read it and maybe we'll get back to the great nation God intended us to be."

She wasn't sure what to say. "I hope so." Then, the light in his eyes changed and she corrected herself. "I pray for it."

His grin was back, and he saw her hand resting on the restroom door's handle. He blushed again. "I'm sorry to have kept you."

She smiled one last time and slipped into the shelter of the ladies' room. Then, she occupied a stall and waited until she heard the old bus turn over and start.

She was back on the road when her phone chirped again. She didn't recognize the number, but knew who it was. "Yes?"

"That," Hunter said, "was what we call making contact."

"Funny," Charity said, "we call it surveillance." Then she hung up. She followed the winding road south, at times through forest and at times within sight of the vast Pacific Ocean. She kept her speed down so that the bus was well ahead of her and out of sight. But she knew exactly where it was and where it was going.

And, more important, she knew Matthew Rodriguez was on it.

George and Molly rode most of the way in silence, the car jostled by a dying highway that curved along steep banks alongside the Columbia River.

The girl looked up from her book about fifteen miles outside of Cathlamet. George gave her a sidelong glance. "So what is it about?"

She smiled. "Healing the world."

George let out a chuckle that was nearly a snort.

She cocked her head. "Don't you believe the world can be healed?"

He shrugged. "I used to. For a long time, I thought I was helping heal it."

She closed the book. "And now?"

He couldn't bring himself to admit he didn't know anymore. And now, something else tickled at his spine. If the things he'd heard about Billy were true, what they'd been doing wasn't healing at all, but harming. He looked at her, looked back at the road, and said nothing.

"I think it can be healed," she said. "Tygre did, too."

He well recalled that kind of fervent belief. "So how are you going to heal it?"

Her smile widened. "Why," she said, "with a casserole."

George laughed and she laughed with him. Then, they lapsed into quiet until they reached Cathlamet.

The town had always been small, but it had shrunk to a bright core in the midst of dilapidation and burned-down houses. Most had fled the decline of the rural Northwest for the dubious job markets of the urban sprawl. Those who remained were those who wanted nothing to do with a reorganized and revitalized United States of America. And the United States took little notice of them, only occasionally raiding illegal fishing and logging operations.

Driving down the short Main Street, passing the Pioneer Church, George could see the charm the town had once possessed. And even now, some of the buildings were still kept up, and at least two businesses—a restaurant-tavern combination and a grocery store—looked open.

"You can drop me here," Molly said, pointing to an abandoned drug store. Its windows were boarded up and weeds grew through cracks in the sidewalk.

George pulled over and put the car in park. They climbed out together and he hefted her backpack out of the trunk. "With casserole?"

She grinned. "Come find out on Friday."

He looked around. "Where?"

She pointed to the drugstore, and he noticed the **SOLD** sign tacked across the doors. "Right here."

He looked at her there in the fading afternoon and saw a lightness in her that made him ache with nostalgia. *But I was never that confident*, he thought. "If I'm still in town," he said, "I just might."

She took the pack. "Thanks for the lift, George."

He tipped his ball cap. "You're welcome, Molly."

She'd already disappeared behind the building when he pulled back onto the street. He continued through town and across an old bridge to Puget Island. It wasn't hard to find the Wahkiakum Bible Temple. It was a sprawling complex of buildings surrounding a large chapel. He pulled into the graveled parking lot alongside a battered pickup with its rifle rack and faded "God is Love" bumper sticker.

He followed the sidewalk along the building to the side entrance with a hand-painted wooden sign that said **THE PASTOR IS IN.** He opened the door and found himself looking at an austere reception area with an old-fashioned counter that appeared to have been pulled from an old elementary school. Muted voices drifted out from a partially closed door, and George paused to see if there was a bell or some other way to announce his visit.

"Just tell him," he heard Billy say, "that we can't afford the attention right now. He needs to hold off that log raft he's fixing to put out there and let us get the Lord's work done."

"He's saying he needs the money, Brother Frost."

"Then we'll take up a love offering for his family. They're watching the river now, watching us even, after that fiasco in Portland. Just tell him another week."

George cleared his voice. "Hello?"

The enthusiasm in Billy's voice sounded genuine. "Holy Jesus . . . that you, George?" A chair creaked. "It took you long enough."

Billy Frost strode out of the office, his arms outstretched. "It's good to see you, Brother."

George returned the hug, a knot suddenly in his stomach. Even the hug was enthusiastic, and for a moment he wondered if maybe the agent from Patriot was wrong about Billy. He hoped so, he really did.

"Come on in here, George. I want you to meet my Associate Pastor." They entered the office where a young man—nearly a brother to the four George had met in the foyer of his church—stood waiting. "George Applebaum, this here is Steve Wilkes. First graduate of our local seminary and my right hand man." They shook hands. "George and me was preaching the streets of Dallas before you were born, weren't we?"

George nodded. "We did a lot of that."

Frost chuckled. "That we did, Brother. You hungry?" When

George nodded, he turned to the younger man. "Steve, I'm going to take Brother George up and introduce him to Rosie's. We have a lot of catching up to do."

And a lot to talk about. He wasn't sure how much talking they could do at Rosie's, but he'd planned three days in town, taking advantage of the guest room in Frost's parsonage. Part of him hoped it was enough time to learn something. But another part of him, a part that remembered the two of them sweating and laughing together as they practiced their zeal and their sermons on innocent passersby, hoped it wouldn't be enough time at all.

"Let's go," Frost said, grabbing up a battered black Bible from his desk. "We'll be back in time for prayer meeting, Steve."

Then, George followed him out of the office. Outside, the sun was trying once again to shine through the clouds. He found kinship in its attempt to cut through the gloom of the day with its watery light, and climbed into the waiting truck with a quiet sigh.

Charity Oxham turned the hot water up all the way and tried to scrub the road out of her eyes. It had been a long, slow drive from Aberdeen.

She'd followed the bus—at a safe distance—to the parking lot of the Wahkiakum Bible Temple on an island just outside of Cathlamet. She'd driven past as the young men filed off the bus with army-issue duffle bags, then she'd taken the long way around the island before heading back to town.

The Bradley House Bed and Breakfast was happy to rent her a room for three nights, and she was happy to pay cash. The room was a bit frilly for her tastes, but it smelled good and the water was hot.

She washed quickly, then dried off and dressed for dinner. After a brisk walk across the street, she settled into a booth in the town's only surviving restaurant. The waitress was an older woman who took her order without writing it down and came back quickly with her iced tea.

When the seafood fettuccine arrived, Charity forced herself to eat it slowly, pretending to read her Bible as she did. Despite her best efforts, she polished it off quickly and paid.

What next? She needed to get Matthew alone and talk with him, see if she could reason with him and convince him to come home with her. But what if he didn't want to? Bring him home by force? And what did Patriot, Inc. have planned here? It was obvious to her that they had this organization under surveillance. She'd read about the bomb-making lab in Portland on the news, and Hunter had referenced it in her notes. So what were they going to do about it?

And what am I going to do? She left the restaurant and set out for the bed and breakfast. But Charity stopped when she heard the singing.

It leaked out of the open door of a rather rundown old pharmacy in a rich alto voice. The song grabbed her and pulled her toward it. The singer was a young woman pushing a broom about the dim-lit, empty store. She wore camo pants and a T-shirt, her blond hair swept back in a green bandana. When the woman looked up to see Charity watching her, she didn't startle, but a deep blush washed her face.

"Sorry," Charity said. "I didn't mean to interrupt." There was something in the song that moved her, but she did not know what it was. It was a foreign, unwelcome feeling, but not because of anything unpleasant it evoked. It smelled of some vulnerable part of herself she had no use for exploring. Still, she had to say something. "You have a lovely voice."

The blush continued as she leaned on her broom. "Thanks. I'm Molly."

"Charity," she answered.

Molly started pushing the broom, shoving piles of dirt and dust to the middle of the room. "So have you lived in Cathlamet all your life?"

She shook her head. "No, I'm just passing through. You?"

"My first day here," she said. "I hitched in earlier."

Charity looked around the store. Even its shelves had been pulled. It still had its counter and the two islands for registers, though the machines themselves were missing. She saw the sleeping bag in the corner next to a grocery sack full of non-perishable food. "You're staying here?"

Molly nodded. "I have a lot to do. I'm opening on Friday."

"What are you opening?"

The girl grinned. "Come back Friday night and see."

There was something about the girl that made her want to nod and say yes. She didn't understand that charisma, and she resisted it. "I'll see what I can do," she said.

Then, the girl surprised her. "Do you believe the world can be healed?"

Charity faltered at the question. It ambushed her and she found herself in a moment of complete candor. "No," she said. "I really don't."

Molly just nodded. "Well, come out Friday anyway," she said.

"I'll see what I can do." Charity departed, making her way back to the bed and breakfast. But despite the cool, crisp sheets and the comfortable bed, she didn't sleep right away. Instead, she lay awake, pondering the girl and her question and the song that she sang.

She'd gone with Edgewater when she got out of the army thinking it was a way she could make the world better. But after the losses of Carter and Murphy and scattered casualties across the years before that, it seemed clear evidence that she was losing more ground than she was holding in this fight.

Charity sighed and rolled over. When she finally fell asleep, it was to the song that Molly sang, only remembered from long ago.

The day they played it at her father's funeral.

George Applebaum tossed and turned in Frost's guest room and finally gave up on sleep at two a.m.

They'd eaten a late lunch at Rosie's and it would've been the best burger he'd had in years under different circumstances. He and Frost had kept the conversation near the surface, catching up on this or that bit of the last decade as they ate fries soaked in ketchup and chased them with sodas. Throughout the three-hour meal, various people meandered by to greet Frost, who enthusiastically introduced them to his guest. They'd been friendly enough, but there were knowing looks he noted between Frost and at least a few of his parishioners.

When they'd finished, the two pastors returned to the church for a prayer meeting that combined a quick exegesis of a section of Ephesians about putting on God's armor and hours of loud praying with men and women kneeling, arms draped over the backs of pews. George noticed a large number of young men in the back of the sanctuary who kept quiet throughout and were suddenly absent when it was time for them to file out and shake hands with the pastor.

It was close to ten when they finally left.

Now, the parsonage was dark and he heard Frost snoring loudly from the bedroom next door. George sat at the tiny desk in the corner of his room and tried to read his Bible. He gave up after thirty minutes and pulled on his sweats, socks, and sneakers, to slip downstairs and out to the front porch.

The island was quiet but for the occasional barking of dogs, and the clouds had pulled back to reveal a night sky scattered with bright stars. The parsonage was a mile or two from the church, an old farmhouse sitting in the middle of a field at the end of a long driveway. Not sure what else to do, George set off at a brisk walk.

He moved out onto the abandoned road, marking the mailbox so he could find his way back. He pointed himself in the direction of the church and wondered what Hunter had made of his conversations with Frost so far.

"With your help," she had told him that evening he'd agreed to this, "we can take him and his group out of business before anyone else is hurt."

Despite the evidence he'd seen, nothing in Frost's words or demeanor so far had suggested he could be the ringleader of a terrorist movement. But he also hadn't confronted the man with what he knew so far, and Billy hadn't brought it up.

Yet. But George knew he would.

He gave himself to walking and found himself thinking about the hitchhiker, Molly, wondering what she was up to with her world-healing casseroles and her run-down pharmacy. There was something about her that stuck with him, and he thought it was her strange combination of zeal and zen.

A sound on the road ahead brought his focus back, and he slowed his pace. It was a distant noise that grew closer, and it took him a minute to place it. It was the sound of feet slapping the asphalt—a lot of feet—and just as it registered, he saw them. They ran in formation, completely silent but for their feet and their breathing. They moved past him quickly; he thought there were maybe twenty of them. As they passed, the man at the lead nodded an acknowledgement, and George realized it was Steve Wilkes, the associate pastor. He nodded in return and kept walking.

A dark thought crossed his mind. *Twenty to replace four.* Of course, there was no way to know if the four he'd met in Portland were the only ones sent out as Frost's missionaries. For all he knew, there were other young men in other cities, buying up their supplies with stolen cards from other churches, building bombs to serve their dark gospel.

He shivered and continued on, taking an hour to walk the loop that eventually brought him back around to Frost's driveway. There were lights on in the house now and he found Billy waiting for him on the porch, up as early as any weekend fisherman.

"Taking care of the temple," Frost said with a grin. "Good man."

George nodded, feeling winded from the walk. "I don't do it enough," he said.

Frost tapped the coffee mug he held in his hand. "Hot coffee inside if you want it. I thought I might play hooky today and get us out on the river for some fellowship and fishing. Sound good?"

George nodded. "I'll grab a cup and be right back."

He went into the house and navigated around old furniture, following the smell of coffee to a well-lit kitchen. A clean mug waited beside an antique percolator that sat bubbling on a hot burner. He poured it and returned to the porch.

Billy sat in the creaking wood rocking chair, his slippered feet moving it back and forth as he sipped from the mug. George sat in the matching chair and shivered suddenly as a light wind moved over his sweat-soaked clothes. He took a drink, savoring the strong flavor of chicory and the warmth that flooded him. He thought of the young men, running in formation like soldiers, and looked at the man he'd considered such a good friend. "So," he said as nonchalantly as he could muster, "what's the Lord been up to in your life, Brother Bill?"

Frost looked at him, and in the dim light of the dirty porch bulb, his broken nose, high cheekbones, and bushy eyebrows took on a sinister quality even as his eyes sparkled. "He's been up to a lot, Brother George. There's a work begun—a revival the likes of which we've never seen before—that I've been meaning to talk with you about."

The kind that involves bombs and militia? he wanted to ask. But he forced himself not to. "I'm always interested in hearing about revival."

Frost chuckled and slapped his knee. "We sure enough preached some, didn't we? I don't think Texas was ready for us young Turks." Then, he sighed and looked around. He lowered his voice. "We'll talk about it out on the river."

There was a sound on the road then, and George looked up. He couldn't see them, but he heard the quiet whisper of their sneakers on the asphalt.

They finished their coffee in silence and twenty minutes later, piled into Frost's pickup with rods, reels, Bibles, a thermos and a stack of peanut butter and jelly sandwiches wrapped in waxed paper.

The town still slept when Charity slipped out of the bed and breakfast in her dark tracksuit and started her morning run. She wore her glasses but found herself wishing she'd had her Edgewater ops goggles with their night vision and boosted WiFi signal. Out here, she picked up little but static on the set she'd gotten from Forrester.

She ran over the bridge, listening to the water below as it moved against the concrete pillars that held the old structure in place, and when she reached the other side, she set out in the direction of the church. She kept a steady pace, her eyes scanning what little could be seen in the charcoal gloom. Twice, she interrupted the prowl of what she hoped were cats, pleased with how little their scampering startled her.

She saw a lone pair of headlights on the road ahead as she approached the series of buildings that made up Wahkiakum Bible Temple. She moved off the road to squat in the underbrush as a pickup truck as old as her own slipped past, then turned her attention to the church. There were several outbuildings, but only one had any lights on. There, behind old floral-patterned curtains, Charity saw movement.

She studied the terrain, marking a path that gave her optimal cover, and suddenly wished she'd insisted on having a firearm waiting for her in Seattle. Of course, it hadn't seemed particularly useful when she thought she was dealing with a college kid who'd joined a cult. But now that it was a senator's son who'd joined a domestic terrorist cell, it raised the stakes a bit. Cultists didn't typically make bombs. And people who weren't afraid to use explosives weren't usually afraid of using bullets, either.

She moved in slowly, grabbing cover where she could, until she reached the building with the lit windows. Inside, she heard quiet voices, and for a moment, she thought they were chanting. She moved closer to one of the doors and realized that what she heard were men, in unison, reciting scripture together.

"Blessed be the Lord my strength," they said, "which teacheth my hands to war, and my fingers to fight." Something in their tone raised the gooseflesh on her arms and she thought of her father and the man who killed him.

Otis Meyer was still in prison somewhere, still quoting his scriptures and even teaching Bible studies, she'd been told. And he still believed that what he'd done to her father was an act of obedience that cleansed the world of at least some of its unrighteousness.

She pushed the memory aside and focused on the voices inside.

Charity knew better than to try and see exactly what they were up to. Considering the reconnaissance a success, she withdrew quietly and resumed her run once she reached the road. She pushed herself hard now that other headlights were on the road and the sky was moving from black to gray.

She slowed to a brisk walk for the last half-mile, letting the cold air dry the sweat on her. The shops along Main Street were still dark for the most part, though she saw lights on in the back of Rosie's as they prepared to open early for breakfast. And when she passed the old pharmacy she saw there were lights on in there as well, though she didn't hear any singing this time.

Her phone chirped when she was back in her room. She looked at the number and took it. "Oxham," she said.

Abigail Hunter's voice was flat and the connection was poor. "You're pushing the limits of my good graces," she said.

Charity laid her clothes out on the bed. "I didn't make contact," she said.

"You're dealing with dangerous people here," the woman said. "And you're jeopardizing our own operation."

Our own operation. She wondered what that operation entailed but knew better than to ask. "I'm not interested in jeopardizing your operation but I *am* interested in getting Matthew Rodriguez and taking him home." She started peeling off her wet clothes. "So how do you propose I go about that?"

"With a modicum of patience," she answered. Then, her voice warmed. "Look, Charity, I'm not trying to be a hard-ass. And truth be told, I've gone over your file three times now and I think you could be an asset to us there. Our other asset doesn't have any combat or law enforcement experience."

Our other asset. She noted this and kept listening.

"You'll get your shot at Rodriguez," Hunter said. "But you can't just take him home at this point; he's already gone too far down the wrong road. Your friend's son is an active member of an organization committed to the violent overthrow of the U.S. government and is already documented as an enemy combatant."

She nodded even though there was no one to see it. "I do realize that." She'd tried not to think about it, and not knowing enough details about what the Sons of New Jerusalem were up to, she could only hope that what he'd done so far—if he cooperated—was minor enough that he'd weather that storm. It would likely destroy his mother's political future though, and knowing her tenacity, it would be a slow death. "And at some point soon, one of you needs to bring the senator into the loop on this. She has a right to know that this is far more than her son running away to join a cult."

"We have a timeline for that," Hunter replied. "And we're close to having enough to do something. Meanwhile, you're either part of the problem or part of the solution."

Charity bit her tongue. She was naked now and the room's air felt cold on her clammy skin. "What do you want me to do?"

"Help Molly," Hunter said. "Stay near that girl. Some folks aren't going to take kindly to her and she might need your help."

How does Molly fit into this? "Is she your other asset?" She asked the question though she was convinced she'd get no real answer.

Hunter surprised her. "She isn't. But we work for separate sides of the same foundation. Her assignment there is entirely funded by them. I'd like you to keep an eye on her. Get her through her first event safe and sound and we'll do what we can about the boy."

"If you're setting up a raid, I want in."

She could hear Hunter's smile on the other end. "I'll take it under advisement. Until then, stay away from the church."

The phone chirped off and Charity turned the water on as hot as she could get it. She showered quickly, dressed faster, and was at the door of Rosie's, Bible in hand, when they opened for breakfast.

George Applebaum watched the tip of the rod bend violently and reached for it even as the line started spinning out.

They were anchored at the mouth of the Columbia within view of the new bridge that connected Astoria, Oregon to the remote corner of Pacific County, Washington. There, in plain sight, they poached salmon with a dozen other small boats.

"State Wildlife does a fly-over every few weeks and grabs what IDs they can," Billy had told him when he'd initially blanched at the idea. "They send someone around maybe once a month by boat." Frost grinned. "But I have affiliates in Olympia who make sure we get a phone call on those days. We activate the prayer chain and sure enough, no one goes fishing then. And for the most part, they look the other way if we're only taking one or two." Then, he tapped the leather book that rested open on his lap. "Way I see it," Frost continued, "the earth is the Lord's and the fullness thereof."

George forced a grin that he didn't feel. "God's fish?"

"Yes sir," Billy said. "God's fish for God's boys."

So, reluctantly, George had baited up and dropped his line in the water.

Now, something large and full of fight pulled at the line and he gripped the cork-wrapped handle with a white knuckled fist as his other hand worked the reel. When the fish broke the surface, it startled him and he almost dropped the rod over the side.

Frost laughed deep from his belly. "Now don't fall out, George."

He braced himself and kept reeling, feeling the salmon pull this way and that as it tried to escape. When he got it close enough to the boat, Billy bent over the side with a net and scooped it in. It thrashed about until the more experienced fisherman could get a hold of it, remove the hook, and club it. There was a tag on its fin that George pointed out and Frost's knife was out, removing it and tossing it over the side.

"What tag?" he asked, holding up bloodstained hands to heaven.

They paused to offer a prayer of thanks before slipping the fish into the cooler of ice to lay alongside the two Frost had caught earlier.

Then, they re-baited George's hook and slipped it over the side. "We'll barbecue one of these up tonight, I reckon. Serve it up with lemon and garlic butter and a bit of pilaf. I might have some of Sister Mary's squash laying around."

George nodded. "Sounds good."

It was a gray day, but the rain had let up and the sun hung like a white disk behind its veil of cloud cover. A brisk wind on the water bordered on cold. Billy reached for the thermos and topped off their mugs, then dug out two sandwiches, passing one over to George.

"So I figure," he said, "that we need to talk some."

George nodded slowly, wishing the hot coffee would warm the ice forming in his stomach. "What happened with those boys, Billy?"

Frost looked around as if to be sure no one was in earshot. "You want it soft serve or hard?"

"I want the truth," George said. "The *honest-to-God* what happened."

Frost sighed, was quiet for a moment, and then looked up with hard eyes. "I'll tell you everything, George. But first, I need you to do something for me."

George tried to read the expression on the man's face but couldn't. "What?"

"Take off your clothes, George."

George blinked. "Take off my clothes?"

Frost nodded. "Take 'em off. Every stitch."

"Why would I—"

Frost's eyes narrowed. "If you want to talk, I'm fine with talking. But it'll be between you and me and the Lord God His Ownself. No one else."

George thought about the suitcase, packed for travel, and ready a day ahead for the agents to pick up. *He knows.*

The wiry man reached beneath the seat and pulled out a wad of clothing. George saw pair of sweats, a CHRIST IS LORD T-shirt, a lightweight windbreaker, and a pair of rubber boots. "You can put these on. It wouldn't do for folks to see a naked preacher in my boat." His grin seemed sincere.

George kicked off his shoes and started peeling off his socks. Billy grabbed them up as they came off and tossed them over the side. George started to protest but Frost raised his eyebrows. He fished his wallet and keys out of his pants and looked for a place to set them. Frost extended a hand.

"Not these too," George said.

"Every stitch," Frost answered.

George placed them in the waiting hand and watched them plunk into the water. Then, he watched as his Bible followed.

"That part grieves me," Frost said, "but I've got another you can have."

George stripped in silence, realizing suddenly that if they really *had* doctored everything he'd brought, it meant they knew this was happening. But he knew better than to expect them to swoop in now and pull him out. When he was finished, Frost pushed the clothing into his hands and he dressed, already shivering from the cold. He sat heavily and glared.

"Now tell me," George Applebaum said.

Billy Frost nodded. "I sent those boys out your way, George, on the Lord's work. I did it and I'd do it again." He leaned forward. "I feel bad that they blew themselves up and I feel bad that I involved you and your church in any way. But I'd do it again." He sighed again. "Hell, I *am* doing it again right now."

George didn't know what to say. He simply blinked and waited for Billy to continue.

"World's going the wrong way," Frost said in a quiet voice. "Moving away from Armageddon and back toward a false and godless Eden. And isn't it funny how the further we move down this road—sustainable this, recyclable that—the less relevant and more sinful this once great Christian nation becomes. We're making Jesus weep, Brother." He tapped the Bible in his lap. "Now I know you believe this book. I remember preaching it with you on the highways and the byways of Texas."

The memory of it intruded involuntarily. For a moment, the smell of fish and coffee and peanut butter was replaced with the smell of hot asphalt and sweat. George opened his mouth to say something, then closed it to let Billy continue.

"And I know you know how it's *supposed* to end," Frost said. "Once this world is used up, a new one awaits God's faithful." He licked his lips, then recited the verse from memory. "'And I saw a new heaven and a new earth: for the first heaven and the first earth were passed away; and there was no more sea.'"

George nodded and picked up where Frost left off. "'And I John saw the holy city, new Jerusalem, coming down from God out of heaven, prepared as a bride adorned for her husband.'"

Then, they were reciting the words in unison and George felt a collision of emotions—nostalgia and doubt and regret—as they finished. "'And I heard a great voice out of heaven saying, Behold, the tabernacle of God is with men, and he will dwell with them, and they shall be his people, and God himself shall be with them, and be their God.'"

They stopped there, though George knew well what followed. Tears wiped away. No more sorrow. No more pain. *For the former things are passed away.*

They were quiet together for a minute and George thought about it. He'd not heard anything that surprised him, but he realized now that knowing it rather than supposing it added a layer of sadness he was unprepared for. The man he'd known had become someone else. Somehow, his faith and zeal had crossed that line into something dangerous for anyone who didn't agree, and George realized now that the line where that happened was blurry indeed. And here, in the rural outlands, with small towns largely abandoned by government and left to die a slow and lingering death, George could imagine Frost's message of hastening Armageddon with a zealous push here or there was gasoline on a mountain of dry sticks.

"So it's true," he said quietly, looking away.

"Yes," Frost said. "It's true."

George hesitated before his next words, not sure if he should say anything or not. "You know that they know, right?"

Frost shrugged. "Sure I do. And when they come for me, I'll go. I've got no trouble telling the truth with my hand on God's holy book. His work is bigger than the folks He uses to do it." He paused for a moment and George saw the lines of conviction on his face. "I'm doing the right thing here, George."

No, George thought, but you think that you are. *Just like I thought for most of my life.* Only this man who used to be his friend had taken a road that he could not fathom. He'd done his share of railing against the system and complaining about the emerging new world order that his own grandfather had likely preached against. But what did it take to tip a frustrated, backward grasping toward a perception of better times into a quiet, resolved rage? A rage that turned to violence to force change?

He tried to think of something to say but could find no words.

Frost offered a strained smile. "I know this is hard. And I'm sorry for it. But it's the truth, Brother. And the Lord himself said he did not come to bring peace but a sword." He lifted his rod and started reeling in the line. "I've got some work today. Visitations to make. I'd like you to come with me."

George felt sick. "I think I should head home, Billy." He thought about the keys now at the bottom of the river. "I can call someone. Or maybe get a ride from someone."

But Billy shook his head. "Too late for that, George. I'm afraid I have to keep you around for a bit longer."

When he opened his mouth to protest, Billy drew an old revolver from his jacket pocket with a heavy sigh. "This," he said, "is one of those moments that you accept the thing that you cannot change, Brother."

After throwing up over the side of the boat, George Applebaum reeled in his own line, stowed his rod, and sat in silence while Frost fired up the engine and pointed them upriver.

As the water slapped the boat and the wind moved over him, George closed his eyes and tried once again to pray.

But now, more than ever, he suspected strongly that no one was really listening after all.

Charity Oxham lowered the handles of the wheelbarrow and wiped the sweat from her forehead. It was a cool day, overcast yet dry so far, but running up and down Cathlamet's residential streets hauling Molly's donations was tiring work.

She'd approached the girl after breakfast, catching her as she mopped the tile floors of the storefront. She'd transformed the space into something passable and had hung a cardboard sign on the door declaring that the Cathlamet Community Club would open on Friday with its kick-off event.

The girl was surprised at Charity's offer of help and took one look at her navy blue skirt, gray blouse, and pumps before grinning. "I'd love your help," she said, "but you're not dressed for it."

So fifteen minutes later, she was back in a sweatsuit and ball cap still damp from her morning run. They walked to the hardware store and bought the wheelbarrow first. From there, it was a morning of walking and pushing.

They went out together from house to house. Molly introduced herself to each person who answered, telling those who'd listen what she was doing with the old Cathlamet Pharmacy and dropping off simple fliers with anyone who'd take them. If a person expressed interest, she shared more and then put what she called "the ask" to them.

"What's one thing you have lying around that you can live without?"

Charity had never seen anything like it. Slowly, the wheelbarrow filled. Old candles. Tattered paperbacks. Cans of food and bags of beans. Sacks of clothing and an old blanket. Some even had larger items—an old sofa, a paint-splattered wooden chair—that they promised to put out on the street. She had no idea what Molly would do with it all, and when she asked between houses, the young woman shrugged.

"Hard to say. But I'm sure we'll find a use."

Charity shook her head. "And this heals the world how?"

"Just watch," Molly said with a grin.

They pushed the latest haul through the glass doors and unloaded quickly, stacking like items with like items around the edges of the room. Then, they sat against the wall and nibbled on salami sandwiches while Molly checked her list and Charity read the flier again.

"A casserole cook-off?" she asked between bites.

Molly looked up, her pencil poised above the sheet. She grinned. "I make a pretty bad-ass casserole." She slid the pencil behind her ear. "It's just an excuse, really, to get people together."

"And once they're together?"

The young woman sipped her Dr. Pepper. "We'll just talk. And we'll keep getting them together. We'll find out what needs doing around here and then we'll go do it. Towns like Cathlamet have lost the tax base for government sponsored community programs. There are other groups filling in those gaps but some of them are—" Here, she paused and Charity watched her look for more careful wording. "Some of those groups have a less positive agenda."

She knows. It wasn't clear just how much, but it stood to reason she'd know something. This foundation intrigued her more and more—a charitable organization that combined guns with casseroles to do its work.

She opened her mouth to ask another question but a knock at the door interrupted her. She looked up to see two men standing in the doorway. The first was tall and nearly gaunt, his salt and pepper hair close-cropped over jutting ears and his intense blue eyes and crooked grin oddly charismatic. He wore jeans and a dress shirt with a western-style tie. His companion looked less comfortable. He was a larger man wearing ill-fitting slacks and a sweater, his gray hair thinning and his expression blank.

Molly stood. Charity did the same.

"Good afternoon, ladies," the first man said with a lazy southern drawl. The man behind him said nothing.

Charity watched recognition flash across Molly's face, then watched her subdue it. The young woman stepped forward and extended her hand. "I'm Molly Clark," she said. "This is my friend Charity."

"Pastor Billy Frost," the man answered. "And this is my friend

George Applebaum. A visiting pastor from Portland. We wanted to come by and introduce ourselves, welcome you proper-like."

Frost. He didn't look the way she'd imagined the head of a terrorist organization might look, but Charity knew from experience that they rarely did.

She glanced at Molly, whose posture and tone suggested something more formal, more guarded than what she'd seen of the girl so far. "I appreciate the welcome, Pastor Frost."

Frost held up one of her fliers and his smile widened. "I love a good casserole. When I heard Bob Drexler's old pharmacy had been bought, I had no idea it was going to be used for the community."

"It was centrally located and empty," Molly said. "It seemed like a good spot."

The minister looked around the room. His friend was oddly silent, and when Charity made brief eye contact with him, he looked away. She saw something in his eyes that gave her pause.

He's afraid. And he should be, she thought.

"So do you both work for this so-called foundation?" Frost asked, walking over to one pile of donated odds and ends.

"Just me," Molly said. "Charity is helping out for a day or two."

He looked up and at Charity. She watched his eyes move over her in a calculating way. "You're also new in town."

"I'm on my way back to Longview," Charity lied. "I've been on vacation at the coast."

Frost nodded. "Not much of a place for a potluck."

"It'll do." Molly's smile was brief.

His own smile was expansive. "Why don't you let me help you out some. How about I make my fellowship hall available for you out at Wahkiakum Bible Temple? We have ovens and tables and chairs. Nice comfortable place."

Molly shook her head. "I've already distributed the fliers."

"Oh, most folks round here are easy enough to contact," Frost said. "We've got enough time to get the word out."

"I really appreciate the offer," Molly said, "but I think we need to stay with our plan. We want folks to see this as their gathering place and they can't do that unless they . . . well . . . *gather* here."

At first, she thought Frost would argue, but instead, he turned those calculating eyes to Molly, sized her up, and then nodded. "Fair enough."

But there was ice in his voice when he said it.

Molly repeated herself, this time firmly but with a smile. "I really do appreciate the offer, though, Pastor Frost."

He stared at her for a moment longer, his eyes hard beneath furrowed eyebrows. "Just keep in mind, Miss Clark, that Cathlamet is a town that was chock full of community before you and your foundation ever showed up. And that community is Wahkiakum Bible Temple . . . God's community."

Her smile was sweet but challenging. "Not everyone believes in God, Pastor Frost. Those folks need community, too."

"Around here," he said, "they *do* believe. So you just be careful which boats you go rocking."

With a last smile, he and his friend left.

Molly sighed and shuddered after he left. "That man is dangerous," she said in a quiet voice.

Yes. He is. "Even his friend is afraid of him," she said.

She wanted to ask Molly how she knew George Applebaum but decided not to ask. Instead, she went back to her sandwich as Molly went back to her list.

Outside, the rain started up again.

What started as a drizzle became a downpour as Frost's pickup made its way back to the church buildings.

After their conversation in the boat, Frost had made only a half-hearted effort to conceal what he was up to, taking calls on an old-fashioned brick-style cell phone with frantic voices on the other end. They spoke in some kind of code, George thought, making references to pies and chickens or to obscure scripture references that even he couldn't conjure up in memory. But still, he was talking . . . a lot. And he'd even taken him to visit Molly.

She'd done a good job of pretending they'd never met, and he wondered why. Of course, his conversation with Frost on their way to the old pharmacy was enough to convince him to do the same. It was obvious from the time he took the call from Steve Wilkes that Frost bore the girl ill will. They'd exchanged words, Billy's voice rising in frustration. "No," he told the associate pastor, "*you* wait for the doctor. I'll see to her."

Truck tires crunched the gravel of the church driveway and

George looked up to see a scattering of cars in the parking lot. He saw Steve Wilkes getting out of one, accompanied by a dark-skinned man in a green windbreaker, carrying a black case. He watched them walk quickly to one of the side buildings and disappear around a corner.

The doctor. For whom? He thought about the young men he'd see running earlier. And the four others he'd met in Portland. George looked away quickly, hoping Billy didn't notice. They parked and went inside.

Frost led him past his office and into the foyer. The doors to the sanctuary were open and George heard angry voices inside. "Now, listen," Frost said. "I'm bringing you with me to this. I don't have to, you know. We could do this without you."

George's look of puzzlement must have been obvious.

"This meeting," Frost said, "is about what to do with you, Brother George. Among other things."

"What to do with me?"

Frost nodded. "I don't make all of the decisions around here. I figure the least I owe you is an opportunity to hear the argument with your own ears." He scratched his gray hair. "It'll save me explaining it to you later, I reckon."

Frost slipped into the room then and George followed after. The room went quiet when they did. He felt the eyes upon him as they walked to the front and sat.

"So boys," Billy said, "I figure we have some things to sort out. First, there's the matter of the arrests. A lot of us are going away and we have families to provide for and chores to finish." He looked at George. "And some messes to clean up." He glanced across the circle of chairs to an older man. "Brother Tom, will you open us with a word of prayer?"

They bowed their heads. When the "amen" was uttered, Billy launched right into business. George noted that Wilkes had slipped into the room and now sat just outside the circle. He and Frost exchanged a look.

"We are underway, Brothers," Frost said. "I'll keep this brief. We have strangers in the yard. Two women up at the pharmacy. One says she's passing through but I don't like the look of her. Her friend's staying up at Drexler's and she'll be having her first event tomorrow evening. Let's make sure it's her last." He thought for a moment. "Don't hurt her. Just help her out of town."

The man to his left nodded. "I'll put out a call."

"Good. Now, I won't always be around to keep the wolves out of the pasture. So make sure whoever you call understands that more are no doubt coming." He raised his eyebrows in Wilkes' direction. "What do you have, Brother Steve?"

"Tomorrow night," he said. "Two by two, just like you said."

Frost smiled. "That's what I like to hear." He looked at George. "Now we have another decision to make." He stood and smoothed his slacks. "I've known Brother George here for a good long while. We preached together. We studied together. We're going to have to keep him quiet for a few days and I don't take to the notion of shooting him in the head, though I will if I need to." He raised his eyebrows and nodded slightly in George's direction with the words. "But I think he's harmless enough now. We've burned or drowned all his things."

"Leo's son says they were riddled with bugs," another of the older men said.

"I'm certain of it," Billy said. "But notice that they haven't come rushing in to rescue him." He gave George a hard look. "Tossed aside, Brother. Used and discarded."

George said nothing.

"And that tells *me*," Frost continued, "that they already know what they need to know and it's just a matter of time. So: What do we do with my friend here, meanwhile?"

"I could call my nephew," said one of the men. "We could stash him in the solitary at County for a few days."

Frost shook his head. "Frank's with us and so are a bunch of the others, but not everyone is. Last thing we need is more curiosity from Johnny Law."

Wilkes looked up and George saw his eyes were cold and far away. "I still think you should've put him in the river, Brother Bill."

Billy smiled. "I know you do. But that's a permanent solution for a temporary problem. And he can't learn if he's dead." He put a hand on George's shoulder. George flinched from the touch. If Frost noticed, he hid it well. "George here is a good man. Of that I have no doubt. And it was unfair of us to involve him and his flock in our little venture without discussing it with him first, though that would've been a bit . . . impractical. And frankly, if our boys hadn't blown themselves up it would've never been an issue."

George sat and listened to them go back and forth for another twenty minutes and as he did, he realized that though he was afraid, another emotion was kindled alongside that fear. He was angry. He felt it build and finally, he looked up.

"I'd like to say something," he said.

Frost stopped mid-sentence and George felt all eyes upon him. The room was quiet and he took a deep breath. Then, he looked at each of the dozen men slowly. "What you're doing here," he finally said, "is wrong."

One of the men started to protest and Frost quieted him with a glance before sitting down. "You have the floor, Brother George."

George stood and felt his legs shaking beneath him. "You all can do what you want with me," he said. "But hear me: What you're doing is against everything Christianity teaches. You're killing people to make your point. You're sending young men out—" Here, he looked at Wilkes, "—two by two with their bombs and your agenda. This is not the way to change the world. Find a better path."

The words fell from his mouth awkwardly, all the anger burning itself out before it had a chance to blaze. He looked around again and sat.

"Actually," Frost said, "way I see it, we're actually quite right, George. The Lord brought a sword, not peace. The Good Book says he fashioned a whip—a whip, mind you—and chased the moneylenders out of his Father's house. The Good Book says beat your swords into ploughshares, but also says beat your ploughshares into swords. 'The kingdom of heaven suffereth violence *and the violent take it by force.'*"

Then the Good Book is wrong. Clarity dawned from the fog of doubt. "Look," George finally said, "there's no way I can convince you you're wrong any more than you can convince me that you're right. So make up your minds and do what you want with me."

The rest of the meeting moved quickly. In the end, George left the same way he came, riding next to Billy in his old pickup truck. They took the long way around the island and they didn't talk. When they reached the parsonage, one of Frost's elders was leaving with a toolbox in hand. He handed Billy a set of keys. "It should hold just fine," he said on his way out.

George went straight to the room and sat on the bed. Frost followed, placing a Bible on the bed beside him. He looked at the book, but instead of finding comfort, he found violence and bloodshed, a fascination with Armageddon with no regard for Eden.

"I'm truly sorry about this, George," Frost told him, patting his jacket pocket. "Three days, tops. I'll bring up some food later."

George said nothing. When Frost left, he heard the padlocks snapping shut in their hasps and he realized that despite the locks and the man with the pistol outside, he had a sense of freedom he'd not possessed before.

The sky was growing dark when Charity and Molly wheeled the last load of donations into the pharmacy. They quickly stacked the items and then stood back to admire their handiwork. Tomorrow was Friday. They'd spend the day putting finishing touches on the space and then enlist other volunteers to help carry folding chairs from the County boardroom and the library. Then, Molly would cook up her casseroles in the Bradley House's oven—an arrangement Charity had helped broker—and the Wahkiakum Community Center would hold its first event.

Charity wondered what they might expect in the way of a turnout. She also wondered about Frost and his fundamentalist friends. She'd not liked the cold, calculating look in his eye, and it wouldn't surprise her if he himself appeared or at the very least sent some of his men to keep an eye on things.

Or close them down.

She pushed the thought away and turned to the girl. "So . . . how about dinner?"

Molly smiled. "Rain check?"

Charity nodded. "Sure. What time do you want me back tomorrow?"

Molly looked surprised. "You're coming back for more?"

She grinned. "Wouldn't miss it."

The girl looked thoughtful for a moment, as if she were working out a math equation, and walked quickly to her pack. "You've been really helpful today. I want to give you something." She reached into her backpack and drew out a plain book, which she handed to Charity. "It's what I believe," she said. "It's why I'm here."

Charity took the book and looked at it. *A Symmetry Framed.* She'd never heard of the author—a one-word name. Bashar.

"Thank you," she said.

Then, they hugged and she headed to Rosie's for a quick meal—

meatloaf, mashed potatoes and rich, dark gravy that she soaked up with fresh rolls and chased with ice-cold milk. She looked over the book while she ate. It was a collection of stories about a man she'd never heard of who'd showed up unexpectedly at the mythical city of Cascadiapolis, supposedly hidden in the Cascades somewhere near Portland. It followed his brief time there and included bits of cobbled together information about his earlier life, the anecdotes and fables he told and the songs he sang, his famous stews and soups. And it chronicled his death at the hands of violent men who did not comprehend his message.

The man who'd written it all down—this Bashar—had been head of security for Cascadiapolis. Other than his first person narrative, though, any other details about the man were absent from the book. If he still lived he had to be past eighty by now.

Curious, Charity opened the book to the copyright page. It had been published last year, from a surprising source.

The J. Appleseed Foundation. Neither Hunter nor Molly had mentioned the name of the foundation before. Now, the symbolism in the name made Charity smile.

Closing the book, she finished her dinner, paid up, and walked across the street to the bed and breakfast.

Mrs. Cooper was having tea in the dining room with two other guests when she arrived. "Miss Jensen?"

Charity nearly kept walking, her mind not registering the name as the one she'd registered under. She stopped, midway up the stairs. "Yes?"

"You've a message, dear." The woman stood and bustled off to her desk to recover a slip of paper. "It was family." She studied the note. "Your Aunt Abigail. She wanted you to call right away."

Why is she calling the bed and breakfast?

She used the house's single landline phone.

"Charity," Abigail Hunter said, "it's good to hear your voice. How's your vacation?"

Charity played along. "It's going very well. I've been helping out at the local community center."

"I'm glad to hear it," Hunter said. "Now, do you remember I told you we had family there in town? His name is George. I think he's out on that island there. We've fallen out of touch. I'm hoping you can look in on him for me."

George. The man with Frost earlier, who had looked so uncomfortable. "I think I might've met him today."

"Well, I'd love for you to look him up for me. I'm sure he'd appreciate a *friendly* face."

"I'll see what I can do," she said. Hunter's meaning was clear and Charity only hoped any listening ears weren't clever enough to follow the subtext of the conversation. Their man in Cathlamet had been found out and was likely in trouble. She sighed.

Back in her room, she sat on the bed and watched the darkness fall outside. There'd been no point in showering or changing her clothes. Not with another night run coming up.

So instead, she read more of the book Molly gave her and waited for the middle of the night.

George lay still in the bed and collected himself, ignoring both the book and the food Frost had brought him hours earlier. Outside, he could hear the rain against his window. Downstairs, he could hear Billy's voice again. Something about Sam's blankets nearly being ready for delivery. More coded conversation, he suspected, spread over several calls received over an old-fashioned landline with a shrill ring.

The longer he lay there, the more he thought. And the more he thought, the more his head hurt.

Two by two. If it meant what he thought, then more teams were going out into the world to carry the message of Frost's twisted faith.

George stood slowly and went back to the window. They'd been bolted shut, the wood shavings left on the sill in the deacon's hurry. The window itself would be easy enough to break, but not without alerting Frost. And it would take more time to climb down from the second story than it would for Billy and his pistol to reach the back door.

Still, it was either climb or try to overpower Billy.

Or do nothing. But doing nothing, he realized, meant people could die.

George sighed and returned to the bed. He glanced to the clock radio to check the time and then blinked. He reached for it, slid the lever to radio and heard the static. Feeling along the side of it with his fingers, George found the volume dial, and slid it down and then up. Then, he glanced at the wooden chair at the small desk.

It might work. He could use the radio to lure Frost upstairs, maybe even drown out some of the sound of breaking glass and buy him a few extra precious minutes to climb down and make his escape.

He could feel his heartbeat in his temples, keeping time with the throbbing of his head as he turned on the radio and spun the AM dial. When he reached Frost's own voice, he stopped and smiled. He was shouting, impassioned, about the Shekinah glory of Christ, and it must have been a live recording played on the airwaves by some small local station.

Turning the volume as loud as it would go, he stood and lifted the chair. He heard Billy below.

"What are you up to, George?"

He heard the creaking of the stairs as Billy approached. George waited until he heard the footsteps in the hall. Then, he shoved the chair through the glass. He crawled out of the window, slipped, slid and caught himself on the gutter before falling into the yard below.

The air went out of him and he felt a sharp pain in his shoulder as he rolled into a ball.

"George!" He could hear the anger in Billy's voice. "Goddammit, I told you." George looked up and saw him leaning from the window of his room. "It was only three days." He turned away, moving quickly.

George climbed to his feet and lurched into a clumsy run. He had to get into the scrub by the side of the road if he was going to have any chance of getting away.

And he had to hope that Frost would find it harder to kill someone with the gun in his own hand instead of through one of his young disciples.

George pushed himself and heard Billy behind him somewhere now, shouting for him to stop. He didn't and he flinched when he heard Billy's first shot ring out. He heard a cry—something too low for a scream and too high for a shout—then realized he was the one who made the sound. He cut to the left.

"This is pointless, George," Billy yelled, his own breath ragged. "There's no place for you to go."

He kept running and heard another shot behind him. Almost simultaneously, he heard the bullet tearing up gravel as it nipped the ground just ahead of him. He reached the brush and crouched, changing direction again, running parallel to the road.

Suddenly, a dark shape leaped up ahead of him from the ground and strong hands grabbed his shoulders. He was pulled in and down and he felt hot breath at his ear. "Get down," a woman's voice whispered.

He let her force him to the ground and he lay prone, trying to slow his heavy breathing. His side ached and he only now became aware of just how badly his shoulder hurt.

Whoever had pulled him down had moved off quietly and all he could hear now was the sound of Frost approaching. He rolled onto his back in time to see the man striding toward him through the brush, the pistol raised from an extended arm. As frightening as the gun, the look on his face was one of dangerous rage. When he spoke, his voice trembled and spittle flew from his lower lip. "Goddamn you, George. God *fucking* damn you."

He's going to shoot me.

But suddenly, Frost's head rocked to the side and George heard the sound of something cracking. The pistol dropped and the man went down hard in the dirt. The woman scooped up the pistol. He couldn't make out her features in the dark, but when she spoke, the voice was familiar.

"Hi, George," she said, holding the pistol in a way that told him she knew how to use it. "Aunt Abigail says hello."

Frost was coming to just as Charity finished duct-taping him to the chair. She'd sent Applebaum upstairs to find darker clothing and better shoes, and now she could hear him clattering around up there. Frost's eyes were fluttering and she dropped the pillowcase over his head. He and the dining room chair barely fit in the small ground-floor restroom but he'd be less likely to tip the chair over.

When he spoke, his voice was heavily distorted by the broken jaw. "You're declaring war on the Most High God," he said. "And His angels will smite you for raising your hand to His people."

Charity ignored him, turning away from the bathroom to find the phone lines and cut them with the rusty old Leatherman she'd found in a kitchen drawer along with a handful of .38 rounds and the tape.

Then, she checked the house quickly again, whistling loudly for George. When he came down the stairs, he was dressed in a dark tracksuit and a pair of sneakers.

She nodded toward the door and he moved to it. She closed the bathroom door and followed him outside. Charity wasn't sure how much time this would give her, but she doubted it would be much. By morning, when they couldn't find their pastor, they'd come looking. By then, she needed to be leaving with Matthew Rodriguez. And George, too, it seemed.

She studied him. He was a large man with dark circles under his eyes. He was going to slow her down. Still, she could hide him with Molly for a few hours and then track down Matthew. But what then? Extricate him by force? She had maybe ten shots, and these antique revolvers were painfully slow to reload. Still, it was better than nothing.

She pulled Frost's keys from her pocket and pointed to the truck. "Get in."

He climbed into the cab, and once he was in, she looked back at the house, now dark, for one final check. Then, she climbed behind the wheel, turned the engine over, and backed down the driveway with her lights off, letting the feel of the tires on the gravel guide her.

"You work with Patriot then," he said as the surface beneath them changed to blacktop.

"Not really," she said. "But Hunter told me to come find you. I'm looking for one of Frost's followers. Matthew Rodriguez. Do you know him?"

He shook his head. "I don't."

She turned the truck toward town. "He came in to the church on a bus with about twenty other men."

She heard the man swallow. "They're the ones staying at the church. Billy is sending them out soon."

Not to preach or pass out leaflets, she thought. *To build more bombs.* "Not if I can help it," she said.

Charity knew Hunter would not be happy about this, but she was the one who sent her in for George. And Charity was the soldier on the ground. They took several turns, and when the bridge was in sight, she switched on the lights.

"You remember Molly?" she asked.

George nodded.

"I'm going to leave you with her. Stay out of sight until I get back. Then we'll find a phone and get Hunter down here."

He nodded again. They pulled up to the pharmacy and she left the truck running as she jumped out and ran to the door. Molly opened it on the third knock, rubbing sleep from her eyes.

"Charity, what are you—"

"I need you to keep an eye on him," she interrupted, nodding at George. "I'll be back in an hour, two tops."

She could see the confusion on the girl's face. "I don't understand what's going on."

She looked at George. "He can fill you in on some of it; I'll explain the rest later. Just keep him here until I get back."

The girl nodded slowly, reluctance fighting with trust. "Okay."

Charity climbed back into the truck, pulled the pistol from her pocket, and placed it on the seat behind her. She saw them vanish into the building and close the door, then backed into the street and sped to Puget Island.

She turned out the truck's lights as she approached the church and parked near the door marked "Office." There were no other cars in the lot other than the white bus, and none of the buildings were lit.

She didn't bother concealing the pistol. Charity jogged along the sidewalk toward the building she assumed was a barracks ... the long low building where she'd heard them reciting scripture the night before. There were doors at either end and she tried the one facing the street first. It was locked.

Charity moved around to the back of the building, listening for any sound of them. It was nearly two o'clock, and if they were keeping to a three o'clock run they'd be waking up soon.

She tried the next door. Also locked.

She placed her hand flat upon the door and pushed, testing its sturdiness. She'd dislocate a shoulder on this door. And she didn't want to waste a bullet on the deadbolt. Not to mention the attention the noise would draw. She retraced her steps next, checking each window until she found one with open curtains.

She stretched onto the tips of her toes and squinted into the dark room, her eyes picking out the shapes of bunk beds and wall lockers arranged barracks-style.

The beds were empty.

That bastard's already sent them. Two by two, George had told her. Enough to fit into a car or a boat heading up or down river. Portland and Seattle were in close reach, and there they could swap cars and pick their next city. She envisioned a network of churches, all happy to lend cars they could later report stolen, or sold ridiculously cheap.

Eventually, the young men would reach their destinations and do what they'd been trained to do.

Charity turned away from the empty barracks, tossed Frost's keys onto the roof of his church and set out at a run for the bridge.

As she ran, she tried to use the exercise to bring her focus. She pulled her breath in at a count of four, then pushed it out, feeling the solid slap of the ground against her feet.

I'm sorry, Sandra, she thought. This one had turned on her. Another so-called bag and tag gone wrong. She felt a stab of guilt and quickly pushed it aside. Matthew had made his own choices. And she'd tried to help a friend without fully understanding what her friend's son had been planning. This was a criminal matter now and she needed to contact Rodriguez and let her know what was happening. *Fuck Hunter and her operation.*

Charity ran, stretching her legs, and turned her mind to what would come next. She'd leave with George in her rental. She'd kept the tank full. It would take her less than ten minutes to throw her things into her bag and they could be in Portland at the local Edgewater office in about three hours.

It was as good a plan as any at this point.

Outside, a solitary dog barked, and George jumped at the noise. His shoulder still throbbed, and every noise caught his breath in his throat.

When Molly saw him trembling, she put on water and mixed him a concoction of instant coffee and instant cocoa, boiling hot and served up with four Ibuprofens. He held the old ceramic mug and sat in the corner.

"What's going on, George?" she asked.

Something in her eyes—compassion he supposed—prompted him, and he found himself laying the entire story out before her. As he did, it suddenly struck him just how far afield from his own life and experiences this had taken him, and he found himself fighting tears. When they did finally leak out, the girl put a hand on his shoulder and squeezed it. "You've been through a lot," she said.

He nodded. "I surely have." And out of all the events of the last three days, the one thing that stood out most for him was that look in Frost's eyes just before Charity hit him with the board. He'd seen rage there mingled with something dark and insane.

Something capable of killing.

Maybe, he thought, a religion founded upon the principle of shedding blood in exchange for life was destined to breed that level of crazy. If the God you worshiped was willing to kill to make His point, why wouldn't you be willing to do the same? He shook the thought away, foreign and frightening. "I just don't get it," he said. "Billy and I were friends. We preached the streets together in seminary. I don't understand how things could go so differently—so wrongly—for him."

Molly's voice was low and soothing. "People change. Mix in a sense of being disenfranchised with a bit of religious zeal and it can be pretty toxic."

He nodded.

She said nothing for a minute and he realized that her hand hadn't moved. It felt good there, reassuring. And even though there was nothing sexual about it, he still blushed. It was more familiarity with a woman than he'd experienced these last thirty years or so.

Molly continued. "These rural areas are riddled with pockets of discontented, angry people who feel trapped in poverty and cut off from the mainstream. The urban will for rural subsidy vanished during the economic collapses. Not even the reform years could help the shrinking tax base, and without the natural resource industry to support them, towns like Cathlamet are awash with bitter citizens longing for change. Add a little 'pie in the sky by and by' to that and . . . voila."

George could see it. Was it Marx who'd said religion was the opiate of the masses? He realized it may well be in some instances.

But in others, it's a lit match to the kindling of discontent and anger.

Molly moved her hand when his shaking stopped, and she sat beside him as he slipped the hot beverage. After maybe an hour, he heard three light taps at the door, and Molly went to it quickly to let Charity in.

The woman was dressed now in a plain navy blue dress. She carried a suitcase as she closed the door behind her, working the lock. The pocket on the right side of her open raincoat bulged where she no doubt kept Frost's pistol. George found himself admiring the strength he saw there. Her eyes were hard and level, moving over the room with practiced care, and her posture and jawline were confidently set. "My truck's in front of the bed and breakfast," she said. "We'll hit the highway, find a signal and call Hunter, then head for Longview."

He felt relief flooding him. He looked at Molly. "Are you packed, too?"

She shook her head. "I'm not going. I have work here to do."

He blinked. "But Frost has people coming for you. They want you out of town."

She shrugged. "Not everyone gets what they want."

George looked at Charity. "You tell her."

Charity shook her head. "She's her own woman, George." He watched her pull a pair of glasses from her purse—expensive, top shelf ones like the glasses Hunter and her partner wore. She passed them over to him. "Wear these. If you get a signal, call Hunter."

He took the glasses and put them on, rolling his eyes to synchronize them. Nothing but white light and white noise. He set them to search for a signal and turned down the glare. Then, he looked at Molly.

She smiled at him. "I'll be fine, George."

He wanted to believe her, and he marveled at the faith on her face. No, he realized, not faith but confidence. He hugged her briefly and then joined Charity by the door.

"It's the gray Ford across the street," she told him before looking to Molly again. "Are you sure about this?"

The girl nodded. "I am."

Then, she held open the door with one hand as her other slipped into her pocket. George moved through the door first and she caught up quickly, her eyes scanning a main street dimly lit by dirty streetlamps spread too far apart.

They reached the Ford and she tossed her suitcase in the back. He climbed into the cab and buckled in, glancing across the street again. George sighed and Charity looked at him.

"She's a tough one," she said. "And I'm willing to bet Hunter and her team aren't far away."

"I hope you're right."

There was something profound about the girl that he struggled to name. Beyond her earnestness she was . . . good. She knew something *true* in a real sense. What he'd felt, when he started his road to the pulpit so many years ago, had *seemed* true, but it was more of a hope or a wish. Otherwise, he wouldn't have felt the need to defend it so strongly and conserve its values so strictly.

He turned his thoughts away from Molly and toward Charity.

He wondered what her story was. She didn't talk much and worked with a matter-of-fact precision that marked her as a professional. And though now she looked the part of a conservative woman with a Bible tucked in her purse, he'd seen her in action. He suspected she was military of some kind.

She started the truck and they moved away from the curb, building speed as they headed uphill past the hardware store to the highway. The road was empty and wet and he saw no traffic even out on what used to be State Route 4 and was now just called the Longview-Wahkiakum Road. But as they turned right and headed east, a lone pair of headlights approached and a van sped by. It was full of men and painted white.

George saw the black letters stenciled above its cab as it flashed past. *Wahkiakum Bible Temple.* He craned his neck to look behind him, and when he looked back to Charity, he saw she was watching the rearview mirror as well, biting her lip.

Thirty seconds passed.

"Fuck," she said.

"Fuck," he agreed.

George grabbed for the dashboard when she braked suddenly and pulled into the parking lot of an abandoned gas station to flip the truck around. Accelerating, she put them back on the highway, heading swiftly west.

The church van sat empty outside the pharmacy, its side door still open, as Charity approached. The door to the pharmacy was open, too, and the lights were on.

She slowed the truck and pulled it to the side of the road about a block away, casting a sidelong look to George as she handed him the keys. "Stay here. Stay low. Honk if there's trouble." She waited for his nod before climbing out of the cab.

She walked quickly but quietly toward the pharmacy, her ears straining at the conversation she heard inside.

"I don't think you understand, Miss," she heard one voice say. "We're not here to ask."

Molly's response was too quiet for her to pick out the words, but her tone was confident and unafraid. She'd have labeled the girl naive if she hadn't seen her in action, working the people with more skill than Charity had seen in most officers. Even under pressure, the girl was a leader-in-charge.

She paused outside the door and quickly counted the heads she could see. Three from her vantage point, not counting the man who spoke. Slipping her hand into her pocket, she curled her fingers around the butt of the pistol.

When she walked in, she finished her head count even as she opened her mouth. *Six men.* "Is there a problem here, Molly?"

The girl's posture was calm, but she saw a momentary flicker of relief in her eyes. She started to talk, but the oldest of the men—a sandy-haired man in his thirties—spoke over her. "We're just having a conversation," he said. "You can go about your business."

She smiled. "It's four o'clock in the morning and I see six young men with a girl backed into a corner. I'd say this is my business."

The man turned on her. "And who are you?"

She drew the revolver and pointed it at his chest. "I'm an armed citizen," she said, "who's thinking perhaps *you* and your boys here should be going about *your* own business."

His face turned red. "We're on the Lord's business."

Charity glanced at the wide-eyed faces around her. None of these young men were the caliber of trained soldiers she'd seen earlier, now sent out to scatter their seeds of violence. These were just members of the local Bullies for Christ chapter.

Except for their spokesman. She could see violence in his eyes and a calculating quality that she recognized. Still, smite the shepherd and scatter the flock.

"So what you're telling me is that the Lord has you out at this ungodly hour harassing this solitary woman on her own property with a gang of well-dressed thugs?" She didn't wait for him to answer. "I think you should all be moving along."

The man sneered at her. "There are six of us and you're just a girl with a gun," he said. "The worst you can do is send one or two of us to Glory."

"I'm a *woman* with a gun," she said, "who's served two tours in Iran and one in Honduras. I've participated in police actions in Nigeria and Pakistan." She waved the pistol. "And you're the only one I'd need to send anywhere."

The sudden honking of the truck's horn outside shifted her attention for just a moment and the man surged forward, raising his hands.

She didn't even blink. She squeezed the trigger and put a bullet in his right thigh. He fell to the side, cutting loose with a string of profanity.

She watched the other faces go white. All but Molly's. The girl continued to exude calm. "You boys can leave now," Charity said.

"Help me up," the man she'd shot demanded, but when he moved, she cocked the pistol and shook her head.

"Your friend stays."

Not a word was said. As they crowded their way through the door, she looked beyond them at the mud-spattered SUV that pulled up behind the van. She closed the door and locked it, hoping George was doing what he was told and staying out of sight.

Then, she moved over to the man she'd shot. "And who might you be?" When he didn't immediately answer, she kicked his wounded thigh. "Answer up, Altar Boy."

"Pastor Steve Wilkes," he said, gritting his teeth against the pain.

She knew the name and smiled. "Things are going to get ugly in a minute," she said. "It'll go easier for you if you tell me where Matthew Rodriguez is going."

His initial look was surprise, but she watched him cover it over with something more resolute and less easy to read. "I don't know any Matthew Rodriguez."

There was hammering at the door now, and shouting. She kicked the man's leg again and when he swatted at her, she hit him alongside the head with the barrel of the .38. "Of course you know who he is, Steve. Thou shalt not bear false witness."

His face was purple now with rage. "You fucking bitch," he said. "You have no idea what kind of holy wrath you're bringing down upon yourself."

"I don't believe in holy wrath," Charity said. And then she hit him again. She looked around the room, saw the duct tape, and nodded to it. "Help me out here, Molly. Tape our boy up."

She counted the minutes that passed. A pistol fired, even indoors, was certain to be heard. And the commotion outside at this hour would wake someone up. The sheriff's office was just down the street.

They're not coming. And she doubted it was budgetary constraints that kept them away. They were looking the other way, letting the town's *real* law enforcement take care of local business.

Good, she thought. *I can use that to my advantage.*

The door was cracking at the hinges as something or someone

heavy fell against it. Charity divided her focus between that and the girl working the roll of tape. "Just his hands," she said, then as an afterthought: "And his mouth."

The door was going to give soon and she needed to be out the back with her prisoner when it did. If there was going to be a firefight two blocks from the sheriff's office, she wanted the citizens of Cathlamet to hear it and see it.

She hauled Wilkes up by a bicep. The tape muffled his cry as he forced weight onto his leg. Without being asked, Molly came to his other side and gripped that arm.

They shuffled toward the back room and were halfway there when the front door caved in.

Despite the slur, she knew the voice she heard next, telling her to stop. More familiar than that was the sound of Frost's pump action Remington as he chambered a shell.

George heard the gunshot and found himself fumbling for the door handle, a panic rising in him before he remembered what Charity had told him.

He saw the SUV approaching next, and it all seemed to unwind like a slow-motion action sequence. As it pulled into the parking lot behind the van, the door to the pharmacy opened and five men came tumbling out before the door slammed shut again behind them. Three older men climbed out of the SUV, all holding rifles, and George's mouth fell open.

Frost was already barking orders, and the larger of the men grabbed up an old cylindrical public ashtray and used it to batter the door. Frost and the others huddled with the young men, talking in low tones.

The conversation was brief and Frost's companion took two of the boys around back. Billy and the other three stood by and watched the door as it cracked and groaned.

George felt that panic rising again, but this time, it was accompanied by focus and one clear need.

I have to do something. He looked around the cab for some kind of weapon, then looked at the keys in his hand. He slipped into the driver's seat, buckled the seatbelt, and glanced around the street as he inserted the key. Then, before turning it over, he took the brake off.

The door fell in and Frost moved in with his shotgun raised, shouting for Charity to stop.

George fired up the engine and floored the accelerator, hauling the wheel to the right and jumping the truck onto the sidewalk. He pointed its nose at the door where Frost and his men gathered and forced his eyes wide open to watch as they turned and tried to get clear.

Two of the younger men were just barely fast enough. One was clipped and thrown into the front of the van. Frost flew backwards into the pharmacy, his shotgun discharging as it clattered to the floor. The man with the ashtray threw it up into the air as the driver's side bumper pushed him into the exterior wall with a crunching noise that George could hear over the roar of the engine and the man's sudden, piercing scream.

The air went out of George as the seatbelt caught his forward movement, wrenching his wounded shoulder. Everything was gray for a moment, and then he was free of his seatbelt and sliding from the passenger door to scramble over the smoking hood of the truck.

Frost was stirring when George kicked him back down. He aimed for the shoulder but got the preacher's face instead.

He didn't feel bad about it.

Charity already held the shotgun, and George felt a moment of inadequacy when she turned to Molly. "Do you know how to use this?" she asked.

The girl shook her head. "I can't. I'm a pacifist."

Charity scowled and turned to George. Before she asked, he snatched the shotgun from her hand. "I used to hunt ducks with my dad," he said. He looked down at his former friend's broken nose, the blood running into his mouth as he gasped for air. "And I reckon I'm not much of a pacifist at the moment."

Then, for the first time, he noticed Steve Wilkes. The man was lying on the floor, bound and gagged with duct tape and his leg bleeding. His eyes were still cold, and for a moment, he wanted to kick him in the face, too. George held his breath and then slowly released it.

Charity stepped over him to tower over Frost. "You'll serve better," she said before looking around again. George followed her gaze. The pinned deacon's screams were subsiding to whimpers as he lay limp over the fender. The others were gathered around him, looking like lost sheep. George watched her counting them.

"Frost sent three around back," George said.

Billy was stirring again and George was surprised at the ease with which Charity dragged him to his feet. Molly was ready with the duct tape.

They approached the back door together with Charity holding her pistol just beneath Frost's rib. George's hands slowly remembered the weapon, though he'd never thought he might use it on a person before. The notion of it made his stomach churn.

"I have your preacher here," Charity shouted through the door. "I don't want to hurt him."

Frost's voice overpowered hers in a bellow that George could barely understand. "I'm glory-bound, boys, if she puts me down. So you stand firm in the armor of God and send her to the judgment seat of Christ."

Charity punched him in the side of his head with the revolver. "I'm not talking about putting you down, Billy," she said. "I'm talking about *hurting* you." Her voice lowered, and George knew that if he could see her eyes now, what he saw there would frighten him. "And you don't want me to do that."

"You all fall back," she shouted again. She nodded to Molly. "Open the door and stand clear."

Charity slipped an arm around Frost's throat, standing behind him for cover, bending him backwards and forcing him to shuffle forward slowly. George raised the shotgun as the door swung open.

The waiting men had faces bathed in uncertainty. Even the older one didn't seem to know what to do. He lowered his rifle when he saw the woman moving forward, using his pastor as a human shield.

George moved forward, shotgun raised. "You should put down that rifle," he said quietly.

Frost protested; Charity squeezed his windpipe. The man stooped and laid it down, stepping back with raised hands. "I think things have gone a bit too far here, Pastor Bill." Then, he backed away.

"I agree," Charity said as she continued moving forward. George followed, the butt of the shotgun still firmly tucked into his shoulder. "Things *have* gone a bit too far. We're going to slip over to your County sheriff's office and sort it out right now."

George could see the glass door, brightly lit, at the base of the County building just down the street. They moved slowly and he tried to imitate the way Charity scanned the terrain. He heard the sound of

another car and flinched at the thought of more of Frost's men showing up. But this one continued on down Main Street, its engine growing fainter as it moved away. He blinked the sweat out of his eyes.

It took them just a few minutes to reach the sheriff's station,
Molly trailing behind. When they did, Charity peered through the
glass. "Lower the shotgun, George, and open the door."

He did and she moved past him. As soon as she entered the lobby,
she called out in a loud voice. "I'm Sergeant Charity Oxham," she
said, "Edgewater Security, D.C., on assignment for U.S. Senator Sandra Rodriguez. I'm armed and have a prisoner. I'm coming in."

George waited outside the door with Molly, his eye on the back
of the pharmacy. Frost's men still lingered there, and he saw that two
of them now propped up their Associate Pastor between them. The
gray halo of a nearby streetlight added something sinister to Wilkes'
angry glare.

When he glanced to Molly, the light she stood in painted her
angelic, her face calm but concerned.

She's not afraid; she's sad. And then it dawned on him that at least
some of how a world was healed was exactly that. Sadness—rising up
from the recognition of a species' potential and an understanding of
its failings and successes—replacing fear and all of its machinations.

Because we could be so much more than this.

He looked at Frost. Fear had driven the changes they were seek-
ing. And fear had governed his own life for as long as he could remember, coring it into something hollow that pretended to be joy.
Even his slow crawl away from faith had been riddled with it, as the
fear kept him behind a pulpit he hated, preaching words he could not
believe.

George blinked at the power of his realization.

He felt a hand on his arm and looked over at Molly. "You look
sad, George," she said.

He smiled at her. "I guess I am," George said.

Charity came through the door and let it close behind her. The
man at the desk looked up, surprise obvious on his face.

Charity repeated herself. "I'm Sergeant Charity Oxham, Edgewater Security, D.C."

His eyes went wide as he recognized Frost. His voice was muffled by the clear bulletproof partition that separated him from the small lobby. "Pastor Billy, what—"

"Reverend Frost is in my custody," Charity said. "The way I see it, you and your men can either complicate an already complicated situation or you can help simplify things. At this point, failing to respond to shots fired is your only complicity in the matter. Don't make it worse."

He blinked and she watched the fight go out of him. But one look at him when she entered the room, and she knew he'd cave fast. "What do you want?"

"I want an all channels broadcast that Frost is in my custody."

He looked at the radio and then back to her. "Sheriff called radio silence three hours ago."

She thought for a moment. "Do you know who Patriot, Inc. is and what they do?"

He nodded slowly.

"This situation is going to unravel really fast, Deputy, and I can assure you that no one will be unsoiled in the shit-storm that is coming your way. You have a choice to make."

Thirty minutes later, Cathlamet was crawling with men and women in dark windbreakers and ball caps. Black helicopters, running silent, shuttled additional agents into town through the high school's football field where they were met by colleagues in SUVs.

Charity sat in a cluttered office. They'd taken Frost and she suspected he was en route to Portland already. She'd seen Hunter only briefly and the woman had frowned. "Wait here for me to debrief you," she said in a sharp voice before she was off barking orders to other men and women. From what she could see, an elaborate net had been laid out here and the events of the night had forced things faster than anticipated.

So she waited.

When Hunter finally came in and sat down, the sun was up, shining bright despite the dark clouds north that threatened. "We've taken twenty six ECs," she said, "including Frost and Wilkes."

Enemy combatants. Semantics that she understood well. These men would not be facing a trial any time soon. Instead, they'd spend the next few years answering questions over and over again. "Where are they going?"

Hunter looked at her and Charity felt her eyes measuring her.

Finally, she spoke. "Seattle for now. The foundation owns a facility offshore. Eventually, they'll be taken there for rehabilitation." She paused. "I don't know if you want to know this or not but I'm going to tell you anyway, Charity. Your father's book, *Unmasking the Fear in Faith*, is required reading for all of us on this particular team, including the counselors that will be working with these prisoners."

It was his first book and it had broken out, taking Dr. Jeremy Oxham out of his psych classroom in Maryland and into a life of signings and speeches and debates. Five books later and he was dead. She shook off the memory. "And what about the twenty men they sent out?"

"It'll take us some time," Hunter said. "We've got a lot to sort through here. They've managed to block most wireless traffic these last two days so we've got nothing there. But we'll start interrogations later this afternoon in Seattle. We know they left by boat and by car but our surveillance has been spotty. The river has a lot of shipping activity on it and there's a maze of old logging roads in and out of here—far too many for us to watch. We'll get them."

"You sound confident."

Hunter nodded. "I am. We have another development that gives me a bit of hope. It involves you, actually."

Charity felt her eyebrows raise. "Really?"

"I'll send the details over by wireless after we're done. Approximately two hours ago, your boy—Matthew Rodriguez—turned himself in to the Portland Edgewater offices with an attorney retained by his mother."

She leaned closer, blinking. "He turned himself in?"

Hunter smiled. It was tight-lipped and devoid of any real happiness. "He did. It seems he changed his mind. Called his mommy and she pulled some strings. He'll be held at a facility in D.C. and has agreed to cooperate with us in the investigation. I argued for him to stay with the others, but your friend has some significant connections. The senator also insisted that you be assigned as his transport officer. We've got a jet waiting for you at PDX."

After all of this. And he'd turned himself in. It made no sense to her and she opened her mouth to say so, but thought better of it. Better to take what she could and get the fuck out of Dodge.

Hunter continued. "We'll have a lot more to talk about with you, but we can do that by vidcon later in the week. The senator was most insistent about having her son back in D.C. by tomorrow." Her tone told Charity all she needed to know about how the woman felt about this, and she wasn't sure she disagreed. "So I'll have Magnuson run you out to the ballfield and put you on our next chopper out."

The agent stood and smoothed her pantsuit. Then she extended her hand. "You've been a bit of a wildcard, Oxham," she said, "but you did good work here today. My report will reflect that."

She wanted to say something snarky about endangering civilians in their game of cloak and dagger, but she bit her tongue and shook the offered hand. "Thanks," Charity managed to spit out.

When Hunter left, she stood and collected her things. She stepped into the hallway and saw both George and Molly in separate offices, nodding and talking to the suits and their digital recorders. She felt a compulsion to say goodbye to them, particularly to Molly, and it surprised her.

She's the girl I might have been, Charity realized. If she hadn't lost her father at fourteen. If she'd never gone to war and learned to kill. There was a strength she shared with Molly, but hers had bent in a different direction with life's stresses and fractures. The girl's strength was gentler, fueled by her idealism and confidence.

Tonight was her first event as director of the Wahkiakum Community Center, and Charity knew that regardless of what else happened today, six o'clock would find Molly opening the doors and welcoming any who took her up on her invitation.

And Charity would head to Portland, collect her friend's son, and return him to D.C. She would wait out her administrative leave and consider Patriot's offer if it came through. She would go back to work, regardless. She would do her part to heal the world in the only way she knew how.

The girl looked up as Charity watched her. She smiled and raised a hand in farewell.

Charity returned the gesture. Then she stepped outside into a crisp autumn day and climbed into the backseat of a car that was waiting for her.

The sun was down and the single streetlamp cast the church parking lot in a dirty light. George had spent the day talking with one agent after another, breaking only to wolf down the burger and fries that Hunter had delivered from Rosie's.

After lunch, she'd taken him to Frost's house where a dozen men and women pored over the property with white cartons, gathering evidence. He'd spent two hours there answering questions.

And then they'd arrived at the church. *Three hours.* He rubbed his eyes and stifled a yawn. His shoulder throbbed and his head wasn't far behind. He could feel the dull ache growing.

"You're doing great, George. We're almost finished. Do you remember anything else at all?"

He looked at the barracks and then back to Hunter. "There was a doctor," he said, surprised he'd not remembered it sooner.

"A doctor?"

George nodded. "Frost and Wilkes were talking about it on the phone. When we pulled in yesterday, he was going into the barracks with Wilkes. Dark skin, green jacket, black case."

The look on her face told George that they weren't almost done after all.

An hour later, George's head pounded when she dropped him off on Main Street. Patriot had arranged a room for him at the Bradley House, but he was hungry and didn't want to be alone. He felt cored out, hollow with exhaustion.

He looked down the street at Rosie's, saw its welcoming lights.

No, he thought. It would be busy and his head couldn't stand more chaos. Across the street, the pharmacy lights were on as well.

Molly. It was Friday night. The casserole cook-off.

He walked across the street, driven by curiosity. He heard quiet music playing on the other side of the door and he paused. But there was no other sound. No conversation. No dinnerware clattering.

George pushed open the door and took in the room. The tables were arranged to easily seat thirty. In the corner, a radio played classic rock from the last century, and at the far end of the room sat a table with a solitary casserole dish and serving spoon.

"George."

He looked up and saw her framed in the door to the back room. She had a glass of iced tea in her hand and a towel over her shoulder. She was the only person here. "I guess I'm early," George said.

She shook her head. "You're two hours late, actually."

He looked around again. "Everyone's already gone?"

She smiled. "No one came," she said. The smile widened. "But *you're* here. Let's eat."

She sat him at one of the tables, brought out the pitcher of iced tea and another glass. Then she dished them both generous portions and they ate while Bono sang about not finding what he was looking for.

When they finished, they carried their plates into the kitchen to wash them. As George dried the plates, he looked over at her. "So what next?"

She shrugged. "I do the same thing next week. And the week after. And the week after."

"And if no one comes?"

She smiled. "Someone will come. It's only a matter of time and persistence."

"And when they do?"

"I'll teach them to be the answer to their own prayers," she said. "I'll help them create a sustainable community that works to connect what they already have rather than focusing on what they *don't* have."

He looked at her and he could see that she believed it. Even *he* believed it if he was really honest with himself. It might not happen fast, but he did not see her giving up. Instead, he saw her winning hearts one at a time. He wasn't sure at all how she would do it, but he knew that she was going to heal at least this part of the world.

"I think you're right," George finally said.

"About what?"

"About casserole healing the world."

She grinned. "Wait here. I have something for you."

She left, drying her hands, and came back with a package. It had been wrapped in newspaper and duct tape. "Don't open it here," she said.

"What is it?" But he knew what it was, just as he knew he'd be up late tonight reading a new gospel that put humanity's well-being squarely upon its own shoulders.

"It's just my casserole recipe," she answered.

Charity pushed back into the airplane's seat and stared out the window at the darkness. There had been delay after delay in Portland as she waited for Patriot to release Matthew into her care. It was past dark when they boarded the private jet Rodriguez had arranged.

She'd only talked to her friend briefly, long enough to tell her she had Matthew and was getting on the plane. She could hear the strain in Rodriguez's voice and she heard others talking hurriedly in the background before the senator was rushed off the phone.

Damage control underway, Charity thought. A U.S. Senator's son arrested in a domestic terrorist plot couldn't possibly help Rodriguez' newfound political career. Of course, Charity hadn't seen or heard anything all day about the incident in Cathlamet in Portland's local news. She wondered how long Patriot and its foundation could keep things quiet?

They were alone in the cabin of the plane, and she glanced over at Matthew. He wasn't the boy she remembered years ago. He had an edge to him that his close-cropped hair and dark eyes accentuated. He sat quietly, reading his Bible. He'd spent most of his time with the book, moving from passage to passage, and she saw the pages covered in small, cramped notes with verses underlined or bright yellow from a highlighter.

In their time together, she'd seen no evidence of remorse and had gotten no sense of regret. It perplexed her and she found herself not grasping why he would turn himself in.

But then again, the whole notion of her friend's son becoming a terrorist perplexed her as well.

"Why?" She didn't realize she'd asked the question aloud until he looked up.

"I don't have to talk to you without my lawyer," he said. His voice was cold.

She sighed. "I just don't get it, Matthew. I don't understand how you could've possibly thought this was the right way. And I don't understand why you would turn yourself in after all of this."

Their eyes met and she saw a fervency there that unsettled her. When he smiled, she shuddered. "'Fear none of those things which thou shalt suffer,'" he quoted, his eyes closing as he called up the words. "'Behold, the devil shall cast some of you into prison, that ye may be tried; and ye shall have tribulation ten days: be thou faithful unto death, and I will give thee a crown of life.'" He opened his eyes and fixed them upon hers. "I'll pray for you," he said, "that you'll be given ears to hear what the Spirit is saying."

She recognized the reference to the Revelation of St. John. "No thanks," she said. She knew the answer to her own question; she just didn't want to apply that knowledge to him. She wanted to remember the four-year-old, the eight-year-old, the twelve-year-old boy she'd met when visiting Sandra.

She'd read her father's books enough times to understand. And the mindset was the same regardless of the specific articles of faith. She'd seen it reproduced in most religions. There were always small extremist, literal groups, usually led by someone charismatic and compelling.

She turned back to the window.

"You're an atheist." His sudden statement surprised her and she looked up.

"I guess I am," she said. "I certainly don't believe in *your* God."

"When this is over," he said, "you'll bend your knee unto the Most High. Everyone will, and when they do, America will be great again."

When this is over. She opened her mouth to remind him that it *was* over, then closed it. There was a certainty to his voice and, beneath the cryptic words, an arrogance dressed up in servant's clothing. And there was something cryptic in what he'd quoted; it unsettled her. *Ye shall have tribulation ten days: be thou faithful unto death.*

They settled into quiet again and she found herself picking at the information like fingers at a knot. She was still pondering when he leaned toward her. "I need to use the bathroom."

She looked up, then fished the keys from her pocket. She unlocked the handcuff and escorted him to the back of the plane, checking the lavatory before she cuffed him to the handrail. "Call me when you're done," she said.

She moved back up the aisle to their seats and glanced down at his tattered Bible. Looking back over her shoulder in the direction of the small restroom, she gave in to curiosity and picked up the book.

The place marker was set to Exodus and a verse there was underlined.

For I will at this time send all my plagues upon thine heart, and upon thy servants, and upon thy people; that thou mayest know that there is none like me in all the earth.

Scribbled next to it was a reference from Revelation and she flipped to the back of the book quickly, her eyes moving to the back of the plane. Once there, she found that verse underlined as well.

And I saw another sign in heaven, great and marvelous, seven angels having the seven last plagues; for in them is filled up the wrath of God.

And then, what she read next, written in his pinched and careful script, raised goosebumps on her arms. It was a one-line prayer written in the margins.

Lord, make me a worthy vessel for your wrath.

There were other references, too, and she spun quickly through them. More about God's wrath. More plagues and disease from Heaven as punishment for the wicked.

"I'm finished," he called out.

Charity moved back to the restroom, reached for her keys, then paused. She opened the door. "There's more to all of this, isn't there, Matthew?" There had to be more.

He said nothing but the look on his face was all she needed. Leaving him, she moved to the front of the plane and tapped on the cockpit door.

A flight officer poked his head out. "Yes?"

"I need to make a call," she said.

"Against regs, ma'am."

She looked back to the lavatory. "I need to make a call *now.*"

He shrugged and passed her a wireless headset. She slipped it on. She had the Patriot, Inc. controller patch her through, and a few seconds later, she heard Abigail's voice. "Hunter."

"It's Oxham. I think we have more going on here than we realized."

There was a moment of quiet on the other end. When Hunter spoke, there was no surprise in her voice. "What do you have?"

"A cryptic-talking kid without remorse and a Bible full of markings about plague."

"Fuck." She heard something in Hunter's curse she'd not heard before. *Fear.* Then, another pause. "Okay. We have something new over here, too. I'm going to hope I'm wrong. I'll call you back."

She left Matthew in the lavatory. He was starting to shout now, but Charity wasn't listening. Instead, she waited by the cockpit door for twenty minutes until the headset chirped again.

Hunter's voice was tense. "Okay," she said. "We're diverting you to Kansas City. I'm on my way now."

"Does Senator Rodriguez know we're—"

Hunter interrupted. "No," she said. "Not yet. Not until we're sure."

Charity handed the headset back and then went to the lavatory.
Matthew looked up and stopped shouting when she uncuffed
him and pointed to his seat. "What's happening?" he asked.

"Change of plans," Charity answered. "We're going to Kansas
City."

When he moved, it was fast but not fast enough. Even as his fist
came up, she knocked his feet from beneath him with a well-placed
kick, grabbed his arm, and let his own body weight spin him around
and onto the floor. She put a knee in his back and cuffed him.

Charity leaned down, her mouth near his ear. "I take it you're not
pleased with this development."

Then, she hauled him to his feet and guided him back to his waiting seat.

He's afraid of something. For the rest of the flight, he fidgeted in
his seat.

When they landed, figures in HAZMAT suits waited on the
tarmac. Still, they sat locked in the aircraft for another two hours
until two HAZMAT response trucks pulled up. Then, the hatch was
opened. Three of the figures, one armed with a rifle, shuffled forward
as they descended the stairs. Charity saw Hunter's face in the visor,
her eyes shadowed by dark circles of sleeplessness. Two men took
Matthew by either arm and escorted him toward a waiting truck. He
walked stiff-backed, his face pale.

"Do we know more?"

Hunter nodded toward the second truck. "Get in. I'll brief you
on the way."

Charity climbed aboard, and before she was seated, the vehicle
was moving, building speed and running without lights or sirens. She
felt a knot, cold and aching, in her stomach.

Hunter sat across from her. "Chances are very good that nothing's
happened yet, but we can't be sure until we run some tests."

Charity blinked. "Can't be sure of what?"

"It was a fucking shell game," she said. "It was never about the
twenty. It was about Rodriguez."

She felt the knot twisting into anger and she heard it leaking into
her voice. "What the hell are you talking about?"

Hunter took a deep breath. "We've identified another involved
party—a Middle Eastern concern with ties to the fossil fuel industry.
Two weeks ago, a biomechanical virologist—Dr. Ibrahim bin Yosef—

went off the grid in Sudan. Applebaum's given us positive ID on the doctor in Wahkiakum County."

"How's that possible?" But even as she asked the question, Charity saw the obvious. By boat. It was a big ocean and a big river. Something small—a yacht, perhaps—could slip into U.S. waters easily enough. Especially with the accessibility of stealth technology for groups that had the funding.

Her mind spun the possibilities, the knot growing colder as she did. Biomechanical virology. Her mouth went dry as she thought about the scriptures she'd read. "And you think Matthew's been exposed to something?"

Hunter nodded again, slowly. "We think he was voluntarily infected. We've got a working theory and we've advised the president to take us to threat level red."

An imminent threat of terrorist attack.

The agent continued. "Bin Yosef's thesis was on latent biomechanical viruses—nano-enhanced, manufactured diseases on timed release with a built-in expiration date. You can kill or incapacitate an enemy without creating a pandemic. Our own government looked into it years ago, but with reductions in military research funding in favor of ecological recovery, the work was discontinued."

Charity felt the wind go out of her. "Time-released viruses?"

"Yes. With a limited range and a high kill-rate."

She didn't need Hunter to paint the rest of the picture. Recruit the disillusioned son of a new senator, shoot him full of a nanobug on an alarm clock and send him home to Mommy. And, through her, to Congress. And to the president.

And to me. She'd spent most of the last twenty years being shot at, chased, tossed about from one threat to the other, but this felt different, and the reality of it staggered her. "How sure are you?"

Hunter sighed. "Pretty sure. Once we reach the hospital, we'll quarantine you both and start running tests. Ideally, we'll catch bin Yosef in our net and learn more. Or get Frost talking." She paused. "But again, if their goal was exposing Senator Rodriguez, then the virus is likely on a longer fuse."

Charity sat back, words fleeing her. She couldn't be in her line of work without putting some thought into her own mortality, and what she felt settling over her wasn't unlike the tingling awareness of every small sensation that showed up on each chopper ride into combat. She closed her eyes. She breathed. She waited.

When the HAZMAT truck came to a stop forty minutes later, Charity found herself in an underground parking garage segregated by walls of clear plastic. More HAZMAT-suited men and women waited with wheelchairs. She saw that Matthew was now shackled and cuffed, one eye puffy and bruised. They were wheeled through automatic doors, down white tiled hallways that were empty until they pushed her into a small room.

A young man took three vials of blood, and then Charity spent another hour waiting until Hunter appeared, smiling but sober-faced, without her protective gear. "You're fine," she said.

The relief she felt was tangible, and for a moment—just a moment—she felt tears working at the corner of her eyes. She took a deep breath. "And Matthew?"

Hunter shook her head. "We'll do what we can for him. There's no real way for us to know when it will release. But at least we'll be able to contain it."

"Have you called his mother?"

"No," Hunter said. "We haven't."

There was awkward silence and Charity closed her eyes. When she spoke, her voice was matter-of-fact. "You want me to do it."

"You don't have to."

But I do. Of course she did. And with that realization, images of Matthew grinning at her as a child flashed unbidden across her memory.

Charity pushed back the tears, hoping another deep breath would keep the sob that suddenly rose within her at bay for just a few minutes longer. "Okay," she said. "Get me a secure line."

When Hunter left, she wiped her eyes and wondered just what the right words would be for the call she had to make.

George Applebaum paused, looked up, and stepped away from the pulpit. He left the resignation letter he'd so carefully written and had planned to read folded into the black leather book he was also leaving behind. As he walked, he looked out over the congregation, his eyes moving over them.

Some he'd brought into this fold he'd played shepherd to for so many years. Some had arrived from other folds. He saw Heather

Thompson, sitting beside her husband Henry, and remembered the day he'd baptized them, pushing them under the water as a metaphor of death, raising them up in a resurrection he'd leaned toward his entire life.

And yet he'd found a real resurrection in the oddest of places, spurred by a betrayal by someone he'd once called a brother. The taste of fear in his mouth as Frost fired on him. The slow motion of the truck bearing down on Frost's thugs and the building scream of the man he'd pinned with the fender. The cold sweat from his hands making the stock of the shotgun slippery. The calculated precision of Charity Oxham moving like an unstoppable machine of war.

They'd driven him home on Saturday morning, and that night he'd sat down with his board after scheduling a guest speaker for the next eight Sundays.

He continued looking around, picking them out now in their pews, their faces still grief-struck from last night's brief meeting.

Andrew Simmons actually had tears on his face. He'd had them the night before, too, when George had broken the news. And there had been pleading in his voice when he looked up from the letter Applebaum had passed around. "I don't understand," he said with shaking hands, "how a man like you could lose his faith, Brother George."

His own words surprised him in their clarity. "I haven't lost anything, Andrew," he said. "I've laid it aside. I've ... changed my mind."

They didn't understand. *And they won't unless they walk my road*, he realized. But as far as he was concerned, they didn't have to. He'd spent his life shepherding everyone else. It was time to shepherd himself.

"I have an announcement to make," he said as he came down the two steps that had kept him above them, hidden behind his pulpit, for so many years. "We've been together a long time, but I've recently realized that I need something different."

He still wasn't sure what that was, but he had some idea. This week, he'd pack his things and start getting the parsonage ready for whoever they brought in after him. He'd sit down and give thought to what kind of resumé a man who'd spent his lifetime preaching might be able to construct, and figure out just how long he could float on his savings. And though there was much in his life that George felt uncertain about, he did know what he would be doing Friday night.

He'd already pulled a recipe from the Internet and dug the casserole dish from the back of his cupboard.

He looked out over the people and took a breath for the words that were to follow. But before he spoke them, George Applebaum smiled upon them, and for the first time in a long while, there was nothing false or forced about it.

The nearly deserted facility was wrapped in a tomb-like silence, especially at night, and Charity found herself unable to sleep despite the exhaustion that rode her. After hours of tossing and turning, she got up, turned on the overhead lamp, and raised her bed. She picked up the book Molly had given her and read a bit more about Tygre before she finally gave up and dressed herself in the clothes someone had picked up for her from a local department store.

At this point, they played the waiting game. When Matthew Rodriguez's fever-wracked body finally gave out, she'd return to Washington with his mother. She and Sandra had sat silently over coffee together a few times over the last two days, but little had been said. Charity had no words for the loss the woman faced.

She pushed her feet into the slippers and left the room, shuffling down the hall. She nodded at the suited woman who stood near her door, and the woman returned the nod, speaking quietly into her throat mic.

It would be another hour before the canteen opened, so Charity headed to the ICU first. She felt compelled to look in on Sandra again, though she knew what she'd find. A broken mother, sitting in her HAZMAT suit by her son's deathbed, holding his hand while Matthew Rodriguez reaped what he'd sown.

When she reached the waiting room, she paused. Over the last two days, the room had been empty, but now an old man sat there, reading a book.

His hair was white, his age-worn features and dark skin offset by the high-end suit he wore. He looked up when she walked in and smiled at her. When he shifted, she saw the book he read and paused.

Serpents and Doves. By Jeremy Oxham. It was the last book her father had written, hastily edited and rushed to print six months after his murder by a publisher eager to cash in on the publicity of his tragic death.

The old man stood, and though he had to be at least in his eighties, he was a formidable figure. "Ms. Oxham?"

She blinked. "Yes?"

He moved toward her, legs carrying him with a quiet confidence that she recognized even through a slight limp. "I'm so glad to finally meet you."

He extended a hand, and when she shook it, the grip was cool and firm. "You have me at a disadvantage," she said.

"I do," he said. Then, he held up the book. "I'm a great admirer of your father's work. We actually corresponded before he was . . ." The man let the words trail off, his dark eyes softening.

She looked at the book again. She wasn't sure what to say.

His own gentle voice filled in the silence. "I'm certain that current events make this a difficult time for our introduction, but I wanted to meet you and thank you for your part in our work."

Our work. Surely, he was too old to be on Patriot's payroll. Her eyebrows furrowed. "And you are?"

"Someone who'd like to talk to you about a job," he said. He followed her eyes to the book he held. "Behold," he said, " 'I send you forth as sheep in the midst of wolves. Be ye therefore as wise as serpents and harmless as doves.' " He paused. "That duality has always fascinated me, even as it fascinated your father. So much so, that I expanded upon the idea in my own book. Though I'm more interested in sending forth wolves in the midst of sheep."

She blinked as the realization of who he was settled in. "You're Bashar," she said.

He nodded once. "I am. And I have work for you if you're interested." He reached into his pocket and withdrew a simple white card. She took it and studied it.

There were no words on it—only numbers—and she quickly recognized them as coordinates. "For the next four Fridays," he said, "I'll wait at this location at sunrise and sunset. There's a stone marker there that should be relatively easy to find."

"And if I come?"

He smiled. "I'll show you something amazing. I'll show you what happens when the serpents and the doves work together using their very different methods to bring about a shared outcome."

"Healing the world?" she asked.

"Maybe," he said. "Or at least some small part of it."

Their eyes met and she saw a fierceness there that countered the gentleness she'd seen in Molly. This man's tools weren't casseroles and community gatherings. His hands were made for silenced pistols and surgical strikes.

Like me. And right or wrong, she apprehended it and to some point even agreed with it. Doves to offer peace and serpents to protect it. "I'll think about it," she said.

He nodded again. "It's all I can ask. But I'll be there waiting. And I think you know how to pack for this."

She did. A backpack with whatever of her former life she might want to keep and a canteen of fresh water. Sturdy boots and a book she was only now beginning to comprehend.

He extended his hand again and she shook it once more. Then, he turned and left the room. Her eyes followed him as he went, and she saw in his stride not just the confidence of a soldier but the care of a hunter on the move.

Charity Oxham looked down at the card again and already knew that she would have to go. Too many ghosts were whispering, her father's loudest of all, that now was the time for change.

Real change. Intentional change.

She'd join the Foundation in its work of guiding that change with both an open hand and a ready fist. She would walk the quiet of the Cascade forests until she reached that simple marker, and then Charity Oxham, swaddled in this unexpected newness of life, would let Tygre's grave become her cradle.

AMAL'S LAMENT

Do you think, my love
I do not know just what you do
You up there upon the dock
You of the land
Me here your loving ghost beneath the water
As you play
Upon your harp the very song
I taught you
A song of night sowing
Like the love we made with our voices and sighs
Late into our silver crescents
Only to, after giggles, fall asleep together
And wake up with the tears of our separation
As the distance of sky between us grew
You play it, our song,
To remind me who I am to you
And to share what we can share
Me beneath the waves
You bathed in the blue green light of me
On this moonless night
As I sing with you and shine in the shadows
Your moving fingers cast.
I will bargain Rufello from his grave and
Bid him bear me from the water
And wrap me in glass and hope and steel
You will no longer weep
My lover, my Czar,
When I stagger uncertain, drunk on love and metal legs
Into your waiting embrace
Once of the moon and then of the water
But shipwrecked now
Upon the island of you.

OF GOLDEN BIRDS AND CAGED DREAMS

The golden bird dreamed of its misplaced cage even as the snow blew against its gemstone eyes and wind tugged at its metal feathers. Wings flapping, it pressed on for a home that it could not find.

Somewhere behind, the cage was swallowed and in the belly of the sea. Cold water spilling in through the very porthole the golden bird scrambled through. Behind, its owner's voice gurgled out, but the golden bird did not recognize it as one of two hundred sixty-seven words scripted into its memory scroll. It did not stop. It lifted into the night, its metal talons scrabbling at the porthole, clawing for purchase against the rush of icy seawater until it could leap up and spread its golden wings.

It fought the storm until dawn came white and somber, spilling light onto the ice fields below. If it had felt pain, its eyes would have stung from the brightness of its first morning in freedom.

It flew on, northward, until it crested the pole and north became south. Its wings grew heavy as the condensation froze in its feathers, and then the sea returned and the air became warmer. Land formed to the west and it banked towards it, finding altitude as the sun warmed its metal skin.

There on the edge of a bay, a trickle of smoke met the sky. A cottage took shape, and as the bird descended, its scrolls spun and clicked at the sound of muted humming beneath the rasp of a saw.

The golden bird landed on the window sill and cocked its head. "Cage?" it chirped.

Through jeweled eyes, the old man was a blurry giant, but his voice was soothing, preceded by a soft chuckle. "No cage here, my metal friend, and you are far from home."

"No home," the metal bird said. "Cage."

If it could smell, the golden bird would've inhaled the scent of fresh cut wood. But it could not. So it watched instead as the old man worked his trade, taking the wood and cutting it to size, planing it smooth, fixing the pieces together with dowels until a chair took shape. The old man sat on it and regarded his guest.

"You want a cage?" the old man asked.

"Cage."

Nodding, the old man stood and went to his pile of scrap wood. He drew a small round post and a flat bit of planking, holding them to the sun and squinting to them. He drew another length from the pile and went to his tools.

"Sometimes," he said, "what we think we need isn't really so." The golden bird watched as the big hands worked. "For instance," the old man said, "I came to this place at the end of a storm thinking I must spend my remaining years alone, away from the weather of misguided mortal dreams."

The golden bird cocked its head, grabbing one of the words it knew well. "Dreams?"

The old man continued his work, long silences between his few words. "I've been lonely," he said, "within this cage I've made. Oh, they come for their chairs and their tables and they pay me well for them. And for the longest while, I disdained their company until they learned that Mad Martin hates the world despite the beautiful things he makes from it and for it." The old man chuckled. "I don't hate the world. If I did, that hatred left me long ago."

The woodworker stepped aside at last to reveal what he'd made. Lifting it, he carried it into his cottage and placed it near the open window.

Hopping from the sill onto the newly made perch, the golden bird sank its talons into the soft pine.

"Cage?" it asked again.

"No cage," the old woodworker said. "But a home if you wish it. You may come and go as you please, and if ever my window is closed, tap at it and I will open to you."

Tiny eye shutters blinking rapidly, the golden bird ruffled its metal feathers and opened its beak to sing.

AFTERWORD:
A Third Trip through the Imagination Forest

*H*owdy folks! Welcome back. It's hard to believe that it's time for a third trip through the Imagination Forest. If you've read the other collections, you'll recall that this is the point where I talk a bit about each of the stories and how they came to be . . . and then thank the many people who brought this whole venture about.

It's April 2015 as I write this and I'm just coming out of the dark. Last year, I lost one of my closest friends and most significant influences—Jay Lake—and that was a tough loss. I did a little math and that man is responsible for about a third of my short stories and all of my novels. They wouldn't have happened without his friendship in my life and his foot kicking me in the ass. So of course, I've dedicated this book to him.

And this is a milestone year of sorts for me. 2015 marks the fifteen year anniversary of my time on stage as a writer. My first short story, "The Taking Night," appeared in *Talebones* magazine in the winter of 2000. I'd written the tale for Patrick Swenson's class back in 1998, and then he'd bought it for his magazine. Fifteen years later and he's publishing my third short story collection. I love it when a plan comes together.

So . . . three passes through the Imagination Forest. Y'all sit down and keep your hands in the bus. Let me tell you a bit about this stretch of woods.

*

<u>All Our Tangled Dreams In Disarray</u>
In March 2013 I took a roadtrip to the Bay Area to teach in a high school classroom and catch up with friends and colleagues. I'd

heard lots of stories about Highway 1, a narrow and winding stretch of road hugging the cliffs of the California coast, and decided to take that route home.

It took me about six hours to drive a hundred and thirty of the most beautiful miles I've ever driven, and that night, I found myself in a little Italian restaurant, V'Canto's, in Fort Bragg. I had a wonderful chat there with the owner and his bartender. The next day, I found myself dwarfed by the Avenue of the Gods—old and massive Redwoods that reminded me of my place in the universe.

Those and other bits of story ingredients turned into this tale when my friend, Nayad Monroe, reminded me that I had a story due soon for her anthology. I sat with those experiences and mixed in the dark machinations of a cult centering around super-powered children inspired loosely upon the notion of the return of the Nephilim of old. Then I added a dollop of the ancient tug-of-war between our need for free will and our longing for destiny. This story came together over a period of two or three weeks in the spring of 2013, and I recycled an old title from an unfinished story and lined up the ending to fit the title. It came out in *What Fates Impose* later that year.

The Starship Mechanic (with Jay Lake)

In March 2009, Jay and I did our first and only write-in together at Borderlands Books in San Francisco. It was just a month after *Lamentation* came out . . . and just a month after my dad's death. So it was a challenging time. In hindsight, I'm pretty amazed that I was able to pull this off.

We arrived at the store and set up our laptops. There was a small audience gathering. And the deal was we'd each start a story, write about a thousand words, and then turn it over to the other to finish. Then, we would read the finished stories to our audience. So I started "Looking for Truth in a Wild Blue Yonder" and Jay started "The Starship Mechanic." Now that you've already read it, I can tell you that my first line in this story is "It was raining men in the Castro."

Prior to this, my only other collaboration had been with John Pitts. We'd taken our time and certainly didn't have the pressure of an audience expecting to hear the fruit of our labor as soon as we finished. I rarely crank out a story in a single sitting these days. But we did it. Jay's confidence and energy were contagious. We wrote them and read them on the spot and much fun was had by all. And later, the stories were picked up by Tor.com along with an essay about the write-in by Shannon Page. And imagine my delight when this one was selected for *The Year's Best Science Fiction*! Pretty good for a tale written in a handful of hours in the back of a bookstore.

A Chance of Cats and Dogs

This is the newest story in the collection, written in October 2014. My favorite stories are usually the ones I'm dared in some way to write, whether it's three word prompts or an anthology theme.

In this case, the editors at a new magazine, *Urban Fantasy*, had invited me to be the cover story for their inaugural issue. Early on, I suggested that they get the art first, and I would write a story to literate their cover. Paul Pederson did a sketch, and I made a few false starts on this one—something very rare for me—until I saw the cityscape in his final version. Then this noir story about Angus Wolfe, Monica Evenheart, and the world of the Rending Hounds, mixed in with a bit of my own internal processing around Patriarchy and class, took shape. It's my first intentional attempt at urban fantasy, and it's a universe I could see myself going back to down the road.

Annual Dues

Nestled right up against the newest story in the collection is the oldest. "Annual Dues" was written in November 1997—the same month that I met John Pitts and launched one of the closest friendships I've ever experienced. This was back when I was re-reading the sword and sorcery from my teen years, and shortly after I came back to writing seriously as an adult. Once my newer stories started selling, most of these older ones went into the trunk. Most of them deserved to stay there. In Fall 2013, I'd been invited to donate a story for the anthology *Fantasy for Good* that Jordan Ellinger and Richard Salter put together to raise money for The Colon Cancer Alliance. This was around the same time that Jay's own colon cancer prognosis was looking dark. I went through my inventory and rediscovered this story. Of course, I was unsure of it, because it pre-dates my earliest publishable fiction, so I ran it past Jordan, and he liked it. And amazingly enough, *this* story spawned a sequel set in the same world and introducing a character that I suspect I'll do more with. But we'll talk about that later.

This one stretches back far enough that I can't recall its origins beyond the fact that I was reading a lot of Robert E. Howard and Fritz Leiber at the time.

Jay Lake and the Last Temple of the Monkey King

I remember it as the last shiny, golden JayCon. It was June 2007. Nearly a year before Jay's cancer diagnosis. I'd just picked up my first agent with my first novel, *Lamentation*, and I was writing *Canticle*. My book deal and the sudden rush of losses that—combined with the birth of my twins—set match to the PTSD bonfire that was buried in me was still ahead of me on the trail.

JayCon was an amazing gathering held each year for Jay's birthday at the Flying Pie Pizzeria in Portland. It was packed out every year, and for three years running, I brought a new "Jay Lake and the ..." story to read and give him for his birthday. In 2005 and 2006, I'd inflicted "Jay Lake and the Inscrutable Alien Story Device" and "Jay Lake and the Mole Men of Mars" upon the celebrants. And for 2007, I'd worked up this one. It features both me and Frank Wu as supporting characters with a gigantic nod to the story that birthed my friendship with Jay —"Edward Bear and the Very Long Walk"—and more inside jokes than I can count.

And that year, I ran a contest online for the story title. Scott Roberts, a friend from my Writers of the Future year, won, so he was written into the story as an assassin. It was great fun. And it was the last of the "Jay Lake and the ..." stories. By the next year, my mother had died, my nephew had been killed in the war, and Jay had cancer. We went straight from my nephew's memorial to the JayCon afterparty so that Jay and the posse could hug us, and so that we could hug him. It was the beginning of a long stretch of dark.

Later, I shared the story with our editor at Tor, Beth Meacham, and when Jay passed away just shy of his 50th birthday, she recommended it up to Tor.com as a tribute on his actual birthday. The story came out the day before I officiated his small family memorial service. It had been seven years since that JayCon reading where he and Frank acted out parts of the story as I read it aloud.

When I read it now, it makes me laugh and it makes me cry all at the same time.

Fuck cancer.

Time Dancing in the Key of E Minor

I was at Norwescon in Spring 2011, fresh from my first experimental treatments for the PTSD. I'd been stalled writing-wise because of my health's sudden turn south—the first of many stalls to come. My experience with the blocks was still new enough that I hadn't figured out that it took a few months after each block for my brain to settle down and for the word fountain to flow. I was sitting in the bar waiting for a friend to join an already crowded table when author and editor K.C. Ball asked me to write a story for her market *Everyday Fiction* for $25 and a chair. She knew I'd been struggling, and her invitation to write flash fiction for her was just the nudge I needed. She gave me the issue's prompt, "It's quiet . . . too quiet," and I went off to ponder.

Now, back in the days before the PTSD went active duty, I could do things like write stories in bookstores and turn around fiction quickly under deadline with relative ease. This kind of story was something I could crank out in my hotel room at a con in about an hour right after the editor asked for it. I could write full length short stories usually in a week or so. But that changed with the PTSD, and this little flash story dogged me for a few months. Finally, I went off to lead a group of workshoppers for Cascade Writers at the coast in June, and arranged to go a day early. I sweated this one out of me at long last—a short, light-hearted parenting yarn—and got myself unstuck for a season.

Fish and Bird, Current and Falls (with Liz Coleman)

I met Liz Coleman at Radcon in 2009 just a few days after my Dad passed and a few days before *Lamentation* came out. As a matter of fact, I left Radcon early that Sunday to attend his memorial. Liz quickly became a part of my tribe, and her friendship is a great gift in my life. K.C. helped me get unstuck with "Time-Dancing . . ." earlier in the year, and when she suggested a prompt for her upcoming issue—"The falls are beautiful this time of year"—I had already decided I would tackle something. In December 2011, I invited Liz to play along, and I started this ghost story of sorts, went about half way into it over the course of twenty minutes or so, and then passed it to Liz so she could finish it up. I like the poetry of it and the way our muses worked together.

If Dragon's Mass Eve Be Cold and Clear

In October 2011, Tor.com invited me to write their holiday story, and I decided early on that I wanted to explore the losses and gains in my life—particularly around what it meant to become a parent while losing my parents. That's usually two major intersections in a person's life, but losing my parents and becoming a parent within about eighteen months of one another made it feel like one big intersection. I decided I would write it as a follow-up to the love story of Drummond Farrelly and Harmony Sheffleton in "The Doom of Love in Small Spaces" and that I would use their daughter as the POV character as she processed her father's death. It also gave me an opportunity to explore my slow movement away from religion and which bits of that life I kept and which I released back into the wild.

But I had no idea what the Department of Horrific Timing had in mind. Early in the month, my wife's grandmother died. It was expected. But we didn't expect her father to pass just a week or so later, and it plunged us back into deep, overwhelming loss. Watching Jen lose her father and go through the most painful, horrible experience of her life while writing a story about a woman losing her father . . . well, it was a lot. We hid out at the coast for a weekend in late October, and I finished it up in a flurry of words. It's one of my most treasured stories, and I see it as part of a handful that have the most of my metaphorical heart and soul in them. I think this one and "Last Flight of the Goddess" showcase the things that are most important to me as a person. I dedicated it to Jen, but it was a few years before she was ready to read this one, and it's as much for Lizzy and Rae as it is for Jen, because this story is where I first articulated—in the final scene—just what their birth meant to me. They are my continent of love.

Someday, I'll do more work in the World of the Santaman and the Bureaucracy. I'll likely pick up with Melody's son and tell the next generation's tale as he goes off to figure out who his father is and where he vanished to with that fabulous sword . . .

Tor.com released this one in December 2011 with amazing Santaman art by Greg Manchess. It was reprinted in the anthology, *Seasons of Wonder*, the next year.

Cowardly Lion's Slipper Wish

So I've said many, many times that it took me seventy-five rejections to sell my first short story. But I don't think I've ever mentioned that the first time I submitted a poem, it was selected for publication. This was back in 1992 in Robert Hughes' writing class at Highline Community College. He required that students submit for publication in order to pass his class, and I submitted a poem I'd written to a magazine. This was in the midst of my preaching days after burning my D&D books (as Satanic) and giving up writing (as idolatry) to pursue the ministry. And it was just a few months before I started pastoring up in Bellingham while I finished my degree at Western Washington University. The poem was accepted and the magazine folded a few months before publication.

Flash forward to June 2006, and I was establishing myself nicely in the genre as a short story writer and getting ready to tackle my first novel. I cranked out this post-apocalyptic, alternate-history Oz poem as a loose sequel to the song "If I Were the King of the Forest" from the classic film adaptation. What would the Cowardly Lion, after years of bullying and fear, wish for if he had the slippers?

It's a nice little slice of dark, and I lobbed it over to Patrick Swenson back in the *Talebones* days. It became my first (and until now, my only) published poem.

On the Freedom of Agency and the Finding of Lost Hearts

As I've noted elsewhere, most of these stories come out of a pretty challenging time in my life filled with fits and starts and stalls as I've adjusted to losing people, gaining children, launching my series, and dealing with the PTSD that emerged from it all. I went from being a writer that met most—if not all—of his deadlines to a writer who missed them more often than not if I found any words at all. A frustrating time indeed. I was stuck and my writing was stalled. All of the losses had me feeling a bit like my heart had been ripped out of my chest and put into a freezer. Not optimal for someone who writes with his heart more than anything else.

I think I was about a paragraph or two into this when I realized that it was set in the same world as "Annual Dues." I'd recently re-read that old story of mine while I vacillated between writing something new or finding something previously unpublished in my inventory for the benefit anthology. As the story took shape, I discovered that Gilga

Yar and his pocket demon were still very much alive and well. And I discovered aspects of that world and its pantheon that I'd not realized before while playing with the idea of what would happen if a love god lost part of his heart and a thief were sent to fetch it.

Ultimately, I finished this one without a market in mind, and I think that was part of what got me unstuck. I'd not written a story that didn't already have an editor waiting for it since 2008, and there was something freeing in writing a story just for the sake of writing it rather than doing it under contract or by request. And it went on to find a home at *Beneath Ceaseless Skies*.

Looking for Truth in a Wild Blue Yonder (with Jay Lake)

This is the story that I started as Jay started "Starship Mechanic" at our Borderlands write-off. I was deep in the throes of complicated grief with the death of my parents and my nephew, and writing is a tool that I use for processing my life. In this case, I started with the title and went forward from there. The Verity character is actually a nod to the same Verity that you'll see again in a later story here, based on a good friend of mine, Alethea Kontiss. This got a little uncomfortable when Jay's turn brought about the sexing up of the character, but she was very understanding. I turned the tale over to him just as the Blue Yonder took hold of the protagonist and Jay took wicked glee in planting words and imagery into the story just to keep me blushing as I read it aloud later. Because, of course, we didn't have time to read the stories to ourselves first. We typed END and then the reading started.

I can close my eyes and still hear him chortling as I blushed my way through that reading. But more than that, buried into the ending of the story, Jay planted a message to me about grief that I took great comfort from after losing him.

Awash in Autumn, the Queen Reflects

This is one of those playful stories spawned from art. Michaela Eaves asked me if I'd be willing to literate one of her drawings in her annual art book *42 Sketches*, and it sounded like a ton of fun. I'm really pleased with how the story turned out, and if you want to see the drawing that inspired it, track down Michaela's book. I'm a bit of a hopeless romantic, so the idea of a coffee wizard courting a hotel housekeeper through foam art magic appealed to me. It's what I saw in the sketch that she sent me, though I'm not sure anyone else would've seen it there. I love turning my muse loose to play with other muses, and this story is a good example of why.

Verity Saves the World

Alethea Kontis and I were instant friends much like Jay and I were.

We met at the 2007 World Fantasy in Saratoga Springs. It was my Cinderella Convention experience just a few weeks after my five book offer from Tor for the Psalms of Isaak. I met a lot of amazing people there, including Lee. Funny thing, later when she asked me to write something for her, I had no idea it was for publication. I just fell into a magic realism freewrite based on a picture I'd seen of her in a bowler she'd bought while wandering Saratoga Springs. I think she was wearing the hat when I met her, actually. So I was delighted to learn she intended to publish my little homage to her in *Beauty and Dynamite*. And since she's also a character in my collaboration with Jay, it seemed appropriate to include this little tribute to her here.

A World Done in By Great Granny's Grateful Pie

In Spring of 2014, Kevin J. Anderson invited me to write something for his anthology *A Fantastic Holiday Season*. It had to be about a holiday, and I pitched a few different ideas to him, including one about zombies in a trailer park.

I'd never given much consideration to writing zombie stories, but he liked the notion of me doing something lighthearted to counter a darker zombie story he'd already purchased. And I'd been recently impressed by the Southern-flavored zombie tales in Katie Cord's *He Left Her at the Altar; She Left Him for the Zombies*. So I took a stab at this tale about family and pigs and pie and a Thanksgiving zombie apocalypse.

Thanksgiving is, after all, my favorite holiday.

And I'm fittingly grateful for Kevin giving me this opportunity to stretch my zombie-writing wings. I may go play in this particular zombie apocalypse again one day.

A Symmetry of Serpents and Doves

In 2011, Jay took over the editorship of Audible's *Metatropolis* series, and as he often did, he dragged me along into his success. He invited me to write for Cascadia, the second volume in the audio series, and as we talked, I realized that what I really wanted to do was tie our stories together.

So I read *In the Forests of the Night*, his novella from the first *Metatropolis*. The character of Bashar grabbed me instantly, and I found myself wondering what if his experience with Tygre brought about a Saul of Tarsus-type conversion? What if he wrote a book about it all that was being used to change the world? The tale of Charity Oxham and George Applebaum came together seeded with a lot of my Preacher Boy past. It allowed me to play in a familiar pool around ministers losing faith and finding their humanity. Later, my story was narrated by LeVar Burton, which was a high point in my Geek Life . . . and even a higher point when he remembered the story fondly when we finally met! *Metatropolis: Cascadia* went on to win an Audie award for best original work.

In 2014, Jay and took our novellas and novelettes from the *Metatropolis* trilogy and, because of how interconnected they were, published them with Wordfire Press as the collaborative collection, *Metatropolis: The Wings We Dare Aspire.* The book came out just a few weeks before Jay passed, so I'm sad we didn't get to sally forth and promote it together. As a matter of fact, it was so close to Jay's death that it really wasn't promoted much at all. But I'm glad he and I had a chance to put that paper child into the world before he left.

So if you like this story, you'll likely love the book with the other four stories set in this world. Help a pair of brothers out and go buy a copy.

Amal's Lament

So I reckon this is my second published poem, published for the first time here. Along the writing of the Psalms of Isaak, I've had these little pieces that have shown up along the way. This one is a poetic sequel to "A Weeping Czar Beholds the Fallen Moon" and is from Amal Y'Zir's point of view. It is set in the final scene of that novelette.

It's about overcoming impossible love. There's an entire mythos around Frederico the Last Weeping Czar and Amal Y'Zir, the Moon Wizard's Daughter that I've set up for future exploration if I keep writing in the universe of the Psalms of Isaak. And yes, it includes a mechanical spider designed by Rufello. Naturally.

Of Golden Birds and Caged Dreams

I often say that my favorite part of being a writer is the people I meet. Early on, as my stories started selling, I was approached by *Shimmer* magazine. Memory is sketchy but I think I first met the editor, Beth Wodjinksi, after she'd already published me. And then later, met her awesome boyfriend (now husband) Sean Markey. When they were first together, he wanted to give her an amazing gift, and went to several of her favorite author friends to collect short flash pieces about birds as a personal book he was building for her as a gift. A hopeless romantic myself, I couldn't say no. So I worked up this little slice of life from an earlier time in Lasthome, the world of the Psalms of Isaak. It was later used as a promotional piece for the series, I think, along with other bits. I thought it would be nice to collect it here as well. And it seemed a good note to close this third collection on.

*

So there you have it. A third tour through my Imagination Forest. Stories from a largely apocalyptic season in my life now collected together at this intersection. Fifteen years of story lumber logged from the Imagination Forest as I sit on the edge of finishing the fifth and final volume of The Psalms of Isaak.

There are so many people to thank here. More than I could ever list because each short story has so many different players who contributed the various ingredients of story. I'm especially grateful to all of the editors who patiently worked with me through the fits and starts of my PTSD-fueled writer's blocks. And those editors who kept asking me for stories, keeping my hands on the wheel as I drove onward.

I'm also especially grateful to the massive tribe of friends who carried me through this most recent loss—Jay—and to him particularly for such a massive thumbprint on my writing life. I couldn't have done any of it without you, pal, and I still don't know most days how I will keep doing it without you around. But I know that I will. I know it's what you're whispering for me to do under the surface of all my words.

I also want to thank Patrick Swenson for fifteen years of publishing joy and a third collection now in the Fairwood Press catalog. I'm glad for your thumbprint on my literary life.

And of course, I have to thank Paul Swenson—Patrick's brother —for another fine cover. I love that this trilogy of collections has your art setting them apart. As I write this, I've not yet seen what you've cooked up for this one but after the first two, I know it will be amazing. [Note: I have now seen it and it is indeed amazing. Thank you.]

Thank you, Mary, for agreeing to introduce this volume. You're another of those instant friends, and I'm glad our paths crossed back in 2005. Watching your star rise has been amazing, and I'm grateful you're in my life.

I'm also grateful to Jen, John, Jerry, Alaina and Robert for keeping me sane and grounded and writing. And to Lizzy and Rae for giving me two fantastic reasons to keep at it regardless of how dark the forest gets around me. And to Dr. Eugene Lipov for helping find a dial on that darkness with his ground-breaking work in treating PTSD. If you or someone you know is suffering from PTSD, please find and watch my video at wwww.kenscholes, "Silence of the Chattering Head Monkeys."

Also, a big thanks to Charity Benham and Joy Matthews for proofing the manuscript.

And last but not least, thank you, Dear Reader, for picking up this book. I write these for the people who enjoy my stories. And I hope that if this is your first trip through my Imagination Forest you'll consider going back and picking up my other books. If you're a returning reader, thank you for staying with me through it all. I hope you'll keep coming back for more.

I know I surely will.

Ken Scholes
April 2015
Saint Helens, OR

ABOUT THE AUTHOR

From his first publication in *Talebones* magazine back in 2000, Ken Scholes has gone on to become the award-winning, critically-acclaimed author of four novels and over fifty short stories.

Ken's eclectic background includes time spent as a label gun repairman, a sailor who never sailed, a soldier who commanded a desk, a preacher (he got better), a nonprofit executive, a musician, and a government procurement analyst. He has a degree in History from Western Washington University. He is a winner of the Writers of the Future award, the ALA RUSA Reading List award, the Endeavour award, and France's Prix Imaginales for best translated novel.

Ken is a native of the Pacific Northwest and makes his home in Saint Helens, Oregon, where he lives with his wife and twin daughters. You can learn more about Ken by visiting www.kenscholes.com.

COPYRIGHTS

OTHER TITLES FROM FAIRWOOD PRESS

A Funeral for the Eyes of Fire
by Michael Bishop
trade paper: $17.99
ISBN: 978-1-933846-49-1

Cracking the Sky
by Brenda Cooper
trade paper: $17.99
ISBN: 978-1-933846-50-7

Pandora's Gun
by James Van Pelt
trade paper: 14.99
ISBN: 978-1-933846-53-8

The Child Goddess
by Louise Marley
trade paper: $16.99
ISBN: 978-1-933846-52-1

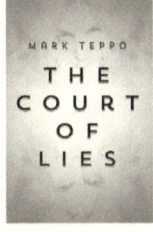

The Court of Lies
by Mark Teppo
trade paper: $17.99
ISBN: 978-1-933846-44-6

Bravado's House of Blues
by J.A. Pitts
trade paper: $15.99
ISBN: 978-1-933846-41-5

The Best of Electric Velocipede
edited by John Klima
trade paper: $17.99
ISBN: 978-1-933846-47-7

A Cup of Normal
by Devon Monk
trade paper: $16.99
ISBN: 978-0-9820730-9-4

www.fairwoodpress.com
21528 104th Street Court East;
Bonney Lake, WA   98391